THE HOB AND HOUND PUB

SEANA KELLY

The Hound and Hob Pub

Copyright © 2022 by Seana Kelly

Ebook ISBN: 978-1-64197-174-4

KDP POD ISBN: 979-8-80622-979-4

IS POD ISBN: 978-1-64197-219-2

NYLA Publishing

121 W. 27th St., Suite 1201, NY 10001, New York.

http://www.nyliterary.com

For Mom & Dad
I can't remember a time when you didn't absolutely believe I could accomplish anything I set my mind to. I set it to books

And a pre-emptory apology to all my British readers. I tried very hard to get the details correct but I'm sure I made mistakes. Please be patient with the poor American

ONE

City of Lights...and Shadows

P aris is my new favorite city! Granted, I haven't been many places, but still. I'd thought we were headed straight for England. Instead, we flew into the City of Lights.

Aldith, Leticia's mother and the woman who had declared war against Clive almost a thousand years ago, was in England. We needed to skewer the heart of the hydra or more vamps would be coming for us. And we would *soon*, but not now.

I had to admit, this whole marriage thing was kind of embarrassing but also sort of amazing. I felt like an idiot referring to Clive as my husband, but then the giddy bubbled up and I found myself grinning for no particular reason. Like now, when we were strolling hand in hand around a glowing glass pyramid between fountains at the entrance to the Louvre. Although, I supposed being at the Louvre was reason enough. I stopped at one of the smaller glass pyramids to look down into the museum. I had to keep pinching myself. I was in Paris!

It was after hours, but Clive knew a way in, one Rémy, his French vampire friend, said still worked. The expansive high baroque palace surrounded a vast courtyard on three sides. Clive walked us away from the lights toward a shadowy corner between the Richelieu and Sully wings. Once the immediate area had cleared out, Clive swung me around so I was clinging to his back and then scaled the wall to the roof.

We jogged along a narrow metal beam between the stone façade of the building and the glass-domed roof. I followed, not looking down, as heights were not my friend. Clive ducked behind a statue and circled to the back of the gorgeously ornate attic in the center pavilion of the wing.

"The last time I was here," he whispered, "these were government offices. The finance department, as I recall."

He took my hand and led me to an ornamental hexagonal medallion. It appeared fixed in place and yet when he pushed, it swung in. "The Louvre used to be just that one long wing." He pointed to the building opposite us, across the courtyard. "Remy said this wing was gutted and remodeled to expand the museum."

His grin flashed in the darkness. "Let's take a look."

He sat on the lip of the opening, his legs dangling into the darkened hall below. "No heartbeat. The guard is elsewhere." He pulled me onto his lap, my legs swinging into the void beside his own, his arm tight around my middle. A moment later, we were dropping forty feet. Clive took the impact before he loosened his grip and my boots hit the polished floor.

I looked up at the open panel, a tiny piece of starlit sky visible. "You left the hatch open," I whispered.

"All the doors are alarmed. That's how we're getting out. Now, where to first?" He took my hand and we strolled down the airy halls, pausing to study paintings and sculptures.

I knew there were guards walking the museum with us, but Clive's sensitivity to heartbeats meant he heard them coming long before they appeared, giving us time to move on or hide.

We wandered for hours, only seeing a small portion of the enormous collection. It felt almost religious, this realization over and over of the greatness, the near divinity of some. We all leave our fingerprints on the world, to greater and lesser degrees, but some have created art so remarkable that tens of thousands flock to experience it daily. It was staggering.

I enjoyed the surprises too. The *Mona Lisa* was small and roped off to keep visitors far away. Clive and I didn't want to trip any silent alarms, so we stayed behind the lines. It was intriguing, if a little underwhelming.

The *Winged Victory* sculpture, however, was magnificent. She stood atop a staircase in a large open hall, an artery for other galleries and floors—easily seen by guards entering from every direction. I couldn't tear my eyes from her. Power, glory, confidence, she awed and inspired me. I wanted to hold her essence deep within, to call upon it in moments of darkness and fear.

I was studying the marble statue one minute, the folds and movement of her skirt, the detail and lift of each feather in her wings, when I was picked up and raced down multiple halls, turning this way and that. When Clive finally put me down, we were standing in front of Botticelli's *Venus and the Three Graces Presenting Gifts to a Young Woman*.

"What the heck?" I whispered.

"Guards from different sectors were all about to converge on that hall. We have a little time before the guard for this sector returns." He pointed to the painting. "And I thought you'd enjoy this one."

Moving in closer, I tried to take in the fresco, the soft colors, the delicate beauty of the women in their billowing robes. The age and cracking of the plaster did nothing to diminish the beauty. If anything, it lent to it.

Turning to Clive, I said, "And you were around when this was first painted." It hit me at the oddest moments. My new husband was ancient. One thousand being the new thirty, if you were a vampire.

He quirked an eyebrow at me. "Problem?"

I shook my head and shrugged, turning back to the fresco. "Decrepitude looks good on you." I'd just leaned in to study the bride's features when I was snatched up, thrown over his shoulder, and carried down darkened passages again.

When my feet hit the floor, we were tucked away in a shadowy corner, away from the art. Clive's mouth was at my neck, his hands dragging down my body.

"Decrepit?" His lips skimmed my jaw.

"Elderly." I gasped when he nibbled my earlobe. "Infirm." One of his hands snaked up my sweater and palmed a breast. Breath uneven, I added, "Frail." The last word ended on a moan as he unzipped my jeans and slid his other hand into my panties.

Clive took my mouth to muffle the sounds I was making, his hands and lips working me over like a virtuoso.

I crushed him to me as I flew apart. Panting, resting my head against the wall, I tried to recover. My knees almost buckled when he did some kind of secret, vampy finger twirl as he slid out.

He leaned in, his lips hovering an inch from mine. "Decrepit?"

"Doddering." I rezipped my jeans with shaky hands.

"That's it." And just like that, I was picked up and we were racing down darkened halls again.

Giggling silently, I smacked his butt. "I want to see the Egyptians before we go."

A few minutes later, I was put down again, my hand in the crook of Clive's arm as we walked through the gallery holding Egyptian antiquities. Display cases held sculptures, jars, jewelry. Some pieces towered over us; some were kept safely behind glass. I studied hieroglyphs longer than I should have, as I had no idea how to read them, but the idea that a story was being told drew me in.

Rows of sarcophagi were lined up in a case, some gorgeously painted, inside and out, others without decoration save for the faces carved at the top, the etchings on the chest. They were—each of them—extraordinary art.

Sometimes it made my head hurt to think I was looking at pieces fashioned by hand four thousand years ago. "Hey, do you know any Egyptians?"

Clive was studying a small cat sculpture with ruby eyes. "Of course."

"I mean ones who were alive in ancient Egypt."

Straightening, he turned to me. "Yes. Well, one, really."

"And let me guess. You dated." I rolled my eyes and kept walking.

Catching my hand in his, he walked with me. "Actually, no. He's quite striking, but not my type." He twisted our hands so the blue diamond in my wedding ring glinted in the low light. "For some unknown reason, my type seems to be bookish bartenders who give me far too much lip."

I spun him around and kissed him soundly. "You mean like that?"

His eyes had gone vamp black, so I knew I was a heartbeat from being thrown over his shoulder and taken back to the hotel—which, granted, any other night would have been mind-blowing—but I wasn't done. I extricated myself from his arms and went in search of a mummy. I was sure they had one here.

Perhaps my necromantic abilities were on overdrive in this gallery, but it was almost like I felt him calling to me, waiting behind a row of sphinxes. Like the Mona Lisa, he was much smaller than I was expecting, nothing like the mummies described in books or depicted on film. Linen strips had been woven in a geometric pattern over his face. He also had a hand-painted chest piece, neckband, and apron laid over the linen wrappings.

"Nenu," I breathed.

"Hmm?"

"His name was Nenu…and he was loved." Someone had taken painstaking hours to weave his wrappings as they had, someone who grieved his loss.

I was stepping away when I saw movement out of the corner of my eye. Nenu's faceless head had turned toward me, the fingers of one hand twitching.

Shhhhiiiiiiitttttt.

"Um, just to be clear, I did not read from the book." Yes, most of my mummy knowledge came from a movie. What's your point?

Clive had his head tilted toward the arched entrance of the hall, listening. "You didn't what?" he asked absently.

"Clive?"

When he turned, he found my shaking finger pointing at a mummy, one who now showed movement in both hands.

His eyes widened. "Oh, good Lord."

We both watched in horror as an arm moved, causing the neckband to slide off and into the side of the glass box.

"Fix it, darling. Now. We are not setting a mummy loose in Paris. We'll never be allowed to return." Nudging me, he stood transfixed.

"I don't know how to—" The head lifted an inch and then dropped.

"Figure it out. And hurry. The guard is coming back."

I closed my eyes and sought out the dead, not all of them, just the one right in front of me. *Rest, Nenu. Your time on this earth is done. Return to Osiris. Go.* I pushed on the last word and felt his spirit leave this realm.

"A bit of a time crunch, my love."

"Done."

Clive snatched me up and raced us through the halls, eventually stopping where we had started. I looked up into the hole in the ceiling. It looked impossibly far away. Clive adjusted his hold on me, so I was clinging to his back, my arms around his neck.

"Hold on," he said, patting my wrist.

When he flexed his knees to jump, I said, "No way."

He leapt straight up, catching the lip of the opening. "Climb up and out, ye of little faith."

I scrambled up his body and out the hexagonal opening in the dome. Once I was back on the roof, Clive pulled himself through and pushed the decorative panel back in place.

Grinning at me in the dark, he asked, "What shall we do next?"

TWO

Should a Hotel Room Be Bigger Than a House?

I woke snuggled up against my bridegroom in the pitch-black bedroom of the George V penthouse. Apparently, if you spend enough—and I didn't want to know how much this place cost, because I was pretty sure it was more than I made in a year—you can ask them to put up blackout curtains to help you sleep or, in Clive's case, not be turned to ash by the sun.

We'd been in Paris two nights, and I was in love with the city. It felt like Paris was America's sophisticated thrice-divorced aunt, who smoked too much, drank only wine, and stayed runway thin by taking rare bites of the world-renowned meals she ordered. She was a total hoot to visit. You learned new swear words and flirted with her handsome neighbor who was far too old for you. Somewhere between the cigarettes, the wine, and the brie, though, you'd grown, become more cultured. I didn't want to live here, but I felt like some of the green had been rubbed off just by visiting.

Yesterday, I'd only woken an hour or so before nightfall, so I'd lounged in the sumptuous living room to wait for Clive. Today, though, I had a few hours. Time to explore on my own!

Dressed in my running gear, I took the elevator down, crossed the elegant lobby, trimmed for the holidays, and hit the streets of

Paris. Clive had sent Russell and Godfrey on to England to do some reconnaissance and secure accommodations. I knew I should be grateful that Cadmael, an ancient Mayan warrior and Clive's vampy friend, was watching over the San Francisco nocturne in our absence, but I hadn't yet forgiven him for rummaging around in my head. Hypocritical, given my abilities, I know.

With Abigail, my homicidal aunt, and Leticia, Clive's psycho stalker, both gone, San Francisco was the safest it had been in quite a while, so I wasn't too worried about leaving my Slaughtered Lamb in Owen and Dave's capable hands. Okay, I was a little worried, but it was mostly centered on Stheno and her sisters permanently scaring away my customers.

At first, my run—like my thoughts—meandered, no destination in mind as I soaked up the sights and sounds of Paris. As I made my way through the Tuileries, though, I realized I was running toward something.

Sunlight glittered off the glass pyramids standing before the Louvre. I wanted to go back, to see something that had barely registered as we'd raced past but had lingered in my mind's eye. Ignoring the long line at the main entrance, I instead went to the Richelieu door, waiting only ten minutes instead of an hour.

I looked up the location of the sculpture on a map. It was in Denon, the wing opposite to the one I was standing in. The museum was, of course, crowded, so I weaved in and out of meandering groups of visitors, slowly making my way through the seemingly endless halls.

Wanting to be there when Clive awoke, I knew I wouldn't have much time. The idea of going back without finding it, though, made me feel unsteady. Finally, after dodging a large student group, I made it to a long hall showcasing an array of sculptures. The one I wanted was at the end.

Psyche Revived by Cupid's Kiss. A half dozen people were standing around the sculpture, taking pictures. I moved to the side, out of the constantly shifting stream of visitors. I tuned out the talking, the complaints about sore feet and boredom, the flash photography—which was prohibited by the Louvre but ignored by the tourists—focusing instead on the marble figures. Psyche reclined, forever reaching up to encircle Cupid as he gazed down, tenderly holding her, as though painfully aware of just how fragile she was, how fragile their love was.

I knew the stories, knew their plight, the distrust, the trials, and yet love had prevailed. Canova, the sculptor, had captured a moment of perfect longing, a moment bursting with anticipation where the world had contracted to two people and the promise of a kiss.

"All right, dear?"

I started at the soft, Italian voice. Turning, I found an elderly woman at my elbow, her expression one of concern.

"Yes, of course," I said, clearing my throat.

"You're crying." She looked back at the piece. "Lovely, yes?"

Scrubbing the wetness from my face, I nodded. "Yes."

Her family gathered her up and herded her on to the next hall, but not before she turned and nodded to me, recognizing another, like herself, who could drop under the noise and chaos of the moment to experience the eternal. I returned her nod as she moved through the arch.

Cupid and Clive bore no resemblance. In the stories, he was too beautiful to look at, which fit, but the sculptural version was softer and more angelic. What touched me, made me weep in recognition, was the love clear in his aspect, the tenderness with which he held her. I identified with Psyche, who appeared to have been through more than she could handle. She was exhausted and ready to give up. And yet, she forever lifted her arms in trembling hope and love.

"Here you are."

I knew that voice. Turning, I wrapped my arms around him and burrowed in. "I missed you."

"Here I am." He squeezed me to him.

"I know, but the missing takes time to fade."

"True." He kissed the top of my head. "When I awoke, you weren't there, but strangely, this statue was on my mind. It was almost like a muddled memory from a dream, but I don't dream anymore. So, wanting to find you, I went in search of the lovers and here you are."

I smiled into his neck, his scent settling something jittering inside me. "You could have just called."

"You mean on this," he said, pulling my phone from his pocket. "You left it charging by the bed."

Grimacing, I took it from him and slid it into my hoodie pocket. "Oops. I intended to go for a quick run through the city and be back before you woke. It's just"—I moved so we could both gaze at the statue—"I couldn't get this out of my head. We raced past it last night, and I wanted to see it again." Glancing up at the clock on the wall, I paused, unable to make sense of it. I'd been standing here for over an hour.

"I imagine you're hungry. Shall we return to the hotel so you can change before we go to dinner?" He ran his hand up and down my back.

"Would you mind if we didn't do fancy tonight?"

"Not at all. What did you have in mind?" He took my hand, and we wove our way through groups of stragglers who were deciding where to go when the museum shortly closed.

I thought a moment. "A leisurely stroll and a café that appeals?"

"Sounds perfect," he said, squeezing my hand.

Once out the main doors and walking across the courtyard, Clive put his arm around me and began the stroll. We walked along the Seine, streetlights dotting the darkening sky. Restaurants and clubs glowed invitingly on both sides of the river.

We made it back to the hotel in no time. After showering and dressing, I almost changed my mind, opting to order room service and eat on our balcony overlooking the city. Almost. I didn't want to miss a moment of Paris before we resumed our hunt for Aldith.

Wearing jeans, boots, a cranberry sweater—in a nod to the season—and the long, warm, black cashmere sweater coat Clive had bought me the night before, I checked my reflection. No braids tonight. I wore my hair long. Clive waited by the door in a charcoal gray overcoat. Vampires weren't bothered by the cold, but he knew how to blend.

Sometimes I was struck all at once by my good fortune. Clive had been born almost a thousand years ago on another continent and yet we'd met and fallen in love. This gorgeous, kind, clever, fiercely protective man was mine. All the days of our very long lives, we'd said when we'd taken our vows. Until I breathed my last, until he was dust on the wind, we'd have each other. The thought stole my breath. Clive would be my partner in crime for all time.

I went to him, wrapped my arms around his neck, and kissed him senseless. When I tried to step back, I found I couldn't move. Clive's hands on my butt held me in place. I looked up into vamp-black eyes and kissed his chin.

"Just making sure you knew I loved you and was looking forward to forever with you."

Palming my butt, he hitched me up around his waist and walked us back to the bedroom. "We'll be making a later start this evening."

I was giggling when he tossed me onto the soft bed.

Considerably later, we were dressed and ready to go again. This time, though, I was famished.

"First order of the evening is food," I said as we took the small elevator down to the lobby.

"We could have ordered room service," Clive said as he lifted my hand, kissing my fingers.

"Nope. I want to see as much of Paris as possible before we have to leave."

A doorman held one of the large double doors open for us, nodding respectfully as we passed.

"*Bonsoir,*" I called back, grateful for the long sweater coat. A late December night in Paris was quite cold. "I thought it snowed in Paris."

Clive tucked my hand into the crook of his arm. "It does, but not this soon. The air isn't freezing yet. As I recall, it's January into February when the snow falls."

Paris was all dressed up for the holidays: Wreaths hung on doors, fairy lights twinkled in denuded trees, storefronts sparkled, bridges across the Seine glowed. I wanted nothing more than to be in the moment, but my stomach started growling.

Clive placed his hand over mine, leading me down a side street. "I know just the place."

We turned again and were on a narrow street where festive lights glittering in windows were dimmed by the warm glow pouring from a restaurant. It was like a Van Gogh painting come to life. Overlapping voices, glasses clinking, a violin playing. It was perfect.

Clive spoke to the hostess in fluent French. A moment later, the young woman led us to a sidewalk table. Most sat inside, but a few, like ourselves, didn't want to be tucked away.

The meal was amazing, both meals. Clive and I had our moves down. He played with his food, occasionally taking what looked like a bite, while I ate mine. Then we switched plates. Being relatively alone meant we didn't have to be quite so clandestine with our maneuvers.

An older woman walked out of the restaurant and said something in French to us. Clive chuckled, taking my hand before responding. I caught 'my wife' and 'American,' but that was about it. The woman nodded, adjusting the thick scarf at her neck. She patted my hand and said something to me. Clive thanked her—I got that much—and then she walked across the street and up the short stairs of an apartment building.

I turned to him, waiting.

He squeezed my hand. "She was sitting in the window and noticed our ruse. She wondered if you were pregnant. I told her we were newly married, and you were not, although I don't think she believed me."

"What about at the end, when she patted my hand?"

"Oh, it sounded like some kind of blessing for being fruitful and multiplying," he said, lifting a finger toward our waiter for the check.

"Aww, that was sweet, assuming we wanted to multiply. Or could." I glanced up when a corner window on the third floor lit up. Hopefully, that meant she'd made it to her apartment. "She had a little buzz."

"Hmm?" Clive placed cash in the red leather folder the waiter had dropped on our table. "Are you ready, and what kind of buzz?"

"Yeah." I took his hand, and we continued our stroll through the city. "I don't know. It wasn't wicchey or vampy—"

"That word."

"But there was some little buzz of power in her touch." I shrugged. "Or maybe she shuffles her feet and built up a static charge."

He pulled my hand back into the crook of his arm, his preferred strolling position. "I didn't sense anything."

Shrugging, I snuggled in. "No idea. It wasn't strong. She may not even know she has magical blood." When we passed under a Metro sign, I stopped and pointed up.

"Oh, darling, must we? Not all Parisian experiences are good ones." At my continued tugging, he gave in and we walked down the steps to the subway trains.

My necromantic spidey senses were tingling. Lots of dead down here. Old, though, not recent. Well, one recent down the white-tiled tunnel to the left. When I paused, looking around for someone to tell, Clive pulled me along.

"I can hear the authorities. They've found him." He led me to a large colorful Metro map. "Where would you like to go?"

Our time was short in Paris. What did I want to see before we left? I pointed to a spot in the 14th arrondissement.

13

Clive looked pained. "Must we?"

I merely grinned in response. He shook his head, took my hand, and led me through the tunnels to the correct platform. Ever since I'd learned about them, I'd wanted to visit the Catacombs of Paris.

THREE

And You Call Yourself a Vampire

"If we don't find an evening tour, they're most likely closed until morning. And wouldn't that be a shame."

I elbowed him. "So you can get into the Louvre after hours but not a catacomb? What kind of vampire are you?"

"One with standards, darling. It's our honeymoon. We could go dancing at L'Arc, perhaps take a cruise along the Seine—"

"Ooh, I heard about a moving bus discotheque. All the benches were removed to make a dance floor. We could dance while seeing the sights. Win-win."

"Pass-pass." The sound of a train approaching echoed off the tiled walls, creating a deafening roar. "If my choices are dancing in a moving vehicle or the dead…" He shrugged, put an arm around me, and led me into the half-filled train car. Most passengers appeared to be heading home from work or going out for the evening.

Clive tucked me in front of himself, wrapped an arm around me, and grabbed a pole by the door. When the train left the station, we began to rock back and forth with the motion of the car. I rested my head against Clive's shoulder and people watched.

"Give us a kiss, love," Clive whispered in my ear.

Grinning, I turned, slid my hands under his overcoat, and then gave him a soft kiss before tucking my head in the crook of his neck. Clive held fast to the metal pole while I held fast to him, swaying with the sudden jolts but never losing my balance.

My spidey senses started prickling again for a different reason. "Is someone staring at us?" I whispered.

"Darling, people are always staring. Have you seen me?"

Snorting, I shook my head into his collar. "Ass."

"Yes, that's exceptional as well." He was teasing, but I'd felt him tense at my question. "I don't see anyone paying particular attention to either of us. Why?"

I tried to shake it off, but the feeling remained. I opened my senses to the dead. Perhaps I was dealing with a fixated ghost. The train was vamp free, save for my espoused. A ghost lingered, but two cars from us. It had to be something I could neither see nor control.

"An itch between my shoulder blades. Someone's paying very close attention to me. I want to know who and why."

Clive's hand moved up my back, a vain effort to shield me. When the train came to a stop, he pulled me from the car, snaking through a glut of people. We walked quickly off the platform, through tunnels, and up the stairs.

Through it all, the feeling of being watched never wavered. If anything, it got stronger. I had to fight to keep from constantly looking over my shoulder.

"Perhaps we should go back to the hotel." Clive lifted a hand to flag an oncoming cab, but I pushed it down.

"No. There are lots of things that go bump in the night, right? I'm not hiding on our last night in Paris. Besides, I'm at my strongest when I'm with the dead. Come on," I said, tugging his hand. "I can feel them. The catacombs are this way."

A few blocks away, we came to the main entrance, the one where tourists purchased tickets. It was closed for the night.

"Well, isn't that a terrible disappointment." Glancing across the empty street, he said, "I know just the place. You'll love it."

I yanked my hand out of his. I wasn't being redirected that

easily. The dark building sitting atop the entrance wasn't terribly secure. Even I, someone with no breaking and entering expertise, saw a number of ways to slip in.

"Clive?" I whispered.

"What?" he responded from a hair's breadth behind me.

I jumped. I admit it. Stupid, silent vampire.

"What kind of scary-ass vampire are you, anyway? Get us in the damn catacombs." I was pretty sure I could take the door off its hinges.

"No."

My shoulders dropped as I turned to him. "No? What do you mean no? We've been married less than a week and I'm already getting no? What about the loving and adoring and obeying? That's it," I said, walking around the back of the building. "I'm telling Russell on you. You have to have just broken a ton of rules right there. Besides, he's the new Master. He'll put you in your place." I tried the knob of the back door.

"Firstly, I can and will say no whenever I please. B, no rules have been broken by withholding consent. And fourthly, he's not Master, as I have not stepped down yet."

Turning, I kissed him quickly before continuing to explore. "You won't distract me by being cute and playful, so just forget it, mister." I stopped near a side alley. "What's really going on? Why don't you want me down there?"

Staring hard at the sign, he shook his head. "I can think of far more enjoyable ways I'd rather spend my evening than traipsing through bloody bone-filled passages." Clive was angry. He so rarely ever was with me, I worried I'd been an asshole, had screwed up in some way.

"We can go," I said. "I'll come back tomorrow during the day if I have time." I took his hand and squeezed, pulling him back toward the city center. "How about Montmartre? We didn't make it there last night."

Sighing, he dragged me back and held tight as a petite car

raced down the quiet road beside us. "Sorry." Tensing, he turned to the dark alley to his right.

"Well, well, well, look who it is." A gorgeous redhead slipped out of the shadows. Vampire. She wore a form-fitting little black dress with stiletto heels as she slowly made her way straight to Clive, her gaze taking in every inch of him. The woman could give TED talks on seduction.

"Suzette, it's lovely to see you again." Clive angled his body so he was partially blocking me. "I didn't realize you were still in Paris."

"Oh." She waved his comment away. "It is my heart. No matter where I go or how long I am away, I always come home." She stepped into Clive, running her hands up his arms and around his neck, her body stretching out like a cat luxuriating in a beam of sunlight as she pressed as much of herself as possible against him.

A low, deep growl rolled down the empty street. Suzette, eyes vamp black, glanced around Clive's shoulder, finally bothering to acknowledge me.

"Suzette, may I introduce you to my wife, Samantha." Humor filled his voice, but I wanted to punch him in the back of the head for letting her turn a hug into something pornographic.

"Wife? I thought she was your"—she shrugged—"I don't know, driver?" She went up on her toes to kiss the corner of his mouth.

Claws sprung from my fingertips. "That's it." I grabbed the wrists of hands currently trying to work their way into Clive's hair and flung them off, forcing her to step back.

Hissing, she flew at me. Clive grabbed her around the waist and walked her back into the alley. Glancing over his shoulder to check on me, he kept her pinned to the brick wall.

"Enough."

"But Clive—" Her voice was a throaty purr and she reached up to touch his face.

He caught her hand and firmly placed it by her side. "No."

It took another minute of her trying to eyefuck him before she finally slumped against the wall. "Eh, fine." When Clive let her go, she moved back to me, the slow, seductive gait gone. "*Félicitations pour votre mariage*," she said before pulling me down to drop perfunctory kisses on both cheeks.

"Thanks?"

Clive moved back to my side, his arm around me. "Why in God's name are you here?" he asked, glancing down the alley.

"A snack. Tourists seek the spooky. I oblige." She shrugged again, a grin pulling at her perfect lips. "The better question is what are *you* doing here? You hate this place," she said, tipping her head toward the entrance to the catacombs.

I raised my hand. "That'd be my fault."

"Ah, first time in Paris?" At my nod, she laughed, a throaty, seductive sound. Damn sexy vamp. "Come. There are many entrances to the catacombs, most of which the humans know." She winked at me. "But not all."

She turned, dashing across an intersection with streets jutting off in different directions before turning down the Boulevard Arago. "Come, *mes petits choux*," she called back to us. "Let us see what we see."

The boulevard was busier than the side streets we'd been on earlier. Cars streaked down the road while a group of young men prowled, crossing the street to head us off. One made a move, breaking from the pack, but was pulled back by a friend, who then hurriedly ushered the group down a side road.

"Friends of yours?"

"The smart ones know they are not the scariest things walking these streets. Eh?" She smacked Clive's shoulder. "We had some fun, *n'avons nous pas?*"

Clive shook his head, grinning. "*Oui.*"

We passed what looked like government buildings and a school, a man sitting on a bench smoking. This neighborhood was quite different from where we were staying: more locals, fewer tourists.

A short way down on the left, we came upon a park behind a

tall wrought iron fence. Suzette paused, looking through the gates, but they were closed and locked. At the corner, she turned left onto Rue du Faubourg Saint-Jacques. The street was quiet. Only two cars passed us and no pedestrians.

Suzette paused, tilting her head and listening. Tall walls towered on either side of the road, so there was no worry of anyone looking out an apartment window at us. With an impish grin, she leapt up and over the back wall of the garden.

Clive turned to me. "Can you make that?" he asked, gesturing to the top of the wall. "Or shall I help you over?"

"I guess we'll find out." I flexed my legs and then shot up and landed with nary a wobble on the top of the wall. I didn't want to end up caught in a tree on the other side. I wanted to see where I was going before I completed the jump.

Clive, barely making a sound, appeared beside me a moment later. Taking my hand, he pointed to our left, to a spot between trees. Nodding, I squeezed his hand and we jumped together.

Suzette leaned against the tree, waiting for us. *"Bon. Allons-y."* She pushed off and streaked across the deserted moonlit park, stopping at a large statue. It was oddly fascinating, like a statue of a man that had been stretched out and then spun in circles. He looked to be made of Silly Putty.

"François Arago, *physicien, mathématicien, astronome.*" She went to the bushes behind the unusual statue. "He is not our destination." She pushed a large branch aside and then motioned for Clive to take it. "This isn't the most accessible entrance, but it is one of the closest."

Brushing leaves off the ground, she revealed what looked like a large manhole cover. Lifting the heavy disc easily, she slid it aside.

A wicked grin spread across her face. "Ladies first."

Clive put out a hand to stop me. "How about if I go first?"

Pouting, she muttered, "Spoilsport."

I took over Clive's job, holding back the branch. He looked down into the hole a moment and then stepped forward and dropped in. A moment later, he called up, "Perhaps fifty, sixty feet. There's a ladder, darling, if you'd prefer."

Suzette held the branch and tipped her head toward the hole. "*Après vous.*"

Not being comfortable dropping sixty feet into the dark, I took the ladder. Suzette released the branch, thwacking me in the back of the head.

"Oops. You're far slower than I was expecting." It was hard to ignore the laughter in her voice. Stupid perfect French vampire.

FOUR

I Use Bones in All of My Decorating...

"Suzette, what did you do?" Clive's voice floated up from the bottom of the shaft.

"Nothing," I muttered, the back of my head sore as I made my way down, rung by rung.

The metal cover scraped back into place and then our annoying French guide plummeted behind me, landing soundlessly beside Clive.

They were silent a moment. "How long do you think this will take?"

"Suzette," Clive warned.

"Do you remember that time we ran into each other in Prague?" Accent thicker, her voice took on the sultry tone she'd used earlier in the evening.

Rolling my eyes inwardly, I continued to stomp down the metal rungs.

"I do, yes. It was a very enjoyable weekend for us both. As I've mentioned a few times, though, I'm now married. See?" I looked down and he was pointing up at me. "Wife."

Unconcerned, she shrugged one shoulder. "I don't mind."

A deep, vicious growl echoed off the walls.

"Ah, but my wife does."

I wobbled a moment. One of the rungs was missing and my foot sailed through the air where it should have been. Screw it. I was only twenty-ish feet up. I dropped a hair's breadth from Suzette, towering over her with my claws extended and my eyes wolf gold.

"Fine, fine." She tossed her hair over her shoulder and turned down a tunnel. "This way."

Clive wrapped his arms around me and squeezed, kissing the back of my neck before letting me go so we could follow.

I held up my phone to light the darkened passages. It was exactly as it had been described in books, and yet wholly unbelievable. Bones were stacked uniformly on both sides of the tunnels. Skulls were incorporated to create patterns. There was a dark, grotesque beauty to it.

Most of the bones were inert, the souls long since gone. Others, though, called to me. I lifted a hand, enjoying the feel of their energy. It was like playing with the wind when you hold your hand out a moving car window.

"Don't touch. You'll cause an avalanche," Suzette said. As she was a good ten feet in front of us, her knowing what I was doing was pretty impressive. Her long red wavy hair glowed like a flame in the phone's flashlight.

"Wait," I said. "They're just loose? I could take a bone, rearrange the patterns, knock them all to the floor?"

"*Oui.*"

"Dang." I slowed, studying the formations more closely. "What about rats or other animals? Do they knock over the piles?"

She shrugged. "Sometimes."

Clive took my hand to speed me up.

"And all these people died during the plague?" It boggled the mind.

Suzette slowed and then turned. "You cannot imagine. Half of Paris gone like that." She snapped her fingers. "Dead bodies lying in the streets, piled wherever there was room." She shook her head, looking around. "Mountains of the dead in graveyards, because there was no one left to tend to them." She turned and started walking again. "Anyone who rhapsodizes about the good old days should be beaten."

"They don't understand." Clive squeezed my hand. "They didn't live it as we did."

Oh. Clive's dislike of the catacombs, his desire to do literally anything else, made sense now. I was a tourist, visiting his past trauma.

Movement out of the corner of my eye made me stop. A nest of rags in a narrow alcove appeared to be breathing. Human, unwashed human. Shining my phone light on the opposite wall so as not to blind this person, I crouched down.

"*Pardon.* Can we help you? Do you need to find your way out?"

"Fuck off." He had a thick French accent, but he got his point across.

"Okey dokey." Popping up, I grabbed Clive's hand again. We sped to catch up to Suzette, who had continued her tour without us.

"…quarries mined to create buildings like Notre Dame and Versailles above. Some tunnels started to collapse, causing structures aboveground to fall through. So, two problems, one solution. Tunnels were reinforced and all the dead who laid moldering above were brought below."

Damn. That sounded interesting. It occurred to me that I was hearing a thumping sound, like a rhythmic pounding. "What is that?"

"Revelers. They sneak in after hours. We have police officers whose only job is to look for trespassers." She turned left at a juncture in the tunnel system and the bass beat got louder.

"They just patrol the catacombs? How big is it down here?" That sounded like the kind of job that would be really cool the first week or two and then get tedious fast.

"I don't remember precisely. A couple hundred miles of tunneling." Suzette gave Clive a flirty look over her shoulder. "Do you remember when we…swam in the lagoon?"

"I do quite well and, again, wife," he said, raising our hands to show my ring.

I tried to ignore the quick flash of jealousy. It wasn't easy, but I tried. "There's a lagoon?"

"*Oui.*" She looked over her shoulder again, interest in her eyes. "Would you like to go for a dip?"

"A big black body of water where literally *anything* could be swimming below me and I wouldn't be able to see it until it wound around my legs and yanked me down to my watery grave? Hmm… No, I'm good."

"The only one wound around me was—"

"Hey," I said, growl in my voice. "How about you zip it already?" The throbbing bass beat was starting to give me a headache.

"Zip? Oh, look." She pointed to her right. "More bones." As every passage was lined with bones stacked five or more feet high, her comment was clearly intended to shut me up.

The nearness of the dead fueled my necromancy. If I'd wanted to, I could have crushed her like a bug with my mind. Granted, it would hurt like hell, but I could siphon off the pain into the wicche glass around my neck. Might be worth it.

"Have a care, Suzette. My wife is quite formidable." Clive saved his next comment just for me, mind to mind. *I apologize. I didn't anticipate her relentlessness. Shall we go? You've seen the bones. It's all more of the same.*

"Yes, yes. Growling and claws. I am most regretfully sorry and quite concerned." The bored tone made me want to punch her.

"Fuck around and find out, sister."

She flew at me, but I was ready. I tossed my phone to Clive, so I had both hands free and then snatched her out of the air by her neck, my claws piercing her skin. I didn't want to kill her, but throttling was definitely on the table.

I slammed her against a nearby pillar, holding her a foot off the ground. I brought my wolf to the fore and let her see I was a predator too. Using my necromancy, I gave her a sharp jab behind her eyes. She winced, and then her gaze darted between Clive and me, unsure which of us had the power to give her pain. If she didn't already know, I wasn't going to tell her it was both of us.

"I have no doubt that if either of us actually wanted to kill the other, it would be a knock-down, drag-out fight until one or both of us was dead. As we clearly don't want to do that, perhaps you could stop trying to seduce my husband right in front of me. I mean it." I squeezed tighter. "I'm done with your shit."

Eyes vamp black, she hissed at me. "I could crush your bones and drink you dry before you made your first move."

"Clearly not." I let go and she dropped to the floor. "I know you could have broken my arm or just yanked it off my body in order to free yourself, just as I could have cut through your neck and beheaded you when you first came at me. We are, both of us, deadly. That doesn't make us enemies. Clive has had many lovers in his very long life, but only one from now on. We're on our honeymoon. How about taking it down a few notches and being Clive's friend instead of pretending there's some rivalry between us?"

"I'd be sorry to lose your friendship," Clive added, "but you've had more than enough time to adjust your thinking."

Blinking, she shook her head, her eyes returning to their normal brown. "Fine. There's an exit just past this party. *Je déteste cet endroit.*"

We turned another corner in the passage and the music became deafening. Colored lights flashed in the dark cavern, an intersection of multiple tunnels. No bones lined the walls here. No caution needed to be taken, and none was. Bodies writhed and bounced to the driving beat. A large screen hung against one wall, violent sex being projected.

Stomach turning, memories surfacing, I looked for Suzette's red hair. I needed out of here now. In the chaos, a woman screamed. I jolted, the pressure in my head at a breaking point. The scream turned to laughter, as I was jostled back and forth by the delirious dancers. A couple grunted, having sex in the corner.

Too many things were hitting me at once. I shrank inside myself, desperate to escape. Clive's arm tightened around me as we pushed through the crowd. I almost broke and ran but then Suzette suddenly appeared before me. Vision tunneling, she was all I saw. She stared a moment and then gently reached down and took my hand, leading me out.

I followed like a child. Disgust with myself for losing it, though, came in a distant second to panic. We traveled down the narrow side passage for quite a while, but even in the relative dark and quiet, I couldn't stop the trembling, my heart rabbiting in my chest.

Nor could I shake the feeling of being followed. It was like the subway all over again. Reaching out with my mind, I searched the catacombs for the familiar cold green blips. Two vamps sandwiched me. A glut of them was deep in the passages, probably miles away. I wondered if they fed on the partygoers. Foggy whisps of the dead, most too ancient for sentience to remain, hovered over the bone piles. Two faint blips of a lighter green were there and gone, making me wonder if I'd imagined them. Stomach fluttering, I realized I was also seeing the purplish smear of an immortal waiting deep underground. Unless my anxiety was playing tricks on me, whatever was out there watching me wasn't something I could sense.

We stopped and Suzette placed my hand on a metal rung. "*Montez.*" She gestured up, so I got the gist. With each step, my nerves settled and I felt closer to safety. I reached the top sooner than I expected. Apparently, the catacombs weren't as deep here as where we went down. Instead of a manhole cover, though, there was a narrow passage forward and then a door.

On hands and knees, I crawled to the door. I sensed Clive behind me as I felt for a latch of some kind. I was about to just break through the door when I felt a metal loop. I tested it, jiggling, pushing, pulling, until I heard the squeal of rusted metal scraping against itself.

I pulled it open a slit, trying to see out. I didn't want to pop out of a wall right in front of a crowd. Water. There was water below the door. Pulling it open, I looked out over the Seine; at least, I assumed that was what I was looking at.

The drop to the path along the river was only eight or ten feet. I looked all around. Seeing no one nearby, I crawled out, hopped over the decorative metal fencing, and landed easily on the path below. Clive stood beside me a moment later. Suzette closed the door on another squeal and then dropped as well.

She studied me as she had in the underground party. "You're all right now?"

I nodded.

Her gaze held understanding. She patted my arm in comfort. "Good. Now fuck off. You," she said to Clive, "I'll see when you dump the dead weight." She climbed the steps to the street above, brushing dirt and webs off her black dress.

Strangely, I kind of missed her. But not a lot.

FIVE

It's Actually over $20,000

"It just occurred to me what that rave reminded me of."

Clive nodded to the stairs Suzette had just used and we began to climb. "Your visit to Hell?"

"No. The Crypt, your nightclub, which I totally don't get. If you hate the catacombs, why do you have a club that mirrors them?" The streets were quiet and empty in the wee small hours of morning.

He looked at me, brow furrowed. "Are you under the impression I go clubbing a lot?"

The question made me laugh, which was no doubt his intent.

Pulling my hand into the crook of his arm, he continued, "Hundreds of thousands of people explore the catacombs every year. Humans are drawn to the macabre. We picked décor that was unusual and would give patrons a heightened sense of danger. The hedonistic drinking and dancing is a reaction to being close to death."

We crossed the wide boulevard, heading back to the hotel. White lights glowed above the sidewalks as tiny flakes of snow swirled in the air, melting before hitting the ground. I was walking through a postcard. On my honeymoon. The world was a strange and wonderful place.

The lobby was decorated for the holidays, with black geometric reindeer, gold ornaments at their hooves, and towering trees decorated in red behind shimmering screens. Clive detoured to the front desk where one sleepy man sat behind the counter.

At our approach, his shoulders snapped back. *"Bonne soirée. Comment puis-je vous aider, s'il vous plait?"*

"Thank you, yes. Our coats were soiled this evening." He helped me out of mine before removing his own. "Could you have them cleaned and then returned to the penthouse. Fitzwilliam."

"Yes, of course, sir." The man came around the desk and took our coats.

I felt kind of bad. I was pretty sure just holding them was ruining his uniform. When he turned to leave, I remembered.

"Wait. *Pardon.* Sorry." I reached forward and went through the pockets of my coat, retrieving my phone. "Thanks."

He nodded, returning my smile, and then headed down a short corridor.

"I could use a shower too," I said as we entered the elevator.

"God, yes. There were times I had to burrow underground to survive the day. Thankfully, that is no longer my life."

We exited and Clive keyed us into our suite.

"I'm sorry I made you go tonight."

"Don't be. How were you to know I hate the damn catacombs? It isn't as though we've discussed it."

We arrowed through the sumptuous penthouse, straight to the bathroom. Clive turned on the hot water as I peeled off clothes covered in grime and spiderwebs. When I'd dressed this evening, I hadn't anticipated crawling through underground passages.

I jumped into the hot, steamy water, a shiver running through me. I stood a moment, soaking in the heat, happy to be washing off the underground. Clive's soapy hands slid around my waist and palmed my breasts, thumbs flicking my nipples while his kisses ran down my neck.

Two could play at this game. I tapped the dispenser, filled my palms with soap, and reached back to run my hands down his sides and over his butt. While one of his hands slid down my belly and between my legs, I took him in hand and stroked.

Fangs pierced my neck and I squeezed. On a groan, he spun me around, hitched me up, and speared me to the wall. Legs wrapped tightly around him, I gripped his shoulders for leverage as we found our rhythm. His hands drove me crazy, his mouth on mine.

Mine. He was mine now and I was his. Forever more. I still couldn't wrap my mind around it.

When the orgasm began to roll through me, I clenched low, my back bowing off the tile. Clive's lips moved back to my neck, fangs descending, hammering home his own release.

Later, when I got my breath back and could stand, we finished getting cleaned up. It was close to dawn, but I didn't want to miss a minute of Paris. I wrapped myself in a thick robe, slid into slippers, and went out onto the balcony.

We had the most amazing view of the Eiffel Tower lit up against the night sky. Paris lay at our feet, twinkling.

"We can come back." He wrapped his arms around me, and I covered them with my own.

"Promise?"

Resting his head on my shoulder, he took in the view with me. "Of course. Once I pass the reins of the city to Russell, we can do whatever we wish."

"I still want The Slaughtered Lamb. Can we live there together, in the apartment behind the bar?"

"Hmm."

"I know it's not a mansion like the nocturne, but it'd just be the two of us." I half turned in his arms so I could read his expression. "We don't need a lot, do we?"

He kissed the tip of my nose. "I'd been looking at homes in Sea Cliff, much closer to your bookstore than Pacific Heights."

"Oh." I loved that neighborhood. Yes, I'd almost died on the patio of Benvair's Sea Cliff estate, but that wasn't the house's fault. I'd spent so many years living my work, maybe having a separate home would help me find balance.

"If you'd prefer, I can have the contractors come back while we're in Europe to add some rooms to the apartment." He touched his lips to mine. "Wherever you are is where I want to be."

"Well, I mean, if you're sure we can afford it. I do love that neighborhood."

"Darling, I'm loaded. Do you have any idea how much this room is costing us a night?"

Grimacing, I looked in the glass doors to the penthouse. "I've been afraid to ask. Five thousand?" This was our third night. Fifteen thousand dollars for a room was obscene, but I would have loved nothing more than to move in and stay a month.

"Significantly more than that, but worth it. Dawn is creeping up on us. Will you come to bed with me, or would you prefer to stay up?" He kissed my shoulder and then stepped away.

"I'm with you. Feeling kind of queasy about the hotel bill, though."

"You'll survive."

We put up the Do Not Disturb sign, checked that all the doors were locked—adding some of our own precautions—closed the blackout curtains, and slid into bed. None of this would save us from a supernatural trying to break in, but it would save Clive from being burned to a crisp by housekeeping barging in and throwing open curtains.

I snuggled in, my head on his shoulder. "The hunt begins tomorrow."

"Hmm." He wrapped his arms more tightly around me and kissed my head. "Hundreds of thousands of nights I've walked the earth, but it's been these last few perfect ones with you that I will treasure above them all."

The sun must have slipped over the horizon because Clive was out. I followed him under. Aldith could wait one more day.

I awoke in the late afternoon, having slept better than I had since we'd been here. I think my body was finally on European time. I'd intended to wander around town before Clive woke but decided not to. It being winter, he'd wake soon, and I was having a hard time shaking that feeling I'd been watched last night. I'd felt it in the subway and the catacombs. I wondered if there was a connection to them both being underground.

Regardless, I was going to have a meal on the balcony and lounge around the opulent penthouse a little longer. We'd be checking out soon. This perfect bubble of romance was coming to an end.

Ordering room service first, I lay down on the couch and closed my eyes, searching out all the cold green blips in my mind that meant vampire. I'd been doing this every day, slowly searching the UK for all their vamps. We believed Aldith was there, and I was trying to find her. I'd started at the southernmost part of England and had been slowly making my way north. Let me just say, there are a shit ton of supernaturals in England.

When I found a nocturne, I'd skim along the blips, looking for Aldith, trying my best not to invade another's mind without cause, all the while channeling the pain into the wicche glass around my neck. It was slow going. After my ham-handed attempt to read St. Germain in New Orleans, though, I'd been practicing. I was able to slide in now without alerting the vamp I was reading. Mostly.

I located a few vamps gathered to the east of London. If this was a nocturne, it was a small one. I only counted five. Maybe it was one of those weekend house parties I'd read about in historical romance novels. I was too busy imagining vampires in period costumes enjoying teacups of blood and giving the cut direct to a social climber who had the temerity to interrupt previously alive Lady Catherine for me to notice that I couldn't read one of the vamps in this small group. Odd.

I tried again, leaving thoughts of my historical vampire romance behind. Nope. One of the little blips had excellent defenses. Perhaps this was Garyn, the vamp who had created both Clive and Aldith. They both had very strong mental powers. This might be where'd they'd inherited them. Leaving that blip for the moment, I dipped into the other four and found boring mundane concerns. They were all sleeping, so their brains were sluggish, but one had a Clive memory close to the surface. The vamp had spoken with Garyn. She'd asked him to surveil us while we were in Canterbury.

There didn't appear to be any menace attached to the request. She just wanted to know why Clive was back and what he was up to. A knock at the door echoed in the silent room. Distracted, I lost the connection. On the plus side, room service had arrived.

Fed, showered, and packed, I was leaning on the balcony rail, watching Paris go by, when Clive came out. He was dressed in jeans and a sweater, his normal shoes exchanged for boots.

"I love waking up with your scent in the room. Every evening I awake with a purpose: Find Sam." He kissed me and we clung to one another just a few moments longer.

"I was doing my vamp sweep this afternoon and I think I found Garyn."

"Really?" He leaned against the railing, looking out over the city. "Interesting. Anything we need to be concerned about?"

"I couldn't read her."

At that, Clive turned back to me. "Isn't that fascinating? Any idea as to why"

Shaking my head, I added, "I was able to read the vamps with her. There was nothing overtly threatening. One of them had been told by Garyn to watch us while we were in Canterbury. She seems to be interested in what you're up to."

"What I'm up to is honeymooning my wife every chance I get."

At my snicker, he kissed my nose.

Tucking a loose hair fluttering in the wind behind my ear, he asked, "Which would you prefer, ferry or chunnel?"

"Ferry."

"I knew you were going to say that. I've hired a car to take us to the coast. Russell and Godfrey have already rented us a vehicle in England. They'll meet us in Dover." He ran a hand down my arm and then returned to our rooms.

I followed after one last look over the rail. "I love you, Paris," I whispered. "And someday I'll be back." Closing the balcony door and taking off my newly laundered sweater coat, I found Clive in the bedroom, his suitcase open. "How late do ferries run?"

"Not late enough, I'm afraid, which is why we'll have a private boat take us across." He folded and packed his clothes.

"Please tell me we're not crossing in a dinghy."

"Not at all. Russell made the arrangements, so I'm sure we'll be in good hands."

"What if I'd said I wanted to take the chunnel?"

"I was pretty sure you wouldn't, but if you did, I've have purchased tickets and we'd be traveling by train." He closed his case and then set it by the door next to mine.

I smacked his arm. "Stop that. You're going to go broke indulging my every whim. You should have just told me that the ferry wasn't an option this late at night and that we'd be taking the train."

He grabbed me and tumbled me onto the bed, kissing me soundly. "Where's the fun in that? And it's our money, not mine. Married, remember?"

"You should have gotten an undead pre-nup, sucker." I giggled as he nuzzled my cheek.

Rolling to the side, head resting on his bent arm, he watched me, a finger drawing lazy circles on my stomach. "And how will you spend all our money?"

Ridiculous things flashed through my mind: a private island, Pemberley, a vintage Jaguar, fancy clothes and dinners, expensive jewelry…

"Books. I'd want a collection of first edition books." And then it occurred to me. "No!" I grabbed his sweater. "You can't leave the nocturne. I'll lose my library!"

"True. *But,* in our new home, you can be a part of the design team and choose the books, first editions included."

I did like that. "But I *love* that library." I may have whined. I'm not proud.

"Almost half of it was blown to bits, darling."

"Don't remind me." Stupid jealous vampire redirecting a bomb to the library door just because I was in there when a perfectly good empty salon sat right across the hall.

He stood and dragged me up, checking his watch. "We should head down."

Pulling my sweater coat back on, I grabbed my bags. Clive tapped my shoulder and shook his head. "Yes," he said into his phone. "Could you send someone up to collect our bags? Thank you." He disconnected and pocketed it.

"Now we have to wait. We're both strong. We're only taking them downstairs. Why have someone else do it?"

"Two reasons," he began, pulling me toward the balcony. "First, we have time for this." He kissed me and all thoughts of luggage and travel disappeared. There was only Clive.

When we finally came up for air, he said, "Secondly, do you really want to deprive the porter of his tip?"

There was a discreet knock at the door. Clive went to answer it while I took one last look around. When I turned to go in, I felt it again, a prickling awareness of being watched. Was it Clive's friend Cadmael? Was he snooping through my mind? Closing my eyes, I focused my magic, gathering it in a ball in my chest, and then flung it out into the world, trying to dislodge whatever had attached itself to me.

The prickling remained. Damn it, what was following me?

"Ready?" Clive stood in the doorway, waiting for me.

"As I'll ever be." I took his outstretched hand and we headed out. It was time to hunt down Aldith.

SIX

Wherein Sam Steals a Car

Our mustachioed driver stood silently by the open back door of a black Mercedes with a silver hood and roof. "Sir. Madam."

Clive held out a hand to help me in, but it was all theater for those watching. *Look how human we are!* He walked around the back of the car and slid in the other side. This was the strangest backseat I'd ever seen. There were two separate seats with a console in the middle holding an integrated tablet. Legroom, there was actual legroom, and screens for each seat, in case we wanted to watch something during the drive. The seats were a buttery soft leather and had their own matching pillows.

I turned to Clive. "This car is now on my list of ways to bankrupt you."

The driver got in and moved out into traffic. "Would you like the screen up?"

"Yes, please." As it slid up, I leaned forward and added, "Nothing personal."

He grinned at me in the rearview mirror before it closed. It was darkly tinted glass, but not completely opaque, giving the impression of privacy.

Two glasses of champagne stood in the console, waiting for us.

Swiping through the tablet, Clive set classical music to playing. It was habit. He enjoyed the music, but more he enjoyed our voices being muted in case anyone was listening. He took a glass and handed it to me before picking up its twin. Clinking his crystal to mine, he said, "I already own a Maybach. It was delivered shortly before we were married. We'll consider it yours."

"Nuh-uh. No hand-me-downs. I want to pick out my own. Knowing you, it's all black, inside and out." I ran my hand along the soft leather. I could live back here.

"It's not, no. It's emerald green with a silver top. I ordered it with you in mind." He took a sip. "And you'd be bankrupting *us*, not me."

"Yeah, yeah. How much does one of these babies go for?" I asked, adjusting the pillow.

"A little north of two hundred thousand."

I choked on my champagne and sat rigid, not wanting to mess anything up. "Are you insane? You spent two hundred thousand on a car? What the frick? There's so much good you could do in the world with that kind of money." I hadn't spilled on the leather, had I?

"I give quite generously to various charities, as you know, but I also have a couple of obsessions: you and cars." He gave me a look I couldn't quite read. "Finding joy in life can be rare. Will you chide me for indulging that joy?"

Well, jeez, when he put it that way. Clive had once said that long-lived immortals often experienced a sort of malaise about life, fading to shadows of their former selves. They'd seen and done it all and had lost interest. If ridiculously expensive cars made him happy and kept him here, present in our lives together, how could I tell him it was wrong?

"No, and tricksily done."

"Lean back and relax. We have a three-hour drive to Calais."

It was the most comfortable and relaxing drive I'd ever taken. Clive and I talked about where we'd live, places we wanted to visit, people he wanted me to meet. It was all so incredibly lovely and normal, I'd almost forgotten the real reason we were here.

The driver took us to the harbor, stopping near a dock where a man in a white uniform stood waiting. Clive got out and spoke to the man, while our driver took our bags out of the trunk. Clive was back a few moments later, shaking the driver's hand and thanking him. The driver slipped the money Clive had passed him into his pocket and then nodded to us both before leaving.

"Sam, this is Captain James." Clive picked up my two bags while the captain carried Clive's.

"Hello. Thank you for taking us across tonight." I followed them down the dock, uncomfortable with the swooping sensation of the path bouncing beneath me.

"Of course, Mrs. Fitzwilliam. We're happy to have you both aboard."

Glowing in the dark was a huge yacht. Another person in a white uniform rushed down the gangway and took the bags Clive carried. We followed the men onto the boat and were passed off to another crew member.

"Mr. and Mrs. Fitzwilliam, would you like a tour?"

"That won't be necessary," Clive said. "We'd like to leave as soon as you're ready."

"Of course," the woman said, nodding to us both before heading up the stairs to the second level.

"Inside or out?" Clive asked me.

I looked through the glass to the outrageous interior. Dark wood, crystal light fixtures, elegant furniture, a huge spray of flowers on a side table. It was like a floating mansion. The deck held a long, horseshoe-shaped couch.

"Let's explore," I said, grabbing his hand.

We moved along the deck to the front of the boat and found another large seating area, with tables and chairs. The interior on this side of the ship appeared to be more of a smoking room. Saddle brown leather couches and chairs, a humidor on the center table, a bar running along the side; it looked inviting, but I kept moving.

Circling around the ship, I climbed the stairs to the second level. It was colder and windier before the yacht had even started moving, but it was open to the stars. The fore and aft decks both had beautiful seating areas, but I chose the fore. I wanted to watch England take shape.

We decided on the soft green loveseat with an unimpeded view of the water and distant shore. As soon as we sat, the boat began to move. Apparently, it was someone's job to keep an eye on us.

A steward appeared. "May I bring you champagne? Strawberries?"

"The strawberries sound great, but can I have hot chocolate instead?"

"Of course."

"Could we also have a blanket and"—Clive glanced at me—"pâté with toast points. Perhaps a charcuterie board."

"Right away, sir." The man motioned up at the lights strung above us. "On or off?"

"Leave them off. We're enjoying the clear night sky."

The steward nodded and returned to the interior of the ship, leaving us in the cold wind under the stars.

"When was the last time you were home?" I snuggled in, pulling the collar of my sweater coat up to block the lower half of my face from the wind.

Clive held my hand, turning it this way and that, watching the starlight reflect off the blue diamond in my wedding ring. "We should have picked you up a pair of gloves." He lifted my hand to his lips, kissing my fingers. "It's been a very long time."

The steward returned with a tray holding two mugs, a carafe of water with two glasses, a plate of strawberries, and an assortment of delicious-looking nibbles. He placed the tray on the table before us and then pulled a thick blanket from under his arm.

"If I may." He shook out the sea green blanket and then handed it to Clive.

"Thank you. That will be all." Clive flung the soft, warm blanket over us and then handed me a mug.

I took a sip and sighed. Delicious. I made short work of the food while Clive stargazed. Tummy full, I leaned back into Clive and followed his gaze up. They were so bright and clear, it felt like I could lift a hand and touch them. We never got to see skies like this back home; too much light pollution. Here, in the middle of the English Channel, we sailed alone between sea and stars.

"After I killed the Atwoods," Clive murmured, "I wanted to get as far away from memories as I could. Traveling was more difficult back then. Horses, as a rule, do not want the dead on their backs. I lived in London for a good long while. Having grown up on a farm, it was difficult to adjust. So many people living so closely together. Filth, poverty, criminals. It was exhilarating and nauseating all at once.

"I didn't realize it then—scrabbling to feed and find shelter doesn't lend itself to contemplation—but I was grieving horribly. My whole family, my farm, my life, all gone. What was left was a mindless, fiery thirst and a drive to survive, no matter who had to be hurt. I'd become a monster."

He glanced over. "I was supposed to be the hero, the one who helped people, who fought on the side of right. Instead, I was slinking in shadows, feeding from the weak, the innocent. I was worse than the Atwoods."

"No," I cut him off. "You did what it took to survive. You didn't hurt people for sport. You didn't attack and rape. You're nothing like those men."

The corner of his mouth kicked up, but there was no humor in his expression. "How would you know? You weren't there."

"No, I wasn't, but I know you. The adolescent who stood in front of a charging horse to save a child did not become vicious and cruel simply because his diet changed."

He released a gust of air. "It was a bit more than that."

"Was it, though? I know who you were through Leticia's memories of you, and I know who you are now. Do you really expect me to believe you were a sadistic sociopath for a few centuries before you regained your moral compass?" I shook my head. "Not buying it."

Clive's phone buzzed in his pocket. It was Russell. Shaking his head, he pulled my hand to his lips for another kiss before answering it. Even with the sounds of the engines and the wind whipping by, I could hear both sides of the conversation.

"Sire, Godfrey and I have secured rooms at The Ducking Stool Inn. Godfrey says you know the owner and that you may be able to get more information out of him than we've been able to."

"Interesting. His name?" Clive handed me the second cocoa cup. It had gone cold but wasn't bad.

"Godfrey says his name is Chaucer."

Clive let his head fall back. "Please tell me Godfrey is joking."

"Godfrey says he's even more of a bore now than he was a few centuries ago."

"Lovely. Where is Godfrey? I don't hear him with you."

"I'm in Dover, awaiting your arrival. He's sitting on the bore's barstool, waiting for a break in the endless rush of words so he can ask a question. He offered to be your driver this evening, but I pulled rank. It didn't take more than a twenty-minute conversation with the man before I wanted to stake myself."

"I'm quite familiar with the feeling," Clive said. "All right. We're perhaps an hour out. We can talk in the car."

Clive was just about to tap the end button, but it seemed Russell wasn't through. "I hope you enjoyed Paris, Miss Qu—Mrs. Fitzwilliam."

I took the phone from Clive. "I did! I could spend a month there and never be bored."

He chuckled, a deep, comforting sound. "And the George V?"

"I want to live there. Rain or shine, I'd have all my meals on the balcony. And the food!" While I rattled on, Clive listened, looking content and amused, which was far better than the annoyance he'd shown earlier at the mention of Chaucer. As we were on our way to Canterbury, I had a pretty good idea which Chaucer this was. I didn't understand what Russell and Clive were complaining about. I enjoyed *The Canterbury Tales*.

"...got Clive to go into the catacombs? It must be true love."

Clive snatched the phone from my hand. "Enough; you're taking up the last moments of my honeymoon. We'll see you soon." He hit end and pocketed the phone.

"Rude," I huffed. "Oh, look. They really are white."

Clive followed my gaze, nodding.

The white cliffs of Dover glowed in the moonlight. England. The home of Shakespeare and Elizabeth Bennet, Jane Eyre and Mr. Darcy, Mary Poppins and Sherlock Holmes, Harry Potter, Willy Wonka, Dracula... I knew we were here to find Aldith and put an end to her homicidal scheming, but I couldn't tamp down the giddy.

SEVEN

The Husband of Sam's Tale

"You're not actually cold, right?"

Clive shook his head.

"Good." I rose and wrapped the long blanket around myself as I strode to the bow. I wanted an unobstructed view. Moonlight bounced off the whitecaps as the ship cut through the water. The prickling along my scalp and between my shoulder blades was back. Who was following me?

"My stalker is back."

"Out here?"

"Asshole kept popping in all around Paris. I was kinda hoping we'd left him behind."

"Why didn't you tell me?" He wrapped his arms around me, retroactively protecting me.

"Nothing happened and I don't know." I shrugged. "I worried it was Cadmael rifling through my head again. The feeling was there and gone. And then, hours later, back again."

Closing my eyes, I sought nearby supernaturals, the ones my mind could identify. My betrothed behind me, Russell's familiar signature ahead. More, though, were crowding in. The light green blips of the water fae swam beneath us. Foggy ghosts paced along the cliffs. I didn't sense the purplish overlay that meant immortal, but I did see quite a few cold, green vampire blips, two close to Russell, the others farther off.

I pulled out my phone and called Russell.

"Hello again."

"Hey, listen, did you already know you have two vampires flanking you?" Clive stilled behind me, his hands resting on my hips.

"I did not." His tone had changed, all business now. "Can you tell me where they are?"

"Distance is hard to judge from this far away. Maybe a hundred yards to your right and above. Possibly a rooftop? The other is closer, only ten yards. Maybe in another car?"

"Can you read them?" Clive asked.

I focused my attention on the closer of the two. My head began pounding the moment I slid into the vamp's thoughts. Lifting Clive's hand to my head, I reminded him I needed pain relief. A cool numbness washed over me, leaving me with a manageable headache.

"It's the one I read before, Garyn's man. He's observing. Waiting." Garyn had wanted Clive to stay with her forever, to be her new family. He'd learned the basics and then set out on his own. He'd had his sister's death to avenge.

Clive had taken my phone when the pain hit. It was just as well, as I might have dropped it in the channel. He had one arm around me, anchoring me to him, while the other held the phone near my shoulder so Russell could clearly hear everything I said.

"Harris. His name is Harris and Garyn sent him to watch for your arrival. She'd heard whispers your men were in town but that you were in Paris. She'd also heard you'd undergone the blood ceremony, and with a werewolf, no less. She didn't believe it but wanted eyes on you.

"He's not a threat," I said, closing my eyes again. I slipped from Harris' mind and dove into... "Isabel. The second one is Isabel. She's watching Harris and therefore now watching you. She wants

45

to know why Harris is waiting, what he knows about you that she doesn't."

I blinked my eyes open. "Both are on reconnaissance missions, Harris for Garyn, Isabel for herself, but she was thinking vaguely about telling 'her' about your arrival. I didn't get a clear picture of who 'her' was, though."

"It sounds as though I'll be safe enough for the time being, then. Thank you for checking, Miss—"

"Sam, Russell. Just call me Sam."

"We'll see," he responded, his voice relaxing.

"Or my lady. I liked it when you called me my lady." I was grinning as Clive shook his head and ended the call, slipping the phone into my pocket.

He grabbed the railing on either side of me and rested his chin on my shoulder again. I leaned into him and we rocked with the ship, the shore growing ever closer.

"How are we feeling about Garyn keeping tabs on you?" I knew he hadn't wanted what she'd been offering all those centuries ago. Had time lessened the hurt for her or embedded it?

"*We* are feeling pleased. Garyn is connected to Aldith. I have no idea if they're still close, but given how Garyn clings to her perceived family, it stands to reason they are. This Harris is connected to Garyn. Much of the hunt is chasing down connections like this. And you found him before we stepped foot on land." He kissed my neck. "Well done, you. We'll let him watch for now, have you monitor him before we pull him in to question."

"All sneaky-like." I took his arms from the rail and wrapped them around me with a sigh. "I know this is why we're here. It's just"—I shrugged a shoulder—"the last few danger-free days have been everything. We're about to jump back into constant worry about our safety."

"I wish you showed more concern for your own safety. As for all this"—he flicked his fingers toward England—"I'd been a fledgling when I last dealt with Garyn. I've gained a great deal of strength and knowledge since then." He kissed the shell of my ear. "You needn't worry."

I turned to the side and looped my arms around his waist, resting my head on his chest. The high cliffs loomed as a fine mist of sea spray hit our faces. I hoped he was right but my spidey senses were telling another story.

He was silent for a while, but I could feel his turmoil. "I haven't been back here, to Canterbury, since my sister's murder and then my mother's death. It's home, but it's mired in heartache. I want you to enjoy your visit, but understand, if I'm—I don't know— short-tempered, it has nothing to do with you or our marriage and everything to do with the memories."

"I'm sorry."

"I know. I am too." He sighed deeply as he crushed me to him. "She'd have liked you, you know."

"Who?"

He chuffed a laugh. "Both of them, actually. My mother wanted me to find a good woman, strong to help run the farm but also kind for me. She thought I was too soft-hearted."

Snickering, I said, "Don't worry. I won't tell your vampy friends."

"Please don't. That cold-hearted bastard reputation took some time to earn." He paused. "No, I meant Elswyth. Like you, she could never say no to anyone or anything in need. She'd have appreciated your irreverence and your love of story. Most of all, she'd have giggled at how easily you conquered me."

"I'm sorry I never got to meet her. Either of them."

"That's the thing, though. If the Atwoods hadn't destroyed my family, I would have died on the farm countless lifetimes ago, and we'd never have met."

"I don't know." I kissed his jaw. "I have a hard time imagining a world where we're not together. I don't think that timeline exists."

"No. Perhaps not."

Soon we docked, met Russell at the end of the gangway, and

were in the SUV. "Harris isn't here anymore, but Isabel is still up on that crane." I searched my mind for Harris's blip.

"A motorcycle drove off perhaps five minutes ago," Russell said, exiting the car park and heading—according to the signs—toward Canterbury.

"Got him. He's ahead of us, a few miles away now."

Clive sat in front, talking with Russell, while I stretched out in the back. I closed my eyes and opened my mind. I wanted to know if there were others now following us.

"We picked up a third one." I felt instant relief from the pain. Good husband. "Not a vampire. This one is fae, I think. I'm not great at identifying them. I think they're the ones with the light green smear over the matte black of immortality. Stheno and her sisters, Meg, Horus, they all have a dark purplish hue that's hard to see. The fae have a vibrant, spring green." Assuming I was correct in my color coding.

"I thought you'd said vampires were green," Russell said.

"You are, but it's a darker, poisonous kind of green, not a healthy lawn kind of green."

Clive and Russell shared a look and then both shook their heads, grinning.

"Do we know anything about our fae admirer?" Clive asked.

"No, *we* don't. I can't read the fae. I don't even know why I can see them. I can't see wicches or anything." I shrugged. My head was a mystery.

"The fae blood Gloriana said you had, I assume," Clive responded.

"Yeah, well, jury's still out on that. I mean, if the old-timey Corey wicche used fae blood to create the first werewolf, how much could possibly still be running in my veins this many centuries later?" I already had wicche and werewolf blood brewing in here. The thought of a third strain made me super uncomfortable.

"Gloriana would know," Russell said, effectively shutting me up. He was right. If Gloriana, queen of the fae, said it was there, it was there.

As we got closer to town, the roads narrowed, becoming cobblestone. Tiny cars skirted around the Land Rover as Russell turned down a side road.

"We can't park on High Street." Russell turned into a small lot and parked. "We'll walk from here."

Russell tried to take my bag, but I wasn't having any of it. I stared him down and he relented. We'd already had this discussion. He did not work for me. I could carry my own stuff. Plus, he'd soon be the Master of San Francisco. Underlings should be carrying his stuff. As a result, though, Russell took Clive's bags and Clive took mine—as was his prerogative as my mate, he reminded me—so I was bagless.

The roads were odd and ancient. I was so used to paved streets, it felt like I was walking into a historical reenactment village. The narrow lane hardly seemed wide enough for vehicles, but both sides were lined with narrow shops, hanging signs jutting out from façades. Shoe repair, key cutters, gentlemen's apparel, coffee shop, watch repair, art gallery, an inn, and more, all were jammed up together on this one short street. I was going to have the most fun exploring tomorrow.

In the distance, between signs and over buildings and trees, the Canterbury Cathedral speared the night sky. Lit from below, the towering Gothic structure watched over the sleeping village.

"High Street," Clive murmured.

We turned left and crossed over the empty road that was perhaps twice as wide as the one we'd just walked through.

Still no cars. "Do people drive here?" It was perfect. No cars to mess up shots. I wanted to take pictures of everything, the Tudor buildings, side by side with Gothic and Georgian ones. And then, every few shops, a modern structure was wedged in between. Every direction I turned, I was met with a postcard view.

"Foot traffic only in the town center. Cars and tour busses need to park farther off, just as we did," Russell replied. "It's just here, on the right." He pointed to a tall Tudor building, with white plaster walls and dark heavy wood framing. The Ducking Stool Inn.

"Is that an autocorrect error?" I pointed at the sign.

Clive gave me a blank look but Russell grinned, opening the door for us. The pub was dim and quiet, with maybe a dozen or so people chatting with friends over a pint. The dark wood bar was L-shaped and stood against the far wall. Booths with deep red velvet upholstery lined the walls with a few tables and chairs in the middle. Mullioned windows looked out on the dark street. Only one person sat at the bar. Godfrey slid off a stool and met Clive, taking my bags from him.

"We'll see to these," Godfrey said before he and Russell left as quickly as human speed allowed.

"Ooh," the barman crooned when Clive and I took the two stools directly in front of him, "I was just getting ready to close, but look who we have here. An old friend has come to visit. And why shouldn't he? Old friends are always welcome. Even those who bring"—he paused, scenting the air—"charming new friends." His eyes flashed vamp black momentarily before returning to his natural brown.

"How exciting," he said, wiping down the gleaming bar. "I was just speaking with our friend Godfrey, relating the interesting tales of my life. He was enraptured, as you would surely guess. In fact—"

"Chaucer, it's good to see you," Clive interrupted. "Allow me to introduce my wife Samantha." He ran his hand down my back in what felt like an apology.

"Wife?" His eyes opened wide in mock shock. "How unexpected. I know a few stories about women who *wanted* to be his wife," he whispered to me.

"Do tell," I said, grinning.

"Let's not." Clive tapped the bar. "Perhaps Godfrey mentioned we're looking for—"

It was my turn to interrupt. I patted Clive's arm, stopping his words. "That can wait. I want to hear one of Mr. Chaucer's stories." I'd felt the instantaneous resentment when Clive had stopped Chaucer from talking. We needed information from the man. I was trying to smooth over the insult.

"You're right," Clive said, following my lead. He rested his hand on my thigh and grinned. "Geoffrey tells wonderful stories. I was merely concerned I wouldn't come off well in them. I'd rather our honeymoon wasn't colored by talk of other women."

Geoffrey's huge smile returned. "Now, now, I'll not cause a rift. Let's see..." He drummed his fingers, pretending to contemplate which story to tell, but I felt the one he wanted ready to burst from his lips.

"Quite some years ago—don't ask how many, as the number will flatter neither Clive nor myself; we'll leave it at some time ago —a young woman was visiting London, where Clive and I were residing at the time. A pretty little thing she was, too. Long blonde hair piled in intricate loops around a stunning face. Flounces upon bows in rosy silk. Big warm brown eyes that never seemed to leave the object of her affection." He nodded to Clive.

"Clive does that to a lot of people."

Chaucer smiled at my comment, but I could feel his annoyance at being interrupted.

"Please, go on."

"The poor child never missed a chance to engage his interest. She hung on his every word, doing anything she could think of to lure him to her, dropping handkerchiefs, losing her balance and stumbling into him so he'd have to catch her, trying to make him jealous with other men. It all came to naught, though, as Clive barely noticed her."

"I noticed. I found her irritating." He turned to me and rubbed my thigh, derailing Chaucer's story. "Would you like something to drink?"

Again, I felt a rush of irritation at being interrupted. "A soda would be great, if you wouldn't mind, and then I'd love to hear the rest of your story." I pressed my foot on Clive's, trying to let him know that we had to let Geoffrey finish the story if we wanted his help. I could have spoken directly to Clive, mind to mind, but Chaucer was quite old. I had no idea what powers he had. As Clive hadn't spoken mentally to me, I kept the silence, just in case.

Pouring me a drink, he continued. "Well, wouldn't you know, while she'd been doing everything within her power to tempt Clive, another had been trying desperately to woo her. He—" Geoffrey glanced up at the dark beams of the ceiling, lost in thought. "John, I believe his name was. He wanted to be her champion, her protector, escorting her wherever she wanted to go, buying her whatever she desired. Alas, her desires had already been claimed."

Clive checked his watch, and again I felt the rush of anger from our storyteller. I flicked my foot, giving Clive a quick kick to the ankle.

"You tell the story too well, my friend. I'm discomfited all over again."

Chaucer stood a little taller, pleased with the compliment. "Well, our doomed John wanted to make her his own, to feed and care for her. To save her prowling the streets at night, he stole people out of their beds, knocking them out and then presenting them to her like tributes to a queen.

"As you might guess," he chucked in a studied and rehearsed way, "he was seen, wasn't he? Seen over and over. He was quite terrifying, and so the townspeople hoped he'd just go away. When it continued, though, they had no choice but to gather their pitchforks and torches."

He laughed. "I'm adding some literary license here. They were smart enough not to set out at night. It creates an evocative image, though, doesn't it? Angry, unwashed faces, red with yelling, spittle flying from their lips as they brandish whatever weapons they can lay hands on, gathered in a mob, trying desperately to bolster one another's courage as they set out to kill the beast." He ran a hand down the vest he wore, smoothing it. "Yes, I rather like that." He sniffed. "Pity it was so much less dramatic.

"They couldn't allow innocents to be taken and killed, so they followed John, discovered his"—Chaucer glanced around, but no one was paying any attention to our murmured voices—"daytime resting spot. Not being complete idiots, they waited until the dawn before they attacked, beheading him. They had a bonfire ready as well, not realizing he'd turn to dust. I believe a few of the more thorough mob members collected the dust and threw it into the flames."

Clive shook his head. "Such a waste. I liked John well enough."

"It was. John lost his life trying to provide for one who was far older and more powerful than she was letting on."

That got Clive's attention. "I remembered her being young and inexperienced. Wasn't she a fledgling?"

Chaucer winked conspiratorially, preening under Clive's interested gaze. "That's what she wanted everyone to think but, no. Never forget a face, do I? She was one of Garyn's. Older than you in life but not in death. I ran across the two of them with a third, a younger one, when I was making my coin through storytelling. We happened upon one another outside an alehouse in the Cotswolds, as I recall. We didn't speak. They were headed in one direction and I another. I remember, though. I've always had an eye for detail. It's the details that make the story, after all."

One of Garyn's people, a blonde with brown eyes, who was desperately trying to get close to Clive, to woo him, have him let his guard down. I had a pretty good idea who the woman was.

Clive and I shared a look. Aldith?

EIGHT

It's All in the Details

"Do you remember her name?" I asked.

"Of course. Details, remember. She said her name was Addie. It was a lie, though," he said, shaking his head and tutting. "It's one thing to enhance the truth, to make a story sing, and quite another to utilize such a mundane fabrication. At least make it interesting and memorable for us."

He shook his head, refilling my glass. "No. Leave the storytelling to those, like myself, with a gift. No one wants your common lies rouged up like tarts on the walk."

"Have you seen her since?" Please, let it be this easy. Let Chaucer tell us she lives 'round the block.

He glanced up. It was only a split second, perhaps less, but I saw it. Deception, no doubt intended to make the final story that much better.

"No." He walked to the end of the bar to collect two empty pint glasses. "I haven't." He turned, his jovial smile back in place. "Why the interest?"

I shrugged. "It's good to be prepared. I wouldn't want anyone to try to steal my fella." I ducked my head to catch his eyes as he dropped the empties into a bin under the bar. "In case anyone was wondering, I won't allow anyone to take him from me. You could

54

let any interested parties know."

He beamed, his expression alight with mischief. "Won't that be fun." He checked his watch and surveyed the pub. Only two tables left. Pitching his voice louder, he announced, "Last call."

"Thank you, for the story and the welcome." Clive left a twenty on the bar to cover my soda and then some. "Shall we find our room?" he asked me.

I stood to follow him and then paused, wanting to know. "What's a ducking stool?" I asked Chaucer.

"This may be of particular interest to you. Come." He crooked his finger and led me to the window overlooking the Great Stour river. Pointing, he said, "Do you see that wooden seat attached to the long beam overhanging the water? That, my dear, is a ducking stool, or chair, if you prefer."

"Okay, but what's it for?" It was like half a see-saw, jutting out over the river.

"Ducking ill-behaved women under the water. The number of times, or the length of the ducking would depend on the offense. It was also used," he added, a finger wiggling toward me, "on women suspected of being wicches."

Stomach dropping, I looked more closely at the foul thing. "So, it's a if-she-lives-she's-a-wicche-and-will-be-burned-but-if-she-dies-I-guess-she-wasn't kind of situation?"

"Precisely."

Chaucer returned to the bar to pour a few last pints while I stared out the window. It happened everywhere, not just this little corner of the world, but thinking about the women who had been scared senseless, even killed, to ensure that they behaved as men dictated took the shine off the town.

Movement across the river caught my eye. Oh, our friend Harris was back, keeping an eye on us for Garyn. When Clive slid his arm around me, I flinched, too absorbed in thoughts of trauma-tized women and peeping vamps. He kissed my temple and led me through an arch connecting the pub to the lobby of the inn.

Godfrey waited for us. "Sire, Missus, your keys." He handed

actual keys, not cards, to both of us. "You're in room six, second floor, end of the hall."

"Where's Russell?" Clive glanced up the narrow stairway.

"Out for a bite. He should be back soon, though." Godfrey extended an arm, inviting us to precede him up the stairs.

"Fine. When he returns, come to our room. We've learned something interesting this evening."

Godfrey followed us down the hall and then stopped before the door to room four, his eyebrows raised. "Truly?"

Nodding, Clive put his key in his own lock and turned. "We'll discuss it." Opening the door, he ushered me in.

Given the age of the building and the narrow passages, I'd assumed the room would be quite small. I was wrong. The room appeared to be twice as wide as normal rooms, running the entire width of the building. Windows to the left overlooked the river. The ones to the right overlooked the town, with the cathedral glowing in the distance.

The walls were the same dark wood as below, with a white ceiling traversed with heavy, dark beams. Most of the furniture appeared to be original to the room, with a king-sized bed, a desk, and a dresser. At the end of the bed was a green velvet sofa facing a fireplace, a thick, hand-carved, wooden mantel above. A polished candelabra sat in the center. On the river side of the room, there was a small square table with four chairs. On the cathedral side, a free-standing tub with a rack of towels beside it.

I checked a door near the tub, hoping for a toilet but fearing it was a closet. Huzzah! I wouldn't need to share a hall toilet with the other guests on this floor. The bathroom was small but modern. There was even a narrow shower beside the toilet.

When I stepped out, Clive was reclining on the bed, watching me. "It's not the George V."

"P'fft. I doubt anything in the world is. This, however, is absolutely perfect. It feels like England. I'm in England!" I ran across the room and dove onto the bed.

Clive caught me, rolling me under him. "Welcome. We're

happy to have you." His lips brushed across mine, exploring, softly running kisses across my cheek, down my throat. I pulled him back and took his mouth with my own, desperate for the kiss he was promising. All thought drained from my head and drifted away down the nearby river.

When a knock sounded in the quiet room, I started, completely forgetting where we were and who we were waiting for.

Clive pushed up on his forearms, staring at me with vamp-black eyes. "Shall I send them away?"

I gave him a quick kiss and then shoved him aside, standing up and straightening my clothes. How did my jeans get unbuttoned? He rolled off the bed, his heated gaze taking in every inch of me, causing me to lose my train of thought again.

"Sire?" Russell's muffled voice came through the door.

I closed my eyes, shaking it off.

"Go away," he said, pulling me back into his arms.

"Wait. No," I said.

He kissed me and I had a hard time remembering why I should care about the guys. Damn it. I pushed him back again and went to the door, pulling it open.

Russell and Godfrey strode in and went straight to the table, taking the chairs that mostly put their backs to us. I shot a finger at Clive, warning him to keep his distance before I went to the table and took a seat.

"I liked it better when these two weren't around all the time," Clive grumbled as he took the last chair.

"He doesn't mean that," I assured them.

"Yes, I do." Looking decidedly disgruntled, he studied both his men. "You've fed?" When they nodded, he said, "Good. Now tell me what you've discovered since you've been here."

"Russell discovered that our host is insufferable. As I was already aware, it was less of a discovery for me," Godfrey said.

"What is it with you three? He's not bad. He just likes to tell stories."

"Ad nauseum, dear." Clive tipped his head back and closed his eyes. "I couldn't even count the number of times I've had to listen to one of his interminable tales. The problem is, he's actually quite old and powerful. As he said himself, it's all about the details, and he pays attention to all of them. If you're able to sit through his stories, you can learn a great deal."

"I beg to differ, Sire. I sat through quite a few today and learned only that I can play an entire chess tournament, both sides of the board, in my head." Godfrey shook his head. "Granted, that was vaguely interesting, but doesn't help us in our search for Aldith."

"Sadly," Russell rumbled, "I couldn't even do that. One story. I was able to make it through one story about a vampire who had done everything for the woman he loved, but she was in love with another, abandoning him to be given his final death by a mob of townspeople." Russell lifted his hands from the table and then dropped them again. "Was that a cautionary tale? A warning not to fall for the wrong person? He ignored every social cue and would. Not. Stop. Talking."

Clive and I exchanged looks again. Wasn't that interesting?

"It seems our host knows exactly why we're here and has been trying to give us information," Clive said.

Russell and Godfrey looked at one another and then back at us. "How so?" Russell asked.

"I'll let Sam explain it. If it weren't for her, we still wouldn't know. I was just as impatient and dismissive as the two of you. Sam is the one who listened and kicked me when my mind wandered."

"Chaucer told us much the same story he told you, Russell, except for a couple of important details. The woman the poor sap was in love with was using him to make Clive jealous." Both men blinked at that. "And we believe the woman in question may have been Aldith."

Russell leaned forward. "How did you get that? There was

nothing in the story he told me to indicate who he was talking about. He talked about fabrics and hairstyle, and then the ways in which every single person had been stolen from their homes and offered to the woman as a snack. That was it. Endless talk of ribbons and lace, interspersed with kidnappings."

"Okay," I said. "But you also made it clear that you had employed every social cue you could think of to get him to shut up."

Russell nodded, his brow furrowed. "How does that follow?"

"He's not stupid or oblivious to your maneuvering. I felt it tonight. Whenever Clive or I interrupted him, there was a flash of anger. Because I felt it, I instantly tried to smooth it over, offer a compliment, show him I was hanging on his every word, and kicking Clive if he tried to interrupt again. My guess is you continued making—in your mind—subtle ploys to end the story and every time you did, he threw in another detour into ladies' fashion. You weren't showing him respect by being a good audience for his storytelling, so you were given a vindictively edited story."

"Oh." Godfrey grimaced. "No wonder I was treated to one mind-numbingly boring story after the next today. I broke into his stories often and when that didn't seem to work, I just stared off into space, playing chess in my head."

"Yeah." I patted Godfrey's hand, which was resting on the table. "He knew exactly what you were doing. He's a storyteller and wants to be appreciated, even lauded, for his talents. He knows a great deal. It would pay to be on his good side."

"Was he lying at the end?" Clive asked. "I felt something. I couldn't name it, but I felt something pass between you."

"Lie about what?" Godfrey asked.

"I asked if he knew where Aldith—or Addie, as she was calling herself at the time—was now. He said he didn't know, hadn't seen her since she'd made a play for Clive and John had been given his true death. It was a lie, though. I felt a flash of deception at his words. It was there and gone in the same moment, but I didn't get the impression he was hiding or protecting her. It was more that our not knowing would make the story better later in the retelling."

"Miss Qui—Mrs. Fitzwilliam, do you—"

"Sam, Russell. Just call me Sam." Although, I had to admit, if only to myself, I was going to miss the Miss Quinns.

The corner of Russell's mouth kicked up, his gaze soft. "I'm afraid I'm not comfortable with that."

"You could refer to me as the Werewolf Formerly Known as Miss Quinn."

Godfrey laughed.

"Perhaps Samantha would work best for you, not as casual as Sam, not as formal as Mrs. Fitzwilliam," Clive suggested.

"I'll consider it," Russell responded. "What I was going to ask is if we still have a tail."

Nodding, I said, "Harris is across the river, watching this place. I don't get menace from him. Isabel, the other one, is gone now."

"Good," Godfrey said. "Perhaps we can table the speculation until tomorrow evening, Sire. Russell and I would like to go have a chat with this Harris chap. The Missus doesn't see him as a threat, but it makes us look weak, not checking on the locals who are watching us."

"Good point. Yes, do that. As a bonus, it gets you both out of our room." Clive stood, looking from one window to the other. "Are the usual protections in place?"

"Yes, Sire," Godfrey replied. He went to each window, tapped something on the top of the frame, and a thick panel slid down, protecting the room—and the vampire sleeping in it—from the sun.

I half expected Russell to take one side of windows, while Godfrey did the other, but Russell merely watched Godfrey along with Clive. Ah, he was making the transition from first to Master. Godfrey was the third, soon to be second? Godfrey was in the San Francisco nocturne because of Clive. Would he stay to be Russell's second? Would Russell want Clive's man as his second, or did he have someone else in mind? I guess we'd need to wait and see how it all shook out.

After they left, Clive drew us a hot bath. We had a little time before the sun rose and didn't want to waste it. He sprinkled in a few drops of bath oil and the whole room filled with a warm citrus scent.

We undressed each other and then Clive stepped in and sat, pulling me in with him. Settling between his legs, I leaned back and breathed deeply. My shoulders dropped and my head fell back to rest on his shoulder.

Voice low, he asked, "Did you read him?" His hands stroked down my arms and over my stomach.

I rolled my head lazily from side to side. "I didn't know him, didn't know how powerful he was. I felt his joy at telling us the perfect story and his annoyance any time one of us interrupted him. You weren't speaking to me, mind to mind, so I wondered if mental acuity was a gift of his."

"You've been practicing. It wouldn't be like St. Germaine again." His hands moved up to my breasts, making it very hard to concentrate.

On a gasp, I said, "He was talking, wanted to tell us his stories. I decided to wait and see what he gave us willingly before I tried to invade his thoughts." I stilled his hands with my own. "It makes me feel like a creep, invading people's minds. If they're clearly bad guys intent on our deaths, I'm on board. But just some random guy tending bar? It's an invasion of privacy that makes me super uncomfortable."

"I understand." He kissed my temple. "I'll always want to know because I'm looking for the threat, but you're right to draw the line. We don't need to steal what Chaucer will give. We just need to sit through his tales."

"Seriously, I don't get why you guys are so negative. I love storytellers."

"And I love you," he said, his hands continuing to explore.

On a moan, I asked, "Are you changing the subject?"

"Every chance I get."

NINE

My Precious

I awoke midafternoon, wrapped around Clive. I gave him a smacking kiss on the cheek, said, "I'm off to explore," and then tried to roll away but he held tight. "Let go, you."

"No," he breathed.

I gave him another kiss and tapped his chest. Relenting, he relaxed his arm. I got cleaned up, dressed, and then checked my pockets for money, phone, and key. I was just about to go when I stopped in my tracks, worried about opening the door and letting in light. Well, shit. Apparently, these vamp rooms weren't intended to also accommodate the living.

What to do, what to do? I considered MacGyvering up the door, but then realized it was far easier to just cover up Clive. I went back to the bed, dropped a kiss on his nose, and whispered, "Sorry."

Pulling the sheet and comforter up over his head, I looked around for other things I could use to block stray sunlight. Hmm, sofa cushions, check. Towels, check. Extra pillows, check. His own overcoat, check. I had a mountain of stuff piled on him—it was actually pretty fun, like chucking stuff at Stheno's head. He was going to be so confused when he rose.

It turned out I needn't have worried, though. The hall was dim.

63

There were no windows and only a few weak sconces affixed at too great a distance from one another. Trotting down the stairs, I wrapped my coat more tightly around myself. The door to the street was just closing and a gust of wind raced past me. This didn't bode well for temps outside. Ah, well. It was winter in England, after all.

Dark, heavy skies hung ominously overhead. I'd checked the weather app yesterday. It had forecasted sunny and a high of forty-five degrees. I got that this was England and overcast skies were not unusual, but this seemed like more than just rai—and there they were. Snowflakes swirled in the wind, slowly making their way to the ground to melt.

I was wearing sturdy boots, so I figured I should be okay. I probably needed to make a pit stop, though, before heading over to the cathedral to explore. Walking in the direction of the towering spires, I popped into the first clothing store I passed. A woman was standing at the window, looking up at the sky.

"Odd, that. It was a nice, sunny day just a tick ago." Shaking her head, she looked at me. "And what can I do for you?"

Grimacing, embarrassed to be the wimpy Californian who couldn't take real winters, I said, "It's a lot colder than I was expecting. Do you have hats, gloves, maybe a scarf?"

"American, eh? Enjoying a visit?" She walked me over to some shelves against the wall that held all manner of cold weather gear.

"We got in late last night, so I'm starting my Canterbury adventure now." I reached for a green and black Glen plaid scarf. It was thick and soft, the two most important qualities.

"That's a lovely warm one." Efficiently, she pulled a few matching caps and gloves for me to choose from. "Now this one"—she held up a knitted cap in the same green—"is lined to help keep your head warm. This one"—she held up a black woolen one with earflaps—"is not as cute, but definitely warmer." She waited a moment for me to speak. "And there are plenty of others, if neither appeals."

"No, it's not that." Earflaps made me think of Holden Caufield.

I loved the book, but it wasn't where my head and heart were right now. "Let's go green."

"That being the case," she said, looking through a pile of fuzzy things, "here are the matching gloves."

The gloves, like the hat, were lined, adding extra warmth.

"I can clip the tags so you can wear them out, if you'd like," she said, taking my purchases to the counter.

"I would, thank you."

After she rang it up, I signed the slip and then wound the scarf around my neck, pulled the hat low so it covered the tops of my ears, and then pulled on the gloves.

"That's a lush coat you've got there," she said, admiration in her eyes.

"Thank you! I love it." I held out the arm of my long cashmere sweater coat. Like the hat and gloves, it had been lined with wool for extra warmth. "My husband got it for me in Paris. My coat wasn't up to European winters."

She touched the arm I offered. "Oh, soft. You look a right picture." Nodding, she swept up the discarded tags and dropped them in the trash. "Hopefully, whatever is brewing out there holds off until you've done your exploring."

"Thank you so much for your help," I said, waving as I walked through the door.

The streets were full, tourists taking pictures, gathering in groups to discuss what to do next. People wandered this way and that. I joined the throng, taking my own pictures and window shopping as I made my way to the cathedral.

A chess set in a window caught my eye. I took a pic but instead of moving on, I walked into the shop. The Slaughtered Lamb needed a chess set with dragons instead of horses and fae warriors instead of bishops. The rook was a pixie, his chest thrown out, expression fierce. The pawn looked like the Orc that had attacked me in The Wicche Glass. The king was shifty, a hand clasping something held behind his back, his eyes cutting to the side, watching the queen. And the queen? Gloriana herself. Who had carved these pieces?

When I picked up a piece, the shopkeeper rushed up. "Madam, please. Do not touch the chess pieces. It's clearly posted right there." He took the piece from my hand and gently returned it to the board.

"I'm so sorry. I didn't see—" My eyes flicked up from the pieces and found a large sign asking people not to touch the chess set. "Oh."

Clearly annoyed, he turned to go back to the desk.

"Sorry, one other thing."

He stopped. "Yes?"

"Is it for sale?" There was something about the set. It was no longer a fun addition to my bookstore and bar. It felt like a message.

"Madam, this is a one-of-a-kind work of art. If you're looking for a game, there's a toy store across the street that carries an assortment of sets." He was less pissy, but clearly not interested in dealing with me.

Glancing around, I realized I was in an art gallery. No wonder he was ticked off at my touching stuff. "Right. But as this is a gallery, you sell the art, don't you?"

He blinked and schooled his expression. "Of course. This was done by a local artist. On this side of the board, he used chalcedony stone with a milky white moonstone base. Each piece carved with such precision, you'd think the stone was touched by magic." He held the queen up to the weak light from the window, the blue-gray stone almost glowing with beauty and serenity.

"And on this side, he used onyx with a malachite base." He lifted the king. The black stone seemed to absorb the light from the window. "The board itself," he said, returning the king, "is made of alternating squares of light and dark green jade. It's an extraordinary piece."

"Who is the artist?" He had to have some connection with the fae to get the likenesses so perfect.

"A.C. Corey. He's a recluse. I've never met the man. Couriers deliver his work and we electronically transfer funds, but the couriers have said they pick up the pieces from his agent, who lives here in Kent. They wouldn't say where, but…" He trailed off, perhaps realizing he was displaying a stalkery level of interest.

Corey. Was he a Corey wicche? Was that why the pieces were so perfect? Like me, had he met the fae? Gloriana had made me promise to discover what was poisoning the fae realm when she'd healed me the night of my engagement party. Frigging kelpies were determined to be the death of me.

This should have been a straightforward transaction, but given his attachment to the chess set, it felt more like I was negotiating with Gollum for the ring. "It's a gift, isn't it? Just standing in its presence?" I was staring at the chess pieces but saw him nod his head out of the corner of my eye.

"It drew me in off the street. I saw it and knew I had to have it, had to take care of it." I shook my head. "I'm sure it sounds crazy but—"

"No, not at all." He stepped closer and lowered his voice. "I come in on my days off to check on it."

Nodding, I worried he'd already spent too much time with a magical object. "I understand completely. The artist needs the money this piece will give him to continue creating, though. If you let me, I'd like to support the artist and protect this art." I gave him my most solemn and trustworthy face. "Can I do that?"

The man had just started to step back, head shaking in refusal when a woman strode out of the back room.

"Oh, the Corey! Stunning piece, isn't it? It almost feels like the pieces are watching me. I sometimes wonder if they jump off their plinths and walk around the shop when I'm not looking." She patted the man's shoulder. "Jeremy, could you unpack those boxes in the back, please. Now," she said to me, "look at this artistry." She picked up the queen, as Jeremy had. "She's exquisite, isn't she?"

Jeremy hadn't moved, even though she'd wedged herself

between us. He stared resentfully at the back of her head, one of his hands beginning to shake. This was going to get ugly fast.

"Thank you so much for all of your help," I said to Jeremy. "I promise to take good care of the set." Turning my attention to the woman in charge, I asked, "How much is it?"

"It's one hundred and thirty-seven thousand pounds. I know it's dear," she rushed on, "but it's magic, isn't it? All the brilliant pieces in this gallery and your eyes went straight to this one, didn't they?"

Nodding, I did an internal spit-take. One hundred and thirty-seven *thousand* pounds. *Shit.* Pounds were worth more than dollars, weren't they? I couldn't walk away from it, though. She was right when she said it was magic. Jeremy was already in its thrall. I had to get it away from humans and figure out what it meant, why it felt important.

Taking a deep breath, I said, "I'll take it." Clive had told me the black credit card could take any purchase. I guess we were about to find out.

"Would you like this sent or would you prefer to take it with you. I should warn you," she said with a smile, dollar signs dancing in her eyes, "it's quite heavy."

Given the way Jeremy was eyeing the board, I had to get it out of here fast. "I'll take it with me. I'm stronger than I look."

"Oh, Jeremy, you're still here. Good. Could you take this set in back and wrap it up for our customer?" She strode back to the counter, swiping through a tablet with a card reader.

Jeremy looked like he wanted to push me down and run out of the store with the chess pieces, so I picked it up myself and carried it to the woman. "I know this probably sounds silly, but I'd like to wrap the pieces myself." The woman looked at me as though I were nuts. "I know. But look at it this way, if anything happens to any of the pieces, it'll be my fault. No blame can be laid on your gallery or the packing."

Nodding curtly, she said, "Right you are. Jeremy, please bring the packing supplies out here, so Ms.—"

"Fitzwilliam."

"—so Ms. Fitzwilliam can wrap the purchase herself."

I handed her the credit card. When she gave me the slip to sign, I said a little prayer of thanks that it had gone through and wondered how much money my stupid rich husband had.

Making short work of the packing—they had excellent supplies —I was soon walking out of the shop, on my way back to The Ducking Stool. I was not walking around town carrying a fae artifact worth a fortune.

The second floor was quiet, the vamps still asnooze. I let myself into our room and laughed at the pile burying Clive. I kind of wished I could be here to see his bafflement upon waking.

Husband,

I'm leaving a box with you. Guard it, please. It's a fae chess set and there is something important about it I need to figure out. It's a magical object that shouldn't be in the possession of humans. Anyway, I made a bold opening move in bankrupting you today. Sorry! I'm off to the cathedral now.

XOXO,

Wife

TEN

An Unexpected Journey

I f possible, it was even darker outside than it was ten minutes ago. The sky looked ready to smother the earth. Jogging up High Street toward the cathedral, I was struck by how the past and present coexisted here. In San Francisco, the old buildings were a hundred years old. I was visiting a city that had begun as a Roman settlement. It was two thousand years old. I was walking the same roads countless others throughout time had before me. Sometimes it hit me just how small and insignificant my problems were in the grand scheme of things.

I stopped at the Canterbury War Memorial right outside the Christchurch gate into the cathedral grounds. Taking pictures all around the open and mostly deserted square—the ominous skies seemed to be keeping tourists indoors—I wished again that we were here on vacation rather than a hunting trip.

This was Clive's hometown. He was one of the legion who had walked the roads before me. Mostly, I was fine being alone during daylight hours. I was almost always working, so no big deal. This was different, though. I kept seeing amazing things and wanting to turn to Clive and point them out or ask questions. Instead, I was just thinking, *Oh look! Yeah, already am. Okay, thanks.*

I loved Clive and would never regret making him my forever guy. It was just sometimes I wished I had a daytime buddy. Silly, I know.

Movement caught my eye. Pretending to take more pictures, I tilted my head down and then slid my gaze to the left. Gollum, aka Jeremy from the gallery, was following me. He quickly turned, looking in a shop front, not realizing his reflection was clear in the window. Damn. I didn't need another obsessed stalker. I already had a supernatural one tailing me. Shaking it off, I went back to sightseeing. I could handle a human. In thrall or not, he was no match for a wolf.

Jogging across the street, I made for the cathedral entrance. Gate wasn't the right word. To me, a gate was a simple affair, wood planks or metal bars to block entrance. Basic. The Christchurch gate to the cathedral was like its own mini castle. It was thirty or forty feet wide with an arched walkway through the middle. Three stories high, with turrets on either side, its design matched the gothic cathedral. The only thing missing was a drawbridge.

Ooh, a drawbridge. Wherever Clive and I ended up living, it had to have a drawbridge.

Walking through the arch felt a little like walking back in time. An elderly couple, hunched against the sudden gust of wind, gave a nod as they passed. The oldest cathedral in England was lit from below, rising impossibly high into the storm-filled sky. I stood a moment, awed.

Human beings built this a thousand years ago. I'd read *Pillars of the Earth* and thought I'd understood what a monumental undertaking it had been to build this kind of Romanesque and Gothic cathedral, but it wasn't until I stood before Canterbury that the weight of it hit me. Hundreds of years, building and rebuilding, thousands of workers and craftsmen laboring from sunup to sundown their whole lives. It was staggering.

The sound of voices raised in song got my feet going again.

Hoping I wasn't interrupting services, I slipped quietly through the huge door. Needing a moment to take it all in, I moved to the side, gaping. Pillars and arches standing atop one another ran down the length of the nave, soaring almost a hundred feet to the curved ceiling.

The choir was practicing, their perfect voices filling the chamber and raising goosebumps. I moved to a nearby pew to sit and listen. Others, like myself, were spread out in the mostly empty cathedral, listening to what sounded like angels singing.

Brushing a tear from my face, overcome by the beauty, I pulled out my phone and hit the voice recorder. When difficult things happened, as they often must, I wanted to be able to listen to this hymn and remember there was also unimaginable beauty in the world.

The last notes echoed off the walls and silence returned. I turned my phone off and slipped it back into my pocket. I stayed for three more hymns before I decided Clive and the guys were probably up. I moved through groups of people making their way down the center aisle. The evening mass must be beginning soon.

I'd return tomorrow to explore the cathedral. I hadn't yet seen the shrine to martyred Thomas Becket. The music was enough for this evening. Beauty before death. Jogging down the steps, I headed back toward the gate. I was almost to it when I saw my guys walking toward me. A huge grin spread across Clive's perfect face. My heart stopped and then galloped. Would he ever stop having this effect on me?

I had taken out my phone, wanting to share the choir with them, when I felt others nearby. Vampires raced around the side of the cathedral. My head swung to the right. They were Aldith's. Unbelievable. People with a link to her were serving themselves up to us. When I turned back to warn Clive, Gollum stepped out of the shadows of the gate. *Shit.* The poor, obsessed dude was about to get ripped apart in a vampire brawl.

Wanting to avoid a death match on cathedral grounds, I

accessed my necromancer side and whipped a coil of magic around the necks of the two vamps streaking toward me.

Got 'em. They're Aldith's. We should—

Out of the corner of my eye, I caught a huge black shape suddenly looming over me and then everything went dark.

A second later, the world had gone bright. I crashed to the moss-covered ground, sunlight in my eyes as something heavy crushed me under its bulk. Wha—? Leering down at me, his head blocking the light, was a—*Oh, shit!* Sun, moss, Orc. I was in Faerie! Ribs crushed, I struggled to breathe. I was in so much trouble.

I yanked an arm out from under him, unleashed my claws through the gloves, and dragged them down his face before he could land his first punch. His hide was so thick, instead of ripping his face off, four distinct slashes drew noxious-smelling blood. One claw, though, went right through his eye, popping it, releasing a foul white mucous. Too busy fighting for my life, I'd need to vomit later.

When he reared back, howling in pain, I scrambled out from under him and ran. Checking over my shoulder, I scanned the meadow to see if he was following. Still on the ground. I turned, putting on speed, and ran straight into something. Bouncing off, I hit the ground hard.

The something I hit turned out to be an impossibly good-looking man in a tunic and breeches. He had dark hair, sun-kissed skin, and golden-brown eyes that considered me.

"You hurt my soldier," he said, not sounding terribly upset. He glanced at my gloved, clawless hands, brow furrowed, no doubt wondering how I'd done it.

"He kidnapped me," I wheezed, still trying to draw in a full breath.

"Yes. True. Of course, he did it on my orders, so..." He shrugged. "It seems only right I punish you in some way."

I struggled to my feet. "The queen promised me safe passage through Faerie." Technically, I believe she only meant that one time, but he didn't know that. Hopefully.

"Did she? Hmm, I don't believe that was intended as a lifetime pass. Still," he said, moving closer, his eyes swirling with amber and gold, "it wouldn't do to upset the queen." He stood before me, sizing me up. "Why the interest in you?"

A dwarf appeared at his side. "Shall I beat it out of her, sire?" Grinning at me with teeth filed down to points, he added, "I can be quite persuasive."

When the taller man leaned in to sniff me, it took all my courage not to cringe and run. Something told me this one held real power, not just the brute strength of the Orc or the sly menace of the dwarf. This one reminded me of Finvarra, the king piece on the fae chess board.

"Safe passage," he echoed thoughtfully. "That means we can do whatever we want to you while you stay with us. When it's time for you to travel back to the human realm, though, we'll make it a safe journey."

The dwarf laughed as the Orc lumbered up behind his compatriots.

"Why have you been following me?" I assumed this was why I kept feeling like I was being watched in Paris and again in Canterbury. Why, though? I wasn't a key player in fae shenanigans.

The man tilted his head, his eyes boring into me. Making sure my mental blocks were still up, I stared right back.

"How did you know you were being followed? My men are quite discreet." The possibly treacherous king's face changed subtly.

Either his form was a bit more fluid than most or he was trying to hit on the most attractive face for me. Vampires could mesmerize. This felt a bit like that. I doubted most would even notice the changes. Beautiful people were more likely to get cooperation and compliance, trust even. They just were. Luckily, Jane Austen novels had taught me to distrust seemingly affable men with handsome faces.

"Clive felt them. He told me." I could have been wrong, but this didn't feel like the time to swagger and boast. The fae scared the shit out of me. They were ancient, made of magic, and powerful as hell. If I were deemed a true threat, they'd kill me without breaking a sweat. If I pushed it off to Clive, who was himself ancient and powerful, they might buy it. Added to that, the fae were sickened by the existence of vampires and therefore didn't seem to know that much about them.

The odd glamour dropped as his expression shifted to disappointment. "This was a waste of my time." He turned to his men. "You both know what to do. I'm afraid I have an audience with Her Majesty soon, so I really must be on my way." He sniffed his own arm and muttered something about needing to bathe before going to the palace.

The dwarf grabbed my arm, his fingers digging into my flesh, yanking me toward a structure tucked into the forest, a rustic, one-room hovel.

"Oh, one more thing." The man was suddenly back.

The dwarf almost pulled my arm out of its socket, turning me around to face the probable king.

"It wouldn't do for you to remember any of this. Can't have you upsetting my charming wife." He flicked me right between the eyes and the world went white.

———

I WAS TIED IN A CHAIR, STARING STRAIGHT AHEAD, MY VOICE UTTERLY without emotion, saying my first name. With barely a pause, I gave them my married name, making sure to speak in the same monotone. The name Sam Quinn might be recognized by a minion. Samantha Fitzwilliam had only existed for a few days.

"Where do you live?" the dwarf asked.

Apparently, I was being interrogated. The Orc paced behind the dwarf, his hands in boulder-sized fists swinging by his side. The slashes down his face had closed, but an eye was missing, and blood still stained his rough skin and tattered tunic.

"Canterbury," I said, pretending to still be in their truth-telling trance. I wasn't sure if it was supposed to wear off quickly so they could enjoy my screams, or if my werewolf healing and wicchey abilities had repaired whatever spell the king had used on me.

"Don't sound English," the dwarf sneered.

"My husband's home. We just moved there." I understood how the truth-while-lying thing the fae did worked. What I'd said was the absolute truth. It also happened to be quite misleading.

While I spoke, I flicked out a claw and began to saw the ropes binding me. I stared straight ahead, eyes unfocused, but I saw movement in the periphery of my vision. Flowering vines were crawling slowly through the open windows.

"What's your"—he paused a moment, as though searching for the word—"occupation?" The dwarf emphasized the last word with a shove to my shoulder, but I saw it coming and schooled my body, neither flinching nor blinking.

"Geh on wiff it," the Orc grumbled.

"I work in a bookstore." My claw did nothing. It had to be a spelled rope. I tried using the spell Lydia had taught me to open something. It was very basic and I was not that kind of wicche, but I'd done it before to release an imprisoned ghost from the Ursuline Convent in New Orleans, so it was worth a try. Unfortunately, it did nothing.

"Why did the queen favor you with safe passage?" The dwarf leaned in, his ruddy, bearded face far too close as he took a sniff. Hopefully, I mostly smelled of the incense burning in the cathedral and the human shops I'd visited. The hat, gloves, and scarf had been touched by many. I was, no doubt, a brew of muddled scents.

Trickier. "I'd been delivering a message to the queen when I was attacked by one of her people."

And then I remembered. The queen had taken a liking to the indigo opal ring Clive had given me in New Orleans. We'd exchanged rings. Hoping the object that allowed me to pass through doorways in and out of Faerie would also have some effect on the fae-spelled rope, I worked my glove down my hand

and pressed the thin gold band I wore on my pinky to the knot around my wrists. It gave way, no claws required. Grabbing it quickly before it hit the floor, I waited for my moment.

ELEVEN

Beware Wee Smol Assholes

"And who were you delivering a message for?" His eyes slitted, suspicion alive in his gaze.

"Russell."

"Who da fuck is Russell?" the Orc asked, genuinely confused. As Orcs didn't seem that bright, though, this may have been his default reaction to most things, ergo the punching.

"A master vampire." The flowing vines continued their very slow progress across the walls and ceiling. Was Faerie listening in or was this a new threat?

At the word vampire, the Orc's expression screwed up in disgust. He shoved the dwarf's shoulder. "Why's da queen takin' messages from a corpse?"

"Don't know, do I?" the dwarf grumped, but he eyed me warily. "How are you connected to vampires?"

This conversation was going nowhere and the longer I was stuck in Faerie, the more time I lost in the human realm. I may have already been gone a few days. Please don't let it be weeks or months. Clive must be going out of his mind with worry.

Wrapping a hand around a wooden dowel in the back of the chair, I responded, "By marriage," and then popped up, whipping my arm around and smashing the chair into the dwarf, sending him across the small room. His head slammed into the wall before he crumpled to the ground.

When the Orc charged, I feinted toward the door, as though trying to escape, and then spun, claws bursting through my gloves again. I scraped them down the other side of his face, aiming for his one remaining eye. I heard the pop as the dwarf sat up, shook his head, and got his feet beneath him. I'd done enough training with Clive, both with a sword and without, to hold my own in hand-to-hand combat.

The dwarf pulled a large hatchet from its sheath on his back and let it fly in one smooth movement that was so fast, it was hard to track. Had it not been for my own quick reflexes, I'd be bleeding out with a hatchet in my chest. Instead, I dropped and rolled out of its path.

Partially shifting, arms bulking up with muscles, jaw elongating to hold a wolf's teeth, I was ready when he sprang for me. I spun out of the way, pulled back my right arm and then slammed my fist into the side of his head. Eyes rolling back, he dropped like a stone.

The Orc was still roaring, spittle flying from his lips, body bouncing off the walls, so I got the hell out. I was pretty sure Gloriana would be pissed if I killed two more of her people, so I decided incapacitated worked for the time being. Now all I had to do was find a door back to my world. Easy peasy.

I jogged over to the spot where I'd come through. I found the impression in the ground where I'd landed. Leading with Gloriana's ring, I ran my hand over the moss, trying to find a spot that gave. Nothing. Trying my best to tamp down the panic rising, I checked the nearby trees. They were too far away. Logically, none of them could have been the doorway, but I checked anyway.

"Little help here," I whispered into the ring. "I didn't kill them, and I really need some help getting home, please."

The Orc came through the doorway, arms swinging in front of him, fists clenched.

Shitshitshit. The chant took up residence in my head. He

couldn't see me, but he'd hear me, and I had no idea which way to go. Padding as quietly as possible, I made my way along the tree line, away from the hut.

Unfortunately, I forgot what I'd learned the last time I was in Faerie. I didn't look where I stepped. I heard an almost inaudible yelp and then a swarm of flower fairies surrounded me, their tiny fists pummeling, their wee teeth biting. It was like being attacked by vicious butterflies.

"Sorry, sorry! I didn't see you!"

Man, flower fairies knew all the best swear words and were quite creative in their construction of insults. The Orc roared, barreling across the mossy field toward me. *Shitshitshit*. I took off at a run, arms flailing, trying to swat the fairies away. Why did they keep going for my face? Smol assholes.

A strong arm looped around my waist and pulled me up short. I heard an odd hiss and the fairies raced away. Fear consumed me before I recognized the scent. Galadriel stood strong and tall beside me, her silvery blonde hair rippling in the wind. Cold violet eyes took me in before setting me aside.

"Wait here."

She stalked toward the rampaging Orc, stopped in his path, drew her sword, and swung. His head rolled away as his body dropped to the ground. She took out a cloth, wiped the blood from the sword, and then replaced it in her sheath.

Turning to me, she asked, "Why did you come back?"

"They kidnapped me." She'd made it sound like this was all my fault. Of course, she probably still blamed me for her wife's— my great aunt Martha's—death.

"They?" She stood with her hands on her hips, waiting.

"The Orc," I said, pointing at our headless friend, "and the dwarf in the shack. I knocked that one out."

Galadriel loped across the field, unsheathing her sword again before entering the small hut tucked into the trees. She walked back out a moment later, wiping down her sword again.

"I thought Gloriana would be ticked if I killed her people."

"She would have been. You're not me."

Fair enough. "They were following me in Paris and then in Canterbury. They attacked right outside the cathedral and brought me here on the king's orders."

"The king? Are you sure?"

"No. But he said he was going to the palace to see the queen and then later referred to her as his wife."

Brow furrowed, she shook her head. "And he let you live?"

"Well, he flicked me between the eyes to make me forget. It worked for a couple of minutes but then it wore off. And those guys," I said, waving to the bloody Orc again, "were interrogating me. Death was probably next on the schedule."

Galadriel's head tilted, considering. "I think it best if we get you out of Faerie."

"That's what I was trying to do before Tink and her friends went savage on me." I gave the delicate flowers a dirty look.

"Don't call them that," she murmured absently, surveying the meadow. "There's no door here, so how did he do it?"

She was talking to herself, but I'd just seen a weird shimmer in the air. "Could they have—I don't know what you'd call it—but could they have made a tear in the air between the realms?"

"Of course not." She glanced up, annoyed, and then her face went blank. She reached out a hand toward the same shimmer I was seeing and then let loose a string of profanity before carefully stepping around the tear.

"Faerie is already incredibly unstable in relation to the other realms. This," she said, gesturing to the shimmer, "makes everything so much worse. It has to be fixed now." She shook her head in disgust. "What was he thinking?

"Quick," she said. "Step through. My queen must repair this, but it will take her time to arrive. The instability throws the time and location you arrive in your realm into question. The longer you wait, though, the more uncertain the time lapse. It could be a week. It could be ten years."

She pulled her sword from over her back, laying the flat of the blade over the silver-swirled Elven mark on her inner wrist before throwing back her head and letting loose an earsplitting, inhuman war cry that made my blood run cold. If I'd heard that sound in battle, I'd know my death was approaching on fleet feet.

Galadriel blinked in the sudden silence. "My queen will have heard me. She'll come." Gesturing to the shimmer, she said, "You can go now or wait for her."

"The longer I wait, though, the more time stretches between our realms."

She nodded. "Even more so because of this. Who knows how many he's made, destroying Faerie with his petty intrigues."

"I'll go," I said, stepping up to the shimmer.

"I would have taken any risk to get back to Martha." She waved a hand. "Go on then."

"It was good to see you again."

She huffed and looked away.

"I miss her too. It's not the same," I hurried on. "I know it's not the same. But if you ever want to talk to someone, I'm here." I glanced over at the shimmer. "I mean there."

She met my gaze, hers defiant and angry. "I wanted you dead. For the longest time, I thought of little else." She let out a deep gust of breath. "I guess I don't want it so much anymore. If I were you, though, I wouldn't push it. Go."

I stepped through, felt myself falling, and then hit the hard frozen ground, bashing my head on a rock.

SOMETHING COLD AND WET TOUCHED MY CHEEK. REELING BACK, I blinked into the darkness. A great hairy beast loomed over me, growling. I scrambled away, my hands breaking the crust of snow. Standing abruptly, I kept the beast in front of me, chancing quick glances in every direction. Where the hell was I?

The beast put its head down, its growl reverberating through the ground. When my eyes adjusted, I relaxed. It was a dog. An enormous dog, but still just a dog. Turning my back to the possible wolfhound, I studied my surroundings. Nothing. Rolling hills with patches of snow as far as the eye could see. Was this a dream? Another vision? The last two had been immediately deadly, a kraken trying to eat me and then hordes of rats attacking. What was coming this time?

Freezing, I stuffed my hands in my pockets and found gloves. I quickly put them on. The fingertips were shredded. Weird. I listened intently. Wind rushed over the fields, small animals scratched and scurried, and the dog sniffed at my pant leg. Was the snow going to rise up, form into a yeti, and kill me? Tension had me jumping when the dog bumped my leg.

Nothing happened, though, other than snowflakes falling from the sky. It didn't snow in the Bay Area. Perhaps this was like the Middle Earth rat vision, only this was an imaginary frozen place. Heart hammering, I prayed for a way out. I didn't think I could take this again. I was holding my breath, expecting something to spring at any moment. Nerves jangling, I needed to move. Anything was better than standing around, waiting for an attack, so I started to walk.

My hand flew to my chest when I remembered. Had my mother's pendant been repaired? It wasn't there. Coco must still be working on it.

Hearing the snow crunch behind me, I spun, expecting claws and fangs. It was the dog. Shaking my head, I continued, the dog following at a distance. There was a lonely, windswept beauty to this place. It reminded me of something, but I couldn't place it.

Flipping up the collar of my coat, I wrapped my freezing arms around myself and leaned into the wind. It hit me then and I stopped, studying the undulating fields stretched out for miles in every direction. I'd read this in *Jane Eyre*. I was on the English moors. Probably. Never having been to England, how would I know, but it felt right.

Hours. It felt like I walked for hours over the moors, the wind whipping through my coat. I pulled the hat down to cover more of my ears, yanking the scarf over my mouth and nose. A flash of something, there and gone: Clive giving me the big warm coat I was wearing. Ha. I wish. I bugged the bejeezus out of that guy.

Teeth chattering, braced for violence, I looked for any kind of shelter. The sun, weak behind the snow clouds, was setting. It was about to get deadly cold. Was that it? Was I going to slowly freeze to death in this vision? A wolf howled. The sound cut through the wind, raising goosebumps. It was the answering calls far closer, though, that had me running. It wasn't going to ice that killed me. I was about to be eaten by a pack of wolves.

TWELVE

People Need to Stop Screwing with my Head

Yes, I was a werewolf, but one of me against a pack of them? I didn't like the odds. Considering the time it took to undress and shift, the pack would be on me before I was ready. Not to mention this was obviously some kind of weirdo vision. What I did mattered less than what the person creating the visions wanted me to experience.

Running faster, I—as I had countless times before—desperately tried to figure out how to extricate myself from the vision. More upsetting than being eaten by the Kraken or torn apart by rats was having no control over my own body, my own mind. While I was trapped in a vision of wolves, where was my body? What was happening to it?

Something was right at my heels. Speeding up, I chanced a glance over my shoulder. The terrain was uneven, with short bushes and rocks everywhere. Tripping and falling now could prove deadly. The wolfhound raced along with me. In the distance, I heard the pounding of many paws.

Ahead, I could make out trees and a church or a castle or some-thing. A deeper black silhouette stood out against the dark, starless sky. I sprinted for it. Any shelter was better than none. My trusty hound friend stuck with me.

A dirt road led to the structure. It ended with tumbled-down rock walls and terraced rises leading to the ruins of a huge church, perhaps an abbey. I leapt easily over the ancient stone walls, the dog sailing over a moment later. There was no shelter. The bones of the building were open to the elements. Snow gathered on the edges of the long-empty, tall Gothic window frames. It blanketed what would have been the abbey floor, the roof having collapsed ages ago.

I raced into the ruins and hunkered down in a corner, in an area that would have been behind the altar. Two solid walls met at the juncture, offering the dog and me some respite from the wind. The dog flopped down, panting heavily. Poor thing. She was exhausted.

Adrenaline dropping, I crouched, rubbing her tummy and listening intently. I didn't hear the wolves anymore. The snow was really coming down now. Perhaps it was obscuring our footprints or our scents. What worried me, though, was that it was muffling their approach.

I was jumping at shadows, but judging by the dog's relaxed state, I didn't need to be. Our corner of the ruin was free of snow and out of the howling wind. It was still freezing, though less so with the big furry space heater leaning against me.

The dog, who needed a name, curled up and fell asleep. Trying my best to follow her lead and settle down, I blew out a breath and checked her neck. No collar.

"What are you doing out here, wandering the moors, little girl?" I scratched her head. Even in sleep, she leaned more heavily against me. The poor pup was starved for love and attention. "Have you escaped Thornfield Hall? Found out the mad woman in the attic was his wife, have you? Not to worry, my plain Jane, I'll take care of you now."

I stayed alert for hours, listening under the driving wind for the sound of paws pounding the earth. Shivering, teeth chattering, I stared into the dark, waiting. It made no sense. I'd never had more than a handful of people in my life. My mother had died seven years ago, and the rest were ones I worked with or served. How had I earned such a relentless enemy, one who understood, who seemed to laugh at, the depths of my loneliness? The Kraken, the rats, they were horrifying but ultimately monsters to be fought. How was one to conquer fear and isolation? This vision was a metaphor for my life: hunted by something keeping to the shadows while I trembled alone in the cold with no protection. I hugged my knees to my chest and dropped my head. I wouldn't give up. I wouldn't. But why did it have to be so damn hard all the time?

When I couldn't keep my eyes open any longer, I lay down beside Jane, huddling against her heat. Without her, I probably would have frozen. With her, I drifted off into strange dreams: Clive carrying me in his arms across the barroom floor, wolves kidnapping me, a vicious wicche, a dragon, waking to find a hand holding mine, a cup of cocoa on the nightstand...

Sam!

Yes? I was in one of those unnerving, lucid dreams, battling a ghost in New Orleans, but fully aware it was a dream. The shout derailed the nightmare, though, which was good, and now I was sitting in a high-backed chair in the front room of a beautiful old house, looking out the window at a tree-lined street, waiting for someone.

Where are you? How odd. My inquisitor had an English accent.

I looked around the front room. *I don't know.*

Are you all right? You sound strange.

Do I? I'm pretty sure this is how I talk.

Have you been injured? The more I listened to him, the more he sounded like Clive, the Master of San Francisco.

No, I—well, my head really hurts, but other than that, I'm fine. This is a weird dream.

You're not dreaming. Where are you, love?

I felt my cheeks burning. Clive called me his love. Ha! Best dream ever.

Sam?

Where was the annoyed, exasperated voice I knew so well?

Uh, yes?

Darling, I need you to open your eyes and tell me what you see.

I don't think you can just open your eyes in a dream.

Sam!

I flinched at the roar in my head. Blinking my eyes open, I looked into Jane's soulful brown gaze and ran my gloved hand over her ears, scratching under her chin. "That was a super weird dream. How about you, my new friend? Did you have a good snooze?" My head was hammering horribly.

Samantha Quinn Fitzwilliam, you answer me! Where are you?

Flinching, I whispered, "Did you hear that?" I peered over Jane's shoulder into the dark surrounding us.

There's something wrong, darling. I can feel it. Look around, think hard about what you're seeing.

"I might be going crazy, little girl. Please don't lock me in the attic." I did as the disembodied Clive voice said, though. I looked around at the ruins. The sky was just starting to lighten. Dawn was probably still an hour away, but there was some definition between the dark silhouette of the ruins and the low, cloudy night sky.

Thinking I might not be giving him the easiest to identify perspective, I remembered how the ruins looked as I was running toward them last night. It was crazy, I know, but I tried to send him that image.

Rievaulx? What in bloody hell are you doing in York?

I cringed away from the anger. I didn't understand what was going on, but I knew I was screwing up somehow.

Sorry. Forgive me. I've been going out of my mind with worry for over a week. I couldn't find you. I can always feel you, your heartbeat a comfort, filling the stillness inside me. I've become so attuned to you, I can sit in my study at home, reach out for the sound of your heart, and hear it beating miles away. For the last week, though, there's only been silence, a Sam-shaped hole in my chest, and it's more than I can bear.

I don't understand. What's happening?

We don't know—

We?

Russell and Godfrey, my second and third. We all came to England together.

I'm in England? I really am lost on the moors?

Apparently so. We went through your phone. Some of the pictures you'd taken walking through the village captured reflections in shop windows. The images seemed to match two of the pieces on that fae chess board you asked me to guard. We have no idea what that means. When you were taken in front of the cathedral, we only saw a blur, but we all caught the scent of fae.

I didn't think I'd ever heard Clive say so many words all at once.

Have you been in York all this time?

None of this made sense, especially Clive loving me and being desperate to find me. We hadn't said much of anything to each other in all the years he'd been making monthly visits to The Slaughtered Lamb, sitting alone at a table, having a drink, and then leaving.

I don't know. The last thing I remember is talking with you on the phone earlier today. Coco was with me in the Presidio. You told her how to pull me out of the rat vision. This is another one, isn't it? Have you figured out how to talk to me when I'm in one?

I wanted to scream. My head hurt so much. This was the monster in this vision, wasn't it? A life with someone who loved me was being dangled before me, but when I woke, it'd be snatched away, making me mourn for a life that never was. I didn't need all this. A devoted partner who couldn't live without me? That was where my tormentor had tipped their hand. It was over the top. All I'd ever longed for was a hand to hold in the dark when I was scared.

I curled in on myself, resting my forehead against my knees again and rocked. What had I done to deserve such cruelty? Jane whimpered and moved in closer. When she laid her head on my shoulder in comfort, the tears I'd been holding in finally came. I was lost in the middle of nowhere, freezing, while someone tormented me with glimpses of companionship and love.

Please don't cry. Oh, love, please. I think I understand the problem now. Darling, listen, I'll help you remember. I'll share my memories with you.

But you're not real. Your memories are just something my fucked-up brain imagined.

Do you remember this? A movie started playing in my head of Clive and me slow dancing in the middle of a loud, throbbing nightclub.

No.

We were meeting with the Alpha of the Bodega Bay pack to ask what he knew about the women who'd been attacked by wolves and dropped into the ocean outside The Slaughtered Lamb. He knew your father and liked him. He didn't like your uncle, thought perhaps he'd killed his own father in order to take over the pack.

I watched myself struggling to relax as we swayed to music only we heard. Clive held me like I was a fragile thing; one wrong move and I'd fly away. His thumb brushed circles on my back. Eventually, his lips touched my temple and the tension eased, my head dropping to his shoulder while he hummed a romantic tune from his youth in my ear.

I was so happy to be holding you. It was the first time I could remember being truly happy in more years than I could count. You were this beautiful, precious, trembling little thing being put in my care. I wasn't being asked to strategize another's downfall or to torture a prisoner. I was being allowed to nurture and protect.

And then we were in his car. He was staring at me, torn, knowing he shouldn't, that a romantic relationship was doomed to end poorly, but being unable to stop himself from leaning in. He wouldn't kiss me, not unless I wanted him to, but I could feel his need. I was the one who moved forward, closing the gap to kiss him. Joy, overwhelming joy and passion, colored the memory. I was seeing my life through Clive's lens.

As he shared memory after memory, the sun rose and my mind

began filling in the blanks. At first, it was a hesitant trickle, but before long my own memories flooded back. Some combination of bashing my head on a rock, coming through a tear in the realms, and the king stealing memories had hidden me from myself. I was back fully in my own skin now and breathing easier.

Jane trotted off to relieve herself, taking my heat source with her.

It's past time for you to sleep. I remember now. I'm okay.

I know. I felt him smile. *You became a participant in the memories a little while ago. I was enjoying myself too much to stop, though. This last week has been hellish, not knowing where you were, who had taken you. Having you safe and sound in my thoughts, returned to the Sam-shaped hole in my heart, is second only to having you in my arms. As soon as the sun sets, we'll be on the road to you.*

It's time to rest now, my pointy-toothed love. Jane and I will occupy ourselves wandering the moors. Perhaps we'll find some nice siblings to take us in.

Jane who?

When Jane came trotting back, I sent him an image of my doggie savior.

She's not some kind of hound shifter, is she? Or a fae spy?

No, of course not. Damn, she wasn't, was she?

I'll see you soon, and then his mind winked out.

Jane flopped down next to me again, her warm back leaning into my knees. Using both hands to scratch her entire length, I thanked my heated blanket for keeping me alive and well all night.

"Apparently, we're in York. We have all day before my vampy beloved comes to pick us up, though." How far was York from Canterbury and how long would it take them to drive it? I remembered studying a map as we flew over, so I knew the moors were north of Canterbury—well, I supposed, most of England was—and on the eastern side of the country. What I didn't know was how many miles that was. Being a Californian messed up my ability to judge distances.

It took twelve to fourteen hours to drive from one end of the state to the other. On the East Coast, that'd be like driving through ten states. In the UK? I had no idea. In fact, I vaguely recalled reading that California was larger than England, which I had a hard time wrapping my mind around.

"We might as well head south, right? I mean, at the very least, we need to find a road." My stomach growled. Jane's ears went up at the sound. "I know. You're hungry too. Let's get moving. Maybe we'll come across a snow hare or something."

The sky was still dark and heavy, the wind relentless, but it was brighter gray now that the sun was up. I could see Jane more clearly too. She was a lovely, mottled gray, with soft brown eyes. She was huge but looked young. No collar. "Are you lost, little girl?"

Feeling stiff, I started jogging, wanting to warm up my muscles. Jane stayed at my side, keeping pace. I rather liked having a running partner. Wolfhounds aren't long distance runners, though, so after a few miles when she appeared to be flagging, I slowed to a walk.

We stopped at a river to drink and rest. There was a dilapidated building that appeared to have been abandoned decades ago. While Jane flopped on the bank, panting like a mad thing, I went to investigate. The windows had all been smashed out. A pub sign hung lopsided, swiveling and swinging in the icy wind, the whining squeal of metal making me uneasy. What a strange location for a pub. The sign had been split. The lower half with the pub's name was lost to time. What remained, though, appeared to be a faded image of wolf's severed head on a pike. Cheery.

The wooden door had four deep slashes, like something with thick claws had tried to get in. Judging by the smashed windows and derelict condition of the pub, it seemed to have succeeded. I peered through an open window frame and saw a tuft of fur caught on a shard of glass. Inhaling deeply, I caught the scent of mold and vermin. Beneath that, though, was whiskey, beer, human, wolf, and blood.

Jane barked. I slapped my thigh, inviting her to join me, but she pranced warily, taking one step toward me, before circling back to get farther away. She did not want to come any closer to this place. Okay. Good enough for me.

We went upstream to a section where the riverbanks were close enough that we could jump across. Farther south, we came upon a pond. Even in the low light, I could see the silvery scales of fish swimming back and forth. My stomach gave another huge grumble. Shifting would cause more stress on my body, hollowing me out, but there were fish right there. Jane needed food too.

I could just unsheathe my claws and hunt like a bear, swatting the fish out of the water, letting them flop on the bank while I found more, but that would require my standing in freezing cold water up to my waist.

Hunting in my other form still required me to go swimming, but I had a thick coat of fur and could shake off the excess. Sighing, I lifted the wicche ball necklace over my head, pulled off my gloves, and threaded my wedding ring and Gloriana's ring through the chain before dropping it back over my head.

Scratching under Jane's chin, I said, "It's still just me, okay? I'll look different. I'll be the thing you were bred long ago to hunt, but it'll still just be Sam. Please don't get scared and run away. I don't want to be all alone again."

THIRTEEN

Manchester United vs. Liverpool

Giving Jane a last head scritch, I took off my hat, scarf, coat, and sweater—Holy crap, it was cold—and shifted to my wolf. It was slower than normal, owing to exhaustion and hunger, but that was still far faster than normal werewolves. My mother's wicche blood helped ease the transformation.

Jane yelped, backing away from me. Once I was fully in my wolf, I stood and shook. At Jane's growl, my heart sank. I plopped my butt down, hoping she'd come sniff me, see that under the fur, the scent was familiar, but she backed farther away.

Barking, she paced frantically back and forth, the hair between her shoulder blades standing straight up.

Since I was only scaring her, I walked into the pond. The cold water was like knives. My lungs seized. I had to do this fast. Snapping, I caught a fish between my jaws and then raced along the mucky pond floor. Emerging, I jerked my head toward Jane, tossing her the fish and diving back in before I could talk myself out of it. We both needed to eat.

Repeating the process four times, I got us six fish, getting lucky and grabbing two in one mouthful. Emerging from the pond, I went to my pile of fish, shook off the water coating me, and gobbled up the food already in my mouth.

Jane was keeping her distance but had clawed at the fish, tearing it open and eating. At least she wouldn't starve on my watch. When she finished, she watched me wolf down a second fish. Once I'd swallowed, I gingerly took two in my mouth and moved toward her. Whining, she backed away.

Understanding fear and boundaries, I dropped the fish near the scales of the last one she'd eaten and then trotted back to my dining spot. After inhaling my third fish, I waited her out, lying down, my head resting on my paws.

Sniffing, whimpering, Jane paced. Finally, her hunger won out over fear and she returned to her meal. When she finished, she moved closer, a sorrowful whine cutting through the wind. I didn't move; kept my body low, my head on my paws. I wanted her to feel safe to approach, to investigate.

Curious, she sniffed me thoroughly, but then moved off, still suspicious.

Freezing from my dunk in the pond, I stood, shook, and trotted off south. Hopefully, Jane would follow. The day had gotten so dark, the clouds so heavy, it felt like night.

A frantic bark punched through the violent wind. I spun as the clouds opened up and the snow began to fall in earnest, a gust pelting me with ice. Jane was surrounded by three wolves. She had her head down, teeth bared, but she was no match for them.

Charging back, I went for the biggest of them. All three turned, backs up. This was about to get ugly. Slamming into a big gray one, we rolled in the snow as I got my jaws firmly around his neck, shook, and then tossed him to the side. I hadn't killed him, couldn't kill him that easily, but I had hurt him. With any luck, they'd skulk off if I made their Jane-meal too difficult.

A reddish one was backing away from me, but a light gray one was crowding Jane, snapping, trying to separate her from me. Claws digging through the snow to the ground beneath, I raced to Jane and leapt on the back of the light gray wolf, bit off part of his ear, and then left him keening in pain as I herded Jane away from the wolves.

We sprinted into the driving snow. I knew Jane couldn't keep the pace for more than a few miles, but I hoped I'd discouraged the wolves from following us. When I spared a look back, though, I saw two more had joined the three.

We were headed north again, back toward the ruins. The snow made it hard to see. The last time the wolves chased us, they'd given up before they'd reached the abbey. Perhaps there was something about the place that repelled them, something that could save us again. It was a weak hope, but a hope nonetheless.

When Jane began to slow, I slowed with her, keeping to her rear, pushing her ahead. The abbey offered no real shelter or protection, but even that was too far off. More wolves had joined the five. We now had seven wolves moving in. That weak hope I'd been clinging to fled.

Good evening, darling.

Hey. No time to chat. I've got wolves on my ass.

What happened?

I caught movement out of the corner of my eye as another wolf moved in from the side. Eight. I sent Clive a mental image of my predicament as I searched the landscape for any kind of shelter, weapon, escape.

Large, rounded, dark shapes rose to the right. I remembered that. There had been boulders and then a drop-off on our left as we'd trotted south earlier. High ground was probably the best I could hope for. Jane was about to collapse. She'd never make it back to the ruins.

Speeding up, I ran beside her, pushing her toward the outcropping. I scrambled to the top of the highest stone while Jane collapsed at the base.

Okay, was I the last of the origin line or not? Hackles raised, I called on my ancestors, wicche and wolf alike, and howled, the sound rolling over the moors, cutting through the muffling storm. The wolves stopped, their eyes on me, Jane forgotten. Growling—the slow, deep vibration traveling through the rock and into the ground—I crouched, ready to attack.

Jane whimpered, but I had to assume it was fear and exhaustion. I had enough to deal with, as the wolves' numbers had risen to nine. The snow continued to fall as I stared them down. I had no influence over wolves as I did the dead.

The one in front crouched, teeth bared, preparing to spring. Putting all the force I could behind it, I let loose another howl, claiming my right as Alpha. I lowered my head and saw eight had backed away, tails tucked.

I wasn't going to get better odds. Leading with shock and awe, I shifted to human, letting my claws slide out and my jaw distend as I leapt from the boulder, landing directly in front of the one not retreating. Before he could react, I swept my claws through the air, raking down his muzzle.

Shifting back to my wolf, I stalked forward. The other eight were lying down, some on their sides, showing submission. The Alpha sprang and I met him, tooth for tooth, snarl for snarl. We grappled, rolling in the snow, claws tearing through fur. He got me a few times, but I bloodied him far more. The snow was becoming red beneath us.

I had him pinned, his throat in my jaws. I could have torn into his jugular, but he didn't deserve it. He'd been leading his pack, looking for food in the winter. Giving him a quick shake, I released him and stepped back. The question was if he'd accept my dominance or if the fight would continue.

Teeth bared, he struggled to maintain eye contact, but was unable. He crouched, tail tucked, fighting against his drive to conquer. My low, rumbling growl rolled under the wind and snow, finding its mark. He dropped to the ground, admitting defeat.

Ignoring the wolves for now, I turned to Jane. Her head was up as she watched, her chest still heaving from the run. When I approached, she stood on shaky legs, ready to go. Good girl.

A strange whistling pierced the roaring of the storm. The wolves heard it as well, their ears up and cocked to the north. I searched with that part of my mind that recognized the dead. Three vampires were racing toward us, but they weren't mine. I moved out to wait between the wolves and our visitors. If they were here to start trouble, I was the one best able to handle it.

A moment later, the three stood ranged around us. The one directly in front of me had short reddish-brown hair and a beard, pale skin, and a black suit, naturally. The other two, though, were wearing what looked to be soccer jerseys. What the hell?

"Good evening. I'm Bram," said the dark-suited one in the middle. "Is one of you Sam?"

Not wanting to shift into a naked human, I gave a woof and ducked my head once.

"Excellent. Clive called to say you were in some trouble and required assistance." He glanced around at the wolves sitting obediently behind me. "He may have been mistaken about that. Well, as we all seem to be getting along so nicely, perhaps you can follow us back to the nocturne. We were told you had a—ah, there she is." Bram inclined his head toward Jane and the Black vamp in the Manchester United jersey went to her, gently petting her before picking her up.

"Does anyone else require assistance?"

When none of the wolves made a noise, Bram nodded. Turning to the South Asian vamp in the Liverpool jersey, he gestured to the far side of the wolves. Apparently, our Liverpool supporter would be bringing up the rear.

We traveled swiftly with our vampire escorts, but it still took a while before we passed the ruins, continuing northwest over the moors.

Have they found you?

Yep. We're on our way to their nocturne now.

Good. We're on our way there too. Considering the speed with which Godfrey is racing down these narrow country lanes, we should be there soon.

Godfrey? I thought Russell liked to drive.

He does, but he's American. He can adjust his thinking to driving on the left when doing so at a normal speed. Godfrey has driving on the left ingrained. Between you and me, though, he's not a good driver, which is why Russell and I are forced to brace ourselves against the doors and ceiling, as Godfrey refuses to slow at turns. I believe we've spent more time on two wheels this trip than four.

Why don't you drive?

Really, Sam. I'm the Master here. I'm not chauffeuring them.

I rolled my eyes at that, and he laughed.

It took a while, but I was finally picking up the scent of the sea. Hopefully, we were close to journey's end. The Manchester United fan set Jane on the ground. She turned and kept pace with me for the last few miles.

When farms and roads began cropping up, the wolves separated, heading off into dense trees. I couldn't see the moon above the cloud cover, but if I'd been in Faerie for a week, the moon was probably full. The pack hadn't felt like natural wolves. They'd probably been out on a moon run when they'd scented Jane. My guess was they'd left their cars and trucks parked on the other side of the trees.

Before long, we were jogging at human speed through quiet, darkened city streets, houses lined up in neat rows, dogs barking behind tall fences. And then we were crossing a bridge over a river, running toward more ruins.

Bram slowed and ran beside me. "The nocturne's over there. Lower floors," he said, pointing to a historic mansion.

"It was a private home but is now a youth hostel. Available food whenever we want it. It works for us." He pointed to the ruins. "Whitby Abbey. The entrance is this way."

I was only sort of listening, though, as I felt Clive nearby. I spotted the SUV parked at the end of a service road near the abbey ruins. Breaking off from the vamps, I raced to the car. Clive stepped out and waited

Shifting midjump, I flew into his arms. He caught me and spun, keeping me warm and covered inside his overcoat. Standing on the tops of his shoes, I held on, breathing in his scent. I was safe now.

"Clive," Bram said.

My espoused turned us, me still clinging to him, naked beneath his coat. "Stoker. Thank you for your assistance."

"Not at all. Your wife had already tamed the pack. We were a bit superfluous, to be honest."

"Nice run," the Liverpool fan said.

"I like the dog," Manchester United volunteered, his hand on Jane's head. "Most don't care for us, but she doesn't seem to mind."

"Can we show you in?" Bram asked.

"One moment," Clive said, spinning us in a quick maneuver that left me wearing his coat. We both looked down at my cold feet on the frozen ground. He picked me up and swung me around, so he was giving me a piggyback ride.

Bram and his men watched us a moment before Bran nodded, as though this was all quite normal. His men went to the SUV to help Russell and Godfrey retrieve the bags.

"If you move the vehicle to the carpark at the end of the lane, no one will bother it during the day."

Godfrey got back in, did a six-point turn, and then raced down the road.

"Thank God I wasn't in the car when he was driving," I said. I'd have been bruised and hurling the whole way.

Russell gave me a look and shook his head. "Never get into a car if Godfrey is behind the wheel."

"I heard that," Godfrey grumbled as he jogged across the field back to us. "Got us here on time, didn't I? If you were driving, we'd still be in Sheffield."

I'd never seen the guys so relaxed and casual in front of other vampires. It was weird.

Liverpool lifted what looked like an oversized metal manhole cover with one hand and then extended the other toward the hole in the ground. "After you."

FOURTEEN

What I Wouldn't Give for Some Underwear Right Now

The underground tunnel was clear and well lit. The cement walls were covered with graffiti, but in what looked to be very sport-specific graffiti.

"Bram?" I called.

"Yes."

"What's with the walls?" They were filled with team names, scores, and dates, all in different pens, markers, spray paint.

Liverpool chuckled behind us and answered for his boss. "We all have our favorites, don't we? Best match. Best team. We record 'em here."

"And then take the piss out of each other over it," Manchester United said, leading the way.

"I gotta say, I've never seen vampires in soccer jerseys before—"

"Football!" Liverpool corrected.

"I mean, ever. I thought the suits came with the fangs." Was someone screwing with my head again? "You guys are the least snooty asshole vamps I've ever met."

"Oi," Liverpool shouted, while Godfrey laughed.

Manchester United led us through a heavy metal door with a keypad into a beautiful dark wood, leather chair, smoking lounge of a room. One wall had the largest television screen I'd ever seen in my life. In front was a huge sectional leather couch holding sixteen vamps, all wearing soccer—football—jerseys and yelling at the screen about a penalty, red card, kick. It was a jumble of shouts and hoots. Jane leaned into me, trembling. The shouts and strange scents were probably too much for her.

"Go ahead," Bram said to Liverpool and Manchester United, both of whom jumped over the back of the couch to sit and join the shouts.

Bram motioned us down the hall into a smaller, quieter room and shut the door. The dark, rich tones and tufted leather furniture continued. It gave off a gentlemen's club feel. We were all just sitting down when two vamps in jerseys came in. One was holding a tray with pint glasses of blood for the guys and a huge burger, fries, and a soda for me. The other had two bowls and a thick blanket tucked under his arm. He put down the food and water for Jane before snapping out the blanket and making an impromptu bed for her.

"That's it. Other than these three, you are all now my favorite vampires ever!"

"We're glad to hear it," Bram said with a smile. "Would you prefer..." He motioned to a small round table.

"Yes. Thank you." I popped up and moved to the table as the server vamp transferred the plate, glass, napkin, and silverware to the table from his tray. Jane was wolfing down her food, so I followed suit.

"It's been a long time. How are you?" Clive asked, his voice warm and relaxed. Whoever these vamps were, they were clearly not a threat. When Clive had introduced me to Rémy, Cadmael, and Liang, he'd been circumspect, more formal, and they were friends. Why were these guys different?

"We're well, as you see." Bram turned his attention to Godfrey. "We've missed you. How has San Francisco been treating you?"

Godfrey laughed. "It's been more interesting of late." He tipped his head toward me. "I must say, though, I do miss the lads and the football."

"No football fans in the U.S.?"

"Oh, some. I've got a smaller version of that room"—Godfrey pointed toward the big lounge we'd walked through—"but there are only a few who watch with me. And they're fucking polite and quiet! Who watches a match like that?" He shook his head, finishing his blood.

"I've tried to watch with him," Russell said, "but I just don't care." He shrugged. "Score already."

Godfrey leaned toward Bram while shooting a hand to Russell. "See what I have to put up with?" He scoffed, "Americans."

"So," Bram said, "what brings you back?"

Jane finished her dinner and trotted over to me, sitting by my side, leaning into me. I ate with one hand so I could keep the other on her. She wasn't shaking anymore but was clearly still wary.

"Do you remember my talking to you about Garyn?" Clive asked.

Bram leaned back in his chair. "That clingy cow? What about her?" He stretched out his legs, crossing his ankles.

"She created another named Aldith. In life, she was wife and mother to the men who raped and killed my sister Elswyth."

Nodding, Bram said, "The origin story. I remember."

Clive glanced at us before focusing once more on Bram. "We've been dealing with a series of attacks, members of my nocturne turned against me, other nocturnes manipulated into declaring war." He flicked his fingers, batting the annoyances away. "We tracked them back to the source. Aldith and her daughter Leticia. The daughter is now dust, so we've come to deal with the mother."

Bram tapped a finger against his lips, thinking. "I don't know that name. Does she go by another now?"

"No idea," Clive said. "We spoke with Chaucer last week and he related a story about a blonde vamp, brown eyes, who did her best to seduce me. The name she was using then—around six hundred years ago—was Addie."

"Wait," I interrupted. "What about those vamps who were going to attack me in Canterbury before the fae beat them to it? They were hers."

"Oh, well." Clive shrugged off the question, while Russell and Godfrey wore similar blank expressions.

What did you do?

"I was very angry. We didn't know what had happened to you." Clive's jaw tightened.

"Got it. Understood. What happened, though? Were you able to get any info about Aldith from them?" It felt like the temperature in the room had dropped twenty degrees, but I wasn't sure why.

"No."

Clive?

He slowly tapped a finger on his knee, four, five, six times. "I gave them pain, more than I'd intended. One of them slurred 'Lady Atwood' before he foamed at the mouth and collapsed. I remembered myself and eased off, allowing the second to speak. That was a mistake."

"Why? What did he say?"

"I won't repeat it, but he decided to insult my wife."

"I assume they've both been given their final death?" Bram asked, his voice pleasant and relaxed.

"You assume correctly."

I could feel it. He was kicking himself for losing control, for destroying the connection to Aldith that we'd been looking for. "That was probably why he insulted me."

Clive nodded.

"A quick death is preferable to a long, drawn-out, painful one, especially if he was concerned that he, like his partner, might talk." I finished the last of the fries, wishing I had dessert.

"I'm smarter than this, damn it." He shook his head.

"Love makes fools of us all," Bram quoted.

I snickered. "He called you a fool."

"In this case, he's right." Clive dragged a hand down his face.

"I was gone for a week. What else did you guys do while I was in Faerie?" I felt Bram's shock at my words.

"What *didn't* we do, Missus. We searched every inch of that town, questioned everyone who might know anything. We scared the piss out of your little human stalker," Godfrey said.

"You didn't lose your temper with him, right?" I watched Clive. "He was mesmerized by a magical object."

"Yes, I know. I had him tell us everything he remembered about the moment of your abduction, but his reactions are human slow. One minute you were there and the next you weren't. We erased his memory and sent him on his way."

"You'd barely arrived in town. How did they even know to look for you?" Bram asked.

While Clive explained our welcome party in Dover, I did what I'd told Clive I hated to do if I didn't have to. All three men seemed so comfortable with Bram, I needed to know if they were right to trust him. If they were, I'd share with him the image I had of Aldith. I didn't like broadcasting what I could do, though. Once people knew, they couldn't unknow it.

I closed my eyes, found his green blip, and slid quietly into his mind. The pain hit immediately. I directed some into the wicche glass around my neck, but most into the streak of white in my hair. The pain receded enough to let me concentrate. I heard the words he was saying, as well as the thoughts beneath them.

He was happy to see the men. He hadn't met Russell before but felt as though he knew him from what Clive had related over the years. He never thought he'd see the day when Clive would commit himself to one woman. And a werewolf. She was beautiful, to be sure—*aww*—but it seemed an alliance riddled with pitfalls.

He wished he knew who Aldith was so he could aid Clive in his quest. He loved and respected Clive, felt indebted to him—Oh! Clive was Bram's sire. He'd created vampire Bram almost two hundred years ago. Wait. The math didn't work—ha! When Stoker had written *Dracula*, he was already a vampire. Clive had encouraged him to write to help him master his control.

I was just about to push the image I'd found in Audrey's memory into Bram's mind when a cell phone buzzed, distracting me.

Russell pulled a phone from his pocket. "My lady, I have your phone. Owen and Benvair have been trying to get a hold of you."

I hopped up and reached for the phone. It was George. "Hey, George, just a second." I heard shouts over the phone. "Where should I take it?"

Clive glanced at my now empty plate and patted the sofa beside him. "I think we'd all like to know why they've been so desperate to talk with you."

"Okay." As I'd already decided to trust Bram, I supposed it was all right for him to hear my conversation. When I sat, the coat pulled open a bit, revealing scarred legs. I felt Bram's eyes on me, shock and concern, before he looked away. I tucked my legs beneath me, the large coat covering me like a blanket.

"I'm back."

"Oh my God, Sam, we've been so worried. Clive said they didn't know where you were. What happened?" Owen had taken the phone from George when I answered.

"I'm sorry. I didn't realize you guys knew."

"Owen, we just found her"—Clive checked his watch—"twenty-seven minutes ago. She's only now finished eating."

"Did you get that?" Wicches didn't have the super sensitive hearing the rest of us had.

"I think so. They just found you?"

"Yeah. A couple of fae goons kidnapped me and took me to Faerie. The king—names have power, so I won't use it—wanted to know who I was and why the queen seemed so interested in me. Luckily, he quickly found me boring, erased my memory, told his goons to employ some enhanced interrogation techniques, and then set off for the palace."

"How did you escape the fae?"

The vamps in the room were extremely interested as well. As I didn't want to tip off anyone about Gloriana's ring, I kept that secret to myself.

"When the king's spell wore off, I was tied to chair and was being questioned by a dwarf, who seemed to have smacked me around a little, as I was sore and tasted blood. An Orc was pacing behind the dwarf, waiting his turn. I misled with my answers as I cut the rope with one claw.

"When the questioning part of our day seemed to be wrapping up, I figured I needed to move before the Orc started punching. I'd already taken one of his eyes, so he was looking for payback. Anyway, I surprised them by getting free, knocked out the dwarf, took the Orc's other eye, and skeedaddled out of there."

Clive tightened his arm around my shoulder.

"The problem was, I couldn't find the door back. I was running from vicious flower fairies when Galadriel found me. She dealt with the Orc and the dwarf—I didn't want to piss off the queen by killing her people—and then helped me find a tear in the air that was the doorway. She said the king was destabilizing Faerie by creating the rips, all because the queen held the real power. Toxic masculinity, am I right?"

The men around me stared blankly. Right. Jane watched me from across the room. I patted my knee and she came trotting over. I'd intended for her to sit near me again, but she decided the floor wasn't close enough. She climbed up on the couch, did a quick circle, and then flopped down, her head resting on my legs under the coat.

I looked at Bram and grimaced, my hand on Jane's head. "Sorry. I know we're both filthy, running around the moors. I can clean it off."

He watched Jane snuggle into me. "Not to worry. I have people for that."

"Sam?" George asked the question, though Owen still held the phone.

"Yes, sorry. I found a doggy friend on my travels." Jane exhaled deeply and snuggled a little farther into my lap.

"Oh, that's nice. Listen, could you describe the king for me?"

"Sure. Tall, dark hair pulled into a leather tie at the back of his neck. Light-colored breeches and a mossy green tunic. Some fae have a light green or blue cast to their skin. He doesn't. It has an almost golden, sun-kissed sheen. Full lips, strong jaw. Everything about him is attractive. His looks invite you in, but his eyes are cold. I know the fae are different, but he's got the eyes of a sociopath.

"He kept trying to very subtly alter his appearance, slight changes to his nose, his cheek bones, his jawline. It was like he was trying to hit on the exact face that I would find the most attractive, that I would trust. Lucky for me, wariness is my middle name and I distrust pretty faces."

"And yet are surrounded by handsome men," Owen said, scoffing.

I glanced at all the very handsome men sitting around me and shrugged. "Eh."

Clive kissed the side of my head and extended his hand to Jane so she could sniff him. I was waiting for a growl, but she gave him a cautious glance and then turned her head away.

"What color eyes did he have?" George asked.

"They were golden brown, with gold swirling hypnotically in them."

"And he's the king?" George sounded worried.

"Yeah, but the queen holds all the real power in Faerie. I mean, he's powerful, sure, but nothing compared to her. Why?"

Owen and George whispered between themselves. I picked up a few words but was trying not to.

"Okay, I'll tell it. We need to know, right?"

George murmured something in reply. Clive's brow furrowed and Russell sat forward, so they must have heard his reply.

"I will. We can trust them. Russell and Godfrey wouldn't do anything to hurt your family."

At that, Godfrey's head tilted to the side.

"Sorry. I should have mentioned earlier. We have another vamp with us."

Owen breathed out a quiet, "Shit."

"His name is Bram. He's the Master of this nocturne."

"Of North Yorkshire," Clive corrected. "Owen, George, I've known Stoker for a very long time. I am his sire and trust him as I trust very few."

"If you would prefer, though," Bram cut in, "I can leave you to your phone call."

"George, he's local. He may know," Owen whispered, forgetting we could all hear him.

"I'll do it. No, you keep the phone. They can hear everything we're saying."

Owen gave another quiet, "Shit."

FIFTEEN

Seconds...Minutes...Hours...Sam

"George, I can call you back when I'm alone." They were checking on me and I felt like we'd ambushed them.

"No, it's okay. Owen is right. It's been a secret for too long." He let out a deep sigh. "I'm a twin. We lost my brother Alec when we were eight—"

"I'm so sorry."

"Thanks, Sam. Growing up, we used to spend every Christmas in Wales with my granddad's clan. This one day I was wandering in the woods and ran into a man who sounds exactly like the fae king. He drew me in with those swirling eyes. I heard him talking in my head but can't remember anything he said. I—I don't know —zoned out for a while. The next thing I remember, I was sitting in the dark in the same spot where the man had been. A woman arrived, said he was right about me being unusual. She said it like that pleased her. Anyway, she put out her hand and I stood and went with her.

"I didn't know vampires could mess with our minds until Russell told us in New Orleans. I can't be sure, but I think she was a vampire. She was leading me deeper into the forest when Alec and my sister Coco came crashing through the underbrush, looking for me. Coco became caught in the same trance I was, but

Alec was always the strongest of us. He cussed the woman out, shoving her away, and then tried to drag me back toward home. He was there, pulling my arm, and then he and the woman were gone. She'd taken him instead."

My hand flew to my mouth. "Oh, George."

"We're very sorry for your loss, but now it's my turn to ask you a question. What did the vampire look like?" Clive gave Jane little scritches under her chin.

"If you remember," I cut in. It had to be about twenty years ago, and he'd been a traumatized kid who'd had both a vamp and the fae king screwing with his head.

"I remember everything. I've been going over it in my head every day since. She was white with blonde hair and brown eyes. I'm guessing on height, as I was shorter. Maybe around five and a half feet. I never saw them standing next to each other, but I had to look up into the fae's face. She was shorter than him."

"Any distinguishing features?" Russell asked.

"Not really. She was just a scary white lady. Well, actually, yeah. The hand she held out had a scar on the side, like an old burn or something."

We all looked at Clive, who shrugged, frustrated. "She wore gloves as Addie and, again, I found her wholly unappealing and so avoided her whenever possible."

"Little details," I said. "I bet Chaucer noticed."

"And that," Clive said with a kiss on my cheek, "is why you are my brilliant wife. I bet he did."

Godfrey groaned. "Please don't tell me we have to go back and listen to that bore. If he knows you want specific information, he'll drag it out, dangling the answer like a cat toy while forcing you to listen to hours of stories."

Bram *hmm*ed in agreement.

George and Owen were whispering again.

"Guys, I'm sorry. All the chatter here is because we think the vamp who took your brother may be the one we're hunting."

Russell nodded slowly at that, expression thoughtful. "Leticia liked to feed from other supernatural creatures. She learned that somewhere. If her mother does the same, that may explain why she kidnapped a dragon child."

"What if that 'somewhere' she learned it was from the fae king?"

"We've been talking about that," Owen said. "We don't understand why a vampire and a fae would be working together."

"He's got a point," Godfrey said. "They hate us."

"It's more elemental than that," Clive explained. "We are anathema to them. They are life, growth, vitality, nature. We are reanimated death."

Godfrey scoffed, "Don't pretty it up for us."

I kissed Clive's jaw. "Decrepit."

He looked at me, eyes going hot. "I thought I taught you about that word in the Louvre."

Resting my head on his shoulder, I said, "You're my favorite dead guy."

He huffed out a laugh. "Thank you, darling."

"I'm just guessing here," I said to Owen and George, "but from what Galadriel said, it sounded like the king did shit—like slicing tears into Faerie—to destabilize the queen. I think Faerie and the queen are synonymous. I mean, all fae are magic, but I think she's the powerhouse that keeps it all going. Without her, the realm would die. The king may be engaged in all these pretty little intrigues, as Galadriel put it, in order to weaken the queen in the hopes of taking over."

"So, leading a dying realm is preferable to being second in a flourishing one?" Bram asked.

"To some," Russell said.

"Guys, George has a question," Owen broke in.

"You said Leticia liked to feed on other supernaturals. Did she take new people every time or did she feed from the same one over and over?" George asked.

The hope in his voice killed me. Best case scenario, his brother had been imprisoned for twenty years while a vampire fed on him.

My mind flashed on that poor werewolf Leticia'd had chained in the Bodega Bay cave. It had been horrific. She'd begun to turn him, wanting to create a mindless monster who would create devastation in Clive's territory, taking the focus off her plotting. She'd tortured him as a distraction, and she was the kinder of the two women. I shuddered to think what had happened to Alec at Aldith's hands.

Clive and I shared a concerned look before I said, "We don't know. Clive is the only one who may have met her hundreds of years ago."

"This is still more info than we've had about Alec in all the years since he was taken. I know he may be dead. Probably is. But if there's even a chance that he's being held somewhere, I have to search for him."

Owen whispered something about bears and a house. I didn't catch it.

"I'll put in for a leave of absence—or quit, if they won't give me the time—and then I'll be on a plane. Where are you headed? I'll meet you there."

"We're in North Yorkshire but heading to Wales. Your memory from twenty years ago matches some recent reports we've gathered," Clive said. "I can send my plane back to pick you up."

"Not necessary. Grandmother has a private jet as well. I'll call when I'm on my way."

"Bye, Sam," Owen broke in. "It's good to have you back."

"It's good to be back." Really good.

They disconnected.

"Well," Godfrey said, putting his feet up on the coffee table, "it looks like we just added a dragon to our party."

"Good," Russell said. "George is intelligent, powerful, a vicious fighter, and knows the area better than we do."

"Yes. We'll head out tomorrow evening. Bram, thank you for your hospitality."

Bram inclined his head. "My home is your home."

"Thank you," I echoed.

I tried to stand with Clive but had a huge doggie on my legs. I pushed and she reluctantly slid to the floor.

When we left the lounge, Manchester United was waiting by the door. "If you'd like, I can clean her up." Jane trotted over and ducked her head under his hand, hoping for pets. He smiled down, scratching her behind her ears. When I nodded my agreement, he turned down a hall and patted his thigh. "Come on, love. You could use a good bath."

Jane hesitated, looking at me. I pointed at the retreating vamp and told her to go ahead. She took a few steps and then looked over her shoulder at me again. "I'm not going anywhere without you. Don't worry." She finally trotted down the hall after him.

"I could use a good bath too." I was desperate for a shower and sleep.

"Actually, before that," Clive said, "Bram, can you tell Sam how to get in and out of the nocturne, as she's likely to wake before we do."

Bram nodded, scratching his beard. "You saw how we got in. You need to be strong enough to lift the manhole cover. The code on the door is simple enough. It's the book I'm best known for."

"Perfect."

"As for getting out with a dog, it would probably be better if you took the stairway. Down here." He beckoned for me to follow. Near the large metal door we'd used to enter was a normal-sized wooden one. He opened it, flicked on the overhead light, and pointed up the stairs.

"At the top is another keypad. Same code. This door goes into the back of a custodian's closet in the hostel above. If someone sees you leaving the closet, you'll need to do some fast talking, but you should be able to walk out from up there. You have to make sure the door closes behind you. There's no way back in. The hostel side of the door is flush with the wall and unmarked. Humans believe it to be the back wall of the closet."

"Tricky." I was all about secret passages.

"We are." He grinned. "To come back in, though, you'll need to use the entrance we used before, near the ruins, and, again, you can't be seen."

"Of course."

"Wonderful. Let me show you to your rooms. Godfrey, you'll be in your old room if you'd prefer to watch the match than go on a tour." Bram shoved his hands into his woolen trousers and waited, looking like nothing so much as a patient professor amused by a rowdy pupil.

"Sire?" Godfrey asked.

Clive nodded. "Go." After Godfrey headed back to join the other vamps, Clive turned to Russell. "I'll come to your room shortly to discuss next steps."

Russell nodded his agreement.

Bram pointed to an open door near the end of a side hall. "This is Godfrey's room. Clive and Sam, the next is yours. Russell, yours is two doors down."

"Thank you again." I felt like an idiot, standing here barefoot, naked under Clive's coat.

"My pleasure. If you need anything, don't hesitate to ask." He left us then, returning down the long hall and turning toward the communal area.

The room was nice. Nothing grand like the George V or the room in Canterbury, but there was a bed and walls and a ceiling and—oh, thank goodness—a bathroom. I took off Clive's coat and headed straight for the shower.

"Sorry. That coat is a mess now."

By the time the water heated up and I stepped in, Clive was right behind me. He pulled me into his arms and just held me.

"I couldn't find you," he murmured. "We searched everywhere. No one knew anything. I was going out of my mind."

Wrapping my arms around him, I squeezed tightly. "I'm sorry."

"Not your fault. If I ever meet this fae king, I'll gleefully take his head, though." He stroked his hands down my body. "And you've lost weight again."

"Time is so weird in Faerie. I think I was gone for a little over a day and I only had three small fishes I snagged from a pond."

He got a handful of bodywash and a cloth and began to clean me. When I tried to take the cloth to do it myself, he said, "Let me, please." He dropped to his knees to get my legs and feet.

"A week, Sam. I couldn't find you for a week." He rested his forehead against my abdomen and held me. "I have discovered," he said, regaining his feet, "that the longest measurement of time for me is the absence of you."

SIXTEEN

How Do I Get My Hands on the First Draft of Dracula?

He poured shampoo into his palm and then began to wash my hair. It was a long, tangled mess. Hopefully, the vamps had conditioner. While he settled himself by tending to me, I had some questions.

"I've never seen you this relaxed around another vamp, other than Russell and Godfrey. Why does Bram get your vampy seal of approval?"

He gave me a big, smacking kiss. "I've never been so happy to hear that ridiculous word." He moved me beneath the water, angling my head this way and that to wash out the soap. Being the good, attentive husband of a wife with long hair, he found conditioner and ran his fingers through the strands, untangling knots.

"And to answer your question, Bram is a good man. He was turned without his consent. When I found him, he was a fledgling, mindless with thirst, and had no one to teach him. I either needed to take him on as his sire or give him his final death. He was too much of a risk to our secrecy as he was." He turned me around to rub my shoulders, working through different kinds of knots.

"He'd been a writer, a poet, in life, so I had him use that training to focus. He needed to find a way to control the thirst."

"And he wrote *Dracula*?" I laughed, returning the favor by

washing him. "You know, looks-wise, Dracula doesn't come off well in that book. Was he a little annoyed with you for not letting him lay waste to entire villages?"

"Please. If he'd described Dracula as Adonis-like, it might have been about me. A hideous creature preying on young women? No. I actually think he based the character on what he remembers of the vampire who'd turned him."

"I don't know. There was that unearthed original draft that said Dracula's washboard abs brought all the maidens to his castle." My soapy hands slithered down his chest, over his abdominal muscles.

"I seem to have missed that version." His lips skated up my neck before he nibbled an ear.

"Yep. He was still super creepy, but the maidens didn't mind as much." I wrapped a hand around him and stroked down his length.

He groaned. "How did the maidens know about the abs? Was he walking around the countryside shirtless?"

"Funny you should ask," I said, squeezing hard. "He did, often flexing on the parapets in the moonlight."

"Really? How odd." His fingers slid between my legs, finding me hot and wet. "You'd think a disgruntled local man would have taken him out with a crossbow while he was posing." He lifted me before pinning me to the slick tile wall.

Wrapping my legs around him, anchoring myself to him, I held on to his shoulders while he slipped inside me. And then his hands were on me, teasing, caressing, while his mouth ravaged my own, muffling my moans. When I was close, he moved a hand from my breast and unhooked my leg from his hip, holding it out, opening me up and changing the angle.

I knew I was in a house of vampires and I needed to be quiet, but it was hard to think about anything other than the feel of him and what he was doing to me. When I felt his fangs sink into my neck, I flew apart and took him with me.

Later, after I'd recovered my breath, I pushed the wet hair from his gorgeous, chiseled face. "The local hunters would have been crazy to take you out. The maidens were getting all hot and bothered watching you flex and then took all that pent-up sexual energy back to the locals to enjoy."

Chuckling, he shook his head against my shoulder. "The original version of that book seems more erotic than horrific."

"Exactly. Prudish publishers needed readers—especially female readers—to be terrified of the unknown, not turned on by it."

Stepping out of the shower, he handed me a towel and then grabbed one for himself. "So the patriarchy is responsible for our horrible reputation?"

"Those bastards are at the bottom of everything, but no. I mean, sure, there might be some guys who are disgruntled that hot Dracula gets all the ladies. The bigger issue is how many of you guys are shitty sociopaths given immortality. Does anyone really need hundreds of years of Aldith?"

Towel wrapped around me, I went back into the bedroom, hoping someone had brought in our bags. I needed clothes. Thankfully, my bag was on a bench at the end of the bed. I pulled out panties and pajamas, diving into them quickly. Finally, that clutch in my gut from being in a house filled with strange men while mostly naked began to relax.

"So, are you contacting Chaucer so I can read him?"

Clive coughed over the top of my words. Right. Forgot. Secret.

"Ask him if he remembers more about Aldith, like a scar on the side of her hand?" I searched through the bathroom cabinet drawers until I found a hair dryer. Thank goodness for thoughtful vampire hosts. "You go talk to Russell while I dry my hair."

He leaned in the bathroom door, gave me a kiss, and said, "I'll be right back."

Once my hair was dried and braided, I climbed into bed, so incredibly grateful to have blankets and a pillow. Sleeping under the stars in the winter in England was not for me. I pulled up the covers, cold just thinking about it. Now that I was safe, the memory of the last day and a half had me trembling. Yes, I was stronger and handled it, but so much could have gone far worse.

Clive returned a few minutes later. He must have seen something in my expression because he sat on the side of the bed, resting his hand on my cheek. "What is it?"

I pulled him down to lie on the bed with me and wrapped my arms around him.

Holding me tight, bruisingly so, he murmured, "I know. I've been out of my mind. Anything could have happened to you."

"It didn't."

"No, but it could have. All I could think, as you were talking earlier, is how at every step, you could have been killed." He toed off his shoes, letting them fall to the floor, and then snuggled me up close beside him with one arm as he pulled his phone from his pocket. Swiping through, he tapped an app and dreamy classical music began playing.

"I felt you pulling me back, so I didn't finish my talk with Russell. There's something I want to tell you before I call him, though. Godfrey was vague about what we'd been doing while you were gone."

I tilted my head up to watch him. "How come?"

"He wasn't sure how much to share. We trust Bram completely, but he was concerned about the artist's safety."

I bolted up and sat cross-legged beside him. "You found the sculptor who made the chess set? A.C. Corey? Is he fae?" We needed to find Aldith, but I also needed to give Gloriana her answers.

"*She* is a Corey wicche—Arwyn Cassandra Corey—and she was quite displeased to see us. I'll admit, I was having a hard time being polite and charming."

I smacked his shoulder. "Did you scare her?"

"Oh, I don't know. I may—"

I lifted my hand to smack him again.

"Yes, fine. I scared the holy hell out of her. In the moment, it felt good for someone else to be experiencing the terror I'd been living with, not knowing where you were, if anyone was hurting you." He shook his head. "I'm not proud of it. I think Russell was almost as worked up as I was. Normally, he's the voice of reason. This time, it was Godfrey who placed himself between the artist and myself.

"It took a while—and a lot of placating words from Godfrey— but she finally started talking. I think she realized the fastest way to get rid of us was to tell us what she knew."

I pushed his leg when he paused. "What? What did she know?"

"She'd been abducted by one of Aldith's fae helpers."

"She was stealing wicches too? But they aren't as strong as dragons. How did she survive?" The poor thing.

"She told us—quite reluctantly—that she is part fae."

When I lifted my hand to smack his shoulder again, he caught it and held it on his stomach. "That must be how she knew all the faces and positions for the chess board," I mused.

He nodded. "Presumably. There's more to the story, though. Understand, some of this she told us, some is conjecture on my part based on her behavior, facial expressions, what she didn't say. I've been questioning people for a very long time, though, so I believe I have it mostly correct."

"Fair enough," I said. "Tell me what you believe to be true."

The corner of his mouth kicked up as he reached for my braid and tugged. "Come back down here. If for no other reason than the position will give your smacks less sting."

I laughed, snuggling back in. "Oh, poor decrepit little vamp, did I hurt you?"

He rolled me over, settling between my legs. "Keep it up. Keep playing with fire."

"It's so cute when doddering old guys still think they're tough."

Clive's fangs skated down my neck, causing all my questions to float away on a wave of lust. When I realized he'd already unbuttoned my pajama top, his hands and mouth everywhere I wanted them to be, I shoved him off and quickly rebuttoned.

"Quit it!" I whisper shouted. "No distracting me midstory."

"Can I distract you poststory?" He grinned, pulling me back against his side.

"Obviously."

"It's difficult, when you're as dodderingly old as I am, to remember stories, though."

I made a fist. "Start talking or you're getting punched in the junk."

He grabbed my fist and pulled it around his waist. "No junk punching. I'll need that later."

I rested my head on his shoulder again.

"Apparently, full fae look down on part fae. I caught the scent of wicche, but only barely of fae. The fae knew she was one, though, and grabbed her. She woke up in a dirt-floored cell. She could sense others around her, guards and prisoners, but she didn't see much.

"Aldith came to her the first night. She wouldn't explain this part. She just said that she heard the bloodsucker's thoughts when she fed on her. Corey could, like you, have an affinity for the dead, but she was able to hear the fae too. Russell believes she's a sensitive. Some are able to use touch to relive memories or hear thoughts."

"She's a fae-wicche-psychic? Damn, that is so cool. Do I get to meet her?" I loved the idea of not being the only weirdo hybrid around.

"Well, as she already hated bloodsuckers before we broke in to interrogate her, you may have trouble—given the bloodsucker status of your husband—getting her to agree to a meet."

"Hmm." I drummed my fingers on his chest. "I'll think of something. Go on."

"It took some...coaxing, but she told us that while Aldith fed, she thought of a farm back when she was a child. Arwyn said the images came as flashes to her, memories jumbled with emotions.

She believes, though, that Aldith's father was a physically abusive man. Aldith learned early to point her father at her mother when he was in a rage. Sometimes, if her mother scolded her for something, Aldith would make up stories about her mother and then whisper them to her easily angered, heavy-fisted father.

"Later, she married Atwood, a man much like her father, strong, cruel, and respected in the community. If she whispered in ears, letting others and eventually her daughter take the punches instead of herself, well, so be it. It kept her safe. She was respected, even envied in the village, until a lying little bastard started spreading rumors about her husband and sons. Women used to stop what they were doing to greet her, to ask after her health, and to offer what little they had as a token of their esteem for her. After the bastard started whispering, they turned their backs on the family, herself included. No more smiles and greetings. Instead, there were whispers behind hands when she walked by."

"Boo hoo."

"Indeed. And I never whispered my accusations. I stated them clearly. Still, I was young, struggling to maintain my father's farm. He was an older, successful man, employing many of the men and boys in town. They needed those jobs in order to feed their families. While they may have believed me, they couldn't say or do anything against Atwood."

"So her outrage has more to do with her own loss of status than the death of her husband and sons."

"Maybe seventy-thirty."

"Ninety-ten," I countered.

He shrugged the shoulder under my head. "Probably. Anyway, the fae shoved Arwyn around when abducting her and then putting her in a cell. She saw glimpses from them, but honestly didn't seem to know how all the pieces fit together. The chess set began as a way to work through the things she'd seen and the inevitable nightmares that followed. She put a lot of herself into the pieces. Once she was done, though, the set made her uncomfortable. She said she felt like they were watching her, so she had her agent take it to a gallery."

"Wait. You skipped a step. How did she escape?"

"Oh, you'll like this. They knew she was part fae, but they didn't bother to find out what the other half was. I'd have thought Aldith would have figured it out when she tasted her blood." He shook his head. "Anyway, no one knew she was a wicche. She waited until daylight, when there was only one guard stationed at the end of the row, and then used her magic to open the lock and walk out."

One beat of stunned silence and then I was doubled up laughing. "She just walked out."

"Apparently."

"Brilliant. Wait! She must know where Aldith is."

He shook his head. "She wandered in the wilderness for quite some time. She states she is not the outdoorsy type. The best she could give us was North Wales."

"Wales again. Sounds like we're headed in the right direction."

Nodding, he dialed his phone. "I still need to finish talking with Russell."

Grinning, I thought about our artist. She'd just walked out of Aldith's clutches. Clive and Russell spoke for a few minutes about logistics for the trip west to Wales. Russell had also called the nocturne back home to check in and relayed the update. Though Cadmael was a vamp of few words, everything seemed to be fine.

Resting my head back on his shoulder, I let their voices and the music blend into white noise as I searched my mind for all the little green blips in the U.K. The vamps in this nocturne were the brightest, as I was virtually on top of them. Continuing the search I'd been doing, a little at a time since we started this trip, I found more pockets of glowing green, some in groups, some alone. London had been the worst. It took forever for me to go through the three nocturnes as well as the countless lone vamps. London was a bloodsucker's playground.

Instead of sweeping north as I had been, I mentally headed

south again to Canterbury. Part of my mind was listening to Clive greeting Chaucer, but the rest was focusing on the blip whose mind was pulsing in time with the words I heard through the phone. Pushing past the surface of the blip, I channeled the spike of pain and then felt Clive wipe away any lingering headache.

Chaucer's thoughts ran parallel to the words I heard. For the most part, he was being truthful and rather chuffed that Clive was consulting with him again. When Clive asked about the burn on the side of Addie's hand, Chaucer told a lengthy story about a soiled glove, but I saw the instant flash of memory. He'd seen the scar. The story he was telling was true, though made far more important and elaborate than the memory.

He saw it. Aldith has the scar George remembers. Ask him about kidnapped dragons—but don't interrupt his story!

He kissed the top of my head. *Not to worry. I learned my lesson there.*

By the time Clive asked about dragons, I was struggling to stay awake. I got as far as Chaucer wishing he knew something, as it sounded like a fascinating story, but...and I was out.

I awoke the following afternoon to a whining Jane, her nose bumping my hand.

"Hey, what are you doing here? I thought—oh, right. That makes sense. Manchester United put you in our room after your bath, as I'm the only one who can get up and take you out. Okay," I said, sitting up and sliding out of bed. "Let's do this. I need a minute myself, though."

Racing through my morning routine, I was ready to go not long after. I wished I had a leash or something, though, and then I saw one on the small dresser by the door. Nice. Manchester United came through again. Where would he have found a leash in the middle of the night in this small town? I had a feeling there was a pet store that was broken into last night. Hopefully, he at least left some cash on the counter.

When I picked up the collar, which had a tag with Jane's name, she plopped her butt down, waiting for me to put it on. Interesting. She wasn't a stray wandering the moors. She was used to a collar and a master to put it on her.

"Who are you, Jane? How did you find me?" Scratching under her chin, I added, "Did someone send you?"

I attached the leash and then led her out of the bedroom, patting my hoodie pocket to make sure I hadn't forgotten my phone. The halls were dark, but I made my way back to the door Bram had indicated the night before.

Although the stairway had a light, I left it off. I didn't want light leaking through the door on the opposite end and Jane and I could see well enough in the dark. At the top, there was a keypad. I tapped the code Bram had given me and then turned the doorknob, listening intently. Nothing. I pulled open the door cautiously. As Bram had said, it was a storage closet. Closing the door securely, I looked around. A bucket, boxes, laundry cart, vacuum; there were so many things that could be knocked over, alerting the house to our presence.

Jane seemed to understand that we were being sneaky. She didn't make a sound and wariness kept her tail from smacking anything. I listened at the hall door for a few minutes, heard a group walk by speaking what sounded like German, and then the hall went still. Distant laughing seemed to be coming from downstairs, but nothing else up here.

Opening the door a hair, I paused again. Still nothing. Now or never. I stepped out with Jane by my side and then strode purposefully down the hall. Nothing to see here. Just a woman and her dog going for a walk. We jogged down the stairs and went straight out the front door. I heard a "Wait," but kept going. I had no plausible explanations for why we were there.

Pantomiming adjusting earbuds, so as to explain why I didn't hear anyone, I glanced over my shoulder. A guy with a bandaged ear started after me. I smelled werewolf. *Shit.* This was the one whose ear I'd bitten a chunk out of. *Shitshitshit.*

Jogging down the steps, I took off at a run, with Jane at my side. Nothing sketchy going on. No reason to call the police. Once we'd passed out of the front garden area, I sped up.

Jane bumped me, pushing me toward a river. I wanted distance from the hostel before we slowed down. We crested the bank, and there was a ten-foot slope down to the water's edge. Long grass, bushes, and tree branches kept us well hidden from passersby.

Jane sniffed furiously, racing back and forth. Perhaps we had a furry forest creature nearby. I thought I heard a faint whistle and then Jane was bolting forward, almost dragging me off my feet.

"Are you a Quinn?" The wolf had followed me.

The leash jerked in my hand. "Stop!" I should have dropped the leash, but I was distracted by the wolf. When she dove through a slit in the air, I barely had time to shout, "Tell Bram," before I was being dragged through with her. *Fuuuuuuu—*

SEVENTEEN

Come On! Not Again

I lost my balance, tumbling over tree roots, the leash yanked from my grip. Jane ran down a paved path before cutting across a lawn. Part of a candy wrapper fluttered in the freezing wind, skewered by a thorn on a nearby bush. Okay, good. This wasn't Faerie. I hadn't just been dragged into another realm. The faint whistle I'd heard before we slipped through the tear sounded again, this time much louder. Jane galloped straight across a road to the small man whose fingers were dropping from his lips. The whistler was leaning against a stone wall outside a beautiful old, ivy-covered tavern, staring in the wrong direction. The sign above the door read The Hob & Hound Pub.

Jane jumped, her paws on his shoulders, licking his face.

"Alice! Where have you been?" He hugged a wriggling Jane, scratching her sides. She plopped down, rolling over onto her back for belly rubs.

I was getting the feeling that Jane was not going to be my new adventure buddy. *Damn.*

The man who seemed strangely familiar turned over the tag on her collar. "What's thi—Jane? Who the bloody hell is Jane?"

Regaining my feet, I brushed myself off and looked at what had tripped me. Turning, I found a rounded, wooden door, flanked on either side by huge, gnarled trees. The trees appeared to be growing into the building, as though this ancient church was built around the towering trees. I had a moment to worry I actually was in Faerie or perhaps middle-earth, as I'd never seen anything like this magical door in the human realm, when a bike bell rang out.

"Behind you." An older woman rode past me on the path around the church.

Once she'd rounded the corner, I tentatively put the hand wearing Gloriana's ring against the knobby tree trunk. I felt it start to give and quickly pulled back. This was definitely a doorway. Pulling my phone from my pocket, I checked the date and time. I hadn't jumped time zones, at least, and judging from the accents, I was still in England.

Jane-Alice barked. Glancing over my shoulder, I found her straining at the leash, trying to get back to me. The man holding her leash watched me, expression dark and distrustful. This was going to be a tricky conversation. I jogged over the frozen lawn, quickly checking maps on my phone. Where the hell was I? The app said this was St. Edward's and I was in Stow-on-the-Wold, Cotswolds. That was no help. Pocketing the phone again, I smiled exactly like a dognapper wouldn't. Jane-Alice pulled, trying to get to me.

"Hi. Sorry about the name tag confusion. Your dog and I found each other out in the middle of nowhere." When I got close enough, Jane leaned into my side and stared up adoringly. I scratched behind her ears. "She wasn't wearing a collar, so I thought she was a stray and named her." Shrugging, I patted her side.

The man, short and muscular, had bright green eyes that tilted up at the sides and tousled brown hair that I was willing to bet covered pointed ears. Had Jane been used to lure me into another fae plot?

"American werewolf?"

"In the Cotswolds. And you are?" If he pegged me as a wolf right from the jump, he had to be a supernatural as well.

"Alice's owner." He scanned the street again, seemed to make up his mind, and waved me to the back door of the pub. "Come on. We're closed now, so we can talk."

"I'll be right in." I pulled out my phone. Jane ran back and forth between us before following him in. I dialed Clive. When it went to voicemail, I said, "First, this isn't my fault. Second, I'm fine. Third, I'm in the Cotswolds—or is it singular? Anyway, I took Jane, who was with me under an alias. Her name is apparently Alice. I took the dog formerly known as Jane out for a walk this morning. She heard a familiar whistle, got all worked up, and ran straight through another of the king's slits in the air. We popped out of the side of a tree at St. Edward's Stow-on-the-Wold. P.S. What the heck is with the way you guys name stuff?"

I knew he'd be in a panic when I was missing again. I wanted him to know I was fine. "Anyway, it was Jane's, aka Alice's, master who was whistling for her. He pegged me as a wolf right off the bat, so I'm assuming he's some flavor of supernatural. My guess is fae, but he doesn't seem hell bent on hurting me, so good. He also doesn't seem too happy to have me around, which is also a good sign. I'm standing in front of The Hob & Hound Pub—Oh! Maybe he's a hobgoblin and Not-So-Much-Jane is the hound.

"So, what I'm saying is, if you can't reach me, rain down hell on all those associated with this joint until you find the short stocky guy with the shaggy brown hair and the bright green eyes. Him you should drain dry, but not before torturing my whereabouts out of him." I was pretty sure the guy was listening. I wanted him to know he'd be dealing with more than just myself.

"Okay, I'm going in to talk now. Please thank Bram and Manchester United for all their help. I love you and will see you soon. Oh, and if Bram is annoyed by a mauled wolf on his doorstep delivering a message from me, tell him I'm sorry. I thought I was getting dragged to Faerie again and I wanted you to know where I was. Okay, still love you." I ended the call and pocketed it, but not before turning on the voice memo app, just in case this was an ambush. I wanted to make it easier for Clive to follow the breadcrumbs to my attackers.

The door was thick solid wood and very heavy. The bright light from outside flashed in the dark barroom. Standing just inside the door, crouched and snarling, was the most ferociously adorable wolfhound puppy. He couldn't have been more than a couple of months old, with a black coat liberally sprinkled with light gray and white strands, and huge paws meant for a much larger dog. I let my wolf out a bit, my eyes going gold and feral. He tucked his tail and then rolled over, exposing his belly.

Poor little buddy. I scooped him up and kissed his nose. "Good job protecting your territory. I was very scared." The tremble I felt when I picked him up was gone. He wiggled in my arms, trying desperately to lick my face. "You, I shall name Fergus."

"Would you mind not renaming all my dogs?"

"I can't help it if I'm better at this than you are."

The maybe-hobgoblin was behind the bar, ~~Jane~~ Alice at his side, her collar suspiciously absent. "Hey, that was a nice collar."

"She *has* one. I'd just given her a bath when she disappeared." He shook his head, either at me or J-Alice.

"I found her wandering the moors alone, which is why I named her Jane, but Alice works too, as she often seems to be falling through fae rabbit holes."

He scratched the top of J'alice's head.

"Is someone else here?" I still didn't know if the fae had to tell the truth, but as they were so good at manipulating language, it probably made little difference. Regardless, I needed to ask.

"Never really know, do ya? But yeah, George, my barman, is below, bringing up a keg."

I snuggled Fergus as a ruse for closing my eyes and opening my mind to the supernaturals around me. The man behind the bar was definitely fae. He had the tell-tale bright green overlay of immortal black. No vamps seemed to be nearby. Lots of hazy ghosties around, but none who were making their presence known. What interested me most, though, was the red afterimage downstairs that told me his barman was a dragon.

"Want something to drink?" The hobgoblin wiped down the gleaming bar top.

Not wanting to willingly ingest poison, I said, "I'm good, thanks."

"Suit yourself." He drew himself a beer from a tap and then walked around the bar, sitting at a table and kicking out a chair in invitation to me.

I chose a different chair, one that kept both the entrance and the storeroom in my line of sight. Fergus squirmed to be let down, so I put him back on the floor.

On guard duty, he sniffed in corners and weaved between chair legs before flopping down with his butt to the bar, putting his head on his paws and looking back and forth between the front door and the storeroom. Good boy.

"I'm Sam. Will you be telling me your name at some point or shall I rename you too?" He was like Puck in *A Midsummer Night's Dream*, but bigger, more muscular. Big Puck. Buck.

"All right. Let's hear it. We both know you've already named me. What is it?" He put his feet up on a nearby chair, crossed his ankles, and leaned back, taking a swig of his beer.

"I was considering Buck but am open to input."

Smirking, he took another drink. He didn't feel like the guys who were after me. Yes, Galadriel beheaded them, but I was sure Finvarra had other minions to send after me. This guy seemed totally unimpressed with me, so maybe the stalking and abductions were done now. A gal could hope.

"Glen." He finished the beer and placed the empty mug back on the table. "My name is Glen."

"Huh. That's less hobgobliny than I was expecting. I thought maybe Newt or Peaseblossom."

He shook his head in disgust. "Do I look like a fuckin' flower fairy?"

"There's a flower fairy named Newt? I bet she's a little badass who flips off the other fairies. Her flower is thistle and she wears a leather jacket, a cigarette hanging from her lip." I bet she said *oi* and *feck* a lot too.

"You don't actually need me for this conversation, do you?" Jane—okay, fine, Alice—trotted over and dropped her head on his thigh. He laid his hand on her head while studying me. "You don't act like any wolf I've ever met."

"I don't wanna brag, but I'm kinda special."

"Uh-huh. Now, why are you here and what were you doing with my dog?" The dark, angry eyes belied the easy voice.

I stretched my hand across the table, palm up. "Can I hold your hand for a minute?"

"No." He dropped his hands to his lap.

"Pretty please?" I gave him my most fakely sincere smile.

"Why?"

"Well, sometimes it can help me get a read on people. I was already fae-napped once this week. I have no desire to repeat the experience. Plus, the king is super creepy."

"King?" He stood abruptly. "Get out! I don't want any interest from Faerie."

"I'll second that." The storeroom door banged open. A mountain of a man carrying a keg ducked under the lintel. He was fair, with long blond hair tied back, bulging muscles, and the same piercing green eyes that George, Coco, and Benvair had. This must be our dragon.

He shoved the keg under the bar and then stood, his head tilting as he breathed in the scents in the room. "Wolf?" His gaze darted between Glen and myself. "Why do we have a wolf on our doorstep?"

I shrugged. "Just lucky, I guess."

The dragon glared at Glen, who appeared unconcerned.

"Before you rename him, this is George. George, Sam." He gave an upnod to the angry man behind the bar. "Bring the Penderyn and three shot glasses. We're going to have ourselves a little talk."

"Why is she here? Since when do we allow stray wolves in the pub?" He pulled a whisky bottle from behind the bar and then stacked three shot glasses and carried the lot to our table.

Fergus woke up and bounded after George, trying to attack the heels of his work boots.

George dragged a chair back and sat, slamming the bottle and glasses down on the table. At least he was going into the conversation with a good attitude.

Fergus sniffed every inch of me that he could reach and then jumped up, with his front paws on my leg. Scooping him up, I sat him in my lap. Looking happily between the three of us, he half crawled onto the table, his butt still in my lap, seemingly content to be within arm's reach of all, in case we were overcome with the need to pet him.

Alice trotted over and tried to nose Fergus off my lap. I kept one hand around him, scratching his tummy, while I scratched under her chin.

"She named the pup Fergus," Glen said.

George huffed, crossing his powerful arms across his chest. "Good name."

I picked up a squirming Fergus with one hand, guestimating he weighed about fifteen pounds. "Two months? Three?"

"Two. We'd sold him to a local family, but he was returned a week later."

Aww. I hugged him to me. No one wants to be returned. "Why? He's a great dog, aren't you, Fergus?" The puppy wiggled until he was able to lick my jaw. "Such a good boy."

"They couldn't handle him. They have little ones. They started worrying about controlling him at a hundred and fifty if they couldn't handle him at fifteen."

"Jeez, isn't that something they should have had a plan for before they adopted him?" I used both hands to hold him in front of me so we were eye to eye. "You just forget about those stupid people. They weren't your forever family. They were just a little vacation from these two bozos." I kissed his nose. "You deserve a person who appreciates what a smart, strong, protective warrior you are."

He growled, his paws kicking, his tail wagging.

"Exactly," I said, letting a deep growl of my own reverberate through the room. Jane moved back to Glen's side. She hadn't forgotten my other form. Fergus, on the other hand, struggled to get closer.

"They named him Daisy," George said.

"What?"

George shook his head in disgust. "Daisy. They let the five-year-old name him."

"That's just disrespectful." I scratched behind his ears. "Shake it off, little man. You're better off without them."

Snuggling Fergus against my chest, I studied George. "I have a dragon friend named George Drake. Is George some sort of traditional dragon name?"

Angry red sparks fired in his eyes. "How do you know Drake?"

EIGHTEEN

Dragon's Fyr

"Why does my knowing him anger you?" I mean, yes, okay, this guy did seem to have only one setting: pissed off. Why he was pissed off at this moment, though, was a mystery.

"Of all the dragons you could have named, you name that one? Are you working for a vampire?" Smoke drifted from his nostrils.

"She was on the phone earlier, telling someone to drink me dry if she went missing." Glen's eyes were on George, though, not me. It was like he was purposely trying to start trouble. Oh, right. Hobgoblin.

George jumped to his feet, knocking the chair over. Fergus whimpered at the huge man with smoke billowing from his mouth. Dang, I was about to get scorched.

Throwing a hand up, I said, "Wait. Stop." I put Fergus down and pushed his butt away from me. He took a few steps in retreat and then came back to stand in front of me. Aww, sweet, brave boy.

Turning my hand around, I showed my wedding ring. "I'm married to a vampire. Clive. As I was telling the shit-disturber over here"—I gestured to Glen—"I've already been abducted once on this trip. I don't know anything about you guys, except that there's a doorway between the realms in your front yard. In my book, that makes you suspect."

His expression darkened even more. "What doorway?"

"The tree on the left side of the church door across the street." Fergus growled at George while backing up onto my shoe. As George didn't seem in immediate threat of spouting fire, I hunkered down and rubbed the brave, trembling puppy. Picking him up, I whispered, "My fierce protector. Good boy."

The fire in George's gaze banked and he turned to an unconcerned Glen. "Did you know that?"

Pulling the stopper out of the whiskey bottle, he poured three shots. "I hadn't heard."

George righted his chair and dropped back into it. Downing the whiskey, he poured another shot and threw that one back as well. "If they've found us, why are we still free?"

"Who?" I asked, balancing Fergus and resuming my seat.

"That fucking bitch bloodsucker and her helpers."

What were the chances? Leaning forward, I asked, "Aldith?"

Both men stared me down. "How do you know her name?"

"That's who we're here to kill! What are the fricking chances?" I pulled my phone from my pocket, paused, and then dropped my hand. "Really, though, what are the chances that after I escape from the king and his thugs, Jane finds me knocked out on the Yorkshire Moors? And then she sticks with me, even though I scare her, eventually pulling me through a tear that leads right to you two?" Pocketing the phone, I put the pup down and stood, moving away from the table and the possibly poisoned glass.

Unsheathing my claws, I brought my wolf to the fore, my eyes lightening to gold. "Who are you two?"

Both men stared at my claws, considering. "You're a Quinn?" Glen asked, suddenly quite interested in me.

"I'm done answering questions. Who are you two and why am I here?"

Glen downed his whiskey and gestured between the two of them. "Glen and George. We were taken, both of us, and given to that bloodsucker to feed on. We escaped and kept on the run for years. After, what, seven or eight years of moving around and no one seeming to be following us, we stayed here and opened the pub."

"My George's brother Alec was taken too. Did you ever see him? She stole him away twenty years ago. His family doesn't even know if he's still alive." My claws snicked in, waiting.

"She kept another dragon chained in a different part of the dungeon." Glen kicked my chair. "Sit down. We'll tell you what we know."

"Why the hell would we do that?" George glared at Glen.

"I'd heard some of this, about the mighty Clive falling for a scarred werewolf." He flicked his fingers in my direction. "And here she is, reeking of vampire, but not ours. She's an American Quinn wolf. How and why would she have anything to do with our situation?"

George studied me a moment. "Like she said, what are the chances she'd just end up here?"

"Were you guys abducted by Fin—"

George coughed over the top of my words. "Don't use names. They have power."

"Sorry. I know better. Was it the king and his thugs who delivered you to her?" I was beginning to get an idea about who was behind my ending up on this doorstep.

The men shared a glance and then nodded.

"Okay. I want to hear the story, but give me a sec." I pulled the phone out again and dialed my George.

"Sam, we're flying over now." At my George's voice, the blond George sat forward in his chair, head tilted, listening.

"Oh, good. I had another unexpected journey through a tear in the air—"

"How are you calling from Faerie?" My George, henceforth referred to by his last name Drake, sounded panicked.

Another voice floated through the line. "Don't be ridiculous. Electronics don't work in Faerie. She's slipped through to some other part of the world." Ah, so Benvair had accompanied her grandson.

Blond George blinked slowly and then looked as though he wanted to rip the phone from my hand.

"Apparently, I'm in Stow-on-the-Wold in the Cotswolds. Anyway, I'm sitting with a hobgoblin and a dragon—"

"What dragon?" Benvair's voice snapped through the line.

"He says his name is George."

"George what?" she demanded.

"Fyr, Aunt Benvair," blonde George said.

She paused a moment. "I knew it! We'd heard you and your parents had died in a car accident. It was a year or two before our Alec was taken. I never believed a car accident could kill three dragons. Once Alec was taken, I was sure it had been a lie." She paused, took a deep breath. "You're all right?"

He shrugged one massive shoulder, not that she'd see. "Mostly. So, my mom and dad are dead? That's why they never came?"

Benvair made no noise, but I could hear her kicking herself. "I'm sorry, child. I shouldn't have blurted something like that. We never saw them again. They disappeared when you did."

Staring down, his hair falling in front of his face, Fyr nodded slowly. "I see."

As we all had excellent hearing, I just placed the phone on the table.

Breathing deeply, he leaned forward. "Auntie, I heard Alec a few times over the years. He was kept far away from me, but every once in a great while, all the doors were open at the same time and I heard him. Sam here said you'd never stopped looking. As of seven years ago—when we escaped—he was still alive."

We all heard the sob through the line.

"You're sure?" Drake asked.

"Wait," I interrupted. "These two were just about to tell the story of what happened. I called you so you could hear it too."

"Yes," Drake said. "Grandmother and I are listening."

"I was little," Fyr began, "maybe six or seven. The before time

139

gets jumbled in my head. It was late at night, but I couldn't sleep. It was Christmas Eve and there were presents under the tree. I was sure Santa was coming soon, so I went out to the back garden and transformed, flying above the house, looking for his sleigh."

"Oh, child." I'd never heard Benvair sound so gentle.

"After a while, I got tired and came back down. I'd shifted and dressed, and then noticed a man leaning against a tree watching me. He was nice looking, but scary. He cricked a finger, inviting me over. In my head, I was yelling for my mom and dad. I was running the other direction—"

"Yes," Drake breathed through the line.

"But I went to him, silently walking over the grass on wet bare feet." He paused, staring down at the phone. "When I got to him, he smiled broadly and ruffled my hair. 'Good boy,' he'd said. My memory goes blank then. The next thing I remember is sitting under the trees on wet grass, my pajama bottoms soaked through, and a blonde lady offering me her hand. I took it and then we were racing through the forest.

"I blanked out again after that. My next memory is being locked in a cold, damp cell, deep underground."

It sounded as though Benvair had started to whimper, but she covered it with a throat clearing. "Did you ever *see* Alec?"

"No, but I recognized his scent. We'd visited the Drake keep the week before I'd been taken. I remembered."

Glen spun his empty shot glass. "We figured out the timing. Based on when I was taken and put in a cell, George was there alone for four or five years, depending on how old he was when he was taken."

"And who are you?" Benvair's imperious voice was back in place.

"Master Peaseblossom of the Glen, hobgoblin at your service, mum."

Fyr leaned forward and gently patted the table beside the phone, as though trying to calm his aunt. One did not snark to Benvair. "Glen is true enough," he said. "And he is a hob."

"I see," Benvair said. "Please, George, go on."

"She had...servants, I guess. Humans that seemed spelled. They'd bring down food and water once a day. Sometimes, there were other vampires around. I got a whiff when the door at the end of the passage opened, but I never saw them. They never fed on us. Only her. We were her menagerie."

We heard Drake give a murmured, "Grandmother." Although silent, Benvair was clearly reacting to the story.

Fyr continued, "We've talked—me and Glen—and we think she was using some kind of mind control on us. She came every night and fed from us. Sometimes it was barely a sip, but she came every night and neither of us ever tried to escape.

"We rarely had a chance to talk to each other. Our jailers didn't like it." Absently, he rubbed his arm, the sleeve rucking up to show a patchwork of scarring. "Sometimes, though, if I was really quiet, I heard a voice in the dark that wasn't my own. Knowing Glen was with me, that I wasn't alone, helped keep me sane."

"Marginally," Glen put in with a smile.

"It sounds like what Leticia, Aldith's daughter, did to Audrey," I volunteered. "She kept Audrey, her lady's maid, compliant and submissive for over two hundred years."

Fyr scoffed. "I guess I should be grateful she didn't keep me longer."

Glen shook his head and refilled their empty shot glasses.

"How did you escape?" Drake asked.

Fyr's shoulder twitched. "I don't know really. She didn't come one night and the next day I wasn't feeling so isolated and cut off. That feeling I always had of being muffled under water lifted. I looked around my cell, at the thick metal bars on the door, and wondered why I hadn't pulled them apart and broken out.

"So I did. The screeching of metal had the guard running, but I just waited until he got close and then opened wide and breathed fire down the passage, burning him where he stood. I stepped through the bars and went down to Glen's cell. More keepers arrived from elsewhere in the dungeon. This time, they had weapons, but not much stands up to dragon fire." Expression haunted, he petted Alice, who had sat beside him and leaned into him during his retelling of events.

I grabbed Fyr's hand and squeezed quickly before letting go.

"Charred bodies were littered down the passage, but I just pulled Glen's bars apart and helped him out. They'd been starving him, so he'd been too weak to walk. I tossed him over my shoulder and busted through the passage door. Men were waiting for us, guns in hand. They shot and I breathed fire. I eventually killed them but not before taking a few rounds."

He paused to gulp down the whiskey. "I'm sorry, Aunt. I should have gone looking for Alec."

"We'd have been killed," Glen interrupted. "He'd been shot twice in the leg and once in the shoulder. They'd got me in the hip. We could both hear it. More were coming. They were pounding the rafters above us. We never would have made it out if George hadn't run. The window was closing. It was escape then or die."

NINETEEN

Dragon Kisses and Other Terrifying Things

Benvair cleared her throat. "You were right to run while you still could."

Fyr closed his eyes and silently let out a deep breath.

"Where's her lair?" Benvair asked.

Glen shook his head, leaning away from the phone. "I won't go back there."

Fyr straightened his spine, though his hand on Alice's head trembled. "She's in Wales. I can take you."

"That won't be necessary," I jumped in. "There are maps. You can just show us where to look." I knew how I'd feel if someone wanted me to go back to the shack where... No. Remembering put knots in my stomach. Fyr didn't need to join our quest.

"She's right," Benvair said. "We would very much appreciate anything you can tell us about the location, the people, the routines. There is absolutely no reason to put you back in harm's way."

"We should change course and head to George and Sam in the Cotswolds. We can make a plan there and together set out for Wales," Drake said.

"Yes. Go talk to the pilot, please."

I checked my watch. "You guys will need to open soon. I can go get us rooms somewhere in town."

Glen pointed a finger up. "We have rooms to let upstairs. Two, but if you guys don't mind sharing, we should be fine."

"I have vampires showing up after sundown. Do you have a basement we could borrow?"

Fyr nodded. "The storeroom is lightless. There's nothing down there but barrels and boxes though."

"They've slept in worse places. They'll thank you for the safe, lightless room."

"The pilot says there's a small private airstrip not far from you," Drake said. "We'll put down there in about three hours. I'm working on getting us a car as well."

"Good," Benvair said.

"Great. Now that that's settled, can we go back to the George situation?" I asked.

"The what?" Drake asked.

Fyr smiled, his expression relaxing, his shoulders dropping.

"What's with the name George and dragons? Two cousins, roughly the same age, with the same name is weird."

Drake huffed out a laugh. "Oh, that. George and I aren't really cousins by blood, but we consider all dragons to be family, so we call each other cousin and auntie or uncle. George is from a different Welsh clan than our grandfather's. He's Fyr. We're Drake."

"There's also Wyvern, Ddraig, Draic, Erwan, Arach, Dreugan, and those are just the clans I know in the UK. We're all over the world," Fyr said.

"Far fewer of us now," Benvair murmured.

"Okay, but what's that got to do with the name George?" Not that this wasn't fascinating.

"You've heard of St. George slaying the dragon, right?" Drake asked.

"Sure. You named yourselves after the guy who slew you?"

Both Georges laughed. "Not quite," Drake said. "See, St.

George was a dragon. He was just screwing around with his brother, who was in dragon form at the time. They were play fighting. Some random human saw them and everyone went nuts about George killing a dragon—his brother Simon was playing dead.

"Anyway, it's a joke. Every generation, each of the clans names a baby George. Part of it is because one of us was sainted for trying to stab his brother. The other part is a reminder of sorts to look beyond the obvious. The human who saw brothers play fighting assumed they were mortal enemies, that the brother in dragon form was going to lay waste to a nearby village, that one was good and the other evil. Rarely is anything in life ever that black and white."

"So every generation, we have a George," Fyr explained, "to remind us that humans are really quite stupid." All the dragons laughed at that.

After I ended the call, I helped George get ready to open. Glen needed some air. The conversation and the idea of returning to Aldith's estate had him crawling out of his skin, he'd said.

"Are you sure he can be trusted? That he isn't a double agent?" I totally understood the anxiety he was feeling, but I also questioned the timing of his departure.

"If you'd seen him when we busted out, you wouldn't question him. He's stuck with me all these years. He's a friend." George finished attaching a line to the keg he'd brought up earlier.

"Okay, but the fae can change their appearance. He could have made himself look emaciated. He may have only been in that cell occasionally over the years, to talk to you, gain your trust. He may have been a jailer in another part of the dungeon." He was probably on the up and up, but I wondered. "And the fae are immortal. A few years wandering around England with you is nothing in the grand scheme of things."

"No. He wouldn't lie to me." He thought a moment. "I mean, what's there to gain?"

"I don't know. I just know that there's a doorway across the street. It could have been placed there because someone wanted me to find you, to right some wrongs. It's possible. It's also possible that he's been using the doorway to report to key players."

"I'm just not that important. Why take the time and effort to keep an eye on me? Why not just drag me back to a cell? I don't see the logic." He flipped the chairs over so they were ranged around the tables.

"What I've learned from dealing with the fae is that their logic isn't ours. Our ideas of good and evil don't match theirs. It could honestly be as simple as he wanted something and to get it, he had to be on dragon duty for twenty years." I flicked the light switch that softly illuminated the bottles behind the bar. "I could be completely wrong. I'm just asking you to consider that Glen may not be the survivor you are."

"I hear you and I'll think about it." He unlocked the front door and came behind the bar with me.

We did a steady trade all afternoon. George had said it wasn't normally this busy, but the week between Christmas and New Year's always saw an uptick in business. Lots of families visiting relatives over the holidays headed to the pub in the evening.

Glen didn't return, but George and I had it under control. It felt strangely familiar but not. Humans were, for the most part, louder and more raucous than supernaturals. There was also no bookstore to check on, no window wall with the Pacific Ocean washing up against it, no Dave or Owen, no Grim, Meg, or Horus. The work was similar to what I did at The Slaughtered Lamb and yet not. I missed my bookstore and bar.

In the late afternoon, the door opened, letting in a gust of freezing wind, along with George Drake and his grandmother Benvair. She looked gorgeous as always, but was more casually attired in slacks, boots, a heavy sweater, and a thick traveling cloak.

Drake came around the bar and pulled me off my feet, hugging me close. He smelled of wood fire, snow, and safety. Wilting in his big, strong arms, I allowed myself a moment to relax. I didn't have to face everything alone anymore.

Benvair hugged Fyr to her. He dropped his head to her shoulder and held on, the strength draining out of him.

A couple of people at the bar needed help, so I tapped Drake's shoulder to let me down. He helped me fill a few orders because we both saw how desperately Fyr needed a moment with Benvair, a kind of surrogate grandmother.

I tapped Fyr's arm and he flinched. "Take Benvair to your office. Sit and talk. George and I have the bar covered." When he hesitated, I pushed him physically toward the office door. Benvair gave me a nod of thanks.

By sundown, Drake and Benvair were in one of the rooms above the bar. Fyr and I had the bar. Glen had not yet returned, and I was waiting for a phone call. When it began buzzing in my pocket, I patted Fyr on the back and grabbed my hoodie, dragging it over my head while making my way to the door. Once I stepped out into the new snow, I tapped the screen on my phone.

"I'm fine. George and Benvair are with us now. Don't let Godfrey drive. There's no need for stunt driving. I'm good, really." I stamped my feet in the sudden cold. The bar had gotten quite toasty, so the snowy evening had me shivering.

He took a moment and then said, "Truly?"

"Perfectly fine." The village was like a Christmas card come to life. Beautiful old brick buildings with peaked roofs, snow glittering in the lamplight, colored bulbs encircling windows and doors. The town was hushed under the snow. Still, Glen had been gone quite some time, so I worried.

While Clive told me of their plans—they were already in the SUV and traveling toward me—I closed my eyes and searched for supernaturals. Glen might really be walking off his anxiety, but I didn't want to be caught unaware.

Lots of misty ghosties hovered in the air. Three dragons were in the pub, right where they should be. Two fae seemed to be moving in my direction. It was far harder for me to locate the fae in my head. They weren't dead, so my necromancy didn't help, but the tell-tale flat black with an overlay of grass green was there. More concerning, though, were the three vampires racing toward me.

"George! Incoming!" Even upstairs, he should hear me. I slipped the phone in my pocket, still live, so Clive could hear.

Fyr appeared beside me a moment before Drake and Benvair.

"Where?" Benvair asked.

I did a quick check. "Two fae, that direction," I gestured to the right. "Three vamps that way." I pointed to the left. "Fae are the distraction for the vamps."

Clive's voice came through the phone in my pocket. "Use the wicche glass. Take them out first. You have dragons to cover you when the fae arrive."

"Already ahead of you," I said as I wrapped my magic around one of the vamps and squeezed with all my might. Channeling the head-splitting pain into the wicche glass around my neck, I felt him pop out of existence. Moving on to the second one, my stomach churned. I did what I could to siphon off the pain while concentrating on the vamp in my hold. A moment later, his dust was floating on the wind. I heard the fae footsteps coming toward us and pushed Drake's shoulder so he'd be facing the right direction.

Meanwhile, the third vamp had slowed. His partners were gone and he was turning to retreat. If Clive had taught me anything, it was that you don't let a serious threat walk away so he can regroup and come at you again. I coiled my magic around him and gave a hard tug. It felt like a spike behind the eyes, but his corpse dropped to the snow. Good luck to whoever found the desiccated, long-dead body in the road.

"Vamps are down," I whispered, trying to push every last bit of nausea and pain into the wicche glass.

I turned to the fae and saw Glen with another guy.

Fyr relaxed his stance. "It's okay. That's Glen and his buddy Win."

Drake and Benvair stayed on alert.

Seeing Glen and Win together did it. I knew now why I hadn't trusted him. They were two of the pawns on Finvarra's side of the chess set. They were the king's men.

I tapped Fyr on the back. "Why don't you go ahead and go back in. They're probably robbing you blind while we stand out here."

There must have been something in my tone of voice because Drake and Benvair spread out, putting Fyr and me behind them. Fyr looked confused a moment, turned to go back in, and then stopped himself.

"Son of a bitch," he spat viciously, moving forward to stand on Benvair's other side. "You son of a bitch! How long have you been messing with my head?"

Glen feigned confusion for a moment. Once he'd taken in our expressions, though, he laughed. "Since you were, what, six?"

None of the dragons moved. I'd expected flames scorching the street or at the very least accusations laced with profanity. Instead, all three dragons appeared to be fighting against a paralytic. None of them were moving, but they were taut, muscles bunching. Those little fae assholes were spelling them. Well, two could play at that.

I pulled the pain from the wicche glass, imagined it traveling down my arms, gathering in my palms. The fae pawns grinned, thinking they'd ensnared us all. As they stepped off the curb, crossing the street to us, I quickly said the 'look away' spell Owen had taught me. I had no idea if it'd work, but I had to try. We didn't need witnesses.

When they seemed close enough so as not to make too much of a fuss and draw the humans out of the bar, I stepped forward and in rapid succession fired a ball of pain at each one. Doubling over, they clutched their heads. The loss of focus released the dragons. Benvair and Drake stepped forward, each grabbing one of the fae by the jaw. They leaned in, their eyes sparking red, smoke billowing from their nostrils, and kissed the fae, breathing fire down their throats, turning them to ash from the inside. A moment later, all that was left of Glen and Win were black smudges in the snow.

"I know that should terrify me," I whispered, "but all I want to do is jump up and down and cheer."

"I assume that means you were victorious?" Clive's voice floated out of my pocket.

"Three vamps and two fae are no longer among the living-ish," I said.

Drake grinned at me. "I could use a drink to get the taste of fae out of my mouth."

"I think we all could," Benvair said. "It's time for cards on the table, Sam. You're going to need to explain to us how you did that."

TWENTY

I'm Going to Be That Kind of a Dog Mom, Aren't I?

When we returned to The Hob & Hound Pub, things were much as they were before. I'm not sure if anyone even noticed we'd gone. Taking the adrenaline out of the situation, we were probably only on the street for a couple of minutes. Which was odd...

I pulled the phone from my pocket. The call with Clive was still live. "How did you know to call me just then?"

"I didn't. I—I'm not sure. I'd started to call you as soon as I heard your message but then stopped. I decided to wait and call when we were on the road. But even then, I didn't call right away. That's very unlike me."

"It really is. Were either of the guys surprised you didn't call right away?"

Russell and Godfrey, who were in the car with Clive, said, "yes" almost in unison.

"It's as though we, too, are pieces on a chess board, isn't it?" His voice was mild, considering, but I could feel the underlying anger.

"Exactly what I was thinking. You still have the chess set I gave you, right?"

"Of course."

"I want to study all the pieces, see if I can identify any other fae. It was hard for me to do it in the shop because the crazy 'My Precious' clerk was hovering while I was packing the set."

"We're here to find Aldith," Russell said, "and we keep running into the fae instead. They normally stay far away from us. What's different here?"

"That's the million-dollar question. How did we end up as pawns on a fae chess board?"

"Speak for yourself, darling. At the very least, I'm a knight."

If I could feel his anger, he no doubt was picking up on my fear. The fae freaked me out. This was what I got for agreeing to investigate Faerie. Of course, it was either that or die, but still.

I stared down at the ring Gloriana had given me in exchange for the engagement ring Clive had put on my finger in New Orleans. The ring had gotten me out of the rope the dwarf had used. I'd seen in it their eyes; the dwarf and Orc were going to kill me. Painfully. The ring had broken the spell on my bindings, probably the spell on me too. When I couldn't find my way out of Faerie, I'd whispered into the ring that I'd needed help and Galadriel had shown up. The ring had been invaluable, but maybe it was also tying me to Faerie.

"Sam?" Clive said it like he'd already said it a few times.

"Sorry. I've had a thought I want to discuss with you."

"We'll be there in about an hour," he said.

"An hour? Is Godfrey driving?"

"I know how to speed as well, your ladyship," Russell said.

"Good. I miss you guys."

"Hopefully, one of us more than the others." Clive sounded put out.

"Don't be needy, sire. It's unbecoming." I heard a smack and knew Godfrey had gotten one to the back of the head.

"Okay, you guys drive safely. And, Russell, if you could speed a little more, I wouldn't mind."

"I'll see what I can do," he responded.

Ending the call, I looked down to find Fergus sitting on my

foot. "I'm not going anywhere. You don't need to pin me in place." Bending down, I scooped him up and carried him to the table where Drake and Benvair were sitting.

"Who's your friend?" George asked—all this Drake business was irritating. He was George. Okay, from now on my George was George and George Fyr was Fyr, which you had to admit was a pretty cool name.

"This," I said, holding him aloft, "is Fergus. I love him and I'm hoping I can talk OtherGeorge into letting me keep him."

George held out a hand and I passed Fergus to him. It was a good test. The pup had to be okay with different kinds of super-naturals if he was going to hang out in The Slaughtered Lamb with me.

Fergus wiggled in George's big hand, struggling to get close enough to lick his face. George laughed, pulling a phone out of his pocket and taking a selfie with the dog. He texted with one thumb while Fergus sniffed George's neck and ear.

Fergus leaned toward Benvair, no doubt hoping for more pets. When she stared back, unmoved, he flopped back on George, his head resting on George's arm so he could gaze ador-ingly at Benvair. It only took two minutes of her ignoring him before she finally lifted a hand and scratched under his chin. George and I shared a look but didn't say anything. Fergus: Dragon slayer!

"Owen sends his love. He's happy we've found each other and guesses Fergus will end up hanging out with Dave in the kitchen." To Fergus' joy, George gave him a full-body rub before setting him back on the floor.

The pup made the rounds in the pub and then came back and took a nap on my foot.

"So, I have some news," George said.

I turned at his words. I supposed dogs didn't *need* to be watched while they slept. "Oh, yeah?"

He nodded, a grin pulling at his lips. "Owen and I are moving in together."

I gasped, waking up the dog. "Yes!" I smacked his shoulder. "His place, yours, or a new one?"

"They bought a house down the street from mine," Benvair interjected.

Eyebrows raised almost to my hairline, I tried to hide my grin. "Really?"

Luckily for me, Fergus decided to try his luck, going straight for Benvair. He popped up, his front paws on the side of her chair. "Oh, very well," she said on a manufactured sigh. "I'll hold you, but don't expect this to become a habit. You are far too large a breed to be a lapdog." So saying, she picked him up and sat him in her lap. He clearly knew this was a person of some importance as he sat still, none of his usual wiggling and licking. Smart boy.

I grabbed George's wrist and squeezed. "I'm so happy for you both. Pictures. Let me see the place." While I scrolled through the gorgeous mansion he was buying, Benvair held Fergus, her eyes on the front door, Fyr, and then back to the door. The guard was on duty.

When George went to the bar to get refills, I took a moment to search my mind for a second wave of vamps and fae. I didn't see any fae nearby, but three vamps were making their way to the pub.

Whooping, I popped up and ran for the front door, not bothering to grab my hoodie. I raced out and around the corner, running straight into Clive's arms. He held me inside his overcoat, like he had outside Bram's nocturne. We clung to one another longer than was strictly necessary, except that it was very necessary.

You're all right?

Right now? I'm perfect.

That you are.

"Missus, I don't want to alarm you, but there's a wee dog trying desperately to get your attention," Godfrey said.

"Oh, Fergus!" I picked him up and held him for the guys to see.

"What happened to the dog formerly known as Jane?" Russell asked.

"She's inside, but she already has someone who loves and cares for her. This is Fergus. He was just returned by the family who had adopted him because they were worried about him being too big."

"He's a bloody wolfhound," Godfrey said, indignant. "Of course he's going to be too big. That's his breed. Was this a family of morons?"

I smacked Godfrey's shoulder. "That's what I said. I'm hoping George Fyr, the dragon who owns this pub, will let me keep him. Wait," I said to Clive. "You're cool with dogs, right?"

"I'd say he's *very* cool with them," Godfrey snarked.

"Wolf, not dog, you limey bastard. Anyway," I said, turning back to Clive. "What do you think?"

Lifting one eyebrow, he shifted his focus to the dog in my hands. "Let's see what he makes of me." Clive took Fergus and held him up so they were eye to eye. "What say you? She and I are a package deal, you know? You can't have her all to yourself." They stared each other down for a long moment and then Fergus strained forward to lick Clive's nose.

Clive handed the pup back while Russell laughed. "My lady, you must know there's nothing he'd refuse you."

I ignored that because although I was pretty sure Russell was right, I didn't want to take advantage of my betrothed's devotion. "Hey, did you hear? Owen and George are moving in together. They bought this amazing mansion down the road from Benvair."

"I wonder if it's the one I was considering," Clive said.

"I've had a thought about that." I pulled him toward the door to the pub.

"Have you now?" Clive took off his coat and wrapped it around me.

Russell stopped by the soot-stained snow. "Is this what's left of Glen and Win?"

When I nodded, he kicked his way through the snow. "Probably best to erase the evidence."

Godfrey held open the door for us. The pub was emptying, which was good. We all needed to talk. I wasn't sure how Fyr would react to having vamps in his bar, though. The specter of Aldith imprisoning him, feeding from him night after night, may have made any dealings with vampires verboten. I knew my guys would never do what was done to Fyr, but he didn't know that. If they were more than Fyr could handle, they'd have to go.

The vamps nodded respectfully to Fyr as they entered, pausing inside the closed door, waiting for the go-ahead. I didn't miss the cold look Clive gave Benvair. He was still pissed off that she'd left me bleeding on the floor after the kelpie attack at the engagement party. Not only left me, but bitched about blood stains. Clive needed info from the dragons or he wouldn't have been standing here.

Fyr took a moment and then reluctantly nodded back. "Okay, all," he shouted above the din. "Time to go now. Drink up. Warm beds are waiting for you."

It took about ten minutes for the pub to clear, during which George and I helped Fyr close down. When the last human left, Russell and Godfrey stood, moving tables and chairs. They placed Fyr's empty chair in between George and Benvair, while the vamps sat on the far side. It was kind and made me want to hug them both.

When I sat next to Clive, Fergus hopped into my lap.

"First," Clive said, "let me thank you for looking after my wife. I've been quite worried. Knowing she was under a dragon's protection settled my mind."

Fyr looked back and forth between Clive and me, as though he was waiting for a surprise attack. "She takes care of herself."

"She does indeed. It was my mind that needed the settling." Clive already had his arm around me, but he snuggled me in closer. "Also, I don't know if she's broached the subject with you or not, but my wife has become quite smitten with Fergus. Would you allow me to buy him from you? We promise to give him a good home."

What's with all the snuggling and 'my wife' stuff?

I'm trying to humanize myself. He's clearly uncomfortable with vampires.

Oh. Good one.

Fyr studied the three of us, vampire, werewolf, and wolfhound. I gave him an overly bright and hopeful smile.

He huffed out a breath. "Yeah, okay. Turns out he's a better judge of character than me. He never liked Glen. That's why we gave him to that family." Fyr shrugged a big shoulder. "The dogs are mine. He didn't much care for animals. Wendy, Alice's mother, didn't like him but she didn't actively dislike him. Same with Alice. This guy, though, would stare at him from across the room and growl."

Fergus settled in for a nap. His back paws were dangling over the side, but he didn't seem to mind. I massaged the top of his head. "Such a smart boy."

Benvair placed her hand protectively on Fyr's back. "Can you tell us what you remember of her lair?"

Avoiding direct eye contact with the vamps, he angled his body toward Benvair. "Yeah. I'll tell you what I remember."

TWENTY-ONE

Who Doesn't Love Dead, Angry Eyes Staring at You?

"When we broke out, it was just before dawn. We were in the middle of nowhere. I don't really remember a lot. There were mountains, lakes, miles of open fields, rocks, wildflowers. We traveled south on foot, trying to put distance between us and the guards."

"Why didn't you shift?" Benvair asked gently.

Fyr opened his mouth to respond and then paused. Alice trotted over and rested her head on his thigh. He ran he hand over her wiry coat and the stiffness slowly drained out of him. "I was afraid to try. I hadn't shifted since the night I was taken. I wasn't sure I could do it, that I even remembered how."

Benvair nodded, her hand still on his back.

"That was probably the work of the fae," Russell said, his deep, quiet voice breaking the charged silence. "The best way to keep one imprisoned—even after they've fled their cage—is to make them doubt themselves. You'd finally escaped your captors. You should have been elated, the moment crystal clear in your memory. Instead of transforming, revealing your true and terrifying nature and flying to freedom, you followed where the fae led."

Fyr lifted his head, meeting Russell's gaze.

"That behavior goes against every instinct of a predator. You weren't yourself because he was still controlling you," Russell said. "I would bet that if you, your aunt, and your cousin were to go to an empty field right now, you'd have no problem finding the fire within yourself and taking to the air."

Fyr sat taller in his chair, smoke billowing from his nostrils, as Russell nodded solemnly.

"Given what you *do* remember, can you give a us a general idea of where we should look?" George asked. He was doing a great job of hiding the urgency he was feeling, but I knew how desperately both he and Benvair wanted to search for Alec.

Fyr nodded, his long blond hair falling forward and screening his face. "I can take you there. I've got all these pictures," he said, tapping his forehead. "The dogs, the work. I can stay busy, keep it out during the day, but I go back in nightmares almost every night."

He took a band from his thick wrist and tied his hair back. "North Wales, Snowdonia, I think." He glanced back at Russell. "Like you said, I guess. I only remember mountains and fields. Walking for days. Sleeping under the stars. In my dreams, though, I see other things."

"Don't question yourself," Clive said. "Close your eyes, think back to what you've seen in your dreams, and tell us. We can help you interpret afterwards. For now, just tell us what you remember." Clive, too, was ready to hunt, but he stayed relaxed, sitting back in his chair, arm around me, as though we had all the time in the world.

Fyr looked between George and Benvair, as though assuring himself he had allies if the bloodsuckers attacked while his eyes were closed. Chair legs scraping against the wooden floor, Fyr pushed back from the table, his broad shoulders behind the other dragons. Alice scooted back with him, leaning heavily into his side. Wrapping an arm around her, he let out a deep breath and closed his eyes.

"The cell they kept me in was deep underground. The stone walls and floor were always wet and cold. They threw straw on the floors, but it would mold. The smell…" He shook his head. "I'll never get that smell out of my head. Sometimes they got rid of the rotting piles and threw fresh straw down, but they did it while I was asleep."

He opened his eyes and looked at Benvair. "How did I always sleep through it? Before, I used to wake when a dog barked a mile away."

Benvair swallowed, getting her emotions in check.

"They probably drugged or spelled you," I said, pulling Fergus up so I could snuggle him against my chest, his head beneath my chin.

Clive rested his hand on my back, tethering me to him, letting me know that no matter what memories this stirred up, he was here now. I wasn't alone in the dark anymore.

"Right," he said, giving his head an almost imperceptible shake. "It was almost always dark down there. Sometimes they lit the lanterns that hung from the ceiling, but not often. Mostly, I was in the stinking cold and dark.

"The only way I could keep track of time was to try to count her visits, but that didn't work either. I'd try to keep the number in my head, but then I'd start thinking that next time she came it'd be whatever number and then I couldn't remember if the number I had in mind was the now number or the tomorrow number. After a while, I gave up. I was somewhere in the mid-three hundreds. I figured I was probably seven by then."

His eyes flew open. "I remember. I'd been six when they took me. I remember realizing I had to be seven by now, that if anyone had been looking, they should have found me. After that, I stopped counting."

Tears streaked silently down Benvair's stoic face, but Fyr couldn't see.

Closing his eyes, he gripped Alice, no doubt reminding himself he was no longer alone in the dark either. "I tried to occupy my brain, mentally walking through my house, trying to remember every detail. Every conversation or outing with my parents, I replayed over and over in my head. Sometimes I changed them, adding what I wished I'd said or done. I'd think about what our lives would be like if I'd still been home with them. Eventually, it hurt too much, so I made up stories to entertain myself.

"A long, long time later. Years. Glen showed up. They threw him in a cell further down the passage. I couldn't see him, just hear him. They shouted and hit him—"

"How do you know?" George asked.

Fyr blinked his eyes open. "I don't know. It sounded like skin smacking on skin"

Godfrey pushed up his sleeve and slapped himself, adding a guttural grunt to the hit.

Fyr looked startled. "Do that again." He closed his eyes.

Godfrey repeated the move. Russell punched his open palm, adding a gasp of pain.

Fyr's eyes flew open again. "That was it. That was the sound. I remember."

Russell repeated the move and sound.

Fyr looked down at the barroom floor. "I really am an idiot."

"No," Clive said. "What you were was a child, one horribly traumatized. You didn't want to be alone and suddenly you weren't. He pretended to be a prisoner so you'd trust him. The fae are ageless and do not possess a human's capacity for sympathy or compassion. They wanted something from you, so they tricked you into being compliant to make their own lives easier. I'm sure they gave no more thought to their trickery than that it was a good way to keep an adolescent dragon compliant.

"In looking back," Clive continued, "try to see yourself for who you were at the time. You weren't the grown man you see in the mirror now. You were a child. Small, skinny, scared. One ripped from his family and thrown in a dark hole to be fed upon by a monster. And still you survived. Remember *that*."

Fyr reluctantly nodded, clearly uncomfortable taking advice from a vampire. Closing his eyes again, he returned to the dungeon. "We weren't allowed to talk. If they caught us—me, I guess—they'd shove a high-voltage prod through the bars, burning me."

I remembered the scarring I'd seen on his arm, suspected he had those scars all over. Stomach twisting, I knew what it was to have a body that was a roadmap of pain. Fergus' big paws twitched in sleep as he no doubt dreamt of chasing rabbits. Needing out of my own head, I kissed the top of his. "I like that too," I whispered.

"My guess," Godfrey said, "is they punished you if he wasn't there to respond."

Fyr scoffed. "So I can thank him for my scars too?"

Russell tipped his head toward the opposite side of the room and Godfrey stood, went behind the bar, and returned with a bottle of water he placed in front of Fyr.

He nodded his thanks, opening the bottle and drinking the whole thing down. "I told you she didn't come one night and by the next day, her hold was sliding off."

Clive leaned forward. "Prior to that, she'd fed from you every night?"

Looking ashamed, he nodded.

"After years of keeping you in thrall, she loses you in a night? It should have taken days—weeks even—before you were able to shake off her influence. You were much stronger than she was expecting."

Benvair shot Clive a glance. It wasn't gratitude exactly, but it wasn't not either, if you know what I mean.

Fyr shrugged a shoulder that seemed a little less slumped than it had a moment before. "I already told you about getting out, so—"

"I'm sorry," Clive interrupted. "We weren't here then. Could you tell us as well?"

Fyr repeated the story about shaking off Aldith's hold, tearing apart the bars and walking out, rescuing Glen, the guards with guns. "There was a long, circular stairway with a ward at the top. I carried him up the steps and then we were standing on a hillside.

Cold air struck my face and I just stopped. I knew the guards were coming, that I needed to run through the pain, but it was the first time I'd been outside since I was six." He shook his head. "I suppose it was a good thing it was still dark out, or I'd have been blinded."

"The guards weren't coming," Godfrey said.

"What?" Even though Fyr knew he'd been set up, all these bits of evidence proving it still took him off guard. It was painful to watch every single time they hit.

"The guards," Godfrey explained. "If you were shot and carrying Glen, the guards should have overtaken you easily. Did you ever see them chasing after you?"

"No. Glen said they were coming, and we needed to run."

"Big of him, seeing as you were carrying him. You know," Godfrey said, looking at Russell, "I'm really sorry we missed seeing this guy burn to death."

Russell and Clive nodded their agreement.

"Then it's just running. Days of running over hills and fields." Lifting his hands, he said, "I don't know. It makes no sense. It's like one of those old cartoons I remembered watching, where Scooby is supposed to be running through a castle or whatever but the exact same room just keeps scrolling behind him."

"So Glen was lazy in creating the false memory," Clive said. "Now tell us what you've started to remember in your dreams."

Nodding, Fyr said, "When we emerged from the stairs, we were on a hillside, but there was a castle ruin around us. I squeezed us through a narrow arrow slit in a crumbling tower. Rock walls cut across the slope, but that was it. The rest was either destroyed or buried under the grassy hills."

I looked around the group. "Does that sound familiar to anyone?"

Godfrey rolled his eyes at me, but Clive shook his head and kissed my temple. "Darling, this is Britain. You'd be hard pressed to take a walk in the countryside and not stumble upon a castle ruin."

"Oh." When Fergus squirmed, I put him back on the floor, where he could sniff and patrol his territory.

"I've been dreaming about this house," Fyr continued, causing Clive to lean in.

"It was dark, but I could see. It's a huge, red brick manor house. U-shaped. Surrounded by trees. Tall steepled roofs and lots of chimneys. Big, deep-cut windows. The center wing is three stories with a kind of tower in the center that rises another couple of stories. The sides of the U are only two stories. Ivy grows up the bricks. There's a rounded arch, at the base of the tower, that looks like a walkway to an inner courtyard." He paused. "Sometimes there are faces with dead, angry eyes in the windows."

I pulled my legs up, heels on the edge of my seat, and rested my chin on my knees, my arms wrapped around my legs. We were going to have to break into the house of dead, angry eyes if we had any chance of locating Alec and Aldith. I knew we had to do it, but I didn't have to like it.

TWENTY-TWO

I Knew This Was Going to Come Back to Bite Me in the Ass

"By midmorning the next day, I'd slowed to a walk. The leg I'd been shot in could barely hold my own weight, let alone his," Fyr explained. "The bullet had gone through, missing bone, so I didn't have to dig it out, but I was...filthy." He shook his head. "It was bound to get infected."

"Yes," George said. "We're naturally fast healers, but given the abuse and neglect, I'm shocked you made it as far as you did."

"I barely got us to the edge of a village. Glen found a small inn and got us a room. The only thing I remember about the room was dragging myself in, curling up in a corner, and passing out."

"How did he pay for a room?" I asked. As someone who had spent her childhood on the run with her mother, money tight, this seemed pretty convincing evidence against Glen.

I saw Russell nod out of the corner of my eye. Fyr, though, looked confused by the question.

"If Glen had really been imprisoned with you for years, how did he have the money to pay for a room? And although you did the busting out and the carrying and the running, you slept on the floor while he took the bed, right?"

Fyr nodded slowly, staring at his hands. Fergus trotted up and reared back, his front paws landing on Fyr's knee. He did little hops, trying to get closer. Fyr scratched the wolfhound's head and then sat back, crossing his arms over his chest and sighing. "What now?"

Clive opened his mouth to respond, but Benvair—control back in place—spoke first. She patted Fyr's knee and said, "You leave it to us. We'll head north, find Alec, and kill the bitch."

"And any of the fae working for her," George added.

Benvair nodded, her expression fierce.

"I'm not sitting here while you go off to fight my battle." Anger lined Fyr's face, his expression adamant.

Russell's deep, solemn voice cut through the tension in the room. "George is right. We'll need his expertise and his help. Your aunt is, understandably, equating your plight with what her grandson has been living for twenty years. She wants to keep you safe, as she wasn't able to properly protect Alec. I'm afraid we"— he motioned to the other vampires and me—"can't be so selfless. We need your assistance and ask that you fight on our side so we can put an end to this once and for all."

Red sparks danced in Benvair's dark eyes, but Russell didn't back down.

"You know I'm right, Ms. Drake. If the fae—even a small portion of them—have aligned themselves with Aldith, we'll need all the help we can get. Mr. Fyr is no longer a child. This is his decision to make, not yours or mine."

Smoke billowed from Benvair's nostrils as she glared daggers at Russell. Proving he was already a master vampire, Russell remained calm but resolute. She could easily breathe fire across the table and incinerate him, but he was unmoved.

"He's right, Grandmother," George said. "We'll need him."

Benvair stood and strode out the front door.

"Should we—"

George shook his head. "Let her cool off. Neither of us are handling this well. It feels very much as though we're sacrificing George to regain Alec."

"No," Fyr said. "I need this." He stood, went behind the bar, and poured himself a shot. "I need to stop looking over my shoulder, waiting for her to find me again." He downed the alcohol and then headed toward the door. "I'll talk to her."

Once the door closed, I turned to my guys. "Do you know the area he was talking about?"

Clive, Godfrey, and George all nodded.

"Not the specific location," Clive explained, "but the general area, yes."

"How long before the fae know we've killed two of theirs, do you think?" I was not looking forward to dealing with Finvarra's stooges and I still needed to talk with Clive about my ring theory.

"You tell us," Clive said.

I closed my eyes. George was as good as family. I didn't care if he knew what I could do. "No fae, but we have some vamps trying to sneak up on our dragons." I pointed. "One from that side of the building. The other—" I started to point right and then pulled my hand up, so I was pointing to the ceiling. "The other is on the rooftop."

The vamps were racing from the room before I'd finished speaking, George a step behind. The dogs tried to follow, but I stopped them.

"You two stay." I put enough Alpha command into it that they both plopped their butts down. I checked one more time, not wanting to accidentally walk into dragon fire, and saw we only had one vamp left out there. Checking over my shoulder to make sure the dogs were staying put, I opened the door and slipped out.

The night was dark and quiet, the street empty but for us. Russell and Godfrey were standing beside a pile of dark dust, toeing the snow over to cover it.

"Well, that was bloody anticlimactic, wasn't it?" Godfrey said. "Here I am, pumped up for a good battle and we get that?" He shook his head. "Pathetic."

The other vamp was close. I couldn't see him, but I felt him, just as I felt rather than saw Clive. The dragons were standing in the middle of the street, talking quietly amongst themselves. They appeared to be trying to convince Benvair of the plan.

The vamp dropped silently from the roof right behind a complaining Godfrey. The second he landed, he crumpled to the sidewalk, writhing in pain. Clive stepped forward, appearing to materialize out of thin air. I'd forgotten he could do that. Godfrey and Russell picked up the vamp and quickly carried him back into the bar.

The dragons stopped arguing midsentence, proving they too were in on the ruse, and followed the vamps.

Fyr ran down to the storeroom and came back with a long length of thick chains. As that seemed an odd item to keep in a bar storeroom, I pointed and asked, "Why?"

He shrugged. "You never know, do you?"

He had a point.

Fyr, with an assist from Godfrey, quickly chained up the enemy vamp. When he was secured, Clive dropped the pain. The vamp straightened immediately, eyes black, fangs locked and loaded.

"Talk," Clive demanded.

While he interrogated the vamp, I leaned against a wall in shadow, closed my eyes, and dove deep into the mind of our prisoner, siphoning off the pain into the wicche glass ball around my neck. Her image rose up in his mind almost immediately. Aldith.

Ask him where Aldith is. He works for her.

Clive asked the question, punctuated with pain. I saw the manor Fyr had told us about. It was even grander than Fyr had described it, though that could have been because I had no experience with these kinds of old-money estates.

Looking every inch a wealthy woman of power and prestige, Aldith sat in a paisley wing-back chair in a pink and gold parlor, looking down her nose at...Bernard, our vamp prisoner.

His name is Bernard and I've seen the estate.

"I have a job for you," she'd said in his memory. "Take another and go to Stow-on-the-Wold, The Hob and Hound Pub. I'm told our little wayward dragon has been joined by a werewolf who was able to use a fae door. As there's only one of those that I can think of, I need you to go now."

Drumming her fingers on the arm of her chair, she stared out a darkened window. "I'll destroy everything he loves—just as he's done to me—before painfully, slowly, handing him his final death."

"You want us to take the wolf?" Bernard clarified.

She barely glanced at him. "I thought that was clear. Glen and Win will capture the dragons when they arrive. I want you to take the girl. Hurt her, if you'd like, but bring her to me. I want the pleasure of draining her dry. I want to watch the life leave her eyes and then describe it all in vivid detail when Clive comes to me, looking for her."

Closing her eyes, a small smile crept across her face. "It's finally happening. He's coming. His cell has been empty too long. He'll soon be mine to torture for all time."

"How did you know we were here?" Clive's voice was like a snap in the barroom.

The prisoner remained silent, but I saw the answer. Glen stepped through a fae doorway, a tree in a grove outside Aldith's home. Bernard was on guard duty at the time. He'd escorted Glen to Aldith's study and left them, but not before hearing that a were-wolf named Sam had also slipped through a doorway and right into their laps.

Ask him how he got here so quickly.

Clive did and then I watched Bernard and his companion slide on rings and then step through the doorway Glen had used.

The rings. I knew it! Pushing off the wall, I crossed the bar, got between Clive and our prisoner, and then yanked the ring off Bernard's finger. Holding it up to Clive, I said, "Fae ring. They're using these to slip in and out of fae doorways." The rest I needed to explain just to Clive.

You're wearing a fae ring too. The wedding was last minute. We didn't have time to shop. It wasn't until the ceremony started that I realized I didn't have one for you. I panicked and then a moment later there was one between my hand and the bouquet. Gloriana gave me an exasperated smile and I knew it was from her.

And you have the ring she swapped for your engagement ring. Is this how we became pawns in the game?

Maybe. I've been considering the possibility, but without the ring, I never would have escaped the spelled rope, or Faerie, for that matter. No fae gift is without danger, but are the rings more of a help or a hindrance? That's what I wanted to talk with you about when we're alone.

"Why are they just staring at each other?" Fyr asked.

Ignoring the question, Clive looked at Benvair and George. "Does dragon fire melt fae metal?"

Benvair stared at the ring in Clive's hand. "Will that take us to Alec?"

Clive wasn't going to answer. I could feel it, but Benvair needed to understand.

"The doorway is guarded. Aldith wouldn't want people just showing up on her doorstep without her knowing. If we find it on our own, our attack will be a surprise. We're outnumbered. We need the element of surprise."

The ring on my finger pulsed once. I closed my eyes and saw them coming. I spun, claws out, and took the prisoner's head. We didn't need an enemy on the inside. As dust and chains fell to the floor, I tensed, counting enemies in my head.

"You're going to get that battle you wanted, Godfrey. Seven more vamps, two fae, and some kind of monster I don't recognize."

I barely got the words out before the door flew off its hinges, sliding across the barroom floor. The ten stepped into the bar and all hell broke loose.

TWENTY-THREE

No, Seriously, What Is That Thing?

The first in was some kind of big, hairy beast. It appeared canine but was definitely not a wolf. Long, shaggy black hair covered a massive, muscled frame. Behind the beast were the fae, an Orc, and a woman who looked enough like Dave's girlfriend that she had to be a banshee. A split-second, that was all the time I had to register the seven vampires behind the fae before they attacked.

My guys stopped them, barely visible streaks of black ricocheting off one another. Russell snatched one out of the air, tore his head off, and then went for another. A pile of dust appeared and then another. All I could do was pray those piles were bad guys. Leaving Clive, Russell, and Godfrey to sort out the seven, now five, I focused on the other three.

When the banshee filled her lungs and opened her mouth, I leapt forward, my arm already in motion, slashing claws through her neck. She blinked once and then her head rolled off her body. I'd heard about a banshee's wail. Given our sensitive hearing, we'd have been incapacitated while the Orc and beast began to tear us apart. A chair sailed through the air. I ducked as George swatted it away.

The Orc's meaty fist whistled through the air, aimed at my

head. I remembered what it was like to fight these dudes. Dropping down, I aimed my claws at his groin and stabbed. A strangled roar vibrated through the floors but then the sound was cut off. Wet, hot, sticky something dropped onto the back of my neck as a vamp crashed into the wall of bottles behind the bar. Glass exploded, the smell of alcohol overpowering the stench of the Orc blood I now had smeared on my neck.

Fergus yelped. Damn it! The dogs must have been hiding behind the bar. I swore, if those freaking vamps hurt my dog, pain was all they had left before them.

Flipping backward, I rolled out of the Orc's reach and straight into the beast. What the hell was this thing? Drool dripped from its razor-sharp teeth, burning holes in the wooden floor. Hellhound? Fae dog? Hypnotic red eyes pulsed in time with its breathing as it stalked toward me. *Shit!*

I touched the magic coiled in my chest and looped it into a ball in my palm. I'd stolen a few spells from my aunt when she'd been trying to kill me. I used the one that had taken me out the first time I'd met her. Flicking my wrist, I lobbed the spell at the hellhound, causing him to go still. I knew what he was experiencing. His brain was shattering, and it was raining glass in his skull. I hated using any of my aunt's magic, but desperate times and all that.

Scrambling away, I popped up, ready to go at him again if the spell didn't take. George beat me to it, though, leaning over, grabbing the beast around the middle, and squeezing. He crushed bones while breathing fire. Howls and whines filled the room and then nothing as ash rained down on the bar floor.

Clive was beside me a moment later, checking for injuries.

"I'm fine, although Orc blood is gross and burny on my neck."

Clive spun me around and wiped my neck off with his sleeve. "Your skin is red and blistered."

"It'll heal," I said, surveying the room. When his tongue hit my neck, I shivered. Right. That'd help me heal faster. A moment later, the pain disappeared. The skirmish was over and we were safe for the moment.

My people were all still standing, though most weren't looking their best. Russell's clothes were ripped and Godfrey had a long, bloody gash down his cheek. Benvair was mussed, George covered in beast ash, but it was Fyr who appeared shocky.

He too was covered in Orc blood, burns splashed across his face. A headless Orc lay at his feet, the missing head hanging from his blistered fist. I couldn't even imagine the strength it took to rip the head off an Orc. The one I'd fought in The Wicche Glass Tavern had a hide so thick, it was almost impossible to cut through.

Benvair took the head from Fyr, tossed it on the dead Orc. As we watched, all the dead fae disappeared, returning to their own realm. Leading Fyr behind the bar, Benvair grabbed a towel and ran it under hot water. When he nodded at her unspoken question, she began to wipe the toxic blood from Fyr's face and hands. It was the most gentle I'd ever seen her.

Russell and Godfrey picked up the door and propped it over the opening.

"So, I'm thinking we should probably get the hell out of Dodge," I said. "They know we're here. They're just going to keep sending more." And I wasn't excited about dealing with one wave after the next.

"The keep," George said. "Let's head to the keep. Mom and Dad will want to know what's going on anyway. We'll be safer there than here."

"How far away is your family's keep?" I asked.

"It's east of Cefndeuddwr and pretty remote."

I stared at him a moment. "Want to run that one past me one more time?"

Grinning, he shook his head. "It'll take three or four hours by car, but we can fly you there."

Benvair's attention snapped to George. She was looking none too pleased.

"Actually, it makes more sense for us to drive," I said. "We have things we need to bring with us"—like a fragile fae chess set —"and we can't leave the dogs here. You guys go ahead, get Fyr up in the air, and then prepare your parents for their vampire guests."

"But—" George began.

"Sam is right," Clive said. "We can't expect Ms. Drake or Mr. Fyr to ferry vampires across the country. If you wouldn't mind giving Russell directions, we'd appreciate it. This will be difficult enough"—Clive's eyes darted to Fyr—"without bloodsuckers watching."

George, too, glanced over at Fyr. "Right." He was no doubt remembering that though he had no problem with these three vampires, the same could not be said for others. Fyr needed to feel safe, to be alone with other dragons.

While Fyr went upstairs to gather his things, Russell and Godfrey tried to reattach the door. As they could bend the metal hinges with their hands, they made short work of it. It wasn't pretty, but the door was attached and could be locked in Fyr's absence. Godfrey even tacked up a 'Closed until further notice' sign.

I found Alice and Fergus hiding down in the storeroom together. Fergus had a cut on his muzzle where flying glass must have caught him. I found Fyr's first aid kit and smeared some antiseptic over the cut. The dogs were shaking, so I sat with them. Both immediately tried to climb into my lap. I struggled to get as much of both as I could and then held them tightly until the tremors finally faded.

I felt Clive nearby and looked up. He came down a few steps but stopped when he saw the dogs tense.

"It's okay, you guys. You remember Clive. He's my hunny bunny."

We both heard the laughter above from Russell and Godfrey.

"Darling, please. You're making me look bad in front of the other vampires." Clive's eyes twinkled in the low light as he sat on a step.

Are you okay?

Perfectly well.

I looked him up and down. *You don't even look like you've been in a brawl.*

I thought you already knew. I'm quite extraordinary.

Yeah, yeah. I smell dog food in the bin in the corner. If you were to bring these two a couple handfuls of kibble, they'd probably be less afraid of you.

He stood, continuing down the stairs. Fergus growled, but Clive went to the food bin, grabbed two handfuls, and then came to us, hunkering down and opening his hands beneath their noses. Both sniffed. Alice whined. It smelled like food but also vampire.

Lean in real slow and give me a kiss.

When he did, I placed a hand on his cheek and kissed him back. The dogs still trembled but they were hungry, never having gotten their dinner in all the hubbub. While Clive and I kissed, the dogs started to eat from his hands. We both smiled and broke apart.

"Let's fill their bowls and let them eat." We were going to need to pack doggie supplies as well.

Clive rose and went to work. Finding a scooper in the bin, he filled both bowls and then went to the sink to clean the dog spit from his hands.

Warily, the dogs gave Clive a wide berth, circling behind him on their way to their bowls. They each paused frequently to look over their shoulders and watch the vampire, but when he pulled me to my feet and hugged me, they didn't seem too upset about it.

He kissed my forehead. "Incoming?"

I closed my eyes and searched. "No one right now, but we really need to leave soon."

"I know. Let's collect what the dogs will need."

I went to a storage cabinet in the corner and checked for doggie things. As it was right next to the food, I was hopeful. The shelves were filled with all kinds of random bar-related whatnot, but among those things were leashes and potty bags, brushes and treats. There was even an unopened forty-pound bag of dog food.

"Hey, Godfrey?"

He appeared at the top of the stairs. "Yes?"

"Can you find me a duffle bag or something? We need to pack up the doggy stuff."

"Your wish is my command," he said, disappearing through the doorway.

When the dogs finished, I grabbed their leashes and some potty bags. Fear of Clive was forgotten in the face of joyful leashes. Both jumped and jostled one another, trying to get as close to me as possible. "I'm going to take them out before we put them in a car. Could you guys pack up everything on those top two shelves, including the food?"

He shook his head, smiling. "Darling, farmer here, remember? I know how to care for animals."

"Right. Sorry."

I started up the steps, dogs racing ahead.

"Russell," Clive called.

"Yes, sire." Russell stood in the doorway as the dogs barreled into him, trying to get to the front door first.

"Sam is walking the dogs. Please go with her."

Russell inclined his head. "Of course."

By the time I got the dogs leashed up, George had joined us.

"Better safe than sorry. Besides," he said, petting Alice, "I want to give Grandmother and George time to talk alone."

I did a quick mental check before we stepped out. Still alone. George took Alice's leash from me and we headed out. Alice and Fergus pulled, wanting to go across the street to the grass at St. Edward's. As that put us closer to the fae doorway, I turned up Market Square and walked in the other direction instead. The dogs were happy to sniff everything they could, but neither was using the outdoor facilities.

"They may have been trained to poop on the grass," George said.

We circled around the block and headed back toward The Hob & Hound Pub.

"Are you sensing anything, my lady?" Russell asked, always on alert.

George grinned. "Yes, my lady, any bad guys sneaking up on us?"

Another quick check and, "Nope."

Once we made it to the grass, Alice and Fergus squatted. I was just throwing away their potty bags when I felt a change in the air pressure. The guys must have felt it too because we'd all swung to face the trees growing on either side of the church door.

A man stepped out and my blood ran cold. Finvarra. The fae king was far more powerful than any of us, than all of us. He studied us one by one, glanced down at the dogs, and then returned his focus to George.

"I remember you."

TWENTY-FOUR

Stop Being a Dick

"It's been quite some time, hasn't it?" Finvarra walked toward George, but neither of my guys moved. "My, how big you've grown."

I checked myself. Could I move? I twitched my fingers. Yep. Unless something dire happened, though, I didn't want Finvarra to know that his spell had slid off. Damn ring; did I keep it or ditch it?

"And you," he said, moving directly in front of me. "You keep popping up, don't you? Why are you alive and my men dead?"

He eyed Russell but neither spoke nor moved any closer to him. Interesting. Apparently, he'd work with vampires if it helped him wrestle power from the queen, but his loathing was clear.

The fae king's focus returned to me. "We'll talk again, quite soon." He moved back toward the tree just as a dwarf carrying a huge axe walked through it. "Set fire to the dead one. The other two, I want kept alive. Take them to the cells in the north."

A smile pulled at Finvarra's beautiful face. "In fact, put the dragon in the cell beside his brother's." He looked George up and down again. "No one would ever guess you were twins. This one, though," he said, pointing at me, "put her in the cell at the end of the first hall. She and I have a few things to discuss."

He waved the dwarf toward us as he stepped back through the tree.

The dwarf swung the large axe back and forth, loosening up his arm. Sneering, he stared up at Russell. "Giant," he muttered. The dwarf circled behind Russell and shoved him over. Russell toppled like a tree. The dwarf strutted down to Russell's neck and drew the axe over his head. Before he could begin the downswing, I jumped forward, yanked the axe from the dwarf's grip and swung, beheading the little asshole. Jeez, two beheadings in one night. I was starting to worry about me.

Trying not to think about my homicidal tendencies, I checked out George and Russell. Neither seemed to be hurt. Taking a chance, I touched Gloriana's ring to George's forehead and he came out swinging, barely stopping himself before he connected with my gut.

I wasn't too sure a fae artifact would work on a vamp, but I gave it a try. When I touched Russell with the ring, he flew up from the ground, grabbed me by the neck, and squeezed, eyes vamp black, fangs descended. George shouted and lunged, but Clive had arrived, dropping Russell with pain while he pried Russell's fingers from my throat.

I fell to my knees, trying desperately to draw in a breath and failing. Black spots blurred my vision. Taken down by friendly fire. The fae ring pulsed in time with my rabbiting heartbeat. Clive's hand was on my back, his lips at my ear, but I couldn't hear anything. It was like being underwater. I needed to breathe but couldn't.

Love you.

And then it all went black.

I awoke in the backseat of the SUV, my head in Clive's lap, his hand resting over my heart. My head was killing me and my throat felt like I'd been strangled, which, come to think of it, I totally had been.

Oww. Why do they always go for my neck? Are George and Russell okay?

Yes. The more important question is are you okay?

My throat hurts like a mofo, so talking is out. Other than that, I guess so. The pain lessened. *Better. It's still hard to breathe, though.*

I know. I've been sitting here listening to you struggle to take in a breath. Your accelerated healing is helping. Your breathing is nowhere near as labored as it has been.

Alice and Fergus hung over the backseat, watching me. When I lifted a hand to pet them, Fergus scrambled to get to me, finally slipping over the top. He would have dropped onto my stomach, taking what little air I could get, but Clive caught him and settled him in the crook of my arm.

"Gentle, little one," Clive said, "or it's back over the seat with you."

The SUV swerved and then stopped. A moment later the back door flew open and a very solemn looking Russell stared down at me.

"My lady, please forgive me. I don't even remember doing it. One minute, that man stepped from the tree, and the next Clive was prying my hand from around your neck." His gaze dropped to my neck and I saw horror in his eyes.

Tell him it's okay. I understand. He looks so upset. Ask him if he's all right.

"She says she isn't sure she'll ever be able to forgive you." Clive's voice was cold.

Stop that! I trust him completely. Tell him.

"She isn't ready to deal with you right now."

"Respectfully, Sire, stop being a dick," Godfrey said. "There's no way she said anything of the sort. Knowing her, she probably asked if *he* was okay. You know he'd been spelled by the bleeding fae king and you're blaming him for fighting as soon as he was able?" He shook his head and looked out the passenger window, avoiding Clive.

I reached out a hand to Russell and he took it, gripping it hard. He leaned in the car, dropped a kiss on the back of my hand, and then closed the door. Circling around, he resumed his seat behind the wheel and pulled out onto the road a moment later.

Godfrey's right. You're being a dick.

He almost killed you! I've been listening to you struggling for air ever since, knowing there was nothing I could do to help and feeling utterly useless.

I'm sorry.

You're sorry? He shook his head and stared out the window. After a few minutes, he laid a hand on Russell's shoulder. "She said none of that. She understands and trusts you. She hopes you're okay now. She also agrees with Godfrey that I'm being a dick."

Smiling, I rested my hand over his. *Thank you.*

He grunted a half-hearted response.

Were they able to get Fyr to shift and fly?

I have no idea. No one's called for a lift, though, so I assume so.

Clive?

He continued to stare out the window.

Tapping the hand resting over my heart, I tried again. *Clive?*

Yes.

Stop.

He turned back to me and brushed a stray hair from my face. *Stop what?*

All of this. This was no one's fault but Finvarra's. Even the dwarf and his axe wouldn't have been there if his king hadn't summoned him. You know how powerful the fae are. Why are you angry and lashing out at Russell when you know none of this is anyone's fault but Finvarra's?

You were just walking the dog! To be safe, I sent you with a guard, the man I trust most in the world. A loyal dragon shifter went along for extra security and still you were targeted and almost killed. We've been married two weeks and you were harassed by my ex, stalked throughout France by the fae, abducted and taken into Faerie for a week—during which I had no idea where you were or if you were even alive. You were almost killed by a different Orc and dwarf. When you were able to break free and cross back, you were immediately hurt, losing your memory, wandering the Moors, almost freezing to death. I finally got you back and you were pulled through another fae doorway, popping out across the country to hang out with a psychotic hobgoblin and a traumatized dragon, only to be set upon by nine vampires, four fae, some kind of monster, and then—his hand fisted on my chest—*and then the fae king returns to try to take you away from me again. You rescue yourself, as well as your guards, and my most trusted friend tries to choke the life out of you.* He let out a gust of breath. *Is this our life now, Sam? Every moment of every day, I have to worry that you're going to disappear or that I'm going to find your lifeless body—one I've been forbidden to turn?*

I wrapped both hands around his fist. *I'm sorry.*

You're sor—He made a strangled sound in the back of his throat. *None of this has been your fault. None of it.*

I know. But while I've been trying to survive the crazy crap, you've been left to worry. I would imagine, for a man who has lived as long as you have, who's fought and won countless battles, to have to wait on the sidelines and hope is a particularly cruel type of torture.

It is.

I wish I could say it was all going to stop soon, but given the last few months, that's probably doubtful. If it's too much, if you need to step back, I unders—

Shut up. He pulled me into his lap and hugged me to him with a strength that was almost painful. *I love you. I'll take insanely frustrating, if I can have this.*

Aww, I love you too. I watched the trees and grassy hills fly by on the dark, empty road for a few minutes. *Where are we?*

Nearing Wales, I believe. I haven't been paying attention. He kissed my neck softly. *I'm afraid I don't handle you being injured well.*

That's better than the alternative.

I felt him smile and then kiss me again. "Sam is asking where we are."

"We could tell you we're near Shrewsbury, but as that will mean nothing to you, let's just leave it at we're about halfway there," Godfrey said.

Could I have some water?

"Water." Clive reached a hand over the seat and Godfrey slapped a bottle into it.

I could only take a few small sips, but they helped. Fergus crawled into my lap and Alice leaned over the seat, resting her head on Clive's shoulder.

Godfrey turned to look at us and started laughing.

Shut up, you.

"She said to shut up." Clive wrapped his arms tightly around me.

"Now, that I believe." Godfrey checked his phone. "Probably only about an hour. Of course, if Russell let me drive, we'd be there in twenty minutes."

"No," Clive and Russell said in unison.

Fergus fell asleep in my lap and then I snuggled in and soon fell asleep in Clive's. What seemed like moments later, the SUV came to a stop and Clive was kissing me awake. "We're here, love."

"Oh," I said, scrambling off his lap. Thankfully, my throat wasn't hurting as much. "We get to meet George's parents."

I hopped out, Fergus on my heels, and looked around. We were parked on a slope covered in snow in the middle of nowhere, with a huge-ass castle at the top of the hill. "No way!"

Russell got out and looked around as well. "Is this it?"

"This place looks even older than our master," Godfrey said.

I opened the back gate and let Alice out. The dogs began sniffing wildly and peeing at will. There was a bulge under the carpet in the storage area. I lifted it and found the dwarf's axe. "How did we end up with a fae axe?"

"No idea." Clive came around the back of the car to stand beside me. "It didn't disappear when the dwarf did. We didn't want a child to happen upon it in the morning, so we took it for safekeeping."

"Weird." I put the carpet back and looked up the hill. "Look, there are lights in the windows. This has to be the place." We were going to stay in a castle! Excitement didn't even begin to cover how I was feeling.

"Leave the bags for now," Clive said when Russell and Godfrey headed to the back of the SUV. "Let's meet our hosts first and make sure they are in fact willing to host us."

"Good point." We closed the car doors and I slapped my thigh, calling the dogs to me. The four of us, plus the hounds, walked the steep path to the main entrance. "They totally need a moat."

"You should suggest that," Godfrey said.

As we got closer, much of it looked like a ruin, but a good portion seemed to still be in working order. The stone walls on either side of us were crumbling, but the gatehouse we walked through was in pristine condition. It was perhaps ten feet long and when I looked up into the recesses, I saw spikes. The old iron gate was up there, ready to drop. Grinning ear to ear, I stepped out the other side into a mossy courtyard, dotted with snow.

"Clive," I whispered quietly. "Later, could you get a horse and a suit of armor and we'll do a little goodbye scene before you head out to battle?"

Clive shook his head, smiling, while Russell and Godfrey quickly turned their heads away. I didn't miss how Godfrey's shoulders were bobbing, though. Stupid vamps messing up my historical romance fantasies.

When we approached the main entrance, the rounded wooden doors opened to reveal a candlelit entry. Silhouetted in the doorway were two people who did not appear happy to see us. They looked like older versions of George and Coco, the same dark, warm skin and bright green dragon eyes. Neither said a word, but the glares of anger said it all.

"Hello. I'm Clive. This is my wife Sam, my second Russell, and my third Godfrey. May we come in…or should we look for another place to stay?"

I was with Clive. If looks could kill, we'd all be dead on the spot.

Smoke billowed from the dragon couple, fiery lights flickering in their gazes.

Well, shit.

TWENTY-FIVE

Wow. They Really Hate Us

"Please, come in," George said, pushing between his parents. "We have rooms for you downstairs." He waved us in, but we didn't move.

"Thank you, George," Clive began, "but I don't believe your parents would like us under their roof." He stepped back, pulling me with him, as Russell and Godfrey headed back to the car. "We need to locate alternate accommodations. We'll call tomorrow to plan the attack." Clive nodded to them all and then we turned to leave. We didn't have much time to find a safe place for them before the sun rose.

"Stop." Benvair's voice cut through the awkwardness. "This is my roof, not theirs." She pushed her son out of the doorway and waved us in. Russell and Godfrey were back, a step behind us.

George's parents stalked out of the entry as we moved in.

"Sorry about that," George said.

"No need. One of my kind has kept their son a prisoner for twenty years. Of course they despise us," Clive said.

Russell turned to Benvair and then I saw the pattern. Clive was having Russell deal with her, as he was still too pissed to do it himself. "While we're grateful for your hospitality, we don't want to cause a rift in the family. We can find somewhere else to sleep—"

"Sleep," George's father sneered from the other room.

"—but we'd need to leave now to find it."

"Nonsense," she said, leading the way across a huge open entry with stone floors and walls, into an adjacent castle-style living room. "We have safe, lightless rooms for you. The boys just added a bed to make it more comfortable."

This time it was George's mom who scoffed.

"You've met my son Griffin and his wife Smoke." The steel in Benvair's voice made me take an involuntary step back and she wasn't even ticked off at me.

"You invited filthy bloodsuckers into our home!" Griffin roared, sparks shooting from his mouth.

Clive shoved me behind him, while Russell and Godfrey stepped in front of him.

Benvair stood in the middle of a huge room, her back to us. I had three men standing in front of me, so I couldn't see what was happening, but the floor began to rumble. My guys moved as one, backing us out.

"You forget yourself, son, because I know you did *not* just raise your voice to me." Benvair's words were low, deep, measured, and could drop a man to his knees at fifty paces.

George ushered us out and into the great hall. Part of me was trying to memorize every detail of the castle, while the other part just wanted to jump back in the car and take off. No one in their right mind would step between dragons battling.

The great hall was amazing. A huge fireplace, perhaps ten feet high and fifteen feet wide, blazed, heating the hall. I wandered away from the men to explore. Long trestle tables that looked to hold twenty or more each took up the center of the hall, with benches and chairs around the periphery. Instead of the rushes I'd expected covering the floors, they had thick rugs. Ancient light pendants hung from the rafters on heavy chains.

"Sam?"

Hmm? Oh. I walked back, gesturing to the tables. "How many Drake dragons are there?"

George looked over my shoulder and shook his head. "Back in the day? Well over a hundred. Now? We'd be lucky to fill one table. We're dying off and hardly any children are being born." He shrugged. "Grandmother's right to be concerned about our future."

Clive ran a hand down my arm. "George is taking us down to our rooms. I want you to come with us."

George led us across the great hall and down a dark, narrow passage with an open arch, stone steps leading down. An icy draft rushed through the passages. Away from the fire in the great hall, I hugged myself and shivered horribly.

"This place must have been the *most* fun growing up." Who was I kidding? I wanted to run around the castle now.

At the bottom of the stairs, he flicked on an overhead light that did little to banish the dark. "This way." He pointed to the right. "And, yes, it was a blast until we lost Alec." He glanced over his shoulder at me. "Just being here…" He paused, looking sadder than I've ever seen him. "I see him everywhere I look. It hits so much harder here than back home."

He looked so lost, it broke my heart.

"I keep waiting for him to run around the corner and nail me with a snowball."

"Even inside the castle?" I squeezed Clive's hand and let go, moving forward to loop my arm though George's.

"Of course. People expect to get hit in the back of the head outside in the snow. No one expects it when they're just walking down the hall on the way to the kitchen for breakfast." He smiled, his expression softening. "Alec would sneak out early in the morning to fill an old messenger bag with snowballs and then hide them on the ledge outside a second-floor guest room."

He stopped at two doors, one on either side of the passage. "Here you go." As Clive, Russell, and Godfrey went to check out the rooms, I stayed in the hall with George.

"How did you know where he hid his stash?"

He stared at nothing, remembering. "I was in the woods, running with the dogs, when I saw a glint off the window as he opened it. I watched him grab a snowball and then duck back in. I was so excited. I'd finally caught him. I tore back to the house and ran upstairs. I had to check a few window ledges before I found the bag, but once I did, I loaded up on the snowballs and went in search of my brother."

Lost in the memory, George leaned against a wall. "I found him in the great hall, eating breakfast with some cousins. I was up above, on the gallery walk. They didn't see me. I leaned over and started unleashing frozen hell on them. The cousins squealed and slid under the table. Not Alec, though. He'd seen me and ran for the stairs. By the time he'd made it to the gallery, I was out of snowballs. I'd expected him to try to beat me up, so I ran, but he wasn't mad. The game had just changed. That was all. Now, it was the two of us against everyone else."

Going up on tiptoe, I kissed his cheek. "We'll get him back."

"You heard that fae bastard. Alec's been imprisoned, starved, and tortured, for twenty years. I went on with my life, moved in with Grandmother. Went to all the best schools, got a great job, fell in love, bought a house. I have everything and my brother has been locked away and suffering."

"Alec loves you," Clive said from the doorway. "He threw himself between you and Aldith to protect you. Chances are, he'd choose no differently now than he did two decades ago. When we find him, you can thank him for his bravery and lead him out of his nightmare and into the light."

George wiped a tear from his lashes and nodded. "I'll let you guys rest. I need to go help Grandmother deal with my parents."

A moment later, Russell and Godfrey came down the stairs with two bags.

"Wait. Where did you two come from?" I tried to take my bag from Russell, but he slipped past me to deposit it in my room.

Godfrey smirked. "Originally?"

"I didn't see you leave." How did I not notice that?

Russell patted me on the shoulder. "Loud, bumbling vampires don't live long."

Godfrey kicked their door closed with more noise than necessary, leaving me standing like an idiot alone in the hall.

I went through the opposite doorway and found Clive standing in a very small, very cold storage closet that smelled as though it had just been emptied of rotting linens. Sneezing, I wished we'd tried to find somewhere else to stay. An air mattress had been wedged into the room and left on the freshly swept stone floor. Sheets and blankets were folded on top. Clive leaned against the wall, arms crossed, watching me.

"Wow. Okay. They really hate us."

"Yes," Clive said. "They really do."

"I'd say let's just go sleep in the car, but that only works for me." Sneezing again, I checked every corner. The scent of rotting fabrics and vermin was thick in the air. There was no way I was lying down on the floor so I could make myself more easily accessible to the castle rats. "Hey, where's Fergus?" At least he'd bark if rats crawled under the door.

"George Fyr is keeping the dogs with him."

"Oh." Well, that sucked.

Relax, darling. Russell and Godfrey are searching the castle for a better daytime resting place. Not having the puppy with us will make that easier.

They're doing that right now?

As Russell said, noisy vampires don't live long. As none of us would like to be gnawed upon by rats or staked by angry dragons, an alternate, secure location is needed.

Oh, okay. Honestly, though, why not just call us on the way and tell us to find somewhere else to stay? Why make the big deal about taking us in just to give us this?

A delicate negotiation is being played out right now. Benvair and George want our assistance and so feel the need to provide for us, not to mention she's trying to make up for her callousness at your near death during our engagement party. Griffin and Smoke want us dead, given how their son has been treated at the hands of a vampire. One group would like to be respectful, the other would like to turn us to ash with their dragon fire. George Fyr is somewhere in the middle. He distrusts and fears us, but we have already proven ourselves helpful to him.

So, they landed on we'll give you a lightless place but it's going to suck and you'll need to contend with rats?

Exactly.

Why not just leave?

Then we would be breaching etiquette. We'll find somewhere safe for all of us and then tomorrow when they realize we didn't stay in the rooms offered, we'll come up with an excus—

Blame me. Sam has a very sensitive nose and couldn't breathe in this room.

He nodded. *Sneeze again.*

I took a deep sniff and sneezed twice.

Good. I'm not sure how sensitive their hearing is, but I'd guess at least some of them heard that.

Just to be safe, I sniffed the corners and sneezed a few more times.

You can stop now.

I'm trying. Those last two were involuntary. I went back out to the hall and forced gusts of air out of my nose, sneezing once more.

My phone buzzed in my pocket.

George: There's a folly in the woods, a ¼ mile northwest of the castle. I checked it out earlier. I think it should work for tonight. Sorry!

Me: Not your fault and thank you.

I showed Clive the text. He didn't say anything, but I assumed he was giving Russell and Godfrey directions.

"I thought—"

He held up a finger, reminding me. *Follies are elaborate or whimsical buildings where the design is far more important than the function. Most are purely garden decorations, but some are constructed more like an actual house for children to play in. Russell and Godfrey just found it. They're going in to see if it works for us.*

I've read about follies, but I thought they were better suited to lovers meeting at a weekend party than vampires hiding from the sun. How do we make a whimsical, hollow house lightless? Listening intently, I tried to track the movements of the dragons above. My hearing was excellent but not as good as vampires. I couldn't hear anything. When I looked back in the storage closet, Clive was still leaning against the wall, but he was nodding. Hopefully, that meant the folly would work for us.

Sorry. You're right. We don't have time to make an open-air building safe for us. Russell and Godfrey say it won't be a problem. They'll be back in a moment and then we'll grab our bags and move there. Take the bedding, though. They believe it'll be quite cold.

TWENTY-SIX

Ah, To Be a Wee Dragon...

A wesome. I grabbed the bedding from both rooms. Clive took the inflatable mattress. When Russell and Godfrey returned, they took our bags, leading us down the passage into a musty room filled with old, random stuff. They zigzagged past piles and pulled at a secret door I hadn't even seen, showing us earthen stairs leading up and out.

Once we were out in the open air, we followed them on a circuitous route, avoiding leaving tracks in the snow. I'd been expecting Greek revival ruins or a gingerbread house, something fabulously whimsical. Instead, the guys stopped in front of a cave opening.

"This?" I whispered. "The folly is a cave?"

Godfrey shrugged. "They're dragons."

"It's perfect for us," Russell added. "I was concerned about sunlight through wooden slats and then saw this and relaxed." He waved us on. "Come see."

The cave entrance was relatively low, given how it opened up into a huge cavern inside. It went deep underground, with lots of offshoot passages. In the center of the cavern floor, though, was a towering pile of treasure that almost seemed to glow from within.

My eyes were still adjusting to the dark when the cavern came to life. Water gushed over a rock terrace high above, creating an almost perfect sheet of blue water before it crashed over black boulders, filling the moat surrounding treasure mountain. Colorful gems in the cavern walls began to glow, as though this was the Seven Dwarfs' mine. Vines, bursting with colorful flowers—like the glass ones hanging from Benvair's ceiling in San Francisco—crawled down the rock walls.

I crossed the cavern in wonder. Once close enough to mount treasure, I could see that it was fake. They'd done an amazingly realistic job, though. It was a heap of huge crystals, golden shields, silver swords—the edges blunted so the children couldn't actually cut each other—gold coins, partially opened chests with more treasure spilling out.

"Did we trip something?" Did the dragons know we were down here?

"It didn't do this when we were in here earlier," Russell said.

My phone buzzed in my pocket. I pulled it out, marveling that I had service down here and then checking the new text.

George: That was me. Sorry about the storage closet. Hopefully, this makes up for it.

Me: Hells yeah it does!! This place is amazing. On a scale of 1-10, how much fun was playing down here as a kid?

George: 100

Me: I bet! Your folks don't know we're here, right?

George: No. Our little secret. Sleep well.

Me: Thank you. We will

"Mystery solved. George wanted us to have the full experience. No one at the castle knows we're here. They think we're in the storage closets." The guys were still looking around. I think they were as blown away as I was.

"This is extraordinary," Clive said.

"How much do you want to bet there's a grotto behind that waterfall?" I was definitely going to explore while these guys slept.

"How much do you want to bet there are a few?" Russell countered. "Look how high up the waterfall starts. If there's only one, they fight for who gets it. A few of them means multiple games can be played at once."

"Oh! Look in the upper corner behind us. The vines and flowers get thick in that corner. I bet there's something hidden behind that too." I hated heights but my desire to visit the flower room might have been stronger.

"Can you imagine a bunch of wee dragons racing around this place, fighting to see who gets to sit on the treasure?" Godfrey shook his head, grinning.

"Do you think there's more down here than this?" We all turned to Russell. "I mean," he explained, "do one or more of these cave entrances lead to other caverns?"

"Now that you say it, I do," Godfrey said. "I want to check every single one because I bet you're right. Maybe one of the high caves. Like those amusement park ride signs. You have to be this tall to ride. Here, you have to be this old and fly this well in order to access the next play place."

"I have a newfound respect for the dragon clan. They're willing to part with a huge chunk of that wealth in order to create unforgettable experiences for their children." Clive leaned over the moat. "Look. Even the moat has subtle lighting. The little ones can find treasure in the water as well."

Godfrey and Russell joined him at the edge of the moat. "I wouldn't mind stripping down and going for a swim and a treasure hunt myself," Godfrey said, to which Clive and Russell nodded.

Aww. My big, scary vampires wanted to play. "How is it so clean down here? George had said they weren't having babies these days, or at least not many."

"You take care of what you value." Clive took my hand, overwhelmed. "At a guess, they have a groundskeeper who maintains the cave as part of his duties."

"The dawn is approaching," Russell said.

"Yes, of course." Clive, though, seemed reluctant to leave the magic behind.

"Sire, we thought that one would be good for you." He pointed to a dark hollowed out den on the second level. "Godfrey and I will take the ones closer to the entrance."

"No. You can't protect us during the day. Choose spots that are safer and more remote."

Russell and Godfrey inclined their heads before taking our bags and leaping to the narrow cave Clive and I would be sharing. I probably could have made the jump, but it would have been super awkward with the sheets and blankets. Clive wrapped me in his free arm and leapt to the ledge just as the guys were leaving.

"Wait, grab your sheets and blanket." I held out my arms to them.

"We don't feel the cold, my lady," Russell said.

"And we'll be dead to the world," Godfrey added.

I stared down at the pile, wanting them to take something. "How about a sheet so your clothes don't get dirty?"

"It's pretty clean—" Godfrey flinched. "Yes, thank you. That's a great idea."

Each of them took a sheet, while I gave Clive my best squinty-eyed look. "I know what you did."

"He did nothing, my lady. Godfrey just thought better of his response. Good night," Russell called as they disappeared into the dark.

"Sure, he did," I muttered, moving into the cave.

Clive had placed the air mattress close to the edge of the small chamber so we could look out into the large, open cavern. Bent over, he snapped on the fitted sheet. My head barely cleared the ceiling, which meant Clive pretty much had to hunch over. When he was done, he dropped onto the bed, avoiding a bashed head.

"Sorry, darling. There's no washroom in here. I believe the little dragons just go outside to relieve themselves."

Shaking out the blankets—rough, thin ones because they really hated us—I laid down and covered us both up. Adjusting, Clive wrapped an arm around me.

"I'll just pretend we're camping."

"These threadbare pieces of fabric shouldn't be termed blankets," Clive said. "You'll freeze."

"I'll be okay. It's not as cold underground as it is outside in the snow." He was right, though. It was damn cold down here. I was just trying to decide if I needed to shift so I had a fur coat to keep me warm when Godfrey appeared at the chamber entrance.

"Here you are, Missus. A much nicer blanket than the ones we were given," he said, handing me a thick, soft one.

"Where did you get this?" I tossed off the gross ones and rubbed the new one against my cheek before throwing it over Clive and myself.

"I have my ways. Good night." And he was gone again.

"Thank you," Clive said, knowing Godfrey would hear him.

Is the chess set with us or in the car?

It's in the second suitcase.

I want time to study the pieces.

What do we do about the rings?

Yeah, that's the question, isn't it? Mine has helped me out many times. It even gave me a heads-up tonight that enemies were on the way. I worry, though, that it's acting like some kind of beacon to the fae, making us easy to find.

The dawn broke a moment later and my guys were out. I was so tired, I just wanted to sleep, but the cavern called, enticing me to come out and play. Deciding I was probably going to lie here wondering anyway, I pushed off the blanket, stepped to the edge, and dropped to the cavern floor.

I considered trying to climb treasure mountain but decided to go for the possible grotto behind the water. If there was one there, then there were probably lots of hidden surprises in here. If there wasn't, there probably weren't.

Jogging around the moat, I approached the waterfall from the side, hoping there was a way in without walking directly through the water. It was *way* too cold down here to be wet. There were no gaps in the water on the left side, so I jogged around the moat to the right.

When I still couldn't tell, I climbed the slippery rocks to get a closer look. There appeared to be a narrow break in the water. I was probably about to get soaked, but I had to check. Sliding through, getting damp from the mist and spray, I slipped onto what looked like half a pirate ship. It was as though the ship was sheared off lengthways. Half was embedded in the cave, while wooden planks and busted storage boxes floated in the water behind the waterfall.

This was better than I could have imagined. A skeleton with an eye patch and a wooden leg sat in the corner, a golden goblet falling from his bone fingers while his other arm was wrapped around a treasure chest overflowing with gold and jewels. A dim, flickering lantern hung from the ceiling.

Some freight boxes were stacked by the back wall of the ship. I tested the box, unsure if it was décor or if the dragons could play with it. That was a stupid question, given this place. The box was heavy but could be lifted. I moved it to the floor so I could look inside. Prying it open, I saw the nails were blunted, really just serving the purpose of aligning the top and keeping it from sliding off. Inside was a stack of ornately framed paintings.

Checking the other boxes, I found gold bars and dusty bottles of grog, rum, whatever it was pirates drank. The bottles were clean, but fashioned to look like they were dusty, and were filled with colorful liquids that sloshed around.

The attention to detail was ridiculous. I was standing on rotting wooden planks, but when I tested the floor, it didn't give an inch. I peered through one of the two portholes and saw a tropical island in the distance. When I looked through the second, I saw another pirate ship heading toward me. Thick ropes and nets hung from the ceiling. I could imagine wee dragons playing in this one cave all day long.

Too distracted, it took me a minute to realize I was hearing something besides the rush of water. What was that? Slipping back out from behind the fall, I crouched in the dark and listened. Footsteps and then two dark figures moved into the glow from the treasure. An elf and a dwarf.

"Kill the bloodsuckers," the elf hissed.

"All of them? I thought we were supposed to take the wolf's mate." The dwarf pulled a heavy axe from the sheath on his back. His voice was so quiet, I could barely make out the words.

"You heard me. I'll deal with the wolf." He pointed unerringly to the cave Clive and I were sharing.

Shiiiiiiit.

TWENTY-SEVEN

I'm Really Starting to Hate the Fae

S crambling down the rocks, I screamed, "Clive!" They were fae. How much did they actually know about vampires? I could have backup. Besides, the main objective was accomplished. They'd been about to leap to our cave and decapitate Clive. Now, they were turning to attack me. Win-win?

The elf's eyes turned swirly, and I quickly looked away, watching the dwarf. I was not getting mesmerized and waiting for the axe to take my head. Springing over the moat, I scaled the treasure mountain with no plan other than to make it weird and to give myself time to come up with something that kept my guys and me alive.

The dwarf circled to the right, the elf left, their focus still on me, so good, I guess. Gems and coins gave way beneath my feet, sliding down the side and dropping into the moat. I grabbed a sword—metal but blunted—from the heap and swung it around like I had no idea how to use one, like I hadn't been trained in swordplay by a master vampire. Unsteady, I stood on top of the treasure, my feet sinking up to the ankles in faceted crystals.

The elf smirked as he hopped easily over the water. "Thank you for making this interesting. I'd thought this such a dull assignment."

Although I'd turned to the elf, focusing on his chin to avoid his eyes, I saw the dwarf move out of the corner of my eye. Tricksy fae. Letting my foot slip, I pretended to lose my balance. The dwarf drew back, hurling his axe end over end at my head.

The pile wasn't all lose treasure, though. There was a solid base of fabricated treasure that I'd already steadied myself on. Dropping the ruse, I shot my hand up, snatched the axe from the air and spun, sending it back at its owner and cleaving the dwarf's head in two.

The elf raced up the pile and I backflipped off the mountain, right through the waterfall and into the pirate ship. Pulling the slipknot on the nets, I let them fall, covering the entrance. When the elf broke through the water a moment later, he was caught in the unexpected ropes. Taking advantage of his split-second of confusion, I slammed my fist straight into his face, breaking his nose and sending him tumbling back into the moat.

Skirting the edge of the net, I sprinted around the falls to retrieve the axe. I needed a weapon that could kill, not bruise.

The dead dwarf had returned to Faerie, but his axe was still here. Weird. I'd just grabbed it when the elf shot out of the water, sword arcing down to split me in two. Rolling to the side, I hopped up. He missed the kill strike but sliced my hip. It stung like hell, but I had more pressing concerns. If Galadriel's skill with a sword was any indication of this elf's abilities, I'd be dying soon.

As his sword was twice as long as my axe, there was no way for me to win this match close up. I was going to have to throw my weapon, and there was no way an elf was slower than a flying axe. Wait. Where'd he go?

And then his sword was at my neck, his body pressed against my back. "That was fun, but it's time to go. I'll come back for your bloodsuckers later."

A dark shape dropped to the cavern floor. Russell. How the hell was he up during the day?

"I'm sorry." His deep voice echoed in the cavern. "I can't allow my lady to be taken by the fae again. She's under our protection."

The elf had flinched when Russell appeared. I'd felt it. Were the fae disgusted by vampires or did they fear them?

Keeping an arm around me, he pointed his sword at Russell. "I guess I'll take care of the bloodsuckers now."

As the elf was distracted, I twisted my wrist, swinging the axe hanging limply by my side. With any luck, I could chop this a-hole's leg off without severing my own. Elated, I felt him crumple to the ground and then watched his head roll toward the center of the cavern. Wait.

I spun and found Clive, eyes vamp black, hands covered in fae blood. Someone was back to his old ripping-off-heads tricks.

"You're bleeding." Crouching, he ripped my sliced jeans open to check my hip.

"Dude, too much." Turning to Russell, I waved. "Hey, thanks for helping. So, uh, is this new or have you always been able to wake during the day?"

Russell didn't move or speak. A moment later, he toppled backward and lay unmoving on the ground.

I tried to go to him, but Clive kept me in place, licking the wound and sealing it. "I was an idiot not to bring a healer with us on this trip."

"But Russ—"

"He's fine. I needed the elf focused elsewhere so I could rip his head off before he hurt you. More than he already had, that is."

I stared down into Clive's eyes, the black fading to stormy gray. "You did that? You can control Russell?" I was happy for the assist, but the how made me *super* uncomfortable.

He stood. "Yes and no. We both woke when you screamed. He'd never done that before. We planned exactly what happened, but when he tried to stand, he couldn't. I helped him stand. He spoke on his own. Once I'd beheaded the fae, though, Russell was out. I'm not sure how he stayed upright as long as he did."

When I took a step toward Russell, Clive tried to stop me. "I can't just leave him on the floor in the middle of the room," I said.

"Why not? A cave is a cave." Clive was still fussing with my wound.

"It's rude. He roused himself to help me. I'm not going to leave him out in the open, where anyone could attack him."

Clive stared at his friend across the dark cavern. "Yes, of course. My brain is quite sluggish, I'm afraid." Shaking his head, he swayed.

"Are *you* okay?"

Pausing a moment, he finally said, "Perfectly well."

I looped my arm around his waist. "Change of plans. How about if I help you first and then move Russell?"

"Darling," he said before kissing me. "Unnecessary." He leapt, taking me with him.

"Show-off," I grumbled.

When we landed, though, I felt his knees buckle before he caught himself. I led him to the mattress and watched him lie down and drop out. Good enough.

Dropping back to the cavern floor, I looked for elf parts and found none. Good. The only helpful thing the fae did was clean up after themselves when they died. I grabbed the axe sheath and wondered why the dwarf's weapon had remained while the elf's hadn't. Odd, that. I went to the moat and washed the blood from my new weapon before strapping it to my back. If more were coming, I wanted to be ready.

Leaning over, I picked up Russell and then squinted, trying to remember which cave he'd called home. I sought out the green vamp blips in my head, finding my guys immediately. Godfrey was in a cave near the top of the cavern. There was no way I could jump that high, carrying a grown man.

"Sorry. You're going to be waking up someplace else." Scanning the second-floor accommodations, I chose a narrow chamber near the waterfall. A smaller cave seemed safer, and I was hoping he'd enjoy the view when the sun went down. I felt like a jerk just laying him down on the rough stone floor, but as Godfrey had said, they were dead to the world during the day.

I kissed him on the cheek. "Thank you."

As I dropped to the cavern floor, I thought for sure I'd heard, "Welcome." Maybe Russell was getting stronger. Maybe prolonged proximity to a necromancer was altering my guys' abilities. Questions for another day.

I was wired, worrying about the next attack while being simultaneously dead on my feet. I couldn't remember the last time I'd had a good night's sleep. Leaping back into our bedcave, I shivered, feeling gross in the cold. Screw it. I set the axe and its sheath aside and then stripped out of my wet, bloody, ripped clothes and shifted to my wolf. Already feeling warmer, I nosed the blanket aside and then used my teeth to pull it back over me. Releasing a huge sigh, I dropped my head to my paws, faced the cave entrance, and closed my eyes, drifting off almost immediately.

In what felt like only moments later, I heard a whisper and was instantly awake and alert. What now? Slinking to the edge of the cave, I scanned the cavern and saw a figure crouched where the dwarf had been killed. Not again.

Leaping soundlessly to the cavern floor, I stalked toward my prey.

"Don't attack, Sam. It's just me." George stood and pointed to the two patches of dried blood. "More fae attacked?"

Nodding, I chuffed and then turned, ran back, and jumped up to my bedcave. Once out of sight, I shifted. "Yeah, as soon as the sun rose and the guys were out, an elf and a dwarf showed up. Give me a sec to get dressed."

"Take your time," he called up.

I opened the suitcase with clothes and quickly dressed, strapping on the axe. Spotting my phone on the floor by the mattress, I snatched it up and then unzipped the other bag, grabbing the box with the chess set. I wanted to study the chess pieces, but doing it with George might be more helpful. He knew a lot of people and might recognize faces.

When I hopped down, he was standing by the cavern entrance. "I should have told you about this." He shook his head, face lined with anger. "I told you to come here and then didn't tell you how to protect yourself."

Waving me forward, he pointed to a recessed section of the cave wall. When he pushed on it, a small, thin square of rock opened, revealing a keypad. "They wanted us to be protected down here if we were ever attacked. It's 999, like the American 911." He tapped in the numbers and a thick metal door slid down, sealing off the cavern from the outside world.

I let out a breath, finally able to relax. "And fae can't get through that?"

"I'm not positive. I never asked. Given how protective the elders are of the children, I'd guess nothing was getting through that thing."

I hadn't realized just how on edge I'd been until I was safe. I put down the box, wrapped my arms around George, burying my head in his chest, and wept. I'd been trying so hard but ever since Paris, when I knew I was being followed, I hadn't been able to relax. Finally, here, underground, behind a thick steel door, being hugged by a dragon, I was able to let my guard down.

Patient as always, George held me, letting me cry off the fear and frustration. "Is this the axe from Stow-in-the-Wold or a new one?"

"New. It was the dwarf's. I killed him with it."

"Ah." He paused. "Does he know?" George whispered. I knew he wasn't referring to the dwarf. He wanted to know if Clive knew how close I was to breaking.

I shook my head. "I said I'd be a partner. No matter what, I'd fight by his side. And I have. I will. It's just been a lot lately."

"It has been," he said, hugging me hard. "Now, what's in this box?"

"Oh." I stepped back, wiping my face dry. "I forgot." Picking up the box, I moved back into the cavern. "Having a decent amount of light would be good. I found the lantern in the pirate ship. Is there a better place with more light?"

George nodded slowly, his gaze moving up at the tangle of

vines, high above the cavern floor. "It'll be tricky. I've done it carrying stuff before, but not in a long, long time." He took the box from me, tucking it under an arm. "You're going to need to get on my back and hold tight."

George was a lot taller than me, so I hopped up on a nearby boulder. He turned his back and I climbed on, wrapping my legs around his waist, my arms around his neck.

"When Clive gives me piggyback rides, I don't have to worry about cutting off his breathing. If I choke you, let me know."

Grinning, he said, "You'll be the first."

He walked to the stone wall directly beneath the vines, putting a foot on a narrow ledge of stone, testing his weight. "I was a lot smaller the last time I did this." He put his fingertips on a high ledge and let his knees go, again checking rock strength. "Okay, let's do this."

Taking a deep breath and only using one hand and both feet, he scaled the high wall in no time, pushing through the vines at the top and depositing me and the box in an open-ended passage, light streaming through the curtain of vines on the opposite end.

"Take a look."

I stood, not needing to duck. At the end, I moved the screen of vines and looked out into a huge, sunlit valley with forests of trees surrounding a dark, imposing castle. Turrets and towers speared the air.

From up here, I could see a small village in the distance, a few groupings of simple cottages hidden in the forest, near a stream.

I turned to George, awed. "How?"

He grinned, his eyes alight with pleasure. "With endless time and bottomless coffers, all things can be accomplished."

TWENTY-EIGHT

Have Fun Storming the Castle!

W e were still underground. I knew we were, but the ceiling was fashioned to look like the sky. It was the most incredible thing I'd ever seen.

"It looks and feels like sunshine. Is it spelled to mimic the time of day outside?"

"Nah. Winter days are too short. It's always a late summer afternoon in this cavern. Although," he said, tapping the rock to his right, "we can change the time of day right here."

Another keypad emerged and he tapped a button. The light in the cavern didn't change, but I did hear a faint whining sound.

"We used to have the occasional night raid of the castle, but mostly we liked playing in the sunlight. No hiding what we were in here. No keeping to the shadows." The sound was coming closer.

"But, when we played in human form, we needed a quick way over to the castle. Otherwise, it's the age-old question of what to do with your clothes when you shift. None of us—well, Stephen was into it—none of the rest of us wanted to be naked while playing knights or guards or whatever the humans were at the castle.

"So," he continued, pointing to the cable that had appeared

over the mouth of the passage we were standing in, "we have a zipline to the castle."

My fear of heights warred with my desire to zipline across this huge cavern. Joy won out over fear. "Tell me what to do."

"Do you want the seat or just to hang?" He tapped a lower section of the wall and a door swung open, revealing ziplining equipment.

"Seat, please."

Crouching down, he grabbed a seat on a rope and attached it to a handlebar before taking the triangular contraption to the line, snapping the handle onto a carabiner welded to a trolley on the line.

"When you get to the end, just let go past the tower roof. It's like a six-foot drop. If you don't, you'll go through the door of the guard tower, which was how it was designed, but Dermot wanted all of us to drop, so he removed the padding attached to the wall. Now, if you wait until the end, you're crashing into a stone wall. I've done it. It hurts. Don't do that."

"I'm surprised the parents didn't put it back up."

George grinned, holding his hand out to me. "We never told them." He waved me forward. "Come on. You can do it. I'll carry the box."

Cautiously, I approached the edge and my stomach swooped out from under me. Almost tipping off, I grabbed George's arm.

"I'll hold it steady. Go ahead and sit down."

Trying my best to hide the fear, I wrapped my hands tightly around the handlebar and then lifted my body, swinging my legs through the triangle and sitting down.

"Perfect. Now tell me when you're ready and I'll let go."

I didn't know that I'd ever be fully ready for this, so I took a deep breath and said, "Go."

George gave me a good shove and I was flying over the countryside, over a forest and then a meadow, over thatch-roofed cottages—one of which had smoke puffing out of a chimney—past a stream feeding into a lake, a blacksmith, an armorer, and inn. As the castle raced closer, I stopped looking around, focusing instead on the huge stone structure I was about to flatten myself—Wile E. Coyote style—against.

Only six feet. Just a six-foot drop. Given the speed, I'd need to tuck and roll. Just let go. Now. Let go now. And now.

"Drop!"

I let go and dropped, the cavern still echoing George's shout. I tried to run with the momentum but ended up tumbling forward. When I stopped rolling, my elbow and knee were banged up. That was going to bruise. Stupid Dermot. I wanted to smack that kid for taking away the soft-landing option.

Brushing myself off, I looked over the edge of the wall. I had to be fifty feet up. This close, I could see a patch of land to the side, dark, rich earth in furrows, an old plow sitting on the ground. It was just like the one I'd seen Clive use in Leticia's thousand-year-old memory of him. Did little dragons pretend to be farmers? How adorable. Oh, or did they fly by and breathe fire on the farmers?

A couple of minutes later, I heard that same high whine. Looking up, I saw George hanging from the zipline one-handed. As soon as he cleared the outer wall of the castle, he dropped onto the far side of the walkway. He was able to stop the forward momentum within two steps and then he was just walking normally to me.

"Show off," I grumbled. "Damn! I should have filmed that for Owen. It was annoyingly hot."

"That's okay. He already thinks I'm annoyingly hot." He pointed to the doorway in the tower at the end of the path. "There are a table and chairs in the guards' room. We can look at your stuff there."

"Actually, do you mind if we just stay out here on the…" I pointed down. "Whatever this is called?"

"Officially, I think it's the *chemin de ronde*," he said. "We just called it the guards' walk. See? It connects the towers. This is the bigger tower, with the guard room. The other three towers are narrower. This one back here"—he gestured to the tower we had to clear before we could drop off the zipline—"it's just an empty, circular room with doorways on either side, so guards could walk the perimeter of the entire structure. It was a good place to dive for cover when the cousins started breathing fire, though."

"I love everything about this." I thought a moment. "That cottage we passed over with the smoke coming up from the chimney? That's always smoking, right? That doesn't mean there's someone in here, right?" It would be just my luck to lock out anyone hell bent on attacking us, only to discover we have fae living inside the folly.

George was staring out over the countryside. From what he'd said, I didn't believe he'd visited the keep or this cavern since he was a child, since his twin Alec was taken. Meaning he'd lost not only his brother but his parents too. Yes, there were phone calls, but they hadn't seen each other in person in twenty years. And then the first day back, they'd been at odds because of the vampires and me visiting.

"I'm sorry the guys and I wrecked your family reunion."

He turned to me then. "That's not on you. My parents are good people. They went a little crazy after Alec was taken, though. They were out of their minds with worry and terrified they'd come back for me, since I'd been the one first led away and given to the bloo —to the vampire."

He sat down on the stone walkway, his back against the outer wall. "Coco and I only got to help search for Alec for a few days and we were under constant guard. When we couldn't find Alec right away, Mom and Dad sent us away. They couldn't risk losing anyone else."

"I'm sorry."

He looked at me then. "Yeah, me too." Letting out a breath, he held out the box. "So, what have I been carrying?"

Sitting down next to him, I reached for the box and pulled open the flaps. "It's a fae chess set I found in an art gallery in Canterbury. It was made by a half-fae, half-wicche artist. The queen is definitely—" I started to say her name and then remembered myself. "The light queen and the dark king are dead ringers for the real ones. I recognized them. I also remember seeing those Glen and Win guys. I'm almost sure." I pulled the polished dark wood box from the packaging.

"The clerk at the gallery had been near a powerful magical object for too long. He was in its thrall and didn't want the set going anywhere. I didn't get a chance to study it in the gallery because he wanted me as far away from the set as possible. I wouldn't have it at all if the owner hadn't stepped in to make the ridiculously large sale."

Hello, darling.

I tapped George's arm. "It's Clive." *Hello, my sweet, pointy-toothed one. Did you sleep well?*

All except for the last part, when I woke and you weren't there. We seem to be locked in. Did you know about this?

Yup. George came and dropped the door so we could—I could—finally relax without worrying the fae were going to pop up behind me.

I followed your scent to the vine-covered cave, but we see what appears to be sunlight behind the wall of vines. We're perplexed. All our phones say the sun is down and it's evening. We're awake, which again says the sun is down. How is it daylight where you are?

"You swear this is magicked to look like sun but is really a rock ceiling, right?"

Nodding, George said, "I've bashed into it enough times to tell you it's rock up there."

I hopped up, wanting to see the reactions.

Come on in, the water's fine.

Are you hoping to be a widow sooner rather than later?

Does the light feel burny?

No, but none of us has moved the vines. Normally, though, even this close to the sun's light, I'd be in pain.

Push through the vines and find me.

Darling...

Okay, shove Godfrey through first to test it. I could feel him chuckle.

Here goes…

Wonder exploded in my mind. I clasped my hands to my chest, eyes on the tunnel opening. A moment later, Clive pushed aside the vines and stood at the edge, staring out over the countryside and then up at the sky. Russell and then Godfrey joined him, all three looking as if they had finally woken from a centuries-long nightmare.

Clive's gaze went unerringly to me. His smile took my breath away. He looked as he had in Leticia's memories, as he'd been when he was a young farmer. Leaping from the passage, he dropped, slower than gravity dictated. Russell and Godfrey looked dumbstruck, unable to move. Clive landed somewhere in the forest. I couldn't see him, but I heard his whoop of joy. The sound broke their trance and then Russell and Godfrey leapt as well. Soon, all three could be heard laughing and shouting.

Tears sprang to my eyes. Blinking rapidly, I tried to clear them, not wanting to miss a moment of this. George got up to stand next to me and watch as well. The men emerged from the forest and then raced over the meadow, past the cottages and the blacksmith, all the way to the castle. In no time, Clive was climbing up the castle wall, still grinning ear to ear. His men began scaling just as he flipped over the battlement, caught me in his arms, and swung me in a circle, kissing me. When he put me down, he leaned over my shoulder. "Nice axe."

"Isn't it? I won it fair and square."

Russell and Godfrey jumped over the wall, laughing.

"I hope your parents don't mind," Godfrey said, "but I'm moving in. After a long day of playing pirate out there, I'll cross the sunny meadow and come home to my thatched-roof cabin. Maybe stir up some local shit at the inn and occasionally storm the castle." Leaning against the outer wall, he surveyed all that lay before him and then snapped his head to George. "Tell me there are other play spaces down here."

All three vamps turned to George, excitement in their eyes.

TWENTY-NINE

The Light Before the Storm

"You guys go explore. I want to study the chess pieces." I sat cross legged on the guards' walk and pulled the wooden box onto my lap again. The men hesitated. "Go. I'm fine. This might be pointless, but I haven't been able to do this since I bought them."

Clive sat down beside me. When I glanced around, though, the other three were gone. "Just because we're married doesn't mean you don't get to go play with your friends."

"Thank you, darling, but we're here for a reason. I was momentarily distracted by the sunlight and the castle." He nodded to the box in my lap. "Let's see if we can figure out what it means."

Opening the intricately carved, wooden box, I was again struck by the beauty of the pieces. One set was a light blue gray chalcedony. The other side was onyx. Unfolding the jade checkerboard, I picked up the light queen, took a quick look, and handed her to Clive.

"This is the queen." Taking the sneaky-looking onyx Finvarra from the box, I gave it another cursory glance and passed him over. "And this is the king."

"The detail is extraordinary." Clive put the queen in her proper place on the board but held on to the king.

"Corey, the artist, had to have started the work on this set a while ago. How did she know who would eventually be sent to kill us?"

"Psychic." Clive seemed to be memorizing Finvarra's likeness.

I picked up two pawns from the onyx side. "These were the a-holes who snatched me from Canterbury and then tried to kill me in Faerie."

"Assholes," he said in solidarity.

I bumped his shoulder with my own, grinning.

Picking up the light knights, I said, "Look! Galadriel!" I handed him the first one. "And this is the warrior form the queen took when she arrested me in Faerie." I grabbed two more onyx pawns. "And this is Glen. This one is Win."

Clive pulled another of the onyx pawns. "This looks like the banshee who attacked us in The Hob & Hound."

"Yes." I grabbed another piece. "And this is that monster hound. I don't recognize the last two onyx pawns, though."

"Something to look forward to." Clive studied the monster. "What is this?" He pulled out his phone and snapped a picture. "I'm sending this to Dave. Perhaps it's a hellhound."

"That's a good idea. We should take pictures of all of them. Going through a fragile chess set every time we meet a new person isn't the most efficient way to identify the players."

Nodding, Clive started taking pics of the other pieces.

"I think it says something that we recognize a lot more of the onyx pieces than the chalcedony ones." I picked up a four-legged gray piece. "Wait. This is Alice." I turned to Clive. "Does that mean she's a fae hound or that Faerie was using a wolfhound to help me?"

"She appears to be the light counterpart to the onyx hellhound."

"Yeah, I get that, but is she herself fae? Fyr isn't going to be comfortable taking care of a fae creature. It's another way for Faerie to keep her eyes on him."

Nodding, Clive added, "On the bright side, I see neither Fergus nor ourselves on the board." He photographed the last few pieces, placing them on the board with the others.

"Wait," I said, grabbing one of the light pieces. "Look. He's missing part of his ear. This is the werewolf I bit."

Clive leaned in to get a better look.

"He works at the hostel above Bram's nocturne. He recognized me when I was taking Alice out for a walk. He chased us to the stream, caught up right before Alice dragged me through a slit in the realms. I shouted for him to tell Bram what happened. No idea if he heard me or did it, though."

"Interesting." Clive leaned back against the wall and crossed his legs at the ankles. "He was intended to be a helper, but he was made useless when you were transported across England. Perhaps the queen *has* been sending helpers, but their efforts have been derailed by the king."

Lifting my hand, I let the fake sunlight glint off Gloriana's pinky ring. "We still need to figure out if these fae rings are a help or a beacon."

Clive stared down at his wedding ring. "Perhaps both."

I picked up two dragons from the board, one light, one dark. "We'll need to ask George if he recognizes them." Studying the onyx one probably longer than necessary, I finally passed it to Clive. "I've only seen our George in his dragon form once, but doesn't that look exactly like him?"

"It does," he said on a sigh. "And you're wondering if his twin has been in captivity too long, if he's been changed irrevocably and is therefore on the king's side of the board."

"Something like that."

"George!" Benvair's voice rang out from a hidden speaker in the cavern. I almost dropped the chess piece I'd been scrutinizing. "Our guests are no longer in their rooms. No one has seen you in quite some time—you know how that unnerves us, especially here. And the security has been engaged on the folly door. Are you in there?"

"Sorry, Grandmother." George's voice was faint. I looked

around, but it was Clive who pointed me in the right direction. The passage to the next chamber was apparently on the far side of the cavern, behind a stand of trees. "We discussed this. The store-rooms were a rat-infested insult. Given Clive wasn't happy with us to begin with—"

"She was unconscious," Benvair broke in.

"His fiancé was dying and you made me leave her on hard, cold tile because it was easier to clean blood from the floor rather than a couch or bed. Clive doesn't take slights to his wife well. We should be doing everything we can to make sure they know we appreciate their help."

"They want Aldith too. They're not helping *us*."

"Grandmother, you sound like my parents right now. You aren't that short-sighted. Yes. Clive wants the vampire. They could easily do this without us, share no information, kill Aldith, and leave Alec trapped and starving in a dungeon. We'd be no closer to finding him."

"We have George. He'll lead us to Alec."

"We hope. His mind was clouded. Even he has no idea which memories are the real ones. Added to that, we'd never have found him, never have had this link, if it weren't for Sam. She's been attacked countless times and none of this has anything to do with her. In fact, two more fae were dispatched this morning. The vamps were dead, and Sam had to deal with them alone. She was afraid to sleep, waiting for more to arrive."

Clive took my hand, rubbing his thumb back and forth in comfort.

"The king sent his assassins to our keep, to our children's folly?" Given how cold and angry she sounded, I was pretty sure smoke was puffing from her nostrils right now.

"Yes. I smelled the fae blood as soon as I walked in. I—shit—"

"Language."

"Forgive me. I just remembered I brought food for Sam. She must be starving by now."

My stomach rumbled in agreement.

"I was so distracted by fae in the folly, I dropped the bag by the entrance."

"Aww," I whispered to Clive. "That was nice of him to bring me food."

Clive shook his head. "I have food for you too, food I forgot in the luggage. I was so worried when I smelled blood and couldn't find you, I forgot to unpack the food."

I bumped his shoulder again. "It's okay."

"It's really not." His voice was so quiet, I barely heard him.

"Collect our guests," Benvair said, "and bring them to the keep. Cook will have dinner ready shortly."

"Yes, Grandmother."

Clive and I quickly put the pieces and the board back into the box and the box back into the outer packaging. We were standing, taking one last look at the manufactured countryside, Clive soaking up every second of sunlight, when the guys arrived. Godfrey was decidedly wetter than the other two.

"Is it raining in the other cavern?" I didn't think I'd ever seen Russell or Godfrey look this happy before.

"It's a vast lake with an island in the middle. And under the surface? Atlantis. There are merpeople down there." Godfrey glanced at George. "I mean, not real ones, right?"

George shook his head. Some of the joy he'd been feeling himself had disappeared after talking with his grandmother. "No, the Kraken, merpeople, selkies, sea serpents, prehistoric sharks, all that was magicked. They aren't real."

"There are sharks and sea serpents? I didn't see those. Do we have time to…" At Clive's look, Godfrey trailed off. "Right. Now's not the time."

"Yes. They're waiting for us at the keep. Dinner will be served soon. Are you guys…" It was George's turn to trail off, clearly not comfortable with asking the vampires about their blood consumption.

"How do we get back to the passage? We had gravity working for us on the way in." The vamps, I'm sure, would have no trouble getting out. I was the only one who was going to need some kind of help.

"Same way we got in. It's motorized for the return trip," George said. "Do you want to go first?"

"Yep. Let's do this." I wasn't looking forward to dangling so high up in the air.

"Would you like my help?" Clive murmured beside me. He knew exactly how afraid of heights I was.

"Nope. I got it." I made it in. I could make it out.

"In that case, we'll race you to the tunnel," Godfrey said, hopping up on the outer wall of the guard's walk.

Russell and Clive leapt up beside him, watching George help me into my seat. Once the line started pulling me up, Clive handed George the chess set and then the vamps disappeared over the edge. Godfrey let out a whoop as they raced across the meadow toward the forest.

I cleared the tower and then was sailing above them. I saw Clive glance up to check my progress and then he overtook his men, laughing as he raced ahead. I knew they'd win. It was a given that vamps were stupid fast.

Gripping the rope tightly, I took mental pictures of the cottages dotting the countryside and considered the lake next door, the waterfall in the primary cave. Clive was looking at homes for us in Benvair's neighborhood. Maybe what we needed were the drag-ons' contractors to dig into the rock and renovate my apartment behind the bar. We could have a sunlit chamber in our home for the vamps to hang out in. Hmm…

Lost in the possibilities, it took me a moment to notice the three grinning vamps lounging around the passage entrance, acting bored, as though they'd been waiting forever.

"Yes, yes, fine," I said while Clive helped me out of the seat and sent the line back to George. "You're all very fast. Meanwhile, how amazing is this place?"

"Darling, I've been thinking."

I smacked his arm. "Me too! We need to hire these contractors. I already have lots of ideas."

He smacked my arm back. "Me too."

Godfrey and Russell laughed. It was wonderful to see them so light, so happy. We needed our own safe place for them to play. The day-to-day of being a vampire seemed pretty dark. They needed the light.

While we waited for George, who was standing on the seat, chess set under his arm, I leaned into Clive. "How about if our bedroom is under the bar? Same glass wall, but fully submerged so we sleep underwater?"

Slipping his arm around me, he said, "No concern about merpeople watching us?"

My face scrunched up. "Well, there is *now*."

"Maybe you can get one-way glass," Godfrey volunteered.

I shot a finger out at him. "Yes. Good one. What will the vamp playroom look like?"

All three men answered at the same time. "A tropical island." "I want Atlantis and sunken pirate ships." "My family's farm, just as I remember it."

"Perhaps we need all three. Russell and Godfrey's could work together. Russell can hang out on the beach, under a palm tree with an umbrella drink in his hand, while Godfrey is under water exploring. And you," I added, poking Clive in the ribs, "can plow a field. Shirtless."

Chuckling, he kissed my neck. "As you wish."

THIRTY

I Think the Lesson Here Is to Never Piss Off Clive

The guys swung by the SUV to get blood packs from the high-tech cooler they traveled with. I ate the sandwich George brought me. It was wrapped up, so a few hours on a cave floor was no biggie. Plus, I was starving. The sandwich helped take the edge off so I could behave properly at dinner.

"Darling, we should probably pack the axe as well. It might appear a tad hostile if you were to arrive at dinner heavily armed."

"Good point." I took it off and then handed it to him by the sheath's leather straps. The last time Clive had held fae metal, it'd burned his hand.

While the guys drank their blood, I took the chess set from George, securing it in an under-the-floor storage compartment. At least it was hidden from random thieves. I didn't want to show it to the dragons, considering how much they crave treasure and how much George's parents hated us. Yes, fae assassins could tear the car apart and find it, but they hadn't yet and Clive had been holding it for me for over a week. I'd hoped it stayed safe for a few more hours.

Looking down at myself, I cringed. I had to be a mess. I couldn't remember the last time I'd bathed. I was pretty sure falling in a moat didn't actually count as a bath. "I assume showering before dinner is out."

"Sorry, but yeah. If Grandmother says soon, she means get your butts in here now."

"We're ready," Clive said.

The SUV chirped when Russell hit the lock. Clive took my hand as George led the way into the keep. When we approached the heavy double doors, one was opened by a man in uniform. George nodded his thanks.

I squeezed Clive's hand and he squeezed back. Making sure, I closed my eyes and sought out the supernaturals, paying particular attention to the man at the door. *Fae.*

Clive was so fast, my eyes couldn't track him. One minute he was right beside me and the next he was down the steps in the courtyard, a headless butler lying at his feet.

"Check his pockets," Russell said.

Godfrey crouched, searching the man's clothing.

"How dare you! I told you, Mother." Tendrils of smoke curling from his nose, George's father Griffin spat, "This is what they are. Demons!"

Lifting my hand to him, I said, "A. Fuck you. Two. Shut up."

Clive turned to me, eyes twinkling. "Come here, darling. I'd rather my wife wasn't singed."

I jogged down the steps as five dragons looked on, expressions varying from concern to fury. The least concerned was our George, who followed me down the steps. "Who was he?"

"Not sure," I responded, knowing the dragons were more likely to listen to what I said, rather than my guys. "He was fae, though." I looked over George's shoulder to his parents. "Given your family's history, you really shouldn't employ the fae." Mostly, I just wanted to poke his parents, who were assholes—understandably, but still.

His mom sputtered, "He wasn—he's not—how would you even—" She grabbed her husband's arm. "Griffin?"

"How long has he been employed here?" Russell asked. Being a vampire, he was, of course, ignored.

"Griffin?" Benvair was not one to be ignored.

He and his wife shared an unspoken moment. Smoke put her hand over her mouth before Griffin finally responded, "Almost twenty years. Dafydd left after Alec was taken. He was the least of our concerns at the time." He shrugged, lost. "After you all moved to the States, Cai arrived, looking for work."

"They probably killed Dafydd to create the opening for one of their own," Godfrey said to Clive, who nodded his agreement. The vamps didn't enjoy talking to people who ignored them, so they talked amongst themselves.

Fyr nodded too. "I'd thought Glen was my friend. He'd been with me for almost that long, but I was just his assignment. He was keeping tabs on me."

I turned to Clive. "If that was how the fae who attacked us knew we were here, maybe we're not beacons."

He slid a hand down my back and then pulled me in close. "Perhaps," he murmured, lost in thought.

"What are you talking about?" Smoke demanded. "There was no fae attack here."

"Not here here," I said. "but over there here, there was."

Godfrey scoffed.

"What? When people are unreasonably pissed off, sometimes confusing them helps stop the rage."

He thought a moment and then nodded. "Fair point."

Griffin and Smoke stalked into the house. They weren't going to stand for vampires mocking them.

"It might be best," Clive broke in, "if we went inside to discuss this. Airing confidential matters out in the open encourages eavesdropping."

Are there any more fae nearby?

I closed my eyes and checked. *A pixie in a stand of trees beyond the outer wall.*

"Should we?" I pointed down to the dead fae. As we stared,

contemplating what was to be done with the body, it faded out of existence, no doubt returning to Faerie. "Well, that answers that question."

"Yes. Please, come in," Benvair said, waving us in the door.

Clive tilted his head, an unspoken request for his men to proceed. As we knew what was out here listening, we'd take up the rear.

We followed the group back into the large living room we'd been in the previous evening. This time, however, we were actually directed to a sofa and chairs. Last night we'd stood awkwardly at the door before being banished to rooms previously inhabited by vermin. So, a step up, I supposed.

Clive and I sat on a sofa, George taking the cushion beside me, Russell and Godfrey the chairs adjacent. Benvair and Fyr sat on the sofa across a coffee table from us, while Griffin and Smoke paced the room. A fire roared in a huge fireplace on the side wall. Shivering, I tried to shake off the cold I'd been feeling since last night. If it wouldn't have looked odd, I'd have sat on the hearth.

Go ahead. You need to warm up and it might help break the tension in here.

Pushing aside the embarrassment of thinking too loudly, I stood up and went to the fireplace, startling Griffin, who had just turned to pace back and almost ran into me. I smiled brightly, pretending to be unaware of his hatred, and then sat on the stone hearth, the fire at my back.

Alice and Fergus trotted in a moment later, the pup coming straight for me. When he reared up, his front paws on my legs, trying to crawl up into my lap, I picked him up and gave him a snuggle, kissing him between the eyes.

"It's a lovely castle you have here." I could feel rather than see Clive's grin.

"How do you even know Cai was fae? Why are we taking the word of a bloodsucker's whore?" Smoke glared, red lights flashing in her eyes.

Clive, Russell, and Godfrey stood in unison. Clive extended his hand to me and I took it. "We'll see ourselves out."

Benvair stood as well. "Please allow me to apologize for my daughter-in-law."

"No, I won't. You left Sam bleeding to death on the floor at our engagement party because her blood would be easier to hose off there. I was ready to cut you off then. Instead, I let Sam, George, and Coco sway me. That was my mistake. You'd already proven you don't consider us worthy of your consideration or respect. The fact that you gave us rat-infested closets to sleep in and have allowed your children to insult us—to call my wife a whore—has come as no surprise."

"Clive," George began.

"We hold no ill will toward you or your sister. The same goes for you, Mr. Fyr." He turned back to Benvair, eyes vamp black. "We'll deliver final death to Aldith. That's why we're here. If your grandson is still being held captive, we'll free him. This we'll do for George and Coco. And for Sam, who is far too tenderhearted to walk away from anyone in need. You, however, are done. Don't approach me for any reason. I will not hear your pleas."

"Good!" Smoke sneered.

"Shut up, you idiot," Benvair snapped out.

I put Fergus down on the floor. If he followed, he was mine. If he chose to stay with Fyr and Alice, then that was where he belonged. I felt him trot along for a few steps and then heard Fyr call his name. Damn. I really wanted that pup.

George followed us out the door and down to the car. I checked. The pixie was no longer in the tree. I didn't sense any fae at the moment.

Lowering my voice to a whisper, I said, "The fae have been watching this place for decades. There was a pixie in the woods earlier, listening. I don't sense him now, but you need to know that you're all being watched and listened to. Clive?"

He turned to me, jaw clenched, but the black was draining from his eyes. "Yes?"

I waved him over. "Show George the dragon pieces. See if he recognizes them."

"Pieces?" George looked between the two of us, confusion clear.

"That chess set I had you carry into the cavern. The light and dark sides are the queen's and king's. We recognized Cai, the butler, as one of the king's pawns. Quite a few of the fae bastards who have attacked in the last week are represented on the king's side of the board. Anyway, there are two dragons, one on each side. We can't identify dragons in their dragon form. We wanted to show your family the pieces to see if they knew who they were. Since that's not happening, can we show you the dragons?"

George already had his hand out for Clive's phone.

The first image was the chalcedony dragon. "That's George." He gestured vaguely toward the keep. When he scrolled to the next image, he flinched, silently staring.

"I know I've only ever seen you in your dragon form once, but…" As quietly and gently as possible, I asked, "Is this your twin?"

George nodded, shoving the phone away from him, back into Clive's hand.

"He may be on that side of the board because he's seen as an unwilling minion. It doesn't have to mean he's been turned against you."

George turned and ran up the path. "I'm coming with you," he shouted over his shoulder. "Let me grab my bag. I'll be right back." He stopped himself before racing through the guard's gate, turning back to Clive. "I can help. You need me. There are things I can do that you can't."

When Clive nodded, George let out a breath and raced back into the castle.

"Son—" Even from this far away, we could hear the emotion in Griffin's voice.

"Don't talk to me. I'm going to get Alec." Footsteps pounded up the stairs.

I ran my hand down Clive's arm. "Thank you."

He shrugged. "He's right. We could use his help." He pulled me into his arms and kissed my temple. "I'm sorry about what she said," he whispered. I nodded, leaning into him.

"Um, excuse me?" It was Fyr.

I turned to see him standing uncomfortably twenty feet away, his arms loaded with stuff.

"We are going to be wedged in tight for this ride," Godfrey groused.

"Oh, no. I don't want to go. I'm sorry. I just—"

"No explanation necessary. I told you at The Hob & Hound we didn't need you to come with us. Stay here. You've already done more than anyone can ever ask of you." The poor guy looked ashamed of his decision.

Letting out a breath, he nodded, not appearing convinced. "No. I came down here because you said you wanted Fergus. Do you still?"

Fergus popped out from behind Fyr's legs and bounded over to me.

"Fergus!" I scooped him up and spun around. "Can we be your forever family?"

He squirmed, trying to lick my face.

Godfrey grinned. "That looks like a yes."

"Good," Fyr said. "I have stuff for you. A dog bed and food and a leash, some toys, food and water bowls. He's had all his shots."

"Thank you so much. I love him already!"

Fyr smiled. "Good. Here, let me help you pack this stuff."

We opened the rear gate of the SUV and stared at suitcases and a blood cooler. How were we going to fit a dragon and a puppy in here?

My George showed up a moment later with his own bag and a handful of bungie cords. "We can strap the luggage to the roof rack so there's more room inside."

I took Fergus a little ways away, where the scrubby grass met snow. "While they repack, you go potty. Go ahead, dude. We have a long drive ahead of us."

Fergus paced back and forth, sniffing everything before he found his perfect pee spot. A few more turns around the patchy grass and he squatted as well.

"Such a good boy," I crooned as he kicked snow over his poop. Checking again, I found the pixie back in the tree. "Come on, guys. I'm ready to go home. This whole trip has been a bust."

"I had my plane routed to the Cardiff Airport. We'll be back home soon, darling. We're happy to give you a ride, George." Clive was always so fast. I never had to explain things to him.

George's gaze scanned the trees. "Thanks a lot. I really appreciate it. If I don't get back to work soon, they'll fire me."

"Wha—"

"George!" Benvair's shout cut off Fyr's question, proving she was keeping up as well. "Cook has dinner ready."

My George pushed Fyr toward the keep. "I'll text you once we're up in the air."

Fyr jogged up the path, confused but understanding he needed to leave now.

"Ready?" Clive asked me.

"You bet. Come on, buddy," I said, smacking my leg for Fergus. "We're outta here."

The Georges had repacked the SUV. All the luggage was on the roof. The third row of seats was put up, while the second row was dropped under the floor into the storage space. The dog bed was placed in the open space between the first row of seats and the third.

We all climbed in, Fergus hopping into his bed where toys awaited him. Clive, George, and I sat in the third row, our legs stretched out before us.

"Good call on the leg room," I said as Russell turned the SUV around and headed down the long driveway toward the road.

Once we'd been driving in silence for about ten minutes, Clive said, "Anything?"

I checked. No fae in the SUV and none that appeared to be following us. "I don't think so."

Tapping George's arm, I asked, "The box I had in the under-floor storage?"

"Box?" he echoed. When I grabbed his arm in a panic, he patted my hand. "Kidding. It's right behind us. There's a small storage area behind this row of seats. The box, the cooler, and the dog food are all in here with us."

Slumping with relief, I leaned into Clive, who wrapped his arm around me. "Everybody's a comedian."

"Sorry," he said, pulling out his phone. "I need to text George and explain what that was about."

"So," I said, "anyone know where we're going?"

THIRTY-ONE

In Which Sam Makes a Disturbing Discovery

"I'm heading toward Cardiff in case we're being followed," Russell said.

Huh. "I know my geography is a little shaky, but isn't that the opposite direction of where we need to go?" I was pretty sure Cardiff was in the south of Wales and the estate where Fyr was held was in the north.

"Yes," Clive said, "but we want our fae spies to stop following us. This will be difficult enough without the fae jumping in to bollocks it up."

"Also, Missus, Wales isn't that big," Godfrey put in. "Even if we drove all the way down to Cardiff before we turned around and drove up to Snowdonia, we're still only talking, what, five hours total. Maybe six with the way this one drives." He jabbed a thumb toward Russell.

"Oh. So, we're doing this tonight." I'd thought we'd have more time to surveil and plan.

"Yes." George stared out the window, a hand fisted on his thigh.

"We'll find him." We *had* to find him.

Nodding absently, he continued to stare into the dark.

"Should we actually go to the airport, pull into the private plane area, and then switch cars?" I had a whole heist movie running through my head.

Godfrey turned in his seat and grinned. "I saw that movie too."

"Ah, but did the fae see it? That's the question."

"She has a point, Sire. I doubt the fae are streaming robbery movies." Godfrey pulled out his phone. "I could order us a different sort of vehicle."

"Or two," I suggested.

"Two smaller vehicles, two different routes. I like it." Godfrey nodded, tapping his phone. "How are we splitting up?"

"George is with Clive and me." Toy clamped firmly in his teeth, Fergus hopped over the lip of the dog bed and scrambled up my legs, settling into my lap. "Make yourself at home, little man." Sighing, he leaned into me and closed his eyes.

George had turned from the window and was watching the pup. "I'm really sorry about what my mother said to you."

I grabbed his wrist and squeezed. "Not your fault. I can't even imagine what they've been going through, that constant struggle between hope and grief. Never knowing what happened. The guilt, wondering what you could have done differently. And the real soul crusher: desperately wanting him to be alive, even though you know he's probably suffering, or, God forbid, wishing him dead so his suffering is at an end. Every day. For twenty years."

"You imagine quite well," George murmured.

"And then," I continued, "three vampires and a vampire-lover arrive, and your parents are expected to be gracious? When it's a vampire who either killed their child or has kept him captive all this time?" I shrugged. "A little name calling and crappy accommodations seem like an understandable and fairly mild reaction."

"Yes," Russell rumbled from the driver's seat.

"Do you think I overreacted?" Clive asked his friend.

"In the moment, I thought you'd underreacted. I expected a head to fly and a war with the dragons." He found my eyes in the rearview mirror. "None of us deal well with insults to you, my lady. But *that* word, given... No, I don't think you overreacted."

Clive nodded and I felt him relax.

"Your wife, though, has the very great gift of seeing situations from another's perspective. I was willing to give them a pass on the open hostility. When they flat out refused to accept that their butler was fae when he disappeared right in front of us—"

"They didn't see that," I cut in. At Russell's furrowed brow, I explained. "They'd just turned from the body to storm into the castle when Cai melted away. If they believe us—the bad guys—then they've been sharing their lives with someone who not only knew where their son is but was actively keeping them from finding him and stopping the torture. How do you forgive yourself —no matter how unwittingly—for being complicit in your child's pain?" I shook my head. "You can't, so you lash out at the messenger."

"Thank you."

I turned to George. "For what?"

He thought for a moment. "For helping me to see my parents more clearly. I've been reeling since we arrived. Back here where I'd been led off into the woods, where Alec had been taken. Where parents I haven't seen in person in decades have been living so they could be close to their missing son, rather than with their present daughter and son. Struggling with all those things you listed before, the hope and grief and guilt." He knocked his fist against his knee. "I wanted them to understand that we finally had a real shot at getting Alec back if only they'd stop being so damned ignorant and short-sighted. You're right, though. I haven't been living what they have."

"You've been living enough."

Unfisting, he took my hand in his and nodded.

Fergus' little paws twitched in his sleep. I nudged Clive and pointed down. He smiled, though his eyes were sad. Talk of Alec being taken and hurt couldn't help but remind Clive of his own sister's abduction and murder. I tipped my head, resting it on his chest, trying to offer comfort to the men grieving on either side of me.

"So," Godfrey said, his phone back in his hand. "What type of car do you want? I already know what Russell wants."

Russell turned to him for a moment before returning his eyes to the road. "What do I want?"

"Some kind of pickup truck," Godfrey responded, scrolling through available vehicles.

Grinning, Russell nodded. "Yes, I do."

"Clive will want a sports car, but we need a sedan. So a roomy four-door—we need legroom and headroom for George—with a lot of power and speed."

"Yes, I do." Clive kissed the top of my head.

When Fergus started to slide off my lap, I had to take my hand back from George. "You should call Owen, when we get to the airport."

Nodding slowly, he said, "Yeah. I will."

"Vehicles are booked. They'll be waiting at the private hangar. I even ordered meals for these two."

"Oh!" I whisper-shouted, not wanting to wake Fergus. "I take back all the things I've said about you, Godfrey."

He gave me a dirty look over his shoulder, continuing to tap his phone. "Side salad it is. George, I got you two bacon double cheeseburgers."

"Thanks, mate."

Sooner than seemed logically possible, we were in southern Wales changing cars. While George spoke with Owen, I scarfed down my burger and fries—Godfrey came through for me—filled Fergus' water bowl and then took him for a pee walk.

Clive drove and George took the passenger seat as the front row had more leg room. Fergus and I took the back seat. While he snoozed, I unpacked the chess set. Taking the carved wooden box from the cardboard, I set it on my lap, opening it while reaching for the small interior light above my head.

Pausing, I stared at the pieces. Some of them seemed to emit a subtle glow from within. In the sunlit cavern, neither Clive nor I had noticed anything. On a dark, deserted highway, in the back seat, away from dashboard lights, I perceived a faint glow.

Flicking on the light, I studied the pieces that had been glowing in the dark. Now that I knew what I was looking for, I saw it. What I'd taken for color variation in the stone was actually the presence or absence of glow. I tapped the lights on and off until I was sure I had it.

"Problem?" Clive asked.

"Is this Aldith?" I tried to hand the onyx queen to Clive, but he shrugged me off, keeping his hands on the wheel.

"I have no idea. Chaucer said I'd met her hundreds of years ago in London, but I don't remember her. I remember an overly ruffled and cloying vampire, but not her face."

"Huh. I wonder if that was intentional. She may not have known if you'd ever seen Atwood's wife. She could have been messing with your head while trying to seduce you." Although, it was hilarious that he remembered ruffles but not her face. Apparently, her clothing deeply offended him.

"Possibly, but I'm not happy she so easily manipulated me." He merged onto another empty freeway and continued our journey north.

"Can I see it?" George reached for the piece.

"Oh! I forgot you saw her in the woods. Good. Is she the black queen?"

George ran his fingers over the piece and then closed his eyes. "Yes. That's her. She's softer in my memory, but that was probably to draw me in, make me feel comfortable walking through the woods with her."

Shoving it back over the seat, he said, "You should take that before I crush it."

Returning the queen to her spot, I studied in turn the other pieces we hadn't yet identified. Fergus whined in his sleep, so I rested my hand on his back. He settled almost immediately. Good boy.

I picked up the light dragon again and almost dropped it. Snatching up the dark dragon, I studied them side by side. *Shiiiiit.* "Uh, guys. We have a problem."

Clive glanced back in the rearview mirror and then pulled onto the shoulder of the road. Throwing the car into park, he turned in his seat to face me. "What have you discovered?"

I held up the two dragons. "The pieces change. This one," I said, holding up the chalcedony dragon, "was Fyr a couple of hours ago. Now it's a duplicate of the onyx dragon. At a guess, I'd say the piece changed because Fyr decided not to go back and fight with us. Instead, George arrived and is taking Fyr's place. Now the dragons on the board are twins."

"That's disturbing," Clive said. "Has anything else changed?"

I scanned the faces, ignoring the glow for a moment, and felt my stomach drop. "Well…on the plus side, we're knights."

Clive ground out a low oath, his fingers drumming on the steering wheel. He paused and then yanked his wedding ring off his finger, throwing it into a cup holder. "Is it still me?"

I watched as one of the knights almost imperceptibly changed from Clive to a faceless, genderless person. What had my heart racing was the way the light went out of my knight. It was still the same color of stone, but the inner glow was gone.

"Why is your heart racing?"

Glancing up into Clive's concerned gaze, I grabbed my water bottle and took a swig, letting my thoughts settle. "Okay, this could totally be wrong. This is just my gut—"

"Tell me!"

"Taking off the ring took you out of play. It hasn't reformed into another face because there's no one to take your place. When you left the board, though, my knight went dark."

"Dark? What are you talking about?"

"When I opened the box in the dark, I noticed an incredibly faint glow to some of the pieces. I was flicking the lights back here to check a theory. All the people still in play have a glow. The ones we've killed, no glow."

Clive snatched the ring out of the cup holder and slid it back on his finger. "If I don't play fae games, you die. Is that it?"

"I don't know." I watched the blank piece become Clive again, while my knight oh-so-subtly began to glow once more. "But I think yes."

THIRTY-TWO

Much Cursing Fills the Car

C live stared at his ring, anger pulsing. "She turned my most beloved possession into something I'd like to fling into a bottomless pit."

"Right. Totally get it. Understandable. *But*, what if she did this to help us?"

Clive stared at me like I was nuts. Given George's expression, he agreed with Clive.

"Seriously. I get the anger. I'm mostly feeling fear, but they come from the same place. Yes, it was a dick move to loop us into fae infighting, but I kind of already agreed to help. Remember, when the queen—names have power and we're trying to fly under the radar, so no names—when the queen healed the kelpie wounds, dragging me back from death, she told me I had to find out what was poisoning Faerie in payment."

"Yes," Clive drew out.

"This is it. The king has been making little tears between the realms, destabilizing Faerie and making it easier for his goons to jump back and forth. He's been helping a vampire abduct and imprison the fae, to feed on them until the vamp either loses control or gets bored and drains them dry.

"Fyr said there were others imprisoned with him. He could

hear and smell them. Who knows how long this has been going on? They could have struck their deal hundreds of years ago. He's been trying to hurt the queen by hurting her people."

"And I don't give a bloody damn what they do to one another!" Clive's eyes had gone vamp black. "You were safe and sound in Canterbury by my side. Since then, you've been ceaselessly set upon by fae assassins. She saved your life just so she can put it in perpetual jeopardy? No! I won't have it, Sam. Saving your life doesn't give her the right to treat you like a chess piece in this eternal match against her mate."

"Again, agreed." I placed a calming hand on Fergus. He was awake now and cowering away from Clive. "*But,* without this ring, I never would have escaped the spelled ropes. I'd have been dead a week ago in Faerie, with you none the wiser as to where I was."

"Don't remind me," he fumed. Noticing Fergus' reaction to him, he turned in his seat and stared out the windshield. After a moment, he pulled back out onto the road. "We have a mission to plan tonight. We'll deal with fae rings later."

"Yes," I said and watched George's shoulders relax. He needed to rescue his brother now. The mission being derailed by a chessboard and rings probably had him ready to explode. Fergus snuggled his warm body into my side and relaxed.

After almost an hour of Clive racing up the darkened highway, no one speaking, I finally boxed up the pieces, faces memorized, and pulled out my phone to dial Godfrey.

"Yes?" he answered.

"I thought we should form a plan," I said.

"Isn't the plan to run in and kill everyone except the prisoners?"

Normally, I enjoyed Godfrey's sarcasm. Tonight, the situation was far too tense to deal with. "Can you put Russell on?" Even if the plan was we'd have to figure it out when we got there, I'd feel more comfortable with something decided.

"I'm here, my lady." Russell's deep rumble helped my stomach relax.

"So, the property has to be spelled, right? George's parents have been all over Wales in the last twenty years, trying to find it, and nothing." Staring out the window at the fog blanketing passing hills, a smattering of houses, I continued. "If it's spelled, we could be sitting in the driveway and not see it. How do we find a hidden house?"

There was a charged silence and then Russell said, "I believe we all thought you could find her. She is a vampire, after all."

"Me? But she's like Leticia, only more so. She's been feeding exclusively from supernaturals for probably hundreds of years. I've been trying to find her ever since we arrived." Knowing that the attack taking place in a few hours was reliant upon me doing what I hadn't yet done successfully was making my voice squeakier than usual.

"We could strap the missus to George's back," Godfrey said. "He flies over Snowdonia while she does her thing. Maybe proximity will help."

"No," Clive said.

Silence again as Russell and Godfrey seemed to recalculate their responses. "Understood," Godfrey responded quietly in deference to Clive's anger.

"Godfrey could scan aerial images as we drive," Russell suggested. "Their spells may not work with satellites."

"Yes," Clive said. "Do that." Voice cold, expression hard, he flew down the road, a good thirty miles an hour over the posted speed limit.

"Okay, well, if you think of anything else, give us a call b— wait! Clive, go back!"

He slowed and pulled to the shoulder again. "What did you see?"

"Nothing. It's what I felt." I pointed behind us. "The fog is thin over a narrow lane back there. It's jutting off from the motorway."

"And?" George asked, not happy with the car stopping again.

"There's a graveyard somewhere down that road."

Nodding, Clive turned the car around. "Yes. Excellent idea."

"What is?" Russell asked.

"I'm a necromancer," I explained. "My powers are stronger when I'm in close proximity to the dead." Pausing, I considered just doing what needed to be done without telling him, as he was already on edge, but that wouldn't be right. "I'll need to pull back whatever imbalance there is in the wicche glass too." When Clive flinched, I added, "But it won't be much. Not like last time. With my magic in balance and my body amongst the dead, I'll be at my strongest. Maybe then I'll be able to find her."

The ghostly silhouettes of trees and bushes crowded the foggy lane Clive turned down, the car bumping along the uneven ground. We passed a sign I couldn't make out. "Did anyone catch that?"

"It's Llandyfeisant church, a historic Welsh site," George said.

We parked a ways away and then walked through patches of snow looking for a church. Fergus raced this way and that, sniffing and peeing to his heart's content. He barked at a tree fluttering in the wind and then sprinted back to my side.

Out of the white mist, an overgrown medieval church rose. A low stone wall surrounded the property. Not sure if he could clear it, I scooped up Fergus and hopped over. It was probably being an American who hadn't traveled much before this year, but really old buildings fascinated me. This church looked like it had been standing here long before Columbus bumped into North America.

"Looks medieval," Clive said.

Built snug against a steep hill, the church was being swallowed up by its surroundings. "Does the snow look weird, or is the church covered in moss and vines?"

"It appears the earth is in the process of reclaiming it." Clive circled around the side. "Gravestones over here, darling."

'Darling.' The word helped to balance my emotions. He wasn't pissed off at me. Shaking his head, he walked back to me, dropping a kiss on my nose before hugging me tightly against himself. "I'm sorry," he murmured. "I didn't mean to scare either of you."

"I wasn't scared. Just worried my shit was getting to be too much for you to deal with."

"Never."

I heard a throat clearing in my pocket. What the heck was that?

Clive reached into my pocket and pulled out my phone. The call to Godfrey was still live.

"Oops."

"We wouldn't mind if you kept it open, so we knew what was going on," Russell said. "We just wanted you to know we were here."

"Okay. Back in the pocket you go." I left Clive and wandered through the graves. The headstones were so old, so worn away by time, the names and dates looked to have been lost centuries ago. The guys waited for me at the edge while I headed into the heart of the cemetery. I found a flat, broken stone on the ground. Brushing off the snow, I said a quick apology to whoever stone this was and sat down.

I closed my eyes and felt Fergus plop into my lap.

"Shall I get him?" Clive asked.

"No. He's a warm ball of comfort. We're fine." Deciding I might as well get the rough stuff out of the way first, I uncoiled my magic, imagining it as a long golden thread. Wrapping it around the wicche glass hanging from my neck, I took back the imbalance stored in the fragile-looking glass. Fisting my hands on my knees, not wanting to squeeze the pup, I drew in the pain.

A gasp escaped me before I could lock it down.

"Sam?" The concern in Clive's voice, knowing he was remembering the last time I'd done this and almost died, made me bite down hard on the pain. "I'm fine," I called. We both knew it was a lie, but he accepted it was something I needed to do.

Fiery pain spread down my body, painting me in agony for a moment, and then it was gone. Clive had been trying to take away my pain, but it was too great. Thankfully it was also brief. Feeling

Fergus lick my chin made me smile. I unlocked my limbs and hugged him.

"It's okay. I'm okay now." I gave him a kiss on the snout and then put him back in my lap. "I've got stuff to do, buddy. Take a nap."

Drawing on the souls of the long dead surrounding me, I opened the necromantic part of my mind. I easily found my three guys. They were so familiar to me, they shone like searchlights, Clive nearby and Russell and Godfrey miles away, driving up a different motorway to Snowdonia. Dimmer but still clear was Bram's nocturne far to the west in the York Moors. There looked to be another nocturne in the south, perhaps near Cardiff and one to the east on the coast.

"There's a lone vamp in what looks like a basement. His mind is a nasty, dark snarl of thoughts and hunger is raging through him."

"I don't understand," George murmured. "Is the vampire with Alec?"

"No," Clive said, his voice almost too low to hear. "She's searching."

I swept back and forth, seeking out the telltale blips of poisonous green that meant vampire. When I hit a nocturne near Edinburgh, I knew I'd missed her again. Opening my eyes, I found Clive waiting patiently. George was on the other side of the low rock wall, throwing a stick for Fergus.

"No?"

"When the vampires had Scottish accents, I knew I'd gone too far."

He walked toward me, a hand held out. "It was a good idea. It just didn't work. Let's get you back into a heated car."

I hadn't moved, though. Another idea occurred to me. "Maybe you're the key."

He paused, eyebrows raised. "How so?"

"You were both turned by the same vamp. Maybe the link is in the blood." The fae ring glowed on my pinky. "And she's been feeding from the fae." I motioned him close. "Remember that thing you did when Abigail was messing with my mind?"

"Giving you some of my blood to break the spell?" He crouched down beside me, resting a hand on my knee.

"Right. It might do nothing but make me queasy, but maybe if I have your blood in my mouth and the fae ring on my finger, I can try to focus my energy on something that combines the two." I sighed. "I have no idea what I'm doing, Clive. I just—I feel like this will work." I stared into his hopeful eyes and felt my stomach drop. I didn't want to give him false hope. "But I could be totally wron—"

He kissed me quiet. "It's a good idea. Let's try." He kissed me again, a long, deep kiss that left the taste of blood in my mouth.

THIRTY-THREE

In Which Sam Discovers a Well of Hate She did Know She Possessed

Holding the blood on my tongue, I wrapped my fingers around the ring and uncoiled my magic, looping it from my mouth to my finger. I searched my mind for the vampire who had both the blood of the same creator as well as that of the fae coursing through her body.

I was vaguely aware of Clive picking me up and cradling me in his lap. I tucked my head under his chin, breathed in his scent, and searched. Finally. Finally, I found a blip that was odd. It had the shape and feel of a vamp blip, but it was black, blending with the darkness in my mind. What I normally saw as faint overlays of color—poisonous green for vampires, spring green for the fae, red for dragons, purple for immortals like Stheno and Meg—was unrelieved black for this blip. Black on black was usually reserved for the well and truly dead, the ones who had moved on and not left a hazy spirit in their wake.

And yet, here was a blip, the shape and feel of a vamp's, but the wrong color, hiding amongst the long dead. It was farther north, at the top of Wales. This had to be her. Diving deep, I pushed into the blip and shivered. Aldith's mind was a cold, angry, and not terribly sane place to be. I felt Clive hold me tighter, which helped.

Memories usually fired up along the electrical nerve impulses of the synapse. When one lit up, I'd hop in and relive the memory with the vamp whose mind I was invading. I waited in Aldith's mind, but no memories flared to life.

Okay. I'd been practicing with Clive. I knew how to sneak in and out without being noticed. Perhaps, I could also... I sent Aldith a flicker of an image, one I'd seen in her daughter Leticia's memory. Clive was plowing a field, stripped to the waist, his tunic hanging from his belt, sweating under the sun—a personal favorite of mine.

Almost immediately, I heard a woman's voice bubble up out of the dark. She screeched about the lying bastard who had ruined her family's reputation, who had killed her hard-working husband and sons, who had caused them to lose the farm. She wished his family was all still alive so she could kill them, one by one, in front of him. She went on and on, Clive the focus of her batshit bile spewing. While she ranted, I tried to discern variations in the black. Did glossy black against matte black signify a memory? Ah, well. It was worth a try.

I stepped into a patch of glossy black and found myself standing outside a large red brick mansion. It was the one I'd seen earlier in the vamp's memory, with a high tower in the middle, a rounded, open-air walkthrough at its base, leading to what looked like a courtyard in the center of the wings. Ivy grew up the walls. Moonlight glinted off the many dark windows.

Aldith stood near the woods with Finvarra. She wore a long formal gown, better suited to a nineteenth century London dinner party than a rendezvous in the forest. The moon hung low in the sky, lending light to the meeting.

"I'm merely surprised. You are, after all, the king. One assumes the king holds the real power and can wield it as he sees fit. If you're concerned how your mate will react were she to find out, I understand." She curtsied and then headed back to the house. Aldith was a handsome woman. She had the same blonde hair and blue eyes as her daughter, but where Leticia was petite, almost fragile looking, Aldith was sturdy.

"You dare insult me?" Finvarra's mouth was set in a scowl, his eyes hard as flint.

She spun back, expression shocked. "Never. I'm outraged on your behalf, a man as…" She looked him up and down, admiration gleaming in her eyes.—"powerful, as charismatic, being asked to take orders from a woman." She shook her head. "I know none of the particulars, so I'm sure I don't understand. I would think the fact that you are as commanding, as skilled, as you are when your power isn't tied to the realm itself would make you the dominant monarch.

"As I understand it, her health and strength are tied to the health and strength of Faerie. Any damage to Faerie is damage to her. Isn't that so? You, on the other hand, wield power in *all* the realms. To my way of thinking, that gives you ultimate command. But," she added with another shrug, "as I say, I know none of the particulars. I'm sure you have good reasons for allowing your mate to hold the reins."

"I know what you're doing." Finvarra's eyes began swirling brown and gold, trying to hypnotize the truth from her as he had me. He couldn't quite hide the satisfaction he felt at her words, though.

"What I'm doing?" Her voice had lost some of its vibrancy; her gaze had dulled. "I'm proposing an alliance that would prove quite beneficial to us both. You will weaken and distract the queen while I am allowed to feed on those who will give me an edge over my own kind."

"Perhaps." He paused, watching her, considering. "Let us go in and discuss the particulars." Finvarra strode past Aldith, heading to the great house, while Aldith followed meekly, her smirk hidden behind his back.

An elven warrior stepped through a tree at the edge of the clearing. I memorized the doorway's location.

Finvarra glanced over his shoulder. "Wait here. We have some details to agree upon and then I will call you to join us." The smile he gave made my blood run cold. The charming mask had dropped and cold, calculating evil took its place. The exchange was fascinating to watch, each side positive it had the upper hand.

The warrior stepped out from under the shadow of the trees, into the moonlight. Inclining his head, he watched his king offer an arm to Aldith, escorting her into the house. I knew that face. He was the one Clive had killed in the cavern this morning. Was it really only this morning?

The memory faded and I was back in the dark, hunting for the next glossy memory. When I saw it, I stepped in and found myself in an earthen tunnel, a weak flickering lantern hanging from a support beam. It smelled of human waste, rot, and unwashed bodies. This had to be the dungeon, but where was—Oh, here she came. Aldith turned the corner.

Disgust lined her face as she glanced into cells on her right and left. From one, the most piteous whining was coming. I made the mistake of looking in. He was a shifter, most likely a werewolf. He'd been broken, though, becoming an unholy combination of wolf and human. His face was gaunt, with open sores, his torso covered in fur, his arms ending in paws, his legs those of a human and covered in bites and bruising.

"Kill. Me," he wheezed.

She made a sound of disgust in the back of her throat and kept walking.

A man who looked too much like Liam not to be another selkie was huddled in the corner of the opposite cell, far from water, with no seal skin in his cell. She wasn't just feeding from these prisoners. She was torturing them on their long, slow road to death.

Aldith appeared quite different in this memory. I'd guess perhaps a century or two had gone by since she and Finvarra had struck their bargain. Her clothing was modern. She wore slacks and a silk blouse, her shoulder-length hair down, pearls at her ears, and what looked like a washcloth in her hand.

Walking to the end of the tunnel, stepping over something foul, she stopped before metal bars. "Good evening, Alec. Have you missed me?"

There was a beat of silence and then a cracked whisper of a voice wheezed, "Yes, mistress. I've missed you very much."

"Good." She took a key from her pocket and opened the door, metal screeching against metal.

Stepping in behind her, I scanned the cell, looking for Alec. It took far too long for my brain to make sense of the heap of rags in the corner.

"You're so beautiful, mistress." Dark eyes, glassy with devotion, shone out of the heap.

A sob choked me. I knew this was Alec, but he looked like my George, only emaciated and beaten. He had burns and bite marks layered over one another on every inch of flesh I could see. His face was ravaged, looking like nothing so much as sick, mottled skin stretched taut over a skull.

How could anyone do this to another being? Tears flooded my eyes as I thought of the child who had been taken from his family to be isolated, tortured, starved, and left for dead. My fingertips itched. I needed to take her head and carry the poor man to safety, but this was a memory. I had no power to help him in here.

"Come, give your mistress a sip."

The man barely covered in rags moved but he didn't have the strength to lift himself, to do more than grunt and fall back to the stinking floor.

She *tsked*, shaking her head. "How hard is it to throw food in here every once in a while?" She pulled his arm up from the floor, used her washcloth to clean his wrist, and then sunk her fangs into him.

Alec barely registered the bite. He sighed when she dropped his arm, and then he fell into a stupor. Aldith stepped out of the cell, locked the door, and then threw the key to a guard I hadn't noticed at the end of the passage.

"Hose him down and feed him. He's useless to me dead. Oh, and let me know when Niall returns. We have a few empty cells."

"Yes, mistress." He bowed his head as she walked by.

"And do something about the stench down here." She held a hand under her nose to block the scent. "It seeps into my clothes and takes forever to fade." As she walked away, the memory went dark.

My hatred of her warred with my need to memorize everything. The only way to help Alec was to find her.

"Why is Sam crying?"

As I pulled myself from Aldith's mind, George's voice was the first I heard, strong and compassionate, everything Alec's couldn't be.

"I don't know." Clive rubbed my back and kissed my forehead. "What is it, love?"

I turned into him and wrapped my arms tightly around him. "It was so much worse than I'd thought."

"What was?" George was suddenly crouched beside me. "What did you see?"

"I found her. Alec—I don't know how he's survived this long."

"What did you see?" George shouted.

Clive tensed, but I held out my hand and took George's. "He was alive, but just barely. He was skin and bones, huddled in the corner of his cell. He didn't have the strength to lift himself from the floor, even under a vampire's compulsion."

I needed him to be prepared for what we'd find. "His condition is far worse than Fyr's." I squeezed George's hand. "I thought he'd be like Fyr, hurt, hungry, but able to break free and run to safety." I held his gaze, willing him to understand. "If he's still alive when we get there, he's going to have to be carried out and rushed to a hospital. There's no way the man I just saw will be able to stand or walk."

He dropped my hand, stood, and stalked away. "We should have found someone like you years ago. I should have never gone to the States. I should have stayed here, searched every fucking house in the country until I found him. I should have..." Lost in self-recriminations, he walked off into the fog.

"There's no one like her, mate," Godfrey said from my pocket. "Nothing could have been done until now, until the missus was here to do it. Russell and I are close to Snowdonia. Where are we going?"

I pulled my phone out of my pocket. "Let me pull up a map and see if I can match what I see in my head to a map of the area." I studied the screen and followed my gut. "I'm not even going to try to pronounce this. I'm just taking a screenshot of this river. I think we're looking somewhere around here."

George looked over my shoulder. "Afon Hafod-Ruffydd-Isaf."

"What he said. You guys head there and Clive'll be racing up the roads behind you."

A sweater fell into my lap. "You drive. I'm flying. Take my clothes, please. I'll need them later."

I started to turn around and then stopped myself, remembering that George was as uncomfortable with nakedness as I was. "Don't do anything until we get there. It has to be all of us. I feel it. In order to kill her and rescue Alec, it has to be all of us working together. Okay?"

"I can't promise you anything, Sam. I can't."

I heard footsteps running, saw a flash of light, and then huge wings were beating the air. I stood then and watched my friend disappear into the fog.

"Let's go," Clive said, grabbing my hand. He scooped up Fergus and then the two of us raced over the hill and down the path to the car. Minutes later, we were back on the motorway, Clive driving like it was the Autobahn.

"Is there time before the sun rises?" I checked the time on my phone. The fae weren't tied to the night, and we'd be losing our three best fighters in a few hours.

"We'll find out."

THIRTY-FOUR

George Was Right

When Fergus fell asleep on my lap, I deposited him in his bed. "You're staying in the car during the battle, little man," I whispered. "You're not quite up to fighting weight yet."

"The problem with that plan is that we'll need to leave the car a mile or two from the property, so she doesn't hear us coming," Clive said. "I'm not sure what we're going to do about your heartbeat."

"Hopefully nothing permanent." I stretched out my limbs and considered hanging my head out the window. My brain was getting muzzy.

"Darling, put the seat back and get some sleep. You're exhausted. If anything happens, I'm here." He turned on the radio, soft classical music filling the car, and then rubbed my leg. "Go ahead."

He was right. I'd do no one any good if I couldn't think clearly. Hitting the button, I fully reclined on the soft leather seat. When I felt it warm, I knew Clive had hit another button. I allowed myself to relax and nodded off almost immediately.

I'm in a room I've never been in before. It's filled with overly fussy antiques, damask fabrics, floral wallpaper, thick Persian rugs. It's cluttered, cacophonous, and cold. Sitting in a high-backed chair by the fire is

Aldith. Niall, the elf Clive had killed in the cavern, is crossing the room to sit opposite her.

"Well," she demands. "What news have you heard? Has she done it?" She stands abruptly, agitated. "She should have contacted me by now."

"Mistress, I have bad news for you."

"No." Eyes vamp black, she picks up the chair she's been sitting in and sends it crashing through the mullioned windows.

Niall stands. "I've heard from the States. It seems Leticia was unsuccessful. Clive took her head."

A mournful howl of "Noooo" follows her after she's left the room, moving so fast as to disappear. Furniture smashes and glass breaks in her wake as she races down the stone steps into the torch-lit dungeon. A guard bows to her and she grabs him by the neck, pins him to the wall, and rips his head off. Dragging her sleeve down her face, she wipes away the blood spatter.

Red sparks light her black eyes as she stalks down the earthen passage to the cell at the end of the row. Alec, still thin and weak but looking more alive, leans against the damp stone wall. When she bares her fangs and hisses, he lifts a hand and flips her off.

With no key and the guard dead, she wails her anger and frustration, tearing the door from its hinges and heaving it the length of the passage. Alec races toward freedom but she's too strong, too fast, and too enraged. She catches him easily, sinks her fangs into his neck and sucks the life from him. He punches and struggles but is no match for her.

What little life was left in him is draining away. She drops him to the dirt floor, tears at her own wrist, and drips the blood into his mouth. She's doing what Leticia had done when she'd tried to turn a werewolf into an undead monster. Aldith is trying to create a vampire dragon.

No, no, no. I couldn't fix this before. I'd had to kill the werewolf to put him out of his misery. Please, I don't want to kill George's twin too.

"You will be my soldier. You'll live forever with the strength of a thousand men, and you will do my bidding. My daughter was too weak. You will be mighty. Your fire and claws will be mine to command."

She leans over, stroking his throat, helping him to swallow. He makes a strange rattling sound, opens his dazed eyes, and then spits the blood *into her face. When she sputters, he wheezes a laugh. That's when she picks him up and throws him against the wall in the corner, leaving him crumpled in a heap of rags.*

George is right. His brother's a hero. He's an effing Titan. It isn't until she's physically broken him, drained him, that he finally succumbs to her compulsion. We have to get him out. Anyone who spits in Aldith's face deserves a long life celebrated in story and song.

I awoke with a start, Fergus climbing over me to look out the window and whine.

"Sorry, darling. You both seemed to be having bad dreams. I put him in your lap and you both settled down. Unfortunately, he awoke, and I believe needs to relieve himself." Clive pulled to the side of a narrow road.

When I opened the door, he shot off to sniff under a large tree. The lower branches kept the snow from the patch he was circling. A moment later he peed, pooped, and came trotting back, the conquering hero.

Once he was back in his bed, toy clamped tightly between his teeth, paws flailing in the air, I turned to Clive. "I had a dream-vision-memory, one of Aldith's, while I slept."

"Tell me."

I explained everything I'd seen while he nodded attentively. "I think whatever we do," I said, "you need to be out in front. You incense her. She won't be able to think straight and will make mistakes."

"Precisely."

The phone rang and Clive tapped it.

"We believe we've found it, Sire. The missus was right. It's about a mile from that river. It's spelled, though, so we can't get close," Godfrey said.

"We smelled both vampire and fae," Russell cut in.

"It's shrouded in fog," Godfrey continued. "When we were getting close, we both felt the need to walk in the opposite direction. We'd just turned to search elsewhere when we realized what we'd done. Once we knew, we concentrated, trying to push through the compulsion and the fog, but we couldn't. All that magic has to be protecting her. Why else would it be here?"

"Have you seen George?" He *had* to wait for us.

"The fog is so thick here, we'd have a time of it if he were standing right in front of the car," Godfrey said.

"If I come to you, will we be far enough away that she won't hear Sam's heartbeat?" Clive turned onto an even narrower road.

"They said a wooded area," I put in. "That means lots of heartbeats to cover mine." As tall woods surrounded the estate, I should be able to get quite close before we blew our cover.

"Human heartbeats don't sound like small woodland creatures, my lady," Russell explained.

Oh. "Should I shift?"

"Wolves were hunted to extinction in Britain hundreds of years ago," Clive said, shaking his head.

"Aye, Sire, but they've begun reintroducing them. I read about a pack in southern Wales," Godfrey said. "It doesn't help us right now, but interesting."

"I wish I'd known that earlier when I ran into that werewolf pack on the moors. Man, they must have a hard time hiding themselves if there are no natural wolves around. Okay, anyway. I'll hang back while you guys go in like the hand of God. George and I will be the second wave."

"We'll keep an eye out for George, as much as we can in this fog," Godfrey groused.

"We're almost to you," Clive said.

"We hear your car," Russell responded.

A few minutes later, we pulled up next to Russell's pickup truck. I walked Fergus around for any last-minute emergencies and then we all sat in the rental sedan. Secret plans shouldn't be discussed out in the open. Voices carried and we didn't know who was listening.

While Russell and Godfrey described the spells that seemed to cocoon the estate, I closed my eyes and opened my mind to the supernaturals in our neighborhood. "Found him!" I jumped out, shifted my jaw and throat, and then howled, prompting Fergus to howl with me. A minute later, I felt an impact tremor in the foggy distance. A ball of fire appeared and then was lost in the murk.

"Do you have my clothes?" George asked.

"Yes! Give me a sec," I whispered as I opened the back door, reached over Godfrey, and grabbed the bag I'd put George's clothes and shoes in. Keeping my eyes aimed at the ground, I jogged over to where I'd heard his voice and placed the bag on a pristine patch of snow. "There you go."

"Thanks," he said as I turned my back to him.

"Thank you for not attacking before we got here."

The bag rustled and then I heard clothes being snapped out. "Wouldn't have done any good. I couldn't see anything through the fog. It's thicker in one spot than the countryside around it, so I figured that was the place."

"Godfrey said the same thing." We both kept our voices so low, it was hard for even me to hear. "He said there was also some kind of go-away spell that made them both detour when they tried to approach the house."

"Done. Let's go talk with the others."

George took the front seat and I made Godfrey scooch over. Fergus was sitting calmly in Russell's lap, which warmed my heart.

"Sam, perhaps you could explain your dream to everyone?" Clive had waited for me to tell it, which I appreciated.

When I told them about the finger, the spit, and the laugh, George nodded, a wistful smile on his face. "That's Alec, all right."

At hearing her reaction to the laugh, he turned away and stared out the windshield.

"How far did she travel down to the dungeon? I mean, is it a basement or was it far below the ground?"

I stared at Godfrey for a beat. "Are there rules for that sort of thing? Basement versus dungeon?" When the vamps stared back, I shrugged. "Just wondering. It felt like a flight of stairs. It wasn't a finished basement. Packed dirt floors in places, stone in others, although some of the walls, like the one in Alec's cell, had brick outer walls. Thick wooden beams braced the ceiling."

"You said she killed the guard. The vision you had earlier tonight, where Alec didn't have the strength to lift himself, was there a different guard on duty?" George sounded hollowed out.

"Yes, there was a guard then too, a different one."

He nodded, still staring straight ahead.

"As we have no eyes on this operation, we need to rely on your observations, my lady," Russell said. "Did you see other fae or vampire servants in the house?"

"Oh, um, let me think. No other vamps. I'd have found them when I was sweeping Britain, looking for vampires."

"What if they drink fae or dragon blood too?" Godfrey asked.

"Could I have missed one, sure, but I only found one vampire color coordinated incorrectly in my head. Also, she's been sending a lot of her vamps to us, and we've been handing them their final death. I don't know how many more she has left."

"In all likelihood, assuming we can get past all the enchantments," Clive began, "we'll be walking into a situation with one unhinged vampire, one to dozens of fae—depending on whether they've been following and listening—any of whom could yank Sam into Faerie to kill her. We'll also have countless prisoners to rescue, all while avoiding the king."

"That sounds about right, and since the night is getting away from us, I suggest we go now." Otherwise, we'd be waiting until the following evening, risking more fae finding us.

George jumped out of the car and started jogging toward where the fog was thickest. We all got out and then Russell returned Fergus' bed to the back seat, placed him in it with a toy, and patted his head. Before closing the door, he grabbed my axe and sheath, passing it to me. The barks and howls started almost immediately. As we didn't need a doggy siren tipping off our enemy, I went back, allowed my wolf to lighten my eyes and growled. He plopped down silently, and I ran to catch up with the guys.

They'd all stopped at what seemed like an invisible wall within the fog. George shoved at it but couldn't penetrate the hazy mist. Clive leapt straight up, his right hand sliding up the invisible wall. When he dropped down a moment later, he turned to me and shook his head.

Any ideas?

THIRTY-FIVE

In Other News, Finvarra Is Still a Dick

Is it okay for George and me to be this close? I thought you guys were concerned about heartbeats.

We are, but there's no way we'll get George to wait, so we're plowing ahead. At least, we were until we ran up against this ward.

Fae had been going in and out of this estate for centuries. Granted, they could have been using the tree I'd seen in the memory earlier. Just in case, though, I led with my right hand, the one with Gloriana's ring. My hand slid through the wall of fog and then out.

"How—" Clive stopped, eyes fixed on the ring.

"Try your left," I breathed. *The one wearing a fae-made wedding ring.* It was harder for him, but he was able to push all the way through. "Everyone hold hands." This had worked when I'd had to visit the queen in Faerie and needed to get everyone out with me. Hopefully, it would work here too.

The men were confused, but when I grabbed George's hand, they understood and linked up. I slid through easily enough. The test was going to be if the guys could cross the ward with me. Once George's hand, gripped in mine, passed through, I knew we were good. The fae despised vampires, so I wasn't sure how fae magic would work on them, but Clive had already made it in, so I

257

was hopeful. Judging by the slow struggle, it was definitely harder for Godfrey and Russell.

Once we were all together inside the ward, the fog was so thick I literally could not see my hand in front of my face. *Shit*. The wall, it seemed, was the least of our problems.

Take Russell's hand but speak to him mind to mind so you know you have his hand and aren't being led astray by a fae trickster.

Lovely thought. Thank you for that nightmare, darling.

I grabbed the front of George's sweater to my left and pulled him down. Once I'd found his ear, I told him to hold tight to both me and Godfrey. We didn't want to lose anyone in the fog. Fisting the hand with the ring—I didn't want anyone to sneak up in the mist and slip it off my finger—I led the way. Without the ring, I knew we'd fail.

Gloriana wanted the problem fixed. I was counting on her help in doing just that. When my fist knocked into a tree, I adjusted and continued forward. I walked through something that felt like another ward. My ring gave a subtle pulse right before hands pounded my back, shoving me forward. I lost my balance, taking a big step forward and knocking my head against a tree, but I never dropped George's hand.

"Shit's getting real. Everyone hold tight," I breathed.

A voice screamed in my ear. I flinched but held the line. I felt George step out of line and grunt, but his grip tightened on mine. From the way my arm was getting tugged this way and that, everyone was under attack. Roots seemed to rise up from the forest floor to trip me.

I understood what was happening now. This was a spell. We didn't actually have fae attackers in the woods with us. Doing my best to attain a calm Zen state, I held my ringed fist in front of me and plowed on.

A hundred yards or so in, I realized I was seeing glowing spots along the ground. I followed. As I got close to one, it went out and another farther along appeared. Will o' the wisp. The question, though, was whether it was here to help us find a way out or to misdirect us. I felt a subtle pull when I followed the glowing specks. Trusting Gloriana had sent them to help, I got knocked into trees, lost my footing, and had my ears ringing, but I held to the will o' the wisp's course.

Stepping out of the fog bank a moment later, I stood on the lawn before the huge brick mansion I'd been seeing in memories.

George, Godfrey, and Russell followed me out, but Clive wasn't with them. Panicking, I tried to run back into the fog, but Russell caught me around the waist.

"He'll make it out," he breathed in my ear. "Losing you doesn't help us."

Where are you? We just got out.

Lost in the bloody fog. I heard your voice scream for help in my ear. I dropped Russell's hand to help. Idiot.

Wait. If you heard my voice, then the spell was tailored to us. They know we're here.

Darling, I'm sure they've known since we turned off the motorway.

Awesome. Just step out already! You always know where I am. Ignore the distractions. Where am I?

Damn it! The opposite direction of the one I was walking.

Hurry. We have a dragon to rescue and a vicious old bitch to behead. We're very busy tonight.

I pushed Russell's arm away and walked the line of fog. I could feel him too. When I was sure he was close, I plunged my hand in, grabbed his arm, and yanked. Clive came tumbling out of the cloudy mist.

Knowing the way fae could alter their appearance and the fact that Clive had been separated from us, instead of hugging him when he reached for me, I stepped away.

How do I know it's really you?

I'm talking to you in your mind.

Sure, but a fae king could probably do that too.

Ah, good point. Okay, quiz me.

I wracked my brain, trying to think of something only Clive

would know, that no one else could have overheard or seen. *How was I finally able to talk you into marrying me?*

Tricksy little wolf. That was all me. You were scared to death to marry me. You said the marriage part sounded okay, but the dress, the ceremony, all the people looking at you were deal breakers.

This time when he opened his arms, I jumped into them. I gave him a quick kiss and then led him back to our friends. Clive stopped by Russell. Kissing my temple, he pushed me into Russell's arms. When I opened my mouth to protest, he held a finger over my lips.

Turning, he walked to the center of the lawn and held his arms out at his sides. "Aldith?" he called in a clear voice, the sound echoing in the fog. "Leticia mentioned you were interested in seeing me before I took her head. As your husband and sons killed my sister, I suppose we can consider Leticia's true death payback."

A shriek rent the air, but the fog was playing tricks with sound. I couldn't be sure where it was coming from. When we heard things smashing against walls, Clive disappeared from sight. A window crashed inward on the second floor and then I thought I saw the bottom of his shoe going over the sill.

Godfrey and George raced in the door, but Russell kept me pinned to him.

"What are you doing? We need to help."

"Sorry, my lady. I've been given my orders."

I struggled a moment and then stopped. "You know I can make you let me go. Why are you two doing this?"

He shifted his gaze from the house to me, one side of his mouth kicking up. "Because he loves you beyond all logic and reason."

I couldn't just stand here. "I'm sorry." I gave him a little zap of pain, but although he winced, he didn't let go. "Damn it! I don't want to hurt you."

Russell's attention was focused on the house and Aldith's incoherent rants, punctuated with crashes. "I know, my lady. Clive counted on that."

"Fine. Go with me then. We'll help George free the prisoners while Clive deals with Aldith, okay?" And then once we'd freed the prisoners, I'd run upstairs to help Clive.

Russell looked torn but finally nodded. We raced in the front door and followed George's scent. I vaguely recalled seeing some of this in Aldith's memories. A loud boom upstairs shook the foundations. It sounded as though someone had been hurled into a wall with a great deal of force.

Russell and I ran soundlessly down the hall, to a thick wooden door that had been wrenched off its hinges, and down narrow stairs. Halfway down, we had to hop over a couple of charred guards. They must have been running to protect their mistress, only to find an enraged dragon.

Night vision was a huge benefit when one had to search a lightless dungeon. Not so fortunate, though, was having a hyper-sensitive nose because the stench was horrendous. Bile rising, I took shallow breaths through my mouth, trying to settle my stomach. I knew we were in a hurry, but something that felt suspiciously like a bone rolled under my foot as I turned left into the first passage. A chill ran down my spine and I did my best to ignore it. This place was evil, and it was messing with my head.

I felt dragons at the end of this row. Russell and I followed the sounds of gentle murmurs. George was rocking his brother's emaciated form. George's head snapped to us, fire in his mouth. Russell shoved me behind him at the same time George recognized us and closed his mouth.

Smacking Russell's arm, I whispered, "You're not fireproof. Don't do that."

"George," Russell said. "How can we help?"

The rags in George's arms moved and my heart clutched.

"I'll take Alec out. Can you get the others? I don't think they left many alive." George rose and carefully carried his brother down the passage.

Russell and I ran down the rows, checking cells. Most were empty. Presumably, the dead bodies of the imprisoned fae had returned to Faerie. Russell found the selkie I'd seen in a memory and brought him up the stairs.

In the cell opposite was the one I'd been dreading and yet needing to take care of, the broken werewolf who been made into an agonizing confusion of man and wolf. When I tore open the bars, one eyelid lifted while a piteous whine filled the cell.

"Please," he breathed.

Placing a hand on his forehead, I took a shaky breath, resolved to do the right thing. "You can rest now. It's over."

"Thank—"

I sliced my claws through his neck. I knew it had to be done but I couldn't let him thank me for killing him. When I stood, hands trembling, my stomach finally got its way and I heaved in the corner.

Blowing out a hard breath, I jogged up the passage, looking for any remaining prisoners. I could feel the battle above, but I tried not to let it distract me or let my fear distract Clive. He and Godfrey were battling Aldith and three of her vamps. Clive was incensed that her mental skills were as strong as his own. It made overpowering her far more difficult than he'd anticipated.

I saw movement out of the corner of my eye and stopped. An Orc was sitting on the floor, his arms and legs chained to the wall. I paused at the doorway, unsure of what to do. I'd never met an Orc who didn't want to kill me, but this one was a prisoner. Deciding I was being an asshole for pausing, I went in and grabbed the keys by the door, unlocking his shackles.

"Can you stand?" I bent over to help him up.

When he opened his eyes, I had a moment of panic. Maybe this had all been a ruse and I was about to get a meaty fist in the face, but he, instead, shook his head.

"No...can try," he grumbled.

The defeat in his voice had me straining to pull him to his feet, but Orcs weigh a frigging ton. Russell returned to help me get the prisoner to his feet and then slung him over his shoulder.

"I'll take him up," Russell said. "There's just one more passage

I haven't checked, down on the right." Demonstrating ridiculous vampire strength, a moment later, Russell was running with the Orc up the stairs and out.

I jogged down to the last passage and turned right. I could feel it. There was someone in the last cell on the left, but the rest all felt empty. I checked each one, just to be sure. Nothing. In the last cell, though, I was stopped cold. Oh, no.

A large, rusted tub sat in the cell. My head was pounding; my breathing had turned to short pants. I wasn't sure how much more of this I could take. They hadn't bothered to lock this door because why would they? I looked in the tub and felt lightheaded. Filthy, stagnant water barely covered the mermaid. A hip, a shoulder, and a bald patch on the back of her head jutted up from the water. Her scales were dull and peeling, blood crusted at the edges.

How could I get her out without making it worse?

Russell returned and we both stared down at our dying mermaid.

"I could pick her up and run, but then what? We have no place to put a mermaid." He looked as sickened as I felt.

"I've been standing here, trying to figure out how to do this. There's a tree that's a doorway to Faerie. I saw it in a memory. If we can get the prisoners there, I should be able to push them through." I looked back at him. "It'll require me going back into the spelled fog."

He paused, wanting to argue, but we both knew it was the only way to save all the poor people who had been tortured horribly. Reluctantly, he nodded, understanding we had no choice. "Yes. All right."

"Let's go."

Plunging his arms into the fetid water, he grabbed the mermaid, threw her over his shoulder, and ran down the passage and up the stairs, me fast on his heels. Once we were outside, I saw he'd left the four other rescued fae at the far end of the courtyard, close to the wall of fog. Perfect.

"I'm going to go in, find the tree, and push her through. You be ready to pass the rest to me, one at a time, okay?"

"Anything could happen to you in the fog and we'd never find you. I should do it." He kept his hand on the mermaid, needing to secure her but clearly worried his touch was hurting her further.

"You can't and you know it." I turned my back, trying to figure out where the tree was. I lifted my hand, whispering into Gloriana's ring. "I have your people. They need help immediately. Please, show me where the tree is."

A pulse of light glowed in the fog. The will o' the wisps were back. "Thank you."

I pushed my right hand through the fog, took a step in, and felt my fingers brush against bark. Spinning, I reached out, half of my body in the fog, half out. "Quick. Give me the mermaid."

Russell shifted her onto my shoulder and I dove back in. I found the right spot on the tree and pushed the mermaid through, yelling for someone to come help her. Hopefully I was heard. When I leaned out again, Russell was holding the selkie upright. I grabbed him and then helped him through the tree. By the time we got to the Orc, we had a smooth rhythm going. I held on to him as best I could, but it was awkward as hell. He had to weigh five or six times more than I did. I almost lost him when he stumbled on a rock, but I finally got him through.

"Please seal this doorway." We didn't need an army of fae sneaking in behind us. I felt the bark firm beneath my fingers. "Thank you."

I stepped out and found Russell without his jacket, folding up his shirt sleeves.

He sighed deeply at my appearance, his shoulders relaxing. "I'm afraid it doesn't really help much with the stench, but I had to try."

I looked down at myself. Rotting scales, blood, muck, and what I preferred to believe was dirt covered my hoodie. Freezing temperatures or not, it had to go. Peeling it off, I kicked it to the side and scooped up some snow, using it to wash my hands and face. Yes, it was freezing, but some things are worse than the cold. Russell nodded, doing the same.

"When you stepped into the fog, I was overcome with dread. I did not want to tell Clive I'd lost his wife," Russell said.

"Whereas I am joyfully anticipating breaking the news of his wife's grisly demise."

I flinched at the familiar voice. Finvarra strode through the passage under the tower with a phalanx of three Orcs, two hell-hounds, and five elven warriors following. How many more were in the courtyard beyond, waiting to appear?

The rescue party had been split. We had to fight together in order to win. I felt it. Clive's fear for me after the light had gone out on my chess piece, though, meant he'd sidelined me, possibly killing us all.

"Why is it always you?" Finvarra tilted his head. "Are you stalking me?" His grin was upsettingly charming. Eyes swirling, he was trying to mesmerize me again.

Scratching my nose, I breathed into the ring, "Are you listening?" I shook my head and, speaking in a normal voice, said, "You'd save everyone so much time and trouble if you and your wife went to couples' therapy. Seriously. You need to deal with your feelings of inferiority in more healthy ways."

The roguish grin dropped away. Much like shoving Clive in front of Aldith, I was hoping if I knocked him off his stride, he'd make a mistake.

As he was looking murderous, I gave him my most concerned expression and continued. "Maybe gardening? I hear people get a lot out of satisfaction out of bread making. You should give it a try."

"Bird watching seems a peaceful activity," Russell volunteered.

Finvarra's lip curled up in a sneer.

Unspooling my magic, wrapping it around myself, I put as much force as I could behind the thought, *Trouble outside! We need you!* Russell and I moved, each giving the other some room. We were sticking together, but we'd both need space once this blood-bath commenced.

"You mock me?" Disbelief was warring with rage.

Was I? Oh, right. I totally was. "You know the queen has given me her protection. What you may not know is that she set me on this quest. She asked me to find out what was poisoning Faerie. Short answer: you. Long answer: All the little doorways you've torn between the realms have weakened Faerie, allowed sickness to bleed into a world that has no natural defense. You're drawing her people out to be imprisoned and killed by a vampire. A *vampire*. You guys hate the dead and yet you struck a deal with one centuries ago to hurt your own people as a way of poking at your wife."

I looked at the soldiers behind him. "Why in the world are you following a guy who would sacrifice your immortal lives in an effort to weaken the queen? The queen, I might add, who is in fact Faerie! If she dies, you *all* die." I returned my focus to Finvarra. "What is the end game here? If you can't rule the realm, all in it should die?" I looked back at the soldiers. "And you guys are cool with this?" I threw my hands up in the air. "Do you all *want* to die?"

"And who are you, wolf, to question me, to think you could ever understand the timeless, the omnipotent? You're weak and outnumbered. My soldiers will silence you, finally swatting an irri-tating gnat and giving me some peace."

Bouncing on my toes, I readied myself for the attack. That axe on my back was about to get a workout.

"It's been an honor, my lady," Russell murmured.

"Right back at you," I breathed.

"Well then." Finvarra grinned, eyes twinkling in moonlight filtered through fog. "Let's begin." His arm moved so fast I couldn't track it.

Staggering back, I felt a punch of white-hot pain in my shoul-der. I couldn't breathe. Turning my head, bile churning, I stared at the elven sword piercing me. It vibrated like a tuning fork. In horror, I watched it slide through muscles and bone, severing my arm from my body.

"Noooo!" Clive's roar sounded from inside the house.

The paned windows on the second floor exploded out, a blonde woman flying over the heads of the elven warriors and landing, crumpled, at the feet of the Orcs. Clive and Godfrey leapt down, placing themselves between the fae horde and us. Our backup had arrived.

I swear on all that is good and holy in this world, if you die, I will burn it all down. I will lay waste to every realm of existence that you do not inhabit. Do you hear me!

"My lady!" Russell ran to me, but I pushed him back. There was no time. The battle had begun.

THIRTY-SIX

In Still Other News, I'm Feeling Strangely Lopsided

I had a moment of clarity as all hell broke loose around me. Russell bolted to intercept the hellhound bearing down on me. The beast had opened his mouth, fangs glistening, when Russell tackled him from the side, pushing him off course and rolling him out of my line of sight. In the distance, Clive and Godfrey battled five Elven warriors. The fae were just as fast as the vamps but had the added advantage of wielding large swords.

Talk to me. How much blood have you lost?

With a deafening groan, the tower rocked, bricks cascading down the façade. A moment later, it fell, burying an Orc and a hellhound. George, in his great dragon form, crawled over the rubble, bricks sliding out from under his massive clawed feet. Lowering his head, red eyes locked on the two warriors who had raced over to dig out the Orc, he sprung serpent-fast, snapping his powerful jaws. Razor-sharp teeth sliced the men in half as he gobbled down his fae snack. I hoped they didn't give him indigestion.

I'm okay. Pay attention to the warriors trying to kill you, not me.

A warrior brought his blade down, attempting to cleave my husband in two. Before the sword could touch him, he blinked out of sight, popping back in right behind the elf, punching him in the back of the head. The elf stumbled forward and then moved, almost as quickly as Clive had. They became a blur, neither gaining the upper hand for long. A body flew through the air. I had a moment to panic before I saw the headless warrior's body crash into the side of the great house. The man really did have a particular fondness for ripping off heads.

George lumbered over the fallen tower, his tail knocking a wing off its foundation. He turned his dark, spiked dragon's head to the right, staring at something in the shadows, and then lunged forward, hooking his claws around the Orc trying to bludgeon Russell to death. Once the Orc was pinned to the ground, George leaned forward and breathed fire on the soldier, turning him instantly to ash.

Through it all, I stood, strangely calm. My arm was lying on the ground beside me, but I watched the battle as if it were a movie that I wasn't terribly interested in. Everything felt dreamily distant and muffled. I'd been close to death before. This wasn't it. I wasn't positive what this was, but it wasn't death. Not yet.

Finvarra held my gaze and laughed. In that moment, it was just the two of us, our own drama playing out while the battle raged around us. He was waiting for me to drop. I could see it in his eyes. I wasn't letting the likes of him put me on my knees, though.

In that weird dreaming place I was inhabiting, I rose above myself and looked down. I half expected to see my dead body staring sightlessly up at me. Instead, what I saw was me, standing paralyzed in Finvarra's gaze, both arms still attached to my body.

I'm okay, really. At least I hoped I was. I didn't want to distract Clive while he was fighting, but I could feel him struggling not to let crushing grief swamp him under. He needed to come to me, but doing so would be a death sentence for his men. He was desperate to be everywhere at once.

The ring on my pinky pulsed. I felt it because that finger was still part of my body. The sword Finvarra had thrown was planted in the ground by my side, the hilt a few inches from my fingers. And then it all made sense. Gloriana had offered me protection. Finvarra ordered underlings to hurt me because he didn't care what happened to them. He would not, however, risk his own safety. Instead, he'd manipulated our minds. He'd created the vision we'd all experienced. He wanted to take me out of the fight and throw my people off their game while holding to the letter of the queen's law.

Not wanting to telegraph what I was about to do, I kept my eyes locked with his and swayed as though ready to collapse. The pain was still horrendous but knowing it was Finvarra fucking with me gave me the presence of mind to channel it all into the wicche glass.

Lurching to the side, with the arm that no longer appeared attached, I grabbed the sword and sent it flying. All the training I'd been doing with Clive on swordplay paid off. Finvarra's grin fell from his face as he stared down at the sword planted in his chest. On a shocked gust of breath, he looked up and found me. His glower promised bloody retribution and then he disappeared, returning to his proper realm.

Yanking the axe from over my shoulder, I raced forward and snatched up the sword—it had for some reason remained when its owner left—and joined the fray. Swinging the heavy axe, I lopped off the head of the warrior battling Clive and then plunged the sword into the back of the Orc trying to crush Godfrey. Twisting the blade, I pushed up and down, trying to hit as many vital organs as possible. When he fell to his knees, I used my trusty axe and sent his head rolling from his body.

Spattered in fae blood, I spun, a weapon in each hand, looking for the next enemy and found only my people.

"Sorry, Sire, but that was hot." Godfrey's gaze traveled up and down before landing on the blades.

"Is it me or the blood you find hot?"

He shrugged with a grin. "Toss-up."

Overcome, Clive threw his arms around me. I dropped the weapons and hugged him back, as tightly as I could with *both* arms. The vision had almost taken him out. They'd all seen my arm severed from my body. For Clive, a man who had fought in ancient battles with swords and shields, he knew the loss of a limb was a death sentence. As there was no medical help anywhere close, the most likely outcome for me would have been death by massive blood loss. He knew that, and still he had listened to me and stayed where he was—a hundred feet away—to fight the warriors trying to kill all his people.

I'd felt it. In that weird, numb, slo-mo moment I'd been experiencing, I'd felt Clive's insane rage and overwhelming grief. He had to protect his men, had to rescue Alec, and kill Aldith, but all he'd wanted to do was go to me, to take me from this place, and keep me safe.

"Aldith?"

He looked over to where her body had landed, but she wasn't there. He shook his head. "Fled."

"We'll find her again," I said, kissing his face. "We're okay and we'll find her again. I know what to look for now."

"Sam!"

I heard Godfrey's desperate shout at the same time I felt a punch in the back. Channeling the horrific pain into the wicche glass, Clive and I looked down at the blade that had impaled us both. It ran through me and into him.

"How does it feel," Aldith sneered over my shoulder, "to lose your love, to watch her blood run cold, knowing you're the reason?"

The sword jolted as Aldith recoiled. Clive pulled himself off the blade, staring at me in horror. I, though, was focused on Aldith, who was staring down at her red, blistered hand in disbelief.

Faster than I could track, Clive had Aldith's neck in his grip. She struggled and tore at him, but it was no use. Clive would never let her go. The last, and possibly most vicious, of the Atwoods was finally his.

Blood stained his abdomen, but he didn't care. All his focus was on Aldith, on finally finishing the job he'd begun a thousand years ago. She was a wild thing in his grip, trying to tear his arm off, but he just kept squeezing. Vampires didn't breathe, but they did need their heads. It appeared this beheading was going to be the long and tortuous kind.

His gaze flicked to me. I knew he was in horrendous pain; both he and Aldith had inherited Garyn's mental abilities and both were trying to drop the other under the onslaught. I couldn't help Clive hurt her. She had too much fae blood running through her for my usual powers to work. I could, however, take his pain away. I drew it out and funneled it into the wicche glass. Standing straighter, he slammed his other fist into her head.

While she was dazed, he shouted, "George! Bring Alec here."

George tilted his big dragon head toward the edge of the building. Moving carefully so as not to crush any of the good guys, he moved from his perch on top of the fallen tower. Once back on the grass, he shifted in a fireball of flame and then ran to the edge of the house. He returned moments later, wearing his pants and supporting a man who didn't look like he should still be alive, let alone slowly staggering toward us.

I felt something clutch in my chest, seeing George and Alec side by side. Twins. They were twins and yet in comparison to George's strength and vitality, Alec appeared at least twenty years older and barely hanging on to life.

Clive's muscles bunched as he held the sadistic vampire in place. "Alec, I think we both should have a share in this death. Are you up to it?"

Aldith's strangled grunts of panic were music to my ears.

Alec wheezed a weak laugh. "Born ready."

"You'll need to yank the sword out of me first," I said. When Clive started to protest, I patted his chest. It had to be done. "The metal shouldn't burn dragons like it does vampires."

George wrapped his hand around Alec's, helping him to grip the sword.

I was funneling the pain into the wicche glass, but I wasn't dying. I had a theory and if I was right, I'd be fine once they removed the sword.

I felt them jostle the sword, but it was okay. Yanking it out felt super creepy, but again, all right. Clive threw her to the ground and pinned her, Russell and Godfrey there in an instant to help.

"Just a downward swing," Clive said. Turning his head, he stared into Aldith's eyes. "Elswyth wouldn't have wanted this, kind soul that she was, kind soul that your husband and sons tore apart. She wouldn't have wanted it, but I do. It's time that your whole bloody family reunites in Hell."

The blade came down a moment later, severing Aldith's head from her body. All three vamps rose immediately. When she turned to dust, I understood why. None of them wanted any part of her on them.

Clive was suddenly in front of me, checking my back and chest, trying to find the wounds. Instead, he found unmarred skin.

"I'm not dreaming, am I? Is she gone?" Alec's voice was weak and heartbreakingly childlike. George's arm kept him upright as he stared down at the pile of dust that had been his twenty-years' torturer.

"No dream," said Clive. "She's finished."

Alec stared down, eyes glassy but hot with rage. "Good."

"So, are we just ignoring the fact that Sam was run through with a giant sword and is now standing around chatting?" Godfrey asked, his gaze darting between the blood stains on both Clive and me.

"I have a theory on that," I began.

Alec swayed. "Would anyone mind if I sat down now?"

George was holding him up, but it was still too much for Alec.

"Actually, Sire, perhaps we should move this conversation elsewhere? The sun will be rising soon and the king's fae know where this house is."

Russell was right. We needed to get out of here.

"Sam?" *Are you all right, love?*

I kicked Aldith's pile of dust, helping the freezing winds to scatter her more quickly. "They could have another doorway around here. I'm with Russell. Let's get the heck out of here and find a safe-ish place to talk." My gaze fell on Alec again. "If we raced, could we make it to the keep before the sun rose?"

Clive squeezed my hand. "Yes, we'll do that. Alec, your parents never left Wales. They've been looking for you ever since you were taken. The fae spelled this property so it couldn't be found. Your parents have probably flown right over this area countless times in the twenty years—"

"Twenty," he breathed, his body somehow losing what little strength it had left.

"They wouldn't have been able to see or sense you. Sam is right. You and your family need each other." He jiggled my hand. "If we get too close to dawn, my men and I will find a sunless place. You keep going. Get George and Alec home."

I nodded, knowing full well that they'd been finding daytime resting spots for hundreds of years. It didn't stop me from worrying, though.

"The fog is dissipating," Russell said. "Does that mean the spell is fading?"

"I'm not sure, but we should hold hands again just to be on the safe side." Bending down, I grabbed the fae king's sword and the dwarf's axe, although I was pretty sure they were both mine now.

"Two axes and a sword. That's a nice little collection of fae weapons you've got going, Missus," Godfrey said.

George gently lifted his twin, putting him on his shoulder.

I grabbed hold of George's elbow, as he needed his hand to keep Alec secured. Godfrey took George's other hand and then grabbed Russell's. Clive took up the rear again.

I speared Clive with a look. "Don't let go this time!"

"I'll do my best, dear." He grinned, and I shook my head.

"Okay, people," I said, sheathing the axe and plunging into the fog, ring and sword hand first, "let's do this." I led them straight through the trees. There were no shoves or screams this time. Russell was right. The fog had dissipated to the point that I could see the trees before I ran into them. Bonus. I had a good, long moment to worry I'd veered to the side and was now walking in the circular path of the fog, rather than through it, when I stepped out the other side, George and Alec, Godfrey, Russell, and Clive following. We'd lost no one. Perfect.

"Okay, everyone, we're racing the dawn. You and Alec drive with Clive and me. Alec can lay down in the back seat."

George nodded and ran with the brother he'd finally found.

THIRTY-SEVEN

Too Close

Fergus was excited to see us until he got a whiff of Alec. He certainly didn't smell *good*, but I was pretty sure it was the fae scent clinging to Alec that upset the pup. Fergus growled and then hopped over the seat to get away from our rescued dragon.

"Should we have the dog ride with Russell and Godfrey?" Clive picked up the pup and held him against his chest. The dog whined, squirming to sniff at Clive's blood stains. He lifted the pup so they were eye to eye. "I'm okay now." Fergus licked Clive's nose.

"No. I'll hold him while you drive like a maniac." I slid in and reached for Fergus. "If he's going to hang out in the bar, he has to take my lead on who's a friend and who's an enemy." Reaching back where Alec was slumped against his brother, I rubbed his shoulder, saying, "Friend," to the puppy.

Fergus sat in my lap, looking suspiciously between the seats, but he seemed to understand that growling was unnecessary.

Russell backed up, executed a perfect turn at high speed, and was gone. Clive gave George and Alec time to get comfortable. I slid my seat forward and heard George sigh. The poor guy probably had his knees digging into the back of my seat.

"Wait." Clive was out and back in a moment, having pulled a

throw blanket from the trunk. He passed it back and George covered his brother. Alec rested his head on George's leg and kept one hand wrapped around his brother's knee. I had a feeling he still wasn't sure if this was real or not.

George murmured to him in a strange language. Alec's breathing changed. I thought he might be crying but then he started speaking in the same odd language. Clive turned on the radio, low bluesy music covering their voices, giving them privacy, as he spun the car around and sped down the narrow road.

Is that Welsh they're speaking?

I don't recognize it at all. At a guess, I'd say they have some special twin language.

Once we were all back on the motorway and everything outside the windows a blur, my phone buzzed. Godfrey. I was pretty sure Alec had fallen asleep, so I didn't want to be too loud.

"Hello," I whispered.

"Why are we whispering," Godfrey whispered back.

"Because I think Alec is sleeping."

"He is," George said, his voice low and soothing.

"Now will you tell us why you don't have a big hole through your stomach?" Godfrey took his cue from George and matched his tone.

"Ah. It's just a theory, but I think the sword is mine now."

"Well, obviously," Godfrey snarked.

"No, I mean with ancient weapons, especially fae ones, there's an inherent magic. I think because I bested the king with his own weapon, the sword changed its alliance. When I sent the king back to Faerie, the sword stayed here. The same thing happened with the axe. The dwarf threw it at me. I caught it and sent it back, killing him. He disappeared but the axe remained. And in Stow-on-the-Wold, I stole the axe and killed the dwarf with it before he could behead Russell—"

"Thank you for that," Russell said.

"You betcha. It's a working theory, but I don't think it's just about killing the fae—or really, sending them back to Faerie. I think it has to do with gaining control of their weapon and then using it against them." Shrugging, I added, "Not sure, though." Like Alec, Fergus was settling in for a nap.

"I was hoping you'd killed the king," Godfrey said.

I thought about it a moment. "I'm not sure he can die, at least not at the hands of any of us in this realm. The queen could probably do it in Faerie." I stroked my fingers up and down Fergus' back and he gave a great sigh. "I think I just gave the king a big ouchie that forced him to go home to heal."

"If that's the case, what stopped him from returning to the fight?" Russell asked.

Fergus' warm puppy breath on my leg comforted me, helping to dislodge the tightness in my throat every time my thoughts turned back to the dungeon and its inhabitants. "Not positive, but I did tell his wife on him."

Godfrey chuckled. Clive turned his head briefly, eyebrows raised.

"I spoke into the ring. I think she can hear me when I do. That was how I told her we were getting married. Ten minutes later, I walked into the Palace of Fine Arts and the queen was standing with the rest of the guests." Cringing a little, I added, "I whispered into the ring that she should listen before the king and I traded barbs. If she was, she heard everything I accused him of, and she heard him fail to deny any of it. So, if anyone could keep him from returning to the fight, it'd be her."

"Niiice," Godfrey drew out. "Here's hoping she keeps him on her side in the doghouse for a few millennia."

"One can hope," I agreed.

"My lady," Russell began, his voice sharing none of the humor of Godfrey's. "I saw his face before he disappeared. You have a very powerful enemy."

"Oh, I'm aware." I breathed a little easier when Clive squeezed my knee. Right. We were in this together.

"So, if that's the case with the sword, why didn't it change allegiance to Aldith?" Godfrey asked.

I shrugged, not that he'd see. "My only guess is that a fae sword would never serve a vampire. It burned her hand when she touched it."

"Whereas it showed its loyalty to you by not killing you when she used your own sword against you," Clive put in. "Fae things respond strangely to Sam. Let's just all be grateful that the sword likes her."

"Heartbeat ahead," Godfrey said. We heard the engine quiet as Russell slowed down. A minute later, it revved back up again. "Just some man who pulled over to sleep. You're clear, Sire."

It wasn't long before we overtook them. A truck was no match for German engineering. When we flew past, Russell and Godfrey briefly bowed their heads.

"Will they make it?" Again, I knew they'd been doing this all their undead lives, but I worried they'd be caught by the sun.

"Doubtful. I'm not sure *we'll* make it. I'll take you as far as I can before I find cover." Clive patted my hand. *I'll be fine, darling. Just don't go anywhere until I wake.*

No worries. I'm so tired, I'll be sleeping all day too. In the cavern, though, where I can lock that big steel door and let my guard down.

After a while, I got used to the speed and began to nod off.

"What have you heard?" Garyn, a woman who appears to be in her late forties, with light brown hair to her shoulders, sits in a cozy room, her cardigan buttoned to her neck. Pictures of family fill the walls as flames flicker in the fireplace.

A man stands at the door, hands clasped before him. "The protections around the house are gone. The tower has fallen. The dungeon is empty."

"Good. I love my child, but she was an experiment gone wrong. I knew it at the time but was lonely and hopeful." She takes a sip of tea. "And Clive? What of him?"

"Joshua was outside, keeping watch. He can't speak to what happened at the house, but he said Clive, his wife, Russell, Godfrey, and a large man carrying what had to be a rescued prisoner all made it out and away."

She hums quietly, staring into her teacup. "He would have done better to stay with me longer. I could have taught him more, but he's done well enough on his own, I suppose."

"Yes, ma'am."

"And has he really married a werewolf?"

The man nods. "All our information says yes. They were married in San Francisco. Russell performed the blood ceremony. They both wear rings."

"Rings?" She smiles, but it isn't quite right. "That's a lovely tradition. Perhaps I should visit soon." Her eyes went vamp black. "I've missed my boy so much."

I jolted awake when the car stopped on a dime and Clive's door flew open. Blinking, I looked around at the forested area outside the car, unsure of where we were.

"We're almost there," George said from the back seat. "The keep's just ahead at the hill's crest."

"Oh, got it." I slid across the console, pulled the driver's door closed, and drove a few minutes more, parking on the snowy hillock where we had before.

George opened the back door, gathered his twin in his arms, and stepped out. Alec stirred, blinking. When he realized where he was, the tears came almost immediately. George threw back his head and roared. The trees shook as birds took flight. Carrying his brother up the path to the gatehouse, George began murmuring in that strange language again. Alec nodded.

I heard the great double doors open, the shouts and cries, the sobbing and questions, but I left them to it. Alec had finally been returned to his family. They didn't need an outsider observing, making everyone uncomfortable.

Instead, I filled Fergus' food and water bowls, letting him scarf up his kibble and then go sniffing around for a potty spot. I stuffed the chess set into my overnight bag, wanting to study it later. A coat was jammed into the back corner. It was oversized and thick, probably George's. I pulled it on, remembering how cold the cave was.

Once Fergus came trotting back, I packed what I figured we'd need for a day of rest. Locking the car, I headed toward the folly. If the door was down, I knew the combo to open it.

Searching my mind for Clive, I found him already in the folly. Perfect. Russell and Godfrey were farther away and resting. Thank goodness we hadn't handed off Fergus to them. What would they have done with him while they were out all day?

I found the folly without too much trouble. Fergus wasn't sure about it, though. He sniffed like mad, occasionally barking and growling. "We're okay, dude. I already took those two out." Finding the control panel, I lowered the thick, metal door and hit a light button. Thankfully, instead of floodlights ruining the pirate treasure feel in here, the walls and ceilings glowed with what looked like inset gems. It was still dim and shadowy, but detail popped into relief.

Fergus wanted to investigate, but I wanted to sleep. *Huh.* Clive wasn't in the little cavern we'd used last time. Smiling, I realized I felt him in the sunny castle cave. I was just trying to figure out how to climb up the walls with Fergus when I realized I was feeling a different signature as well.

Closing my eyes, I sought out anyone locked in here with us. Spring green over black. Fae. Not with me. With Clive, who was defenseless in the day. *Clive! Wake up! Fae assassin nearby.* I picked up Fergus, stuffed him in the deep pocket of the coat I'd found in the trunk. He didn't fit well, but it was the best I could do.

"Shh, stay." I couldn't leave him in the pirate cavern. His barks would warn the elf. Climbing the wall faster than I'd thought possible, I ignored my fear of heights, never looking down, only up. I couldn't let anything happen to Clive. I almost slipped multiple times and Fergus got bounced against the wall too often, but he remained silent, seeming to understand the urgency.

In no time, I was climbing over the edge through the vines and then running down the short passage. An elf was sneaking up on Clive, his sword drawn. I didn't think, didn't stop to weigh my options. Dropping the coat and Fergus to the floor, I breathed, "Please," as I yanked the axe out of the sheath on my back and heaved with all my might, sending it flying, end over end, toward the warrior.

I must have made a noise, or perhaps Fergus did. Whatever the reason, the elf stopped, lifting his head and locking eyes with me a split second before the axe buried itself in his chest and he popped out of existence in this realm.

Knees weak, I dropped to the passage floor, my racing heart pounding through my whole body. All I could hear was it reverberating off the walls. So close. If I'd done anything different... If I'd gone in the keep with George and Alec. If I'd looked for food for myself before heading to the cavern. If I'd snuggled up with Fergus to get some sleep, I'd have been too late. Clive would have been handed his final death.

Fergus crawled into my lap and licked my chin.

"I'm okay." I hugged him to me, unable to stop the trembling. That was too close.

Movement out of the corner of my eye made me jump. Clive heaved himself over the lip of the passage, my axe in one hand.

"Why is your heart racing and why was your axe lying in the grass beside me?"

Grabbing the front of his sweater, I pulled him toward me, tumbling him onto the tunnel floor with Fergus and myself. I couldn't think. I was kissing him and kissing him and kissing him. I hugged him so hard, it was good he didn't need to breathe.

"How are you awake? How did you climb the side of a cavern during the day?"

He held me tight, chuckling when Fergus jumped up, trying to wiggle between us. "I can't say that I know. I have a feeling, though, that it has something to do with this fae ring on my finger. I've been more restless during the day since we married."

He shook his head, relaxing back and holding me close. "I'd thought it was fear for you keeping me more aware than normal during the day. If this thing is returning my mortality to me, the queen and I are having words."

"It was super handy just now, so let's hold off on cussing out the queen."

"Even now, the sun is pulling me under, but there's a restlessness in me trying to keep me awake." He sighed, eyes closing.

"Sleep now, love. I've got us covered. And I've got Fergus as backup. Sleep. Hopefully, we can go home soon." Who would have thought I'd ever long for the nocturne? Right now, though, I'd have given anything for a hot shower, a huge meal—my stomach rumbled in agreement—and our soft bed. Even a house filled with pissy vampires couldn't spoil my anticipation for home.

THIRTY-EIGHT

Who Knew Dragons Ate Crow

Slipping the big, heavy coat back on, I lay down beside Clive. He slept with his head turned toward the sun. Before we left, we were getting the names and contact info of the team who created this folly. I knew Clive was looking for post-Master of the City homes for us, but I'd been thinking—in between bad guy attacks—this was what I wanted. A normal house would, I'm sure, be lovely, but we weren't normal.

There were huge drops on either end of the tunnel between the dragon play spaces. I was afraid that Fergus would go off to investigate and fall while we slept, so I cradled him between us. If he moved, I'd wake up.

Later—no idea how long—he scrambled up and hopped over Clive, running toward the pirate room. "Fergus, no!"

"Sorry, Sam," George said. "It's just me. Is it okay to come in?"

I laughed at that. "It's a tunnel in *your* folly. Of course you can come in."

He stepped through the vines into the tall passage. "I brought food and it occurred to me I never told you where the toilets were."

I sat up straight, my bladder painfully full. "There are bathrooms in here?"

Waving me to him, he scooped up Fergus and then looked me up and down, grinning. "And I see you found my coat, although it might be a little big on you."

I wrapped my arms around his waist and closed my eyes. I knew he was planning to jump down to the floor of the pirate cave. I wanted a restroom and food pronto, but I didn't want to watch us plummet.

He held on tightly to Fergus and me and then leapt straight out.

Burying my head in his chest, I tried to ignore the light-headed stomach swoop of gravity working overtime and said, "I bet this is what Owen looks like when he tries to wear your clothes."

We landed with a jolt. "Pretty much. Some couples can share clothes and end up with double the wardrobe. We are not such a couple." He walked us back to the cave entrance. In the stone wall opposite the control panel was now an open door to a washroom. When I ran for the door, he said, "I'll take this guy out to do his business."

"Watch out for random fae!" I shouted, slamming the door.

Afterward, I wandered out and found George throwing a stick for Fergus. Grateful for the heavy coat, I brushed snow off a fallen tree and sat to watch. San Francisco sometimes got foggy too, but it had nothing on Wales. Fortunately, this was completely normal fog, not fae-spelled super fog.

"Would you like me to get Clive?" George had thrown a normal-sized stick for Fergus, but the pup had returned dragging an entire tree branch. Laughing, George took the limb, snapped off a branch, and denuded it, thereby creating a new stick. Fergus watched with rapt attention. When George threw it in the opposite direction, he went to retrieve the new magic stick that smelled like dragon.

"No thanks. Let him sleep in the sunlight."

Nodding, he pointed to the cave entrance. "Food's inside. And what did you mean about random fae?"

When we walked in, Fergus trailing with his stick, I locked the entrance. George looked confused but didn't say anything. Sitting on the ground by the waterfall, I pulled a big, meaty sandwich out of a paper bag. "Oh, bless you!"

In between bites, I explained about the elf lying in wait for us. George looked ready to breathe fire.

"That's twice they've used dragon property to attack friends of the clan. In the short term, we can keep the door closed and locked, but long term, this is a play space for children. We can't have assassins coming and going whenever they feel like it."

Fergus climbed into his lap, and he tried to shake off the anger. "Are there any in here now? The door was open while Fergus and I were outside."

Closing my eyes, I sought out any supernaturals in the vicinity. One vamp, one dragon, one me. "Nope, just us."

Nodding, he looked up. "Oh, good. You found the lights. I'll let Grandmother know about the fae," he said, stretching out his legs. "She'll probably station a few of our members in here to burn first and ask questions later. If they know coming here is a death sentence, perhaps they'll stop coming."

"Good call. So, we're hopefully heading home soon. Are you planning to stay here for a while, or do you want a lift?" The sandwich was delicious and gone far too soon.

"The clan doctor came while you guys were sleeping." He paused, staring at the waterfall. "I don't know how Alec survived," he said quietly. "There were days I didn't think about him. Not many, but whole days went by when I didn't think about my missing twin."

"Twenty years, George. After a while, the mind tries to protect itself."

"I was living my life, going to school, learning to drive, first boyfriend, college, and then more college, a career I love, working with animals, and the whole time, he was locked in a cold, dark cell, starving, being tortured. I went whole days without even thinking about him." He closed his eyes and dropped back onto the cave floor.

286

Fergus crawled up, resting his head on George's chest.

Wrapping my hand around his ankle, I said, "He loves you. You may feel guilty you didn't share the same fate, but I can guarantee he doesn't feel the same way. I saw the way he looked at you, George. I'm sure there were moments he wished for death, for an end to the pain, but he held on all those years because he's a fighter. Twenty years in, he spat in her face and laughed.

"This isn't going to be easy for him," I continued. "The physical recovery will be hard, but he'll get through it. He's strong. The emotional and psychological recovery will be more difficult and likely take far longer. Through it all, though, he'll need you. There will be times he'll be angry and frustrated and lost, and he'll lash out at you. But that's when it's your turn to be strong for him, to take anything he says on the chin and continue to help him come fully back."

Eyes still closed, George nodded. Fergus scooted up farther, resting his head against George's neck. *Good boy*.

"It's going to feel weird and lonely, like the world passed him by. The rest of you have shared memories he doesn't. Think about what you understood of the world at eight. That's where he is right now. He understands horrible, cruel things you never will because he lived them, but in terms of rejoining the world and his life, he's at a serious disadvantage."

George sat up, expression thoughtful. "So what do I do?"

I shrugged. I'd lived through some of this, but it wasn't like I was a trauma expert. "Start slow. Get him healthy first. Share the stuff you both loved with him again. Watch football and rugby matches together. Give him some new info, a little at a time. Don't overload him with everything you can think of all at once. It's a hard balance, informing an adult of basic things without making him feel stupid."

He nodded, listening.

"Take him to the zoo. I bet he'd get a kick out of seeing what you do, being able to go behind the scenes with you, meet bears and tigers." I smiled, thinking of Alec going from a cold, dark hole to wresting with bears. "Introduce him to Owen. That's going to be a trip for him, unless you'd already discussed your interest in boys at eight."

A grin tugged at George's mouth. "I'd started thinking about it, but I hadn't told anyone." He nodded again. "Owen will help. Maybe we should have him live with us. We're buying a huge house. There's plenty of room."

"Ask. Let him decide. He's been able to make very few decisions for himself. Whatever decision he makes, you accept and are happy that he was able to make it for himself."

"Right."

"So, staying or a lift?" I really wished there was a second sandwich in the bag. It had been a while since I'd had a decent amount of food and my jeans were getting too loose.

"Oh, sorry." He rubbed Fergus and then set him down to explore. "We have the family plane. Thanks for the offer, though. I'll stay until he's ready to travel and then we'll all be flying home together. Mom and Dad haven't been home in twenty years. It's going to be a big transition for everyone."

"As soon as we get back to San Francisco, we can put Owen on the plane and fly him here to keep you company while Alec gets stronger." I felt so guilty that Owen was holding down my fort while his boyfriend needed him.

"We talked about that today, but he's worried about changing the focus from Alec returning home to who's this guy that George is moving in with? Well"—he thumped his knee—"he's probably right. Alec should be ready to fly in a couple of days, a week at the mos—"

"That soon? Really?" He couldn't stand on his own. How were they going to get him ready to fly in a couple of days?

"We heal quickly. The doctor's got him on a couple of IVs, giving him much needed nutrition and medication. He's already looking better. If you wouldn't mind, he'd like to talk to you before you guys leave."

"All of us or just me?" Alec had been in a speeding car with

Clive, but he'd slept most of the time. I wasn't sure if he was ready to deal with vamps again.

"All of you. Oddly enough, he doesn't have the same hatred of vampires that my parents do." He tilted his head, considering. "Or if he does, it doesn't extend to Clive, Russell, and Godfrey. You helped him escape and kill Aldith. You're rock stars."

I felt it when Clive awoke, so his shoes hitting the cave didn't startle me. It did, however, make George flinch. That was Clive being polite. I knew he could do that silently. He was giving George a heads-up that he was there.

"I've tried many different careers in my long life. Alas, rock star wasn't one of them." He stood directly behind me. "How is my thankfully still two-armed wife this evening?"

I leaned against his legs and stared up at him. "Better now."

Bending down, he gave me a kiss. "Oh, good. You've eaten." I smacked his leg and he pulled me up.

"Alec would like to talk with us before we go."

"I heard." He turned to George, who had risen as well. "Thank you for feeding my wife, and we'd be honored to meet with your brother. My men are waking. They're about ten miles away. They should be here shortly."

"You should feed too." Their high-tech blood cooler was in the trunk of the rental. I wanted all of them fed before they entered the keep. Being thirsty made for bad tempers and I was pretty sure George's parents were going to be pushing buttons. "When do we head to the airport?"

"Yes, I wanted to talk with you about that," Clive began.

George whistled for Fergus. Clive grabbed my bag and we headed for the entrance.

"The timing is very close. It takes about twelve hours to get home, with a refueling in New Jersey. Which means we need to take off very shortly after sundown in order to get home before sunrise. In the winter, this is possible, but everything has to go like clockwork. If we miss it, our plane will be sitting in the hangar all day, passengers inside. It's suspicious and we don't need authorities called to investigate."

George closed and locked the door as Fergus ran back and forth between us, sniffing his surroundings like mad.

"I thought," Clive continued, "that we could drive down to London and spend the night sightseeing. We can fly out the following evening at sunset."

"Can I get cleaned up in the hotel before we go anywhere?" I couldn't remember the last time I'd showered and I felt particularly gross, especially as I spent all my time with people who had super-sensitive noses. The look on George's face made me wonder if I was already ripe. "What is it?"

"Oh, just something Owen said. Maybe don't take too long getting home. Apparently, there's something up with Dave. He's been acting strange and missing work after a demon came in looking for him. Owen and Audrey have been covering, but Audrey doesn't arrive until after sundown. Owen's been working every day, opening to closing. By the way, he said the fact you did this schedule for seven years is ridiculous and you need to hire more help."

"He's right. We do need another person, two if Audrey's done with bartending. I'll text him on the drive to London. I don't want to wake him. He can take time off as soon as I get back."

I kicked the car tire while Clive opened the trunk. "Meanwhile, what's going on with Dave? We've never had demons in the bar." The thought scared the shit out of me. My wards couldn't stop them and the last time I'd seen one, he'd made it quite clear how easy I was to overpower and manipulate. I wasn't sure I was up to trouble with demons.

Russell and Godfrey drove up as Clive took out three blood bags.

"Good evening, Sire, Missus, George." Godfrey waved off the bag. "As much as we enjoy cold blood, we've eaten."

Clive nodded, tossing two bags back in the cooler and locking it. He stepped away to drink. If it had just been us, he would have stayed. George, though a friend, was an outsider, so Clive gave us his back as he walked toward the trees to go vampy and drink his blood.

"Where did you guys spend the day?" They didn't look dirty, so digging underground seemed out.

"Castle ruins. Far off the beaten path," Godfrey said. "We found a nice, lightless storage spot under a floor." He grinned at my horrified expression. "Cozy."

"How are you guys not covered in cobwebs and dirt and rat droppings?" I cringed at the thought.

With a flick of his eyes toward George, he said, "This isn't our first rodeo, Missus. We know how to protect ourselves."

"We do," Clive agreed as he returned, dropping the empty bag into a special spot in the trunk. He patted my back, letting me know he'd explain later. They didn't discuss vampire stuff with outsiders.

"Sire, are we ready to go?" Russell asked.

Shaking his head, Clive gestured to the keep. "Alec would like to speak with us before we depart."

"I see." Russell didn't appear any happier about this than Clive did.

It wasn't that anyone had anything against Alec. None of us, however, had any desire to spend time with Griffin and Smoke, who were no doubt by their son's bed. The men were ancient, proud, and not used to allowing insults to go unanswered.

Clive slammed the trunk, took my hand, and led the way to the keep. Given the silent, hard expressions of my guys, I kept quiet too. None of them were in the mood to chat. They wanted this over.

When we approached the door, it was opened by Benvair. "Thank you all for putting aside your anger with us to see my grandson."

With a curt nod, Clive strode past her into the dining hall, stopping short when he saw Alec sitting in a chair by the fire. "It's good to see you up. We'd assumed you'd be abed."

He had IVs in an arm, but he looked remarkably better. It had been less than twenty-four hours. How was that possible? His skin had, thankfully, lost the gray cast. Still painfully underweight, he now bore a strong resemblance to George and Griffin.

"I see you got a shave and a haircut, mate," Godfrey said.

Alec nodded and smiled. "Grandmother insisted." He took a mug that smelled like tea from his mother and sipped. Setting the cup aside, he said, "Thank you. You didn't have to rescue a stray dragon, but you did. I can never pay you back—"

"That isn't necessary," Clive broke in.

"*But,*" Alec drew out, "if you ever have need of a skinny dragon, who may or may not still be able to shift, my claws and fire are yours."

His father Griffin opened his mouth to protest, but Alec gave him a look that shut him up. Yep. This one was a fighter with a spine of steel.

"I'm told," Benvair began, "that you have an interest in the team who created our folly."

"Yes!" I jumped in.

"They would normally never work for vampires." She gave her daughter-in-law a steely glare when it looked like she was going to agree with that policy. Smoke deflated, averting her eyes.

"How about werewolves or wicches?" I asked.

"I will contact them and let them know that I would consider it a personal favor if they were to take the job." Benvair stood stiffly, obviously still put out by the way Clive had dressed her down the last time we were here but swamped with gratitude to have her grandson returned to the clan.

Alec cleared his throat. "Wasn't there something else, Grandmother?"

Blinking twice in rapid succession, she added, "And we will, of course, pay for the work. We are forever indebted to you, and this is the least we can do."

Alec and George wore identical grins. Griffin looked sick,

Smoke chastened, and Benvair resolved. Whether they wanted to or not, we had dragons backing us up now.

"We accept your generous offer and are looking forward to meeting with the team. Alec, it's good to see you up and about. We wish you well on your continued recovery. I know your family has thought of little besides you these past twenty years."

Smoke's scowl disappeared at Clive's words.

"When you're ready," I added, "your brother can bring you to The Slaughtered Lamb. I'd be honored to serve you your first adult beverage."

Alec's laugh ended on a wheeze.

"Since Alec isn't sure what he likes," George said, resting his hands on his twin's too-thin shoulders, "we can do tastings."

"We can also find you some books you might want to read," I said, leaning in and squeezing his forearm. "Consider us your extended family."

Nodding, he said, "I will."

"Okay, we should let them hit the road," George said. "They're headed to London tonight."

"We are," Clive said. "Our door is always open, Alec. We wish you a speedy recovery." Clive nodded to all assembled and took my hand, Russell and Godfrey leading the way out.

"Thank you."

We paused and turned to the speaker. Griffin and Smoke stood shoulder to shoulder, both looking like it was killing them to speak but doing it nonetheless. "Thank you for our son," Griffin repeated. Smoke nodded, tears streaming down her face.

Clive squeezed my fingers, prompting me to respond. I think he knew they'd rather deal with a vampire's whore than the vampire himself.

"You're welcome. You searched for him every day for twenty years. It wasn't your fault you didn't possess the gifts to break through the spells. The people working together to hold Alec, and many others like him, were counting on that. But," I added, not wanting to let them completely off the hook, "it probably doesn't make sense to bite the hand offering help."

Smoke nodded, wiping her face.

———

WE ENDED UP STOPPING IN CARDIFF TO EXCHANGE THE TWO VEHICLES for an SUV. Once we were all together again, Russell and Godfrey in the front seats, Clive and me in the third row, with the second under the floors and Fergus once more lounging in his bed, we were able to talk freely.

"One of the reasons I've stayed with you so long, Clive," Russell began, "is that given the choice between kindness and cruelty, you choose kindness. They'd been horribly rude to us, to your wife, but you both made sure their son knew they'd never stopped looking for him. You didn't do it for them. You did it for him. He may have suffered unspeakably for two decades, but he can hold close, in the dark times that will surely follow this, that he was always loved and never forgotten."

I squeezed Clive's hand.

"Thank you, my friend. I know that I'm leaving the city and the nocturne in right hands. You have the strength, the intelligence, and the integrity to lead and have legions follow."

Russell inclined his head at Clive's words, his eyes never wavering from the road.

"Mind, I'll still be around if you need me, as my wife owns a business in our fair city, but it looks like I'll be learning how to mix drinks. I hear she needs to hire more help."

———

Keep Reading for
ALL I WANT FOR CHRISTMAS IS A DRAGON
A story in the world of Sam Quinn

This holiday short story featuring Owen and George was offered free to my newsletter subscribers last December. The plot intersects with The Hob & Hound Pub. If you'd like to sign up for my newsletter **Tales from the Book Nerd**, you'll get behind the scenes info, book recommendations, deleted scenes, and the occasional short story.

All I Want for Christmas is a Dragon

Prologue

...BUT FIRST A WORD FROM STHENO

So, what do you need to know before you read Owen and George's story? Hmm, that's a puzzler. A lot of shit has gone down, only some of which I was here for. I guess I'll start with the basics. I'm Stheno, one of three gorgon sisters and friend to anyone willing to pour me a drink.

Pull up a barstool and slide me that bowl of nuts, would you? If you're new around here, stick with me for a few minutes and I'll fill you in on what you need to know. If not, proceed at your own risk, for here there be dragons.

Sam Quinn is the werewolf book nerd who owns The Slaughtered Lamb Bookstore & Bar. She's away, though, so I've put on a greeter's vest. I don't work here. I just like to hang out, watch the ocean crash against the window wall in the bar, and drink. It's a good life.

Clive, her new husband, is the vampire Master of the City. He's an ancient bastard, who I wouldn't trust as far as I could throw, but Sam loves him. I tried to talk her out of it, but what are you going to do? To his credit, there doesn't seem to be anything he wouldn't do for her. He even hired a gorgon—me—to guard her when they went to New Orleans to brawl with bloodsuckers. I liked the kid—in spite of getting blinded on that gig—so I visit.

Owen Wong, the guy who's going to be telling this story, is a wicche,

AKA a magical person. He comes from a long line of wicches and is Sam's best friend. George Drake, his boyfriend, is a dragon shifter and a large exotics veterinarian at the San Francisco Zoo.

What else, what else? Dave, a half-demon cook, works at The Slaughtered Lamb. He's a grumpy bastard and sexy as hell. All fiery temper, hard stares, and bulging muscles. *fans self* Unfortunately, he's also taken. Too bad. I wouldn't mind...

Anyway, the newest employee is Audrey. She's one of Clive's vampires and was a lady's maid in life. Her employer was a batshit crazy bloodsucker who didn't want to lose good help and so turned Audrey into a bloodsucker too. Batshit is now dust, so Audrey is trying to live her best undeath.

Anything else? I don't know. I'm already bored with this conversation. Just read the story. Owen will fill you in. Wait. Can you top off my drink first? Oh, and merry, happy, feliz, whatever the fuck. This time of year, I celebrate Dionysis. My case of wine and I wish you well. Now, scram.

ONE

Pizzlies, You Say?

Life rarely follows the path we imagine. All those seemingly inconsequential decisions we make every day nudge the trajectory of our lives this way and that. Every time we say yes to one possibility, we say no, or not right now, to countless others. Really, it's all about choices. Like, do I ask my boyfriend to move in with me?

Everyone thought I'd follow my family's path, that I'd be a healer. My sisters did. They were all about checking the list twice. Me, I was more interested in connecting with people, learning about their lives, listening to their stories. With George, though, I felt like some latent, familial push for success was emerging. I'd been budget planning, researching apartments centrally located to both our jobs, even thinking about how our furniture might blend. It was kind of wigging me out, actually. I didn't even know if George was on the same page as me. What if this was all in my head and he was just having fun dating a wicche?

For instance, this was the kind of seat-of-my-pants decision-making I normally did. When I was twenty, I headed downtown to a little independent bookshop I liked. I was already on my way when I remembered my mom saying a werewolf had opened a bookstore and bar in the Lands End area. I changed direction and drove toward the water. Little choices.

The Slaughtered Lamb was mostly empty, but it was staggering. I must have stood, looking out the window wall, watching the kelp bob, the fish swim by, the waves crash for a good five minutes.

"Can I help you, sir?"

Sir? Me? I turned to find a girl a few years younger than me, eyes huge with fear, standing stiff and wary. Scars snaked out of the neck and cuffs of her long-sleeved shirt.

"I'm just book shopping," I'd said and some of the stiffness went away.

"The bookstore is right through that arch. If you're looking for a particular book, though, I can find it for you."

I'd nodded my thanks and went browsing. There was a counter in the bookstore, but no one was behind it. In fact, I hadn't seen anyone else working here but that one poor girl. When I went back into the bar with a stack of books and a rare grimoire in my arms, there was a dwarf sitting on the last stool, a tankard in front of him. A few wicches were sitting at tables by the window and the girl was behind the bar, dropping a teabag into a cup of steaming water. Oh, honey, no. Not a teabag.

She needed help. I could feel the need the moment I saw her, but I also felt the wall she'd put up. She delivered the cup, picked up a few empties, ran them into a back room, and then returned a couple of minutes later carrying a heavy crate of beer bottles as though it was nothing. Wait. *This* was the werewolf?

Relaxing my focus, I took a peek at her aura. Instead of the usual dark furry snarl I'd been expecting—we think duality of human and wolf messes with auras—it was a bright, shiny gold. So bright, in fact, it made me wince. Angry, livid claw marks left ragged tears and the telltale furry blurring was barely visible around the edges. Odd.

Decision made. She needed a friend so desperately, I felt the clutch in my chest. Sitting at the bar, I set my stack of books aside, and waited until she was done stocking the fridge under the counter.

"Hi," I said when she looked up. "I'm Owen Wong. It looks like you're the only one around." At the sudden look of panic, I knew I'd phrased that wrong. "I mean, it looks like you could use some help. I've worked in a bookshop before and I know how to properly brew tea—from leaves, I mean. You should know, wicches love their teas and they expect the good stuff."

The crone by the window cleared her throat and nodded.

Face going red, the girl stood, gripping the edge of the bar. "Oh. Sorry," she called to the wicche. "I'll fix that."

"That's what I'm saying. I can fix it for you. I can tell you what to order and teach you how to brew. I'm in school but can work part-time if you want the help." I lowered my voice. "And I really think you need the help."

I could have just bought the books and left, happy to have found a new indie bookstore in the city, but instead I changed the trajectory of my life by asking for a job. So, here I was, years later, managing the place while Sam was gallivanting around Europe with her new husband Clive. I'd met and become friends with the most interesting people—ones I never would have crossed paths with in my normal life—while doing a job I loved. I would have missed out on all of this if I'd made a different choice that day, if I'd stuck with my plan to go downtown.

When I graduated from college, I think my parents were waiting for me to announce my desire to be a doctor like my sister Blythe or a physical therapist like my other sister Lilah. Sorry to disappoint, but no.

My family has had strong healers for generations, but the talent seemed to have skipped me. I could help in a pinch, but not like the rest of the family. My mom Lydia said I was a jack-of-all-trades, which was the mom equivalent of a participation trophy. Hopefully, someday I'd discover a special talent.

That spur-of-the-moment decision served me well, though. I loved working at The Slaughtered Lamb. It had been quiet for years and then all hell broke loose about four months ago when Sam started getting attacked on the daily. That was also around the time my niece had dragged me to the San Francisco Zoo. Choices. I could have said no, could have redirected to the park or a movie, but I said yes and met a dreamy veterinarian I've since fallen hard for.

He was everything I never knew I wanted but absolutely needed. I wanted us to find a place we could share every day, not just a few days a week. But what if I was just his walk on the tame side? From everything I've heard, dragons mated for life—with other dragons. It could have been our messed-up schedules or work or whatever, but he'd been different lately, silent and distant. It had me worried.

Speaking of my guy, heavy steps sounded on the stairs. I'd know that sound anywhere. A moment later, George emerged from the stairway, boots, muscular legs in jeans worn tight in all the right places, a narrow waist, a chest and arms carved by gods, and then my favorite, a smile that lit up the room when he saw me, dark, warm eyes that softened when I smiled back. Damn, I had it bad.

George strode straight to me, leaned across the bar, and kissed me. The snap of it made me want to crawl across the bar and into his arms. I was working, though, and this being a nice establishment, live sex shows were frowned upon.

"I missed you today," he murmured against my lips. Glancing down, he took in today's ugly Christmas sweater. I had one for each day leading up to my showstopper of ugly sweaters that I saved for Christmas Day. "This one is definitely worse than yesterday's. Why is there so much orange?"

"It's a mystery and I missed you too." I kissed him back, turning to mush. I'd had boyfriends before, quite a few actually, which was how I knew George was it for me. I pushed aside my worries for the moment. I was in love and my man had missed me.

"Don't go anywhere," I said as I went to deliver a black and tan to Horus, who may or may not have been the Egyptian sky god. We didn't like to pry.

The Slaughtered Lamb was done up in holiday finery. We had Christmas lights everywhere, running down the stairs, along the edges of the bar, inside the arch to the bookstore, draped garland-style around the cash wrap. I used frosty glass spray around the edges of the huge, aquarium-grade window wall that held back the ocean. At low tide, the water splashed a few feet above the barroom floor. At high tide, the water line was well above our heads.

It was festive as hell around here. We had a tree in the corner, a menorah on the bar, the seven candles for Kwanzaa on the book-store counter, strings of dried fruits and evergreens hanging from the ceiling in a nod to an assortment of pagan winter festivities. Sam had put together a book display of holiday traditions from around the world. She didn't want anyone feeling left out or unseen.

With Sam gone, though, Dave and I were working extra hours, meaning George and I were struggling to spend time together. Our schedules right now sucked, him starting not long after daybreak and me often working into the wee hours of the morning. We tried calling and texting during the day, when we were both awake at the same time, but George often didn't pick up or reply until hours later, his job keeping him busy. Hopefully, it was that and not me bugging the crap out of him. It was so frustrating. We were right here but still missing each other.

Even with all the extra hours, we needed more help. Audrey, one of Clive's vampires, volunteered to bartend, and she was doing far better than any of us had guessed. She took to it easily, lacking the arrogance and barely suppressed violence most of the vampires possessed.

When the sun went down, Audrey arrived, ready to work. "Good eve, Owen. Good eve, George," she said, tying an apron around her waist. Unlike most black-clad vampires, Audrey was having fun wearing colorful modern clothes of her own choosing. After being under that vampire Leticia's control for two hundred and fifty years, she was exploring what *she* liked. Today she was wearing a pair of light-washed jeans with embroidered vines and poinsettia blooms crawling up the legs, paired with a crimson blouse. Her long blonde hair was tied up in an intricate style I couldn't begin to name.

"Good eve, Audrey." I enjoyed Audrey's antiquated phrases. Gesturing to the small bag she carried, I asked, "So, what is it today?"

"Tinsel. Have you seen the likes of this before?"

George and I grinned and nodded.

"They're just tiny strips of reflective material." She opened the box and rubbed a few strands between her fingers. "But then on the tree, they reflect the lights, making the tree sparkle grandly." She shook her head in wonder.

This was her first Christmas since Leticia, the vamp who had turned her, was dust. In life, Audrey hadn't even known such things as vampires existed outside of scary stories. She'd been a lady's maid in London. Her employer decided that good help was hard to find and so transformed Audrey, dictating every moment of her long undead life since. Audrey was finally free and finding joy in the smallest of things, like tinsel.

"Dave is making chili and cornbread tonight."

Her eyes flicked to the menu board by the kitchen door. "Aye, beef chili—that's like a kind of stew, isn't it?" she asked, carefully adding tinsel, strand by strand, to the tree.

George grabbed a handful and tossed it like confetti on the branches, demonstrating another way to trim it. "Sort of, but spicier," he responded. Shrugging one broad shoulder, he added, "I don't cook, but I think it has more of a tomato base with chili peppers and ground beef, beans, and I'm not sure what else. It's great, though."

Audrey tipped her head, examining the two methods of trimming, before continuing the chili conversation. "I can smell it. I'll ask if I can try some later. Once everyone's been fed, of course." She grabbed a handful, as George had done, and tossed it at the tree, grinning. Nodding to George, she left the tinsel on the bar for later and then tucked a towel into the waist of her apron, picked up a tray, and went to collect the empty glasses and cups scattered on tables around the bar.

I never thought I'd be able to work alongside a vampire—they were such pompous pricks—but Audrey was different. She was a hard worker, and one I genuinely liked.

Dave, our half-demon cook, pushed through the swinging kitchen door. He had dark red skin and shark-like, full black eyes that scanned the bar. His gaze paused on the newly festooned tree. He took a handful of tinsel, held it above the tree, and then opened his fingers, letting the sparkles rain down on the branches. That done, he grabbed a tall glass, a bottle of cinnamon schnapps, and filled the glass to the brim. Nodding at George, he returned the near-empty bottle to its usual place behind the bar.

He drank half in one gulp. "How's it going?"

"Good," George said. "I like the t-shirt."

Dave looked down at his nod to the holidays and shrugged. The cartoon front displayed drunken, passed out, vomiting snowmen surrounding a keg. "What's going on with that polar bear you were talking about last week?"

George sighed. "He's miserable. The repetitive behaviors are getting worse. He's bored and penned and losing it. I've tried bringing in things for him to play with, giving him a good wrestle when no one's around, but he's having a hard time."

"I guess releasing him into the wild is out of the question, huh?" Dave grabbed a pint glass and poured George a beer.

"At this point, yeah. We're his third zoo. He's been in captivity too long." George stared down at the bar. "Separated from his family, his home."

"How do you deal with that?" Dave asked. "I'd imagine it

would be tough for a two-natured shifter to put one-natured animals in cages."

George's shoulders tensed, his expression hard. "Do you have any idea how many times I've had to defend what I do to my family?" He scrubbed his hand down his face in frustration.

I stopped what I was doing and reached across the bar, running a hand up and down his flexed arm.

"Not trying to piss you off," Dave said. "Just wondering."

George held up a hand. "Yeah. I know. I just hate this time of year. Short-tempered." He downed his beer in one. "Sorry."

"I didn't know you hated Christmas." Growing up, my sister Lilah and I used to go nuts decorating every inch of the house for the holidays. My apartment currently looked like an annex of the North Pole. No wonder he always wanted me to go to his place. *Damn.* Living together meant no more decorations.

"It's not Christmas, so much as…I don't want to get into it now." He turned back to Dave. "Yes, it bothers me to cage animals, but zoos help engender a love and appreciation of animals, a concern for the endangerment of a species. We need the public to care about the plight of animals. This is the easiest, most accessible way for the average person to see lions and gorillas and giraffes up close, to become as fascinated with them as I am.

"But it isn't even just that. Zoos are places of scientific study and conservation. I want the animals as well cared for as I can make them. I want their habitats as interesting and natural as possible. If I'm there, I can help affect change. If I'm not, I can't. For example, I had an idea about that polar bear," he continued, shaking off the frustration. "It's a little unorthodox, but we have a female grizzly who's just lovely. She doesn't like the boys, who can be aggressive brutes. She's sweet and nurturing. I just love her."

"Rosie," I said, remembering him talking about her.

"That's the one. So, I went in earlier than usual and brought them both out into our work area. There was some initial weirdness, which is only normal, but she was new and interesting. My polar stopped rocking and swinging his head."

308

"George!" I knew how much the polar bear's state of mind was weighing on him.

George nodded, the tension in his shoulders dropping away. "I know. I kept the first meeting short, but they were already starting to interact with each other. Now that I know it's possible, I'll talk with the director about giving them shared time daily."

"Huh," Dave grunted. "Polars and grizzlies get along?"

"In the wild, they never used to come across each other. With climate change, though, their habitats are moving closer and closer together, so they're starting to encounter one another. There are even pizzlies out there to prove it." At our looks of confusion, George elaborated. "Polar-grizzly cubs. Pizzlies."

"That's adorable." I lifted my soda glass. "To pizzlies!"

George grinned. "One step at a time. I'll settle for Baffin and Rosie not mauling each other."

Dave turned to go back to the kitchen but stopped himself. "You hungry?"

George nodded. "Always."

"Coming up," Dave called, pushing through the swinging door.

Audrey returned from loading the dishwasher with the empties. Leaning in and lowering her voice, she said, "I have a question, if it wouldn't inconvenience you." At George's nod, she continued, "Owen's mentioned your other nature. I've heard of… people like yourself in Europe, but not here. I know I miss a lot, as no one's breaking down my door to explain things to me, but doesn't living in a city make it hard, secrecy-wise?"

Dave returned with a huge bowl of fragrant chili and a plate of cornbread.

Audrey took a long sniff. "That does smell hearty."

George offered her a spoonful.

"You wouldn't mind?" After hundreds of years with Leticia, Audrey was still unused to kindness.

"Not at all."

She took the bite and let it settle on her tongue a moment before swallowing. "Mmm, that'll burn the roof off."

"I thought vamps couldn't eat," I said while George dug into his chili.

"We don't need it. Most get sick if they try to eat or drink anything other than blood. Nocturnes normally don't have human food, so it doesn't really come up. Now that we have Mrs. Fitzwilliam with us, the kitchen is stocked, and I've tried some things I remembered enjoying before." She shrugged. "It didn't bother me none."

"You know you can call her Sam, right?" I said.

"I tried once. Felt wrong." Her gaze returned to George, waiting.

"Secrecy can be difficult for dragon clans in densely populated cities. My grandfather was from Wales, but grandmother's clan is in the Okefenokee Swamp in Georgia."

"Okefe—did you just make that up?" Audrey looked as though she wasn't sure if she were being made fun of.

"No, indeed. It's a Choctaw—Native American—word meaning trembling earth. It's a huge wilderness area, hundreds of thousands of acres wide. The vegetation is so dense, humans don't notice what's flying above the canopy."

"What about airplanes or helicopters or I don't know what all else?"

He swallowed a bite of cornbread. "We're very careful. The clans in Alaska and Wyoming have it easier, as great swaths of it are empty of humans."

"What about you in *this* city?" she persisted.

"Well…" George shrugged and took another spoonful of chili.

"Dragons don't willingly share—" I began.

"Anything," George interrupted.

"—where they transform. There's a lot of secrecy surrounding it," I finished.

"Aye." Audrey tapped her finger on the bar. "That's the right way of it. What people don't know, they can't hurt you with."

Nodding, she laid a hand briefly on George's. "Thank you for sharing your secrets with me. I promise to keep them." She went off to start delivering meals.

"Speaking of secret dragon things," George whispered. "I need to talk to you about something later."

My phone, with that heavily used real estate app, felt heavy in my pocket the rest of the shift.

TWO

Never Come Between a Dragon and his Treasure

D ave took off at closing to meet his banshee girlfriend Maggie at an after-hours club. George normally didn't stay until closing. He started work at the zoo hours before it opened to the public. I still slept in my own apartment a few nights a week, but more and more lately, I went to George's instead, which seemed to make us both happy. This whole after-work talk George wanted to have, though, was putting angry, buzzing bees in my stomach. Late-night, we-need-to-talk conversations were rarely good.

He'd once told me that dragons needed to keep their treasures nearby. They needed to see them, touch and smell them, in order to calm, to stop mentally pacing. I'd never seen any obvious treasure around his apartment, although I supposed the jewelry store below his apartment was a family treasure.

Anyway, one night, I crept into his bedroom, not wanting to wake him—he was a horribly light sleeper. I was sliding into bed as gently as possible when George's arm snaked around my middle. He pulled me in close, curling protectively around me. Sighing deeply, he murmured something about his treasure before finally sinking under. I kept thinking about that moment in an attempt to quiet the bees.

Tonight, George was awake late and flipping over chairs so they hung off the edges of the tables while Audrey began to mop. When I returned from dealing with dishes in the kitchen, George had moved over to close down the bookstore. He'd watched me do it a few times and had an excellent memory for anything money-related. He checked the cash drawer, ran the totals detailing cash and credit charges, and did the math. Thankfully, it balanced.

He handed me the cash bag and slips and I took them to Dave's desk in the kitchen, as Dave was in charge of the banking. I went back to the bookstore, looking for my guy, and found him shelving stray books. Best boyfriend ever. While he finished up, I went to clean out the espresso machine. Finally done, I found him empty-handed and staring out the window, arms folded across his chest.

I often noticed him staring out the window at the crashing waves, the fog creeping across the water. And too often, like right now, he looked lost and sad. I'd asked what was wrong, of course, but he'd blinked, expression clearing, saying he was just thinking. In my weaker moments, I feared it was us—well, me—that had put that defeated look in his eye. Unlike the polars and the grizzlies, I worried he didn't see a future for a wicche and a dragon.

Sliding an arm around him, I said, "Hey, Audrey and I are all done. Thanks for helping."

Nodding, he relaxed his arms, wrapping one around me before leaning down and taking my mouth with his own, running his fingers through my hair. He loved playing with my hair, so I'd let it grow out a little. If I could make that deep, throaty, contented rumble sound he sometimes made, I'd be doing it now.

On the way out, I turned off the lights and used my own magic to activate The Slaughtered Lamb's wards. Sam and I had worked on it before she left, making sure the wards would recognize me as they did her.

I took George's hand as we walked up the steps. "I can't believe you're still awake. Everything okay?" The sound of buzzing grew stronger.

"Yeah." George nodded thoughtfully before pulling my hand to his lips. "I know my family can make you nervous, so I thought we should talk before I give them an answer about Christmas."

"I'm not nervous—well, not much. I mean, come on. Your grandmother is terrifying." I glanced over, assessing George's reaction. When we reached the parking lot at the top of the stairs, I saw my car but not George's.

Apparently guessing my hesitation, George said, "I was with Coco earlier. She dropped me off." Still holding my hand, he guided me around broken glass at the edge of the pavement and I melted into a pool of buzz-free goo. "Besides," he said, "we don't need two cars if we're going to the same place." He hesitated. "You are coming over, right?"

"Absolutely, especially now that I don't have to worry about waking you up. I don't want you groggy when you're dealing with eight-hundred-pound bears with really sharp claws."

Grinning, George opened my door for me and then walked around the back to the passenger side. "They would never. Even the grumpy grizzlies know not to piss me off. They don't know what I am, but they smell much a bigger predator when I'm around and they behave accordingly."

I drove a small, environmentally conscious car, one George had a difficult time fitting into. I knew he preferred his own Bronco for comfort, but I liked having him snugged in next to me. I felt really bad about the glove box digging into his knees, though. He tilted his seat back, way back. The headroom was fine for me but definitely not for him. Okay, I felt *really* bad. In my defense, I bought the car long before we'd met. How was I to know I'd fall for a dragon?

"I want to make sure you understand," I began as I pulled out of the parking space. "Your family doesn't make me nervous. I love your sister Coco. You know that. The others I only met that one time at Thanksgiving—which was overwhelming, but not the point of this conversation. Your grandmother is another story. I know my own lao lao seems soft and sweet, right before she takes you out at the knees, but yours doesn't even bother with the niceness—which, now that I think about it, I actually prefer."

"Do you know you ramble when you're nervous?"

"Do not."

"It's cute," he said, relaxing back into the seat. The poor guy had been up for almost twenty-four hours. "And I get it. Grandmother enjoys being feared."

"Okay," I admitted. "There's some healthy fear there. It's just— I worry, I guess, that they're disappointed you aren't with another dragon."

George was silent, and the bees swarmed.

"I guess that answers that question." Gripping the steering wheel hard, I headed to the Marina district. Holiday lights twinkled in storefront windows and reflected off the wet streets. George, like Coco, had an apartment above Drake's Treasures, the family jewelry store.

"That's not it at all," he finally said. "Would Grandmother like me to find a nice, female dragon to settle down with and start making little dragons? Yes, she really would. Does she have a problem with you? No. Other than the baby dragon issue."

George rested his hand on my thigh. "I need to explain to you why my family can be so cold and forbidding, especially Grandmother. It's a long, complicated story and one I haven't told you yet only because it's hard for me."

I put my hand over George's and squeezed before returning it to the stick shift to change gears. "You don't have to talk about anything you don't want to."

It wasn't easy, given the narrowness of the car, but George managed to get his arm behind my shoulder, his hand in my black, floppy hair. "It's not that. When we get home, we'll have a glass of wine, I'll lay it all out, and then I'll have an invitation for you."

My eyes flicked to the clock on the dashboard. "It's really late. You're only going to get a couple of hours of sleep as it is."

"I'm off tomorrow. This close to the holidays, our schedules are a mess. I need Christmas Eve off, so I switched with Jenny who wants Christmas Day. I have tomorrow off because Simon needs me to take his New Year's Day."

"Oh, okay." I pulled into the four-car parking lot behind the store. Coco's Jeep was parked beside George's Bronco.

The apartments had excellent soundproofing, as dragons have excellent hearing. I was used to my own apartment building, though, so I often caught myself tiptoeing up the back stairs and past Coco's door.

George and I changed into sleep pants and t-shirts before I went into the kitchen to pour the wine. If George was going to have to discuss difficult things, I wanted him to be as comfortable as possible. He took the glass I offered but then seemed to change his mind, setting it aside on the coffee table. I, on the other hand, took a large gulp and tried to prepare.

"So," George began, "did I ever tell you I'm a twin?"

THREE

Two Villains in League

"What?" The wine glass stopped a few inches from my lips. "Yeah." He took a deep breath and let it out slowly. "There are three of us. Coco's almost two years older than Alec and me."

"I don't understand." I put the wine glass down and took George's hand. "Why haven't you ever told me you have a brother?"

Closing his eyes, George shook his head. "I'm telling it wrong." He studied our entwined fingers, light and dark, and then tugged. "Can you sit with me?"

I didn't hesitate, crawling over and dropping into the narrow wedge of space between George and the back cushion. If he hadn't looked so serious, I'd think this was payback for him having to cram himself into my tiny car. Turning to the side, I dipped my shoulder under his arm. I'd have a hell of a time getting up, but I was fine for now. Wrapping an arm around George's waist, I rested my head on a pec and waited. I'd wait all night if that was what he needed.

George put his feet up on the coffee table, adjusting to give me some breathing room. "Growing up, we spent every Christmas in Wales, visiting granddad's clan, running up and down the countryside, flying after the sun went down. The keep has been in the family for hundreds of years. No one lives nearby, not for miles. The short days, gale-force winds, and cold kept hikers away. We had it all to ourselves.

"I mean, there were aunts and uncles, and cousins, and what-not, but no humans. Alec and I had been kicking around a football with our cousin Jordie, waiting for the bigger kids to come so we could play a proper match."

"How old were you?"

"Eight. Alec and I were eight. Coco was a month shy of her tenth birthday. Anyway, I was getting bored waiting for the others to arrive, so I decided to go exploring in the woods. I wasn't far from the clearing where we played, just a hundred feet or so beyond the tree line. Even over the wind, I could hear Alec and Jordie trying out the new curse words we'd heard our older cousins use.

"There was a rustling in the underbrush, so I went to investigate, thinking I might find a rabbit or maybe a hedgehog who hadn't gone into hibernation yet."

"Even then with the animals," I murmured, my fingers brushing absently over George's chest.

"I went deeper and deeper into the woods, following the noises. I didn't find a hedgehog, though." He hesitated, all these years later, before telling it. "There was a man leaning against a tree, waiting. I know it sounds paranoid, but it felt like he was waiting for me."

I tensed, fearing what George was about to say.

"He was a tall white man with long dark hair pulled back, and light golden-brown eyes that—again, I know it's stupid, but—it was like they pulled me in. Hypnotized me or something. I knew I should've run. I was yelling in my own head to get away from him, but I just kept walking toward him, not stopping until I was directly in front of him. He wore strange clothes, but it was his eyes. It was like the color was swirling in them."

"What happened?" Please don't let this be another story like Sam's. I couldn't take two people I loved being brutalized like that.

"He talked. His lips didn't move but he talked to me. I have no memory of anything he said, but I can still hear his voice, the deep timbre of it." George shook his head. "Maybe it *was* hypnotism. The next thing I remember is shivering on the forest floor beside the tree the man had been leaning against. It was dark. Hours must have gone by, but I couldn't remember anything."

Suppressing a shudder, I held him tighter.

"I heard movement to my right, away from the meadow and my family. A white woman, a blonde, walked through the trees, no outerwear or boots. She dressed like Grandmother, silk trousers and a blouse, high heels. She stared down at me and said, 'He was right. You are an unusual one, aren't you?' I didn't know if she meant because of my dragon blood or my skin color, but I knew she was something to be feared. Like the bears know I'm the bigger predator, I knew that about her."

"What was she?"

"No idea. Not for the longest time. But do you remember when we were in New Orleans and Russell told us that vampires could mess with people's minds, making them forget things?"

"Oh, you mean that little bit of news that keeps me jumping at shadows? Yeah, vaguely."

"Right. Anyway, I've been thinking about that ever since. She might have been a vampire. She didn't say anything else, just held out a cold hand. I stood and took it."

He paused again and I wished I could take it, wished I could hold the memory for him so he wouldn't suffer with it.

"We hadn't gone more than a few steps when there was crashing behind us. Alec and Coco had come looking for me. They skidded to a stop, confused. Coco just stared at the woman, but Alec shouted at her to get her sick fuck hands off me. He charged and shoved her back. Instead of running or fighting, she just smiled down at him. It was the most terrifying thing I've ever seen in my life.

"Alec was always the stronger of us. He jabbed a finger at her and told her to piss off. Then he grabbed my wrist and pulled me toward Coco, who was still dazed. I didn't even see the woman do it. Didn't see anything. One second, Alec had my arm and the next, they were gone. She'd snatched him away."

"Oh, George." I wished there was something I could do to ease the pain in his voice.

"Coco and I ran back and told our parents, told Granddad and Grandmother. Everyone searched. All night. On the ground, in the air, we searched. We went out every day, every night. They questioned us over and over. And every time, Coco and I felt it hit home harder and harder. This was our fault. We had him. He'd been right there with us. And then we lost him."

"No." I levered myself up so I could see George's face, make sure he understood. "That wasn't your fault. None of it. You were eight years old. You were a child being manipulated by two supernatural adults, one that sounds like a vampire and the other a fae. The fae can fuck with your head too. You had two powerful beings messing with three little kids. None of you had a chance."

"Fae?" George sat forward, his feet back on the floor, as though preparing to jump up and continue the search now. "How do you know?"

"The swirling eyes. You said funny clothes. Was it a tunic and breeches?" At George's nod, I continued, "That's what Sam said they wore in Faerie. And she said the queen's eyes became kaleidoscopic, all the colors swirling, hypnotizing her."

"But—" George fell back against the arm of the couch, his brow furrowed. "That makes no sense. Why would the fae be working with vampires? You told me—when Sam had to go into Faerie—that Clive couldn't go with her because the fae despised vampires for being unnatural."

"As far as I know, they do, but maybe this isn't all fae and vampires. Maybe this is one member of the fae and one vampire who've struck an accord. He finds her victims and she...I don't know." I framed his beautiful face with my hands, making him look at me. "But, George, there was nothing either you or Coco could have done."

"You think he's dead, then? That she killed him all those years ago? That we've been looking for no reason?"

My heart cracked a little more. I took his hand and squeezed. "I don't know."

"*I* should know, though, shouldn't I? He's my twin. Sometimes it felt like we shared our thoughts, along with a bedroom, clothes, and toys. I'd feel it, wouldn't I? In here?" he asked, pounding on his chest. "I'd know if my brother was dead."

"I don't know," I said again, feeling useless. I wasn't helping, didn't know how to help.

George stood abruptly. "I need to talk to Coco." He looked down at himself, as though checking to make sure he was dressed.

"Now? It's the middle of the night. She's sleeping."

George shook his head. "She never sleeps. I saw the light flickering from her TV when you parked out back. Twenty years she's been on guard, looking for Alec and watching over me." He rubbed his hands over his face. "The alcohol. The guilt was too much. She fell into a bottle, trying to punish herself. If she couldn't find him, she'd disappear along with him." He stared into the past, eyes haunted. "I almost lost them both. I finally yanked her back out before she drowned, but no, she doesn't really sleep anymore. Penance, I suppose."

George leaned over and gave me a quick kiss. "I'm sorry. Get some sleep," he said, gesturing toward the doorway. "I need to talk to her, tell her we were up against a vampire and a fae. It might help."

"Okay, go." I almost offered to go with him but knew this was between George and his sister. Alone, I did the only thing I could think of to help. I cleaned up the dishes, put the wine away, tidied in the kitchen, and waited.

FOUR

Encounters with Dragons

I woke to George picking me up from the couch—where I'd
apparently fallen asleep—and carrying me to bed.

"What happened? Are you okay?" I scrubbed at my face,
waking myself up. "Sorry. I didn't mean to fall asleep."

He slid us both in under the covers. "We're only an hour shy of
dawn. This seems like the perfect time to be asleep. Come on," he
said, pulling me close. "Lie back down."

"Is Coco all right?"

"We had a long, horrible talk, but I think it's starting to sink in.
She's been carrying the guilt for two decades. It'll take a while for
her to set it down, and even longer for her to stop panicking when
she realizes the phantom load is gone, that she hasn't forgotten
something vital, that it's no longer there because it was never hers
to carry."

"She'll get there. So will you."

George stared up at the ceiling in the darkened room, rubbing a
hand up and down my arm. "We'll see. This is why I hate the holidays. We lost Alec at Christmas." He brushed a hand through my
hair. "Go ahead. Get some sleep."

Sleep was overrated and George needed out of his own head. I
snaked my hand up his t-shirt, fingers playing over his abdominal

muscles. The reaction was immediate. George rolled over, crushing his mouth to mine.

"Soft lips and wicked hands," he mumbled, scraping his teeth over my jaw.

A man's got to go with his strengths. I slid one of my wicked hands south, over the ridges of his abdominals, down the front of his sleep pants, finding what I needed hot and hard. When I stroked down his length and squeezed, George bucked, palming my ass and grinding against my wicked hand.

He ripped my t-shirt over my head and then yanked down my pajamas, taking a moment to let his gaze take in all of me before his tongue followed suit. This wasn't about me, though. I reared up and pushed George onto his back. Unlike the speed with which he'd moved, I slowly peeled the tee from his muscular chest and broad shoulders, my lips skating up his torso, over blessedly exposed skin.

George had trouble breathing and I exulted. There'd be no brooding tonight. There'd be skin and friction and lust and exhaustion. And he'd sleep without memories keeping him close to the surface.

My fingers and mouth were everywhere, and his groans had me going harder. He would know he was loved and cared for. I'd make sure of it. When I made my way back to his mouth, he reached between us, gripped my cock in his large fist and squeezed, his thumb swirling circles around the head.

In a tangle of tongues, he tried to reverse our positions, but I wasn't having it. I pushed him back again, biting his lower lip before feasting on his god-like body. When I finally settled between his legs, George was panting like he'd run a marathon.

"Let me," George breathed, but I already had my tongue curling around his shaft. Exploring, hands gripping, fingertips brushing, I kept him out of his own head and focused on me. He groaned, hips pumping, his hands fisted in my hair and then he was roaring, emptying himself.

When George's breathing finally leveled out, I'd crawled up

and was straddling his stomach. Looking down into his grinning face, I said, "I love it when you roar."

Laughing, he flipped me over. "Let's see if we can make me roar again."

He did roar a few more times before we settled down to sleep.

———

I AWOKE A LITTLE BEFORE NOON. I NEEDED TO GET CLEANED UP quickly if I wanted to open on time. I hadn't really thought about it before I'd had to cover for her, but Sam worked ridiculous hours. Yes, she used to live behind the bar, but still, twelve to fourteen hours a day, seven days a week. Even with Audrey's help, Dave and I were working a lot more hours in Sam's absence.

With a towel slung around my waist, I went back into the bedroom and stopped short. George was still asleep. This was unprecedented. George normally surfaced every time I so much as moved. I had felt guilty for sleeping over in the beginning, but George assured me he slept better when I was there.

Back when our work hours were more aligned, he'd often be in the kitchen making coffee or sitting on the couch reading when I got out of the shower. He was never asleep. My throat tightened, watching my love finally getting a good night's rest. The talk, the realization, it seemed to have helped George forgive himself, at least a little. With any luck, Coco was sleeping as well.

George had given me plenty of room in the closet and bureau, so I grabbed clean clothes, shoes, phone, and then tiptoed out of the room. It was George's day off. I wanted him to sleep as late as he could.

Dressed and ready, I closed and locked the front door, then jogged down the steps to the back parking lot. Checking my watch, I decided it would probably only be Grim, a perpetually grumpy dwarf, waiting impatiently for me at The Slaughtered Lamb's entrance.

I couldn't have been more wrong. Grim was nowhere to be

seen. Standing at the top of the steps leading down to the bookstore and bar was Benvair, matriarch of the dragon clan and grandmother to George and Coco.

She may have scared the shit out of me, but I couldn't help but admire the woman's style. Her hair was pulled back into a classic chignon, with pearls at her ears. She wore a long camel overcoat with black trousers and high-heeled boots. A Burberry plaid scarf was wrapped around her neck and tucked into her coat, a matching handbag at her side. Perfect. The woman always looked perfect.

Benvair checked her watch and then pinned me with an annoyed gaze.

"Mrs. Drake, what a nice surprise." I kissed her cheek as I'd seen George do, hoping I wasn't overstepping. "I'm so sorry I've kept you waiting. I'm afraid George and I were up late talking." I did my best to block out everything else we'd done and hoped she didn't possess the ability to read minds.

"Yes," she said, taking my elbow. "I know."

I kicked myself for not offering my arm before we descended the stairs.

"My granddaughter came over this morning to discuss these revelations with me. I was wondering," she said, as we moved through the ward, leaving the human world behind and stepping into The Slaughtered Lamb, "why you hadn't mentioned any of this before. The timing is interesting."

I led her to a table, pulling out a chair, assuming she wouldn't want to sit on a barstool. "Can I get you a cup of tea?"

Placing her bag on the adjacent chair, she nodded regally. "Yes."

I went behind the bar, her scrutiny making me nervous and clumsy. Because of me, Sam stocked a huge selection of tea leaves. Trying my best to shake off the unease, I busied myself creating a blend that I thought would be conducive to our discussion. Benvair and I may not have much in common, but we had one thing: tea. Starting with my best black tea base, I added lemongrass to lessen the melancholy she was feeling over Alec's loss, golden flowery orange pekoe to soften the sadness that seemed to have already turned to anger, and a hint of peppermint for general emotional well-being.

She said nothing while I worked, which I appreciated. Using a spell I'd created long ago for blending and brewing tea, I infused the inherent benefits of the leaves with my own magic, hoping to help her shed her suspicion and find equilibrium.

Holding a hand over the teapot, helping the tea along, I thought of my mother and settled in my skin. They were similar. I could see that now. Strong women who would do whatever it took to protect their own. If they were ever at odds, it'd be a clash of the titans. Benvair was here, trying to make me cower, because she was protective of George and Coco, still grieving for Alec. She wasn't going to let some bartending wicche change the family narrative until she'd learned everything she could about me and knew whether or not I was to be trusted.

Feeling steadier, I brought the teapot, fragrant with steeped tea, back to her table. I placed a cup and saucer in front of her and then poured, before taking my seat. We both wanted the same thing. We weren't adversaries. Intimidation and fear had no place at this table.

"Mrs. Drake, George told me last night about what happened when he and Alec were eight."

"I'm aware." Her tone would have frozen a lesser man, but I understood her protectiveness now. She took a sip, closed her eyes a moment to savor, and then took another. I accepted it as the compliment it was.

Opening her mouth, she hesitated an instant, and then said, "I don't trust you." Her tone reeked of disdain, but her eyes told a different story. She *wanted* to believe, quite desperately. She wanted to finally have an answer, to know what had happened to her grandson and to lay waste to all involved.

"I love your grandson very much. I think you already know that. I want what you all do, for George and Coco to be safe and content, to finally lay down the guilt they've been carrying for twenty years, and to know what actually happened to George's twin."

"You have no idea what I want." Her hands rested on the cup, not drinking but not letting it go.

"Please, don't let your annoyance with me keep you from your tea." When she finally lifted the cup to her lips, I said, "You're right. We barely know one another, but I can speculate."

She took another sip, eyebrows up, and I continued, "Coco and George interpreted the constant questioning about what happened when Alec was taken to mean you blamed them, that their actions or inactions led directly to their brother's disappearance, that they were at fault."

Anger sparked red in her gaze. I couldn't forget that this woman could breathe fire and leave nothing but ash where I sat if she were so inclined. Dropping her fiery gaze to her cup, she took another sip.

"You hadn't known that. It's why Coco drank. I think they're wrong, though. I don't believe you blame children for being victimized by adults."

"No?" She smoothed her perfect hair, a sure sign of distress in a woman this composed.

"No. I think you were trying to protect them, trying to see and hear everything they had so you could hunt down the predators before they took another child. Especially," I added, "if that child were George. They had originally chosen him, after all. Taking Alec was a spur-of-the-moment decision. They had George's scent. What if they came back to claim him? How could you protect him if you didn't know exactly what you were up against, exactly what they looked like, sounded like? You've been on guard ever since, like Coco, waiting for a glimpse of your enemy."

FIVE

You Had One Job!

B envair stood, looking down her nose at me. "I did not come here to be psychoanalyzed by you."

I stood as well. "I apologize for making you uncomfortable. I was pretty sure you were here to intimidate me, to get me to back off from George. You need to know I'm not going to do that. I understand I'm an unknown, a potential threat. What if I'm passing along info to the ones who targeted your family?"

Faint tendrils of smoke puffed from Benvair's nostrils. I needed to make my point fast.

"The thing is, though, when you hide away the pain, tending it in secret, it never heals. The only reason you now know a vampire and a member of the fae were most likely involved is because George is with me.

"So many of us tend to cling to our own. I understand the history of why we do that, as well as the emotional and psychological reasons for it, but maintaining insular groups means that information often doesn't cross the lines between dragons and vampires, between wicches and the fae.

"George and I flew to New Orleans to help the vampires. In turn, they shared secrets, like the fact they can mesmerize and alter memories. Through Sam, I learned about the fae, which I shared with George. To find what happened to Alec, we'll need the trust and cooperation of those outside the dragon clan."

"And who are you, little wicche, to wield so much power?" Red sparks danced in her eyes again. I was about to get scorched.

"I'm Owen Wong, one of an ancient and respected line of wicches." I made a fist and lifted my hand. Turning it over, I opened my fingers to reveal a blue flame that built and lengthened, a veritable bonfire in my hand. "I am not one to be so easily disregarded, if you please."

Benvair tipped her head, conceding the point.

Closing my fist again, I doused the flame. "I will share a secret with you, as Sam would be the first one to volunteer her help. She has an affinity with the dead."

"I already knew that. She's made herself useful to me in the past." The red sparks disappeared, and she sat.

Following her lead, I resumed my seat as well. "Did you know that vampires are dead enough to qualify?"

"I did. You are not the only one collecting secrets, wicche." She took another sip.

"Owen is fine. Have you already spoken with her about searching for the one who stole Alec?" I needed her to trust me. It was the only way we were going to get anywhere, but trust is earned over time, not given over tea.

"She's overseas."

"True, but cell phones work over there too. I have the numbers for all four of them." The way she clung to her secrecy was making me nuts.

"The request is for her. I'm not going through the men. They have no authority over either of us." She paused a moment. "And I tried her number. She didn't answer."

I opened my mouth, but she cut me off.

"Twice."

"Okay, did you leave a message for her?"

"No. Phones can be lost or stolen. Our family's business is no one else's. I will only speak to her."

"Right. Okay. I understand that. Not returning phone calls isn't like Sam, but losing or destroying phones really is." I checked my watch. "It's past sundown in England. May I text Russell on your behalf to ask if Sam has her phone?"

Letting out a deep breath, she finally nodded.

Me: Cheerio! I have Benvair here. She's trying to reach Sam, who hasn't been picking up. Did Sam lose her phone again?

Russell: ...

Russell: ...

My phone rang. It was Clive. I swiped to answer. "Hi, sorry to interrupt your trip. As I texted Russell, Benvair has a question for Sam."

"Has she spoken to her? Has she heard from her at all?" The desperation in Clive's voice scared the hell out of me.

Benvair's eyes narrowed. "No," she said, knowing Clive would hear.

"What's going on? Where's Sam?" What was happening over there?

"We don't know." *Click.*

Standing abruptly, I knocked over the chair. "Damn it, Sam! You had one job. One. Enjoy your honeymoon." *Fuck!* Yes, fine, two jobs. But the general public didn't know they were also hunting Clive's stalker. I paced the bar. Who should I contact? What could I do?

I'd completely forgotten Benvair was there until I heard the scrape of her chair. "I'm going to go. I know, quite well, what you're feeling right now. If you think of a way I may aid in her return, please contact me." She paused, reaching for her bag. Seeming to make up her mind, she added, "Thank you for sharing with us your suspicions regarding Alec's abductors. I'll contact my son and daughter-in-law, give them this information. They never left Wales. Never stopped searching." Inclining her head, she said, "We are indebted." Grabbing her bag, she walked across the bar and up the stairs, leaving me alone with my chaotic thoughts.

Thirty minutes later, patrons had begun to trickle in. I'd called

Dave to relay Sam's disappearance. He said he'd do some digging and get back to me. I didn't know anyone who lived in England, at least no one who could help with this. Sam's great-aunt had a fae wife. She might be able to search more easily, as the fae seemed to be able to jump around the world using Faerie as a hub. The problem was I had no idea how to contact her, no number, and last I heard, the Wicche Glass had been shut down. In fact, with her wicche wife dead, it was likely Galadriel had returned to Faerie.

The familiar sound of George's footfalls on the steps pulled me out of my own thoughts. Checking my watch, I let out a breath. He'd had a good, long sleep.

Coming behind the bar, he pulled me into a hug. "Grandmother called. She said Sam was missing and you needed me."

Incredulous, I stared into his beautiful, earnest face. "Your grandmother was concerned and sent you to check on me? Come on."

He gave me a quick kiss and then went around to his side of the bar and took a stool. "She said you'd had a talk today. She didn't tell me what you spoke about, but her tone had changed. She actually used your name, instead of 'that wicche.'"

I grinned at that and then shared my conversation with Benvair. I also told him everything I knew about the Sam situation and what was currently being done by everybody *except* me. I was selling books and brewing tea, like always. I was useless.

George snagged my arm as I walked past and pulled me toward him over the bar. He sat and I stood, our elbows on the bar, our cheeks touching. It was something I'd seen him do with Coco, a dragon thing, a message. He was telling me he was with me, sharing what I was going through, ready to take any part of it I was willing to give up.

"We'll find her. She has many powerful friends, not the least of which is her new master vampire husband. She's a trouble magnet—"

"She never used to be. It was downright boring around here."

"What changed?"

I let out a huff of breath. "Sam."

He nodded. "There you go. She's choosing life and adventure and love. That's dangerous stuff. I mean, she gets into weird, dire situations, right? But she gets out of them too."

"Do you know how many times she's almost died recently? I can't believe Clive didn't bring a healer on the trip."

When I tried to pull away, he brought me back to him. "You'll ask Godfrey to give you the full story and we'll figure out how we can help. All right?"

I nodded, feeling better.

"Can I finally give you that invitation?"

"Right. Sorry. Totally forgot. Yes, please."

He dropped a kiss on my nose and then sat back. "I'd like you to spend Christmas Eve with my family. Grandmother hosts a huge family get-together every Christmas. Some of the Welsh dragons are living in the U.S. now; some of Grandmother's Georgia family fly in. Honestly, any stray dragons willing to make the trip are welcomed in like family.

"There'll be a feast the likes of which you've never seen, drinks, gifts, games, you name it. And later, after most of the city is tucked away waiting for Santa, we'll fly up and search for his sleigh. Want to come?"

"Hell yeah, I want to come!" I whisper shouted.

He kissed me soundly. "Good. I'm going to go check on Coco and then do our laundry. I'll be back to have dinner with you. Any idea on what Dave's making?"

I shook my head. "It's whatever he's feeling that day. I can text you when he updates the menu board."

"Nah, I'll be surprised. Everything he makes is good." With a wave, he was gone.

The rest of the shift, I was vacillating between concern for Sam and unparalleled joy at flying with dragons. Wait. I did get to fly with them, right? I didn't have to watch from the ground, did I? Then again, those sort-of reins I used when George flew us to Mount Tamalpais to search for Sam—that woman really needed to stay put—had been janky as hell. I didn't want to drop hundreds of feet and splat. No. George would never let me fall.

The real issue was what kind of gift to give Benvair. I'd already bought and wrapped gifts for George and Coco, but I hadn't been expecting an invite from the grand dame herself. What do you get the woman who has everything and can easily afford the best of anything new?

Hmm, I had until tomorrow night to figure it out.

SIX

All I Want for Christmas Is You

W e'd been planning to close The Slaughtered Lamb on Christmas Eve, but Dave and Audrey said they didn't have anything better to do, so they offered to open for any of our customers who likewise had nowhere special to go. Audrey had even picked up Santa hats for her and Dave.

I went to my own apartment last night, wanting to finish wrapping gifts. My family was Buddhist, but ever since Lilah and I were little we'd loved the twinkly lights and decorations, the Christmas songs and Claymation TV shows so much, our parents let us have a secular celebration.

Bodhi Day on December eighth is actually our big winter holiday. We celebrate the Buddha Siddhartha Gautama achieving enlightenment. Our huge extended family gets together then. Christmas is just the twenty-fifth, except in our family where we have a tree, presents, cookies, and spend the day watching holiday movies. With George's family, I was looking forward to getting an insider's view of the holiday.

I had one thing left to pick up to complete Benvair's gift, but I needed to go to Mom and Dad's house to get it. I grew up in the North Beach district, lots of Italian and Chinese restaurants, lots of little parks. Our neighborhood was very family-oriented. The apartment I lived in now was farther west on Russian Hill. It was on the top floor of an old Victorian boarding house. It wasn't much, but it had a great view of Coit Tower in the distance.

Luckily, I caught Mom before she went out. I was going to need her help.

When I put my key in the front door, she was already pulling it open. "Owen," she crooned happily, like she hadn't just seen me a few days ago. Kissing my cheek, she drew me into a hug. "Look at you. You look so tired." She dragged me out of the entrance festooned with holiday lanterns and closed the door. "I'll fix you lunch. All these extra hours, you're not getting enough sleep. Come." She led me into the kitchen, nudging me toward a chair at the table.

"Mom, I'm fine. Really." But she was already heating up leftovers. Which, now that I thought about it, I *was* hungry, so good. I'd eat and then we'd start searching in the attic.

After she put a piping hot plate of beef noodles in front of me, she sat down. "Are you sure you want to do this? They're family heirlooms."

"Would you be upset if I did?" I hadn't considered Mom not wanting to lose them. I should have.

"Well, you tell me. Is he the one? This is the one you want to spend your life with?"

I swallowed. "I think so."

She pinned me with her mom look. "Be sure."

Going with my heart, my gut, I said, "Yes."

"Okay. When you finish, we'll go up and get them. I'll help you wrap the box. Benvair Drake is a formidable woman, but I know she'll care for our heirlooms like the treasures they are."

I put my fork down and reached for her hand. "Thanks, Mom."

She gave me another kiss on the cheek. "My darling boy, you have found the one you were destined to be with, the one who wears your string. It may have been jumbled and tangled and knotted along the way, but the invisible thread tied to your finger has also been tied to his. To find one's soulmate"—she shook her head, tears in her eyes—"this we celebrate. Fate has found its way. Come, we'll find your new grandmother a perfect gift."

"Mom, I can't speak for George. He's the one for me, but that doesn't mean I'm the one for him. I'm not really sure if he's thinking about a future with me."

"Nonsense," she laughed. "You're just nervous. It's good to feel nervous and overwhelmed when you meet your fate. Just remember," she said, patting my hand, "he's tied to you too."

———

I HAD NO IDEA WHAT ONE WORE TO A DRAGON PARTY, ESPECIALLY IF they were ending the evening shifting. I texted George. When he didn't respond, I tried Coco. She said she wasn't sure about me, but that she was expected to wear a dress and she was none too happy about it.

Deciding it would be better to be overdressed than under, I put on gray wool trousers, a white dress shirt and a midnight blue cashmere V-neck sweater. I even wore the black dress shoes I'd bought for my sister Blythe's wedding. I looked in the mirror, brushed my hair again, and hoped for the best.

I drove to Drake's Treasures, parking beside the Bronco. I needed to transfer the gifts from my trunk to his. George jogged down the back stairs a minute later, dressed much the same as me. Okay, one hurdle cleared.

"Merry Christmas," he said, giving me a kiss. Squeezing my shoulder, he said, "Look at you." He brushed a stray hair from my face. "If we didn't have someplace we had to be..." And then he kissed me. A lot.

"Break it up, you two." Coco came down the stairs wearing an adorable cranberry-colored cocktail dress. For a woman who hated getting dressed up, she did it quite well. Her hair was pulled up in a kind of waterfall of curls. She looked incredible. What seemed to be giving her trouble, though, were the shoes.

She stared down at the cranberry heels, her ankles unsteady.

"Why? Why do women wear these things? Why does Grand-mother insist on them?"

"Do you have any heels with ankle straps? Those are a little more secure. Better yet, any wedge heels? The more sole on the ground, the steadier you'll feel." They looked at me blankly. "I have sisters."

"I think I have both," she said, going back up the stairs. "They're wedges with ankle straps. Brilliant! And the best part is, if Grandmother doesn't like them, I can tell her Owen said it was okay." She laughed maniacally as she passed through the back door.

"Wait, was she serious?"

"Well," George said, transferring gifts to his car, "Grandmother knows she's hopeless. That's why she buys all her clothes. She knows Coco could never put together outfits on her own. Don't worry, though. Coco's wearing a dress. Even if she puts on hiking boots, Grandmother will consider the dress a win. Come on." He opened the passenger door for me.

"Aren't we waiting for your sister?"

George walked around the front, climbed in, and started the engine. "Nah. She likes to drive herself. She always wants to know she has an escape route if she needs it."

"Oh, okay."

"Listen," he said, turning in his seat to watch me. "I know we haven't talked about this yet, but we're already spending most of our nights together. And if you want to maintain your own space, I understand, but if you were open to the idea, I'd like us to live together."

"You would?"

He kissed me again. "I really would. I've been looking for a place and I think I found it. Can I show you on the way over?"

"What?" He'd been looking too? All this time, I thought I was alone in my angsty real estate search and he'd been on the same page the whole time.

"Our schedules have been so off lately. I should have talked with you about it sooner. I downloaded a couple of apps and have been looking on my lunch breaks."

Heart eyes. "I've been looking too."

"Yeah?" He picked up my hand and kissed it. "Have you found our home yet?"

"Not really. I wasn't sure what you could afford in rent. I mean, it doesn't sound like you and Coco pay rent now, so I was just going by what I think you make as a vet and the considerably smaller salary I get." I couldn't get over it. He'd been looking too.

"I found a couple of cool apartments," I said. "The problem is I've been spoiled by working at The Slaughtered Lamb. I want a view, but a view is going to cost us. If we look farther from the water, we might be able to afford a two-bedroom with a little more square footage."

"Hmm." He threw the truck into reverse and then pulled out onto Marina Boulevard. "Let's look at the one I found. If you think I'm nuts, we'll keep looking, okay?"

"Okay." I was waiting for him to pull into an apartment building, but he just kept driving toward his grandmother's. "They're going to let us look on Christmas Eve?"

"Yup." He pulled onto Sea Cliff Avenue.

"Oh, I thought we were looking now. Are we ducking out later?"

He passed his grandmother's house and then pulled into a driveway six or eight mansions down. "If it's too much or you hate it or have any reservations, we won't do it."

"A house? Oh my God, George, these places cost millions, tens of millions. I have $322.79 in my checking account. I couldn't afford a night in a place like this." All I could see from the street was a garage that looked like a carriage house and a doorway to the right, through an ivy-covered wall.

He brushed my cheek with the back of his hand. "Owen, I'm a dragon. Just because I live in a small apartment doesn't mean I don't have a personal treasure. Besides, Coco and I like to keep an eye on each other, make sure the other one is safe." Running his fingers through my hair, he gave a little tug. "I'm loaded, silly. I can afford this."

Wealth on this scale made me uncomfortable, but... "We can look."

"Great." He jumped out and went to my side as I was dropping to the pavement. He slammed the door, took my hand, and led me to the ivy door. Taking a key out of his pocket, he opened the door into a secret garden.

It was ridiculous and magical and perfect and I hadn't even stepped foot into the house yet. Ivy grew up the garden walls and the brick on the lower half of the Tudor house. There was a lawn in the center, with brick paths cutting through the thick, lush plants. I could hear water tinkling, so there was a fountain in here some-where. It was so gorgeously over the top, it felt like we'd walked into Faerie.

"Come on," he said, pulling me along the path. He took out another key and opened the front door.

I'd never seen anything more beautiful. Benvair's home was stunning but cold. This one had the same high ceilings and window walls overlooking the ocean and Golden Gate Bridge, but it felt warmer, homier—if you could call a seven-thousand-square-foot mansion homey. I was guessing on the square footage, but come on, this place was—

"Well? Do you want to see the rest?"

George walked me through the entire magnificent house. All I could do was follow, mute, staring at every gorgeous detail and thinking this must be a dream. Real people didn't live like this.

We ended the tour on the back patio, watching the ocean slam against the rocks at the bottom of our steps. Our steps, because at some point in the tour, I started picturing us living here, imagining what it would be like.

"I know it's a lot for two people, but we both have big families. It'd be nice to be able to host get-togethers with all of them."

I nodded slowly, still in a daze.

"And it's closer to both of our jobs. And"—he glanced over his shoulder at the back of the house—"we can decorate it however you'd like." He paused. "Listen, you're it for me. I want to spend my life with you. If this isn't what you want, that's fine. We'll get one of the apartments you were looking at. I want to be with you, wherever that is, if you'll let me. This place"—he gestured—"I could picture us here. Fumbling around the kitchen, trying to cook. Our nieces and nephews racing up and down the stairs, playing in the garden. Our families sitting at a huge table in that oversized dining room for Thanksgiving. A huge bed in that big bedroom up there." He shrugged. "I pictured it and then I wanted it so badly. And now I'm the one rambling. What do you want?"

Choices. I slid my arms around him and kissed him with my whole heart, as that was what I was giving him. "You, George. All I want is you."

He crushed me to him.

"And this house," I said. "I really want this house."

———

THE PARTY WAS EVERY BIT AS CRAZY AS GEORGE HAD SAID, LITTLE KIDS racing through the rooms, people constantly trying to put cocktails and plates of food in my hands, and more than a few people pulling me aside to ask if I was staying for the second half of the party, if I understood what that meant.

George had explained it to me on the walk to Benvair's home. Dragons didn't share their secrets easily, often at all. Casual dates were never allowed to know where the dragons shifted or to see them do it. Only mates were allowed to attend. As dragons mated for life, I was George's forever plus-one. Which was perfect, as he was mine, that thread Mom spoke about forever connecting us.

"Come on," George said, grabbing my hand. "Grandmother wants to open your gift now."

Terrified I'd missed the mark, overshooting it by miles, I gripped George's hand and hoped she wasn't expecting a scarf.

She picked up the first, smaller box and unwrapped the tea

blend I'd been working on all morning for her. She sniffed at the bag and then called her butler Fyffe, asking him to brew her a pot.

She then picked up the far larger and heavier box, pulling the bow free and raising the lid. She lifted a rare eighteenth-century teapot from the tissue paper. It had a red speckled glaze with a golden Chinese dragon emblazoned in the center. The spout, handle, and rim were a mosaic of gold and black rings. There were gasps in the room. People who had continued to talk amongst themselves went silent and moved forward to see.

George took my hand into both of his.

Very carefully, Benvair placed the pot on the table beside her and took out each cup and saucer, marveling at the treasure each piece was. When she had taken the last piece from the box, she stood and moved to me. The others moved closer to the set. It was obvious they all wanted to touch the pieces but knew not to lay hands on another's treasure.

"Please tell me the story of this set."

"I'm told my family was living in China during the Qing Dynasty. They were more artisans than healers then. They made this set. The wealthy family who'd commissioned it never returned to pay for my family's work or collect the set. Although they needed the money and should have sold it to someone else, my many-times grandfather couldn't part with it. It was his greatest work of art. It's been passed down, generation to generation, ever since."

"Won't your ancestors be angered you've given it away?" She studied me, brows raised.

"I'm passing it to a new member of my family, one who will care for it as it deserves to be cared for."

She almost smiled. "Good answer." Leaning forward, she kissed me on the cheek while patting George's chest.

George was grinning ear to ear as his grandmother walked away. It appeared we'd been given her blessing. "I have something for you too," he said, leading me to the tree.

"I didn't bring your gift here. I was going to give it to you at home." *Damn*. His gift was sitting in my apartment.

"That's fine." He reached under the tree and pulled out a large box wrapped in red foil.

I sat on the bench by the window, box in my lap, and began to unwrap. When I took the tissue paper out, I found a large leather harness, with tons of straps and rivets. I quickly covered it back up and whisper-hissed, "What the shit?"

George blinked and then threw back his head, roaring with laughter. The people nearby who had been watching were laughing as well. Coco walked over and patted my head, smirking.

Crouching down beside me, George moved my hands and the tissue paper. "I'm no one's leather daddy. It's a harness so you can safely ride with me when I shift."

"Oh!" No wonder it was so big.

Later, out on the coast, the dragons began to take turns shifting and flying away. In their dragon form, they were simply too big to all do it at once. Coco walked up to me as George was talking with his cousin.

"Congrats. George tells me you two are taking the house down the street from Grandmother." She shook her head, grinning. "Good luck with that."

I worried about Coco being alone over the jewelry store now. "Are you okay with George moving away?"

Nodding, she watched her family shift and set out over the waves. "He's your responsibility now."

"Accepted."

"Besides, I'm thinking about knocking down the walls between our apartments and taking over the who second floor." We stood in silence a moment and then she turned back to me. "You always say that you're not a healer like your sisters, but you are. George, grandmother, even me, we're all in a better place since we met you. I think you're a different kind of healer. You don't mend bones. You heal hearts and minds."

A rush of emotion swamped me.

She patted my shoulder, still watching her family. "George is up next. Get ready," she said before going to take her place.

Harness secured, I climbed George's back, while all around us people were shifting into their dragon forms and winging out over the Pacific. I scrambled into the straps and shouted, "Ready!"

George's great wings flapped once, lifting us into the air. Once more and we were soaring out over the waves. All around us, dragons swooped and wheeled, racing and diving. I threw spells over the water, causing the white caps to turn holiday colors. The dragons thundered their delight when I created a red and white peppermint stripe in the surf below. It was joyous and playful and the most exciting Christmas I'd ever had.

Clinging to George's back, I shouted along with my new family. Sometimes joy is too great to be contained. Riding a dragon was even more exhilarating than I'd imagined—and I didn't even mean that in a dirty way. If you want to talk dirty, though... Nope. Holiday story. Keeping it mostly clean. Let me just tell you this. All I ever wanted for Christmas was a dragon—and I got him.

Acknowledgments

I was lucky enough to chaperone two student trips to Europe years ago. I know some chafe under the imposed schedule of an educational tour, but my eventual husband and I loved it. I don't care about wandering wherever I want, whenever I want. Give me a tour guide who tells me the history of the places I'm visiting! All of that is to say, I've been to Canterbury and Paris twice, but not the other locations Sam and Clive visit. I did a great deal of research, worrying terribly the whole time I'd get it wrong. If I did, hopefully you're a forgiving lot.

We lost my dad while I was writing this book. When I was very little, I used to crawl onto his lap, and he would make up the most insanely ridiculous stories off the top of his head for me. I cuddled in, knowing I was safe, and let his stories play out in my mind. When I asked him to tell a specific one again, like the one about the boy with a thumb growing out of his belly button, he'd look blankly for a moment, trying unsuccessfully to remember, and would instead embark on a new story.

Thank you to my parents who made reading a priority and filled our house with books. Thank you to my husband and daughters for doing anything and everything to help me with my father's illness, hospital stays, memory care facility, more hospitals stays, death, funeral, and then with selling my parents' house and moving my mother close to us. They never complained, only asking what they could do. Even when I was trying desperately to finish this book in between all the rest, they found ways to make my life a little easier.

Thank you to C.R. Grissom, gifted writer, great friend, and amazing critique partner, who always makes the time to read the chapters I send. Your feedback and support have meant the world to me. Thank you to Norma Jean Bell, my fabulous beta reader for her insightful analysis.

Thank you to Peter Senftleben, my extraordinary editor. You have the enviable knack of getting to the heart of the story and then helping me to see my own work through a different lens. Thank you to Susan Helene Gottfried, my exceptional proofreader who always knows exactly where the commas go (unlike myself).

Thank you to the remarkable team at NYLA! You've made every step of publishing a little easier with your kindness and expertise. Thank you to my incredible agent Sarah Younger, the inimitable Natanya Wheeler, and the wonderful Cheryl Pientka for working together to make my dream of writing and publishing a reality.

Dear Reader,

Thank you for reading *The Hob & Hound Pub*. If you enjoyed Sam and Clive's fourth adventure together, please consider leaving a review or chatting about it with your book-loving friends. Good word of mouth means everything when you're a new writer!

Love,
Seana

Want more books from Seana?

If you'd like to be the first to learn what's new with Sam and Clive (and Owen and Dave and Stheno...), please sign up for my newsletter *Tales from the Book Nerd*. It's filled with writing news, deleted scenes, giveaways, book recommendations, first looks at covers, short stories, and my favorite cocktail and book pairings.

The Slaughtered Lamb Bookstore & Bar
Sam Quinn, book 1

Welcome to The Slaughtered Lamb Bookstore and Bar. I'm Sam Quinn, the werewolf book nerd in charge. I run my business by one simple rule: Everyone needs a good book and a stiff drink, be they vampire, wicche, demon, or fae. No wolves, though. Ever. I have my reasons.

I serve the supernatural community of San Francisco. We've been having some problems lately. Okay, I'm the one with the problems. The broken body of a female werewolf washed up on my doorstep. What makes sweat pool at the base of my spine, though, is realizing the scars she bears are identical to the ones I conceal. After hiding for years, I've been found.

A protection I've been relying on is gone. While my wolf traits are strengthening steadily, the loss also left my mind vulnerable to attack. Someone is ensnaring me in horrifying visions intended to kill. Clive, the sexy vampire Master of the City, has figured out how to pull me out, designating himself my personal bodyguard. He's grumpy about it, but that kiss is telling a different story. A change is taking place. It has to. The bookish bartender must become the fledgling badass.

I'm a survivor. I'll fight fang and claw to protect myself and the ones I love. And let's face it, they have it coming.

The Dead Don't Drink at Lafitte's
Sam Quinn, book 2

I'm Sam Quinn, the werewolf book nerd owner of the Slaughtered Lamb Bookstore and Bar. Things have been busy lately. While the near-constant attempts on my life have ceased, I now have a vampire gentleman caller. I've been living with Clive and the rest of his vampires for a few weeks while the Slaughtered Lamb is being rebuilt. It's going about as well as you'd expect.

My mother was a wicche and long dormant abilities are starting to make themselves known. If I'd had a choice, necromancy wouldn't have been my top pick, but it's coming in handy. A ghost warns me someone is coming to kill Clive. When I rush back to the nocturne I find vamps from New Orleans readying an attack. One of the benefits of vampires looking down on werewolves is no one expects much of me. They don't expect it right up until I take their heads.

Now, Clive and I are setting out for New Orleans to take the fight back to the source. Vampires are masters of the long game. Revenge plots are often decades, if not centuries, in the making. We are expecting one enemy, but quickly learn we have darker forces scheming against us. Good thing I'm the secret weapon they never see coming.

The Wicche Glass Tavern
Sam Quinn, book 3

I'm Sam Quinn, the werewolf book nerd owner of the Slaughtered Lamb Bookstore and Bar. Clive, my vampire gentleman caller, has asked me to marry him. His nocturne is less than celebratory. Unfortunately, for them and the sexy vamp doing her best to seduce him, his cold, dead heart beats only for me.

As much as my love life feels like a minefield, it has to take a backseat to a far more pressing problem. The time has come. I need to deal with my aunt, the woman who's been trying to kill me for as long as I can remember. She's learned a new trick. She's figured out how to weaponize my friends against me. To have any hope of surviving, I have to learn to use my necromantic gifts. I need a teacher. We find one hiding among the fae, which is a completely different problem. I need to determine what I'm capable of in a hurry because my aunt doesn't care how many are hurt or killed as long as she gets what she wants. Sadly for me, what she wants is my name on a headstone.

I'm gathering my friends-werewolves, vampires, wicches, gorgons, a Fury, a half-demon, an elf, and a couple of dragon-shifters-into a kind of Fellowship of the Sam. It's going to be one hell of a battle. Hopefully, San Francisco will still be standing when the dust clears.

Biergarten of the Damned
Sam Quinn, book 5

I'm Sam, the werewolf book nerd in charge of The Slaughtered Lamb Bookstore & Bar. I've always thought of Dave, my red-skinned, shark eyed, half-demon cook, as a kind of foul-mouthed uncle, one occasionally given to bouts of uncontrolled anger.

Something's going on, though. He's acting strangely, hiding things. When I asked what was wrong, he blew me off and told me to quit bugging him. That's normal enough. What's not is his missing work. Ever. Other demons are appearing in the bar, looking for him. I'm getting worried, and his banshee girlfriend Maggie isn't answering my calls.

Demons terrify me. I do NOT want to go into any demon bars looking for Dave, but he's my family, sort of. I need to try to help, whether he wants me to or not. When I finally learn the truth, though…I'm not sure I can ever look at him again, let alone have him work for me. Are there limits to forgiveness? I think there might be.

And for something completely different…
Welcome Home, Katie Gallagher
This romantic comedy was my first book published. Remember, don't judge a book by its (truly hideous) cover.

Nobody said a fresh start would be easy

A clean slate is exactly what Katie Gallagher needs, and Bar Harbor, Maine, is the best place to get it. Except the cottage her grandmother left her is overrun with woodland creatures, and the police chief, Aiden Cavanaugh, seems determined to arrest her! Katie had no idea she'd broken his heart fifteen years ago…

About the Author

Seana Kelly lives in the San Francisco Bay Area with her husband, two daughters, two dogs, and one fish. When not dodging her family, hiding in the garage to write, she's working as a high school teacher-librarian. She's an avid reader and re-reader who misses her favorite characters when it's been too long between visits.

She's a *USA Today* bestseller and is represented by the delightful and effervescent Sarah E. Younger of the Nancy Yost Literary Agency

You can follow Seana on Twitter for tweets about books and dogs or on Instagram for beautiful pictures of books and dogs (kidding). She also loves collecting photos of characters and settings for the books she writes. As she's a huge reader of young adult and adult books, expect lots of recommendations as well.

Website: www.seanakelly.com

Newsletter: https://geni.us/t0Y5cBA

twitter.com/SeanaKellyRW
instagram.com/seanakellyrw
facebook.com/Seana-Kelly-1553527948245885
bookbub.com/authors/seana-kelly
pinterest.com/seanakelly326